Not From Around Here, Are You?

Edited by
Woody Carsky-Wilson

Not From Around Here, Are You?

Published by Cincinnati Writers Project
PO Box 29367,
Cincinnati, Ohio 45229-0367

Edited by Woody Carsky-Wilson

ISBN 978-0-615-25195-0

Cover Art by Tina Clyburn, graphic designer

Book designed by T. Lee Harris

Contents

Not From Around Here, Are You?

Preface

Thanks to assistant editors Marcia Eckstein, Tom Groh and Chris Specht for wading through all the submissions I routed to them and giving me honest feedback. You guys were quick and helpful, providing a perfect mix. Tom carried the axe of merciless critique. Chris was the buoyant spirit of delight. Marcia was the steady rudder that sailed the ship.

I was just Captain Bligh with a damned good crew!

NOTE TO READERS

You are the most important person in the writing process. Without a reader, there is no market and writers are just whistling in the dark. Without a reader, there are no magazines, no books, no reason to write except to impress ourselves.

Impressing ourselves gets boring really fast.

I and my assistant editors, therefore, picked these stories with the reader in mind. For example, Charles Sroufe's story about cats doesn't really fit the theme of this anthology. So what? Readers will like it and let's face it, themes can be pretty silly. Then there's Donnie McGovern's story that fits the theme, but it's not fiction! We included it anyway. Why?

The reader will enjoy it. Enough said.

By the way, we chose not to include those cute and cuddly intros to each story that you see in some anthologies. You didn't come her to read a pontificating editor. You came here to read the stories and poetry.

Enjoy!

Not From Around Here, Are You?

NOTE TO WRITERS

You're a writer, huh. So what? We could pave South America with writers and still do a land bridge to Asia with the leftovers. You're nothing special.

Oh, you want to be a successful writer? Well that's a different story altogether. . .

Writing is a bundled set of skills like playing the violin or chess. No beginner is perfect. Everyone makes the same cat screech on the strings or the same stupid beginner moves that lead to checkmate in a nanosecond. The difference between these beginners and a successful violinist or chess player is simple.

Experience. Hard work. Dedication. A willingness to learn.

Inspiration is great, and it plays well in the movies, but you can force inspiration by monitoring your own creative process. Likewise, a natural ability to craft words is fine, but it doesn't guarantee you'll get published. And knowing the editor of a publishing house is wonderful, but will not automatically sell copies of your book.

You have to want success in this business. You have to work for it.

For many writers, the third best thing they ever did was join a writers group. The second best was to submit their naked, fragile, flawed stories to that group. The first was to take the critique they received and use it to improve their stories.

That's how I, and lots of writers like me, did it. Before my wife forced me out of the house and into the indelicate arms of the Cincinnati Writers Project, I had writing stamina, great ideas, an excellent vocabulary and a real thirst to excel.

But my first stories were crap, and luckily they were never inflicted upon the general reading populace. Instead, I inflicted them on people in the CWP's fiction critique group, and every week sat there with mouth shut and ears open while these fellow writers dissected my stories. My whole creative cycle soon revolved around that group as I struggled to submit a new story every week no matter what.

Preface

I made it a hundred twenty straight weeks, until both the group and I took a well-deserved break from my stories. Even now, years later, I can hear the individual voices telling me where I needed to trim words, how I needed to tighten a plot, which character required more attention. As a result, I became a successful writer, which means a bunch of my stories got published in legitimate, paying magazines.

This is a pretty common success story.

The anthology you're about to read is a collection of stories, mostly written by members of the CWP. There are similar groups all over the place.

Are you jealous? Do you want to be a writer, but you're not published yet? Then join a group! Submit your stories, close your mouth and open your ears while you receive the critique of brutally honest peers who really have a vested interest in you becoming a better writer.

Because that's how it's done.

Sincerely,
Woody Carsky-Wilson
Editor-in-chief

10 Reasons Skyblue Lives

A CWP Dedication: Remembering Dallas Wiebe, Cincinnati Writer's Project co-founder, past president and past board member

Jeffrey Hillard

✍ Seven of us Cincinnati writers met in Dallas' living room on McAlpin Ave. in Clifton in September, 1987, understanding that not one of us knew a writer outside of Clifton. Or, if we did, we did not always see that writer. Dallas, Jon Hughes, and I had discussed the need to connect with other writers—form a network—because we detected a chasm of inactivity among writers at that time. We knew better: we believed writers were seeking other writers, but did not exactly know how to connect. I had literally just been hired fulltime to replace poet Nikki Giovanni, who taught part time, at the College of Mount St. Joseph. I basically thought I was the only literary writer on the west side of town. I was also assistant editor of *Cincinnati Poetry Review*, which Dallas co-founded in 1973. Jon and I were collaborating on a couple of journalism pieces for then-*Everybody's News* alternative paper. Yet, Dallas was front and center. He waved the banner: "Everyone, help yourself to cold beer in the refrigerator. Let's get going on this." Dallas' living room was happening. I took notes. We had three follow-up meetings in five weeks. Most of the writers that evening stayed on. We were confident we could strategize ways to unite, fortify, nurture, showcase, and cheerlead for other writers—in all genres. We immediately agreed all genres were worth embracing; it was early inclusivity at its finest. Even sci fi: Imagine the blessing we felt when in the early 1990s, Ryck Neube showed up at the Carnegie Cultural Arts Center in Newport. Dallas, Ryck, and I may as well have forged blood ties by piercing our skin and

Dedication: 10 Reasons Skyblue Lives

bleeding into each other at the Carnegie, for all the big-hearted love and kindred spirit Ryck has since given CWP—and Dallas and me. Ryck, Karen George, and other stalwarts grew CWP in the late 1990s, when Dallas and I decided we did not want it to seem a "Dallas and Jeff" production.

So, CWP was conceived in Dallas' living room in 1987. It was outright birthed, umbilical cord and all, in October, 1998 at the Butterfield Center on Garfield Place in downtown Cincinnati. The occasion: CWP's first and only major Small Press Bookfair. It was CWP's official launch. It was Dallas' effort to organize the fair that made it huge. Over fifty small press publishers and editors from the Midwest and East (Maryland) lined the all-purpose room displaying books and magazines. It was a beautiful event. We presented awards (money) to winners of a CWP-sponsored, high school writing contest. For the entire year it took to organize, I worked side by side with Dallas, who carried the load. On the day of the bookfair he was battling the flu. I had never seen him sick before.

A community of writers had come together. It's important for you to realize that, because of Dallas' vision and commitment to CWP, you are reading this anthology. Community. Writers. Artists. Publishing. You must realize that Cincinnati in the 80s and early 90s was a vacuum. We did not know how to connect with a workshop or to adventurous publishing. There were only two or three community workshops. CWP vigorously formed a network for writers of all genres. This was key.

Dallas was a truth-teller. He did not tolerate bad writing. If you were around him, you quickly understood this. Any workshop Dallas ever taught anywhere, CWP included, was packed. Even when he held court on the art of story at Arlin's Bar, a literary conference, at a picnic or reception, his notions over the twenty-nine years that I knew him never wavered.

"Keep the writing simple and clear, and let it build. Work your 'patterns' or small details that should recur throughout the story," he'd say. "Get your secondary patterns [below the plot or storyline] working. Pay attention to them. That's what a reader *sees*."

✍ Are you kidding? Dallas took CWP very seriously, and yet he was one of the great comic fiction writers in the country. Characters: Dallasandro Vibini, Gottlieb Liebgott (a palindrome, did you notice?), Abraham Nofziger, Grassgreen, Dirtbrown, William Weary, Peter Seltanzer a.k.a. Skyblue the Badass. The stories' subject matter: a glass-eyed blond boy, a Vietnam vet who created his own fictional world in drawings, a child who could not forget anything, and a Holmesian loser who solved petty crimes. Just a few examples of so very many. He published a novel that invoked much of Russia. We rarely had a CWP meeting when someone didn't come up to Dallas and say, "Jesus, I nearly choked laughing at that recent story you published." He was a comic genius. His erudition was always tempered by the frequent homespun humor. In conversation, he'd have you howling. "I'm not going to read any more crap by that writer [like John Updike, for instance]." Or, he could have meant crap by a colleague at U.C.

✍ Dallas bragged about you in Cuba in 1993. I was there with him. Jon Hughes and Lew Moores were there, as well as several others. Dallas' first of two trips was in 1985. He said to Cuban writers, artists, and professors at the University of Havana how proud he was of the writers in CWP. He talked about how the organization thrived on solidarity, and this truth incited the Cubans to buy another round and toast to CWP's longevity.

✍ Even before CWP, there was Mount Adams. I'm vague on the particulars, but Dallas, in 1963 and 1964, wasted no time hooking up with the literary and artistic scene in Mount

Dedication: 10 Reasons Skyblue Lives

Adams. He befriended the late George Thompson, who published *The Mount Adams Review*. They collaborated on issues. George had a printing press in a small building. A linotype press. There was a thriving literary scene in that heyday, a precursor to what CWP would become.

✍ Dallas cared about a writer's struggles. I never knew one moment when he didn't speak to a writer, go out of his way to encourage a young writer, or get in the car and go have a drink with a writer, if there was time. Until he was seventy-two, he rarely missed community readings. Regularly, he was the scene. Dallas is here; you could hear the echo.

✍ He cared about new writers, young writers, writers with a burning desire. He established the early CWP workshops, taught in them, solicited other writers in the city to help facilitate the teaching. He was a tireless advocate. I often wondered when he had time to write. But he was as disciplined a writer as anyone I have ever known. He taught me how not to fall into an undisciplined pace, a habit into which I confess I sometimes fall.

✍ Dallas left Skyblue for the generations in 2040 to latch onto. The way Fitzgerald left Gatsby for us. Flannery O'Connor and her Hazel Motes. Skyblue the Badass is Dallas' penultimate creation—his epochal fictional character and alter-ego. When people asked, "How much of Skyblue is you, Dallas," he would say, "We're a lot alike, and we're different." I've pondered that remark for twenty-eight years. One of the telltale similarities, though, I most see is that both Skyblue and Dallas view the world as irreversibly lunatic and still entirely needy. These divergent conditions drove Dallas to write. In his novels, stories, and poems, he maximized their outlandish visibility in our lives. He cared about people. Dallas cared enough about writers that he had some of us gather in his living room to make plans to remedy some writers' needs. This is also why Skyblue the protagonist lives.

Not From Around Here, Are You?

Skyblue's words cannot become extinct. Dallas needed that channeling. They remain fresh and they agitate. They drop the bombshells of irreverence and world-weary astonishment that never comply with what someone else expects. And that's to say Skyblue's words are a wake-up call to the world. (But the world will never get it.) Skyblue is about story. Ever story. Story is what bonds humanity, Dallas once reasoned. Because you cannot bury story. You cannot bury one's imagination.

Please read my 1999 *CityBeat* cover story on Dallas' influence on American writing. At www.citybeat.com, type in "Rebel with a Cause" in the search box. The article commemorated the thirtieth anniversary of the publication of his first controversial novel, *Skyblue the Badass*.

Mullins Lake

Ryck Neube

Alicia Kerns demanded my ID before our first date could begin.

"Huh? I've been out of circulation for twenty years, so forgive me if I'm slow on modern dating etiquette." I forked over my license. "Want my fingerprints? A blood sample?"

"You're not from around here," she said, contorting the license under the morning sun to assure herself it was real. "I don't believe your name."

"That's why I like folks to call me 'Lock. Lookit, Mom drank and read a lot, a dangerous combination. So in a rum-induced act of whimsy she named me Sherlock Tanner."

"How do you pronounce N-M-I? Is that Greek?" she asked.

"It's not a name. It stands for No Middle Initial. Hey, is there any way I can avoid this getting around? With a nickname like 'Lock, folks in Thames County think I'm a reformed safecracker. If it gets out I'm a Sherlock, I'll never hear the end of it."

"What a boring secret."

"If you ask me, it was child abuse."

Alicia posed in the doorway, the autumn breeze playing with her curly black hair which matched her simple dress. Pumps accentuated an impressive pair of legs. In the urban turf I had called home for years, she would be considered overdeveloped. In Appalachia, those muscles came in handy as she unloaded crates at LeClair's Warehouse, not to mention dealing with drunks during her part-time job working the graveyard shift at the Morehead Pike mini-mart/gas station/bait shop. That's where I had met her, stopping for a midnight snack, staying for hours of chatting.

"So where are we going?" she asked.

Not From Around Here, Are You?

"I thought we'd go to the lake for a picnic. Drove to Lexington last night to raid a gourmet store. My basket overflows with goodies, and the best bottles of wine in Thames County."

Her forehead furrowed. "But it's October."

I shrugged. "And that portends what exactly?"

"N-nothing. It means there won't be anybody else at the lake because . . . uh, because . . . nothing." Alicia twitched as church bells tolled their message of haste to the gathering congregations.

"Give me a minute," Alicia said, retreating into her shotgun house.

"At least she left the door open. Guess that means she isn't fleeing. Like riding a bike, boyo," I repeated until it assumed mantra mode. This was my first date since the divorce. It was going to be okay.

Alicia reappeared wearing running shoes. "Let's hit it," she said with all the enthusiasm of someone going for a root canal.

It was a long drive from the county seat to the southern border of Thames County, though less than twelve miles as the bird flew. Wending through the Daniel Boone National Forest rewarded us with a symphony of leaves in their Van Gogh finery. Not only were the roads curvy, but narrow, soon giving away to gravel lanes whose flanks were marred by gaps where mountain goats had careened out of control and crashed down the bosky slopes.

Alicia spoke about small town life, people I didn't know doing things that I could care less about, until I started interrogating her about her own life. That triggered a bout of nail chewing between laconic answers.

Great start, I chided myself. I confided to Alicia about my divorce last year, that strange feeling of relief I experienced when Stella confessed she found me as boring as I found her. The information loosened Alicia's tongue.

Twice divorced, Alicia related. Her second ex- was in prison for embezzling from the bank where he was a loan officer. Not only had his gambling bankrupted them, but she had spent

16

a weekend in jail as the prosecutor intimidated her into surrendering her spousal privilege in order to testify against him.

Hard luck. The hills spouted such stories faster than trees grew in its forests. Timber, coal, tobacco, each had dominated the economy only to wane in turn, leaving behind broken hopes and a few smirking marijuana cultivators. The smart, the ambitious, and the lucky fled Appalachia to wherever the jobs were. People remained behind because they were stubborn, or set in the concrete of circumstance.

"There's gossip that you're a super hacker," she said.

"I've cracked a few databases in my career, but I'm working for the frigging governor. Can't get more legit than that."

"Others say you are an undercover agent for the IRS."

I chuckled. "Me? A revenuer? Reckon it was inevitable that the legendary Appalachian paranoia labeled me as an outsider come to do them evil. If you want to experience true boredom, I'll give you an A to Z on my research project."

Alicia replied, "The last time I went on a date with a stranger, we got into a fistfight at the Plum Holler Inn. Boring would be a nice change of pace."

I waited for her to laugh at her joke, but she did not. I cringed at the implication.

"Remember, Alicia, you asked for this. It all boils down to the 2000 Census showing a 17.65% drop in the population of Eastern Kentucky. Now, our benevolent government gathers birth and death records, plus unemployment, welfare, social security, and tax records, all which provides them with an idea of the migration factor. Yet when you add the numbers up, they only account for half the population drop. Therefore, Governor Barnes hired the best data ferret he could find to investigate—me."

"Folks are vanishing? Like a serial killer?"

"Not unless there's an army of murderers living up here. We're talking over a hundred thousand people. I suspect the census overcounted in '90 and undercounted in 2000. Plus, there are a bunch of people fearful of the post-Waco government, so they live lives invisible to the state. Plus, there's significantly more migration than can be tracked by databases."

"A data ferret, I like that," she said. For a while she chewed on her lower lip. "So what data do you have about Lake Henry Clay?"

"TVA era damming of a branch of the Kentucky River. The lake only reached half its proposed size, due to fractures that drain the waters, so it never became a recreational bonanza like Lake Cumberland."

"Your people used to live up here, right? Don't you know more?" she asked.

"Buncha Tanners settled Pawpaw Corners in Daniel Boone's days. Stayed there until the government condemned— or con-damned, as Grandma used to say—their farms."

"If your people lived in the basin, you must know about the Mullins clan." She whispered the name.

"Grandma raised me on Mullins' stories. Oh, oh, I remember a story about a deputy busting one of the Mullins' boys for stealing clothes. Well, the boy said he was just 'borrowing' some clothesline in the dark, who knew there'd be all those clothes on it. And he had no idea how he ended up wearing those bloomers."

Alicia cleared her throat. "My maternal grandfather's grandfather was sheriff for six years until a Mullins shot him in the back. They were bad seeds. Evil."

"You mean the stories about them being witchy?" I asked.

"My ancestral sheriff got tired of their thieving and killings. So he raised a posse. They were going to hang them all and rescue the children who were supposedly stolen from Pine Grove."

I laughed. "Grandma used the phrase 'lazy as a Mullins' all the time. She claimed they were so lazy, they'd only steal children who were potty trained, so they wouldn't have to wash diapers."

"Anyway," said Alicia, "the posse rode into a fog that lasted a week. They got lost in a forest where they had been hunting all their lives. It'd be like us getting lost on Main Street. It wasn't until they decided to go home that the fog lifted."

"So says the folklore. I suspect each man went to battle

Mullins Lake

with a jug of 'shine. Booze-addled, they got lost, and when their hangovers blossomed, they said *hasta manana*."

"It's not all superstition," she snapped.

"Never is. There's a molecule of fact behind every bit of folklore. The Mullins were bad to the bone, Manson family values. When I was fifteen, Grandma caught me shoplifting candy bars. She yelled at me, 'Don't mullins that candy!' They must have been profoundly evil to become a frigging verb."

"The senator who got the dam built came from Pine Grove." Alicia glanced over her shoulder. "His daddy had been murdered by a Mullins. The lake was his revenge. When evil is that concentrated, the best you can do is scatter it. But the Mullins clan refused to leave their holler, so the National Guard burnt them out, but they came back as soon as the flooding commenced."

"Yeah, Grandma mentioned folks who thought they could stop the lake by refusing to leave."

"Except the Mullins clan never left that October," she said. "After their holler was flooded, no one ever saw them again. Poof. Fifty-two of them gone without a trace."

"No doubt there's a block in Detroit or Cleveland that's not fit to inhabit because of them."

"No, they vanished into the lake. People still disappear around the lake during October."

"Are you telling me the lake is haunted?" I tried to read her expression, but her dress kept hiking up, distracting me. Great legs.

"I'm not scared of old wives' tales, but—"

"Hey, I never said you were." I slowed to a crawl to drive around a fallen tree.

She tented her hands in front of her face. "N-nobody goes to the lake in October. They say the Mullinses are hunting for winter."

"A logic flaw, methinks. Lazy as a Mullins. Grandma said they would crime a mile, rather than work an inch. They homesteaded the best bottom land in the Kentucky hills, yet never farmed it a lick. Alive or dead, they wouldn't hunt to

19

stockpile for winter."

"There are darker stories," she whispered. "They ate their dead because it was too much work burying them. That gave them a taste for . . . you know."

"Yeah, Grandma mentioned cannibalism."

Alicia shrugged. "Elaine Johnston last year, Benny Dobson six years ago, Ted Begley when I was in high school— all vanished in October at the lake."

"Lazy as a Mullins."

Alicia laughed. "You are right about that. Still, people vanish all the time in our hills." She gnawed on a thumbnail. "Even our governor thinks so."

"The headline of the PINE GROVE RECORDER yesterday was: Library Gets New Chairs. If folks were being hunted by amphibian white trash, the journalists of this fair county would be covering ghost Mullinses like a quilt to avoid those fast-breaking chair stories."

"Are you making fun of me?" After a long pause, she added, "Well, it is exaggerated, but—"

I slid my Escort into a clearing notched into the forest that I had scouted earlier in the week. It was a scenic stroll, courtesy of a dried creek bed that meandered to the murky waters of Lake Henry Clay, the great compromise lake. Streaks of mica decorated the sandstone, playing with the sun. Wished I hadn't noticed the lack of birds; their silence filled my ears. Following her wary eyes as they darted, I sensed Alicia, too, felt the oppressive silence.

Not that we said one word about it. Instead, I babbled about the day I spent with the governor, the endless local celebrities I encountered.

The lake was shaped like an arrowhead made by a very clumsy child. We settled upon a large, flat slab of limestone on its northern shore. A thin mist muted the far shore, lending a humid thickness to the air, but the slab had been absorbing sunlight all day, so its warmth compensated for the dampness.

I emptied the basket in the rehearsed order onto the blanket I had spread, hummus being trumped by salmon goo trumped by caviar, though the pita expired ere the spreadables. Fortunately, I had fetched along ample soda bread. We exchanged food jokes, whispering as if in church.

Exotic fruits cleaned our palates. Much to my chagrin, I couldn't recall a single name of them, but Alicia enjoyed the weird things. After a test bite or two, I kept heaving mine into the lake when she wasn't looking. Then came the imported cheeses. I discovered she was a brie hound, but I tried not to think less of her for that perversion.

The true secret of the feast, of course, was the vintage Merlot. When the wind picked up halfway through the second bottle, it felt natural to cuddle for warmth.

I made a note to award myself a Dating Nobel Prize for packing a second blanket. Once we tossed it over us, reducing our universe to tented cotton, our snuggling escalated. Her moans echoed along the lake, sometimes coming back furious, sometimes comic. For a few minutes, it sounded like a hundred couples were making love.

Afterwards, I deployed a derby pie, a little worse for traveling; we took turns feeding each other. We washed it down with Antigua coffee from a thermos. Whereupon we returned to the second bottle of wine which inspired a second romp.

I think I dreamed the third. Hoped not, it was the best.

Never had limestone felt so soft; we slumbered as if on a feather bed. Woke with dusk shadows dancing toward us from the surrounding hills. The surface of the lake gleamed like polished obsidian. Dressing was complicated due to our manic disrobing. One of my sneakers had vanished. While I stashed our trash and blankets in the basket, we polished off the last of the coffee. Silence ruled until I kissed her fingertips.

She said, "You must think—"

"That today is the best day of my life."

Fish splashed just off shore. We both jumped at the sudden noise. Both laughed when we recognized what was happening. The sound that echoed back was less laughter than the wail of tortured souls. As abruptly as throwing a switch, twilight became no light.

Not From Around Here, Are You?

"Geez," was the only thing I could think to say.

An echo came from across the lake like a giant's heavy breathing. The noise abruptly stopped.

"What was that?" I asked.

The breathing resumed in the forest behind us. Ragged. Angry.

Alicia hugged her purse. "I used to go hunting with my father every deer season. My first husband and I used to hike these hills every weekend. I love nature. But that racket isn't natural."

Her defiant shout came back as laughter, the voices of scores guffawing.

We ran. I tried to maintain a modicum of dignity as my adrenal glands squeezed themselves dry. Thanks to my missing sneaker, I stayed behind my fleet lover during the uphill charge. We reached the creek bed, turned right for a hundred paces. She waited for me, sucking down great lungfuls of air as I wheezed to her side.

"It's going to be okay," I prattled.

She merely pointed. I scarcely had time to bang her back with the basket as a wall of fog rolled over us. It was so dense I could smell her easier than see her, despite our embrace.

My marrow chilled. We trembled.

"As long as we play smart, we'll get out of this," she whispered. "The Mullinses will expect us to go toward the car, so we need to find a place to hide until the fog lifts. The hunters won't expect that."

"There are no hunt—"

The bay of a hound silenced me.

Hand in hand, we inched down the creek bed, stumbling, often unable to see below our waists. Splashed into several holes which had collected the last rainfall. Each splash, each crunch of woodland debris, each startled gasp thundered in our ears. Occasionally, the echo of distant laughter sliced the fog.

At last we found a pair of boulders on the bank of the dried creek. Behind them was a small, sheltered space. We huddled there, cocooning ourselves against the frigid fog with

22

the blankets. As our nerves settled, the wine mixed with fear and the downside of the adrenal rush to put us to sleep.

I woke as Alicia was digging through the basket for more . . . brie.

"How can I be this hungry?" she whispered.

I snaked from the blankets. The fog was dissipating into cottony ropes and roiling balls. A gibbous moon poured hints of light through the trees bending over the creek. I sniffed nature with paranoid nostrils more accustomed to rush-hour traffic. My ears picked up endless bizarre sounds. I would have sold my soul for the bray of a police siren.

Once I returned to Alicia's side, she kissed me hard. Her lips tasted of feta.

She whispered, nigh panted, "I know how hunters think. We can get through this."

"There's nothing to get through, Alicia. The Mullins ghouls aren't out there. We got a little drunk, got freaked by the fog. There are no—"

"Stop playing Sherlock. This is Twilight Zone city." She groaned as if trying to communicate to a lunatic.

I started to protest, but her hand covered my mouth.

"If it makes you feel better, let's say this is a silly game. Play along with me, 'Lock, and I promise you a weekend that makes this afternoon look like ninth grade foreplay." She sealed the statement with a kiss that curled my toes.

It took me a moment to regain feeling in my lips. "Love your incentive program, boss."

We abandoned the awkward basket. I tied linen napkins around my shredded, soggy sock to protect my foot. We wended down the creek, making good speed courtesy of the moonlight. Alicia moved like a panther on the prowl; I fell down a few million times. An owl screeched five times. Grandma would have known what that meant.

Part of Alicia's game, I kept telling myself. Glimpsing my lover washed in moonlight made any discomfort worthwhile.

Preternatural noises leapt from the darkness, speeding us along the way. It could be twisted voices, echoing from afar.

Not From Around Here, Are You?

From the grave, insisted my fear. Just animals looking for eats, declared logic. Other sounds could be the squishing of Mullins' boots, rotted by their long stay beneath the lake.

"We should be reaching the shore any minute now," I said a dozen times.

Yet our path continued down and down. Waterfalls forced us to descend rock faces. The banks of the dried creek grew further apart, more sharply chiseled into the sandstone. Boulders of limestone grew larger.

What was that sound?

It. . .it gurgled like a drowning man. Was that splashing? A Mullins emerging from the primordial goo of Lake Henry Clay? I cursed the diet of horror films I consumed as a teen. If only my heart would stop jack hammering.

We stopped as the moon slipped free of a cloud. A river blocked our way. Granted, not much of a river, it burbled over rocks, scant inches deep in its center, spitting distance from the bank upon which we stood.

"It's the North Fork," she said.

Duh, I didn't say, seeing the way the moonlight played with her long neck, smelling her hair as the wind blew it into my face.

"There's no river here," she said.

"Uh, it's not much of a river, but—"

"It's the North Fork of the Kentucky River, the one that was dammed for the lake."

"Con-damned, Grandma would say. We've reached the mouth of the lake already? Wow, we made great time."

"No, this is the river before the dam," she whispered. "We should be under thirty feet of water standing here."

I took a deep breath. Apparently a few bottles of vintage vino and Alicia lost her mind. Took a deeper breath. It was merely a game, I told myself.

"Did we time travel?" I barely kept the laugh from my voice.

"Why don't we ask them?"

My eyes followed her pointing hand. As the moon dived

behind a cloud, I glimpsed a trio. They slack-jawed at us, more Neanderthal than Cro-Magnon, more predator than prey. One of them pointed at us. The second grunted. The third lifted his shotgun.

Whereupon Alicia whipped a .38 from her purse and fired. I think she hit all three before the shadows swallowed them.

I did what any man did after his date committed mass murder—grabbed her hand and made like Road Runner. We blazed up the creek bed, no tripping this time. The gallon of adrenaline in my system made gasping unnecessary, made breathing unnecessary, placed faster-than-light travel within my grasp.

We returned to our boulder fortress, ducking behind their stony safety.

"Did you see them?" she kept asking.

"I saw nothing! This never happened. We need to rehearse our alibi and bury that damned pistol."

Thankfully I had kept the corkscrew in my pocket, though it tore a hole in my jeans. Murder was thirsty work. We polished off the last bottle, then deployed the blankets.

"Uh, I didn't know you were packing."

She gave me a kiss that curled my liver. "Wait. I'll hide us properly."

Slipping from our blankets, she threw forest debris atop our ersatz tent. Once she crawled underneath our shelter, Alicia grabbed me. We embraced for an eternity while our bodies exchanged trembles and heat.

She whispered, "Should have stayed hidden to begin with. As soon as the sun is up, the Mullinses have no power."

I swallowed my comment about the powers of grand juries and pesky murder charges. After all, I was merely an accessory. The D.A. would give me a deal if I testified against her. It would be okay.

Her marvelous body soon chased those thoughts away. Exhaustion did the rest. I fell asleep in mid-kiss.

Woke with the sun up, my torso and head exposed. Joints throbbed. I nearly cried. Standing was torture, but the stone was so cold. Alicia woke, stretching like a cat, no worse the wear.

Unable to stand straight, I hobbled off to empty my bladder, returning with a whole new series of aches. It was a long limp to the car.

"You should bury that pistol to get rid of the evidence. Maybe we shouldn't tell anybody we went out yesterday," I mumbled. Had to use my left foot on the accelerator, such were the pains from my shoeless right.

"Last night still has you freaked out, 'Lock?"

"I think you hit all three of them. Where I come from that counts as a felony hat trick."

"He needs killing more than a Mullins—that's another saying, like lazy as a Mullins. Nobody will find a thing. Stop worrying, Sherlock."

Perhaps she was right. If the locals didn't frequent the banks of the lake in October, Mother Nature had plenty of time to remove any clues we left behind, like my sneaker.

The nightmare faded the further we drove from Lake Henry Clay. Maybe I'd seen nothing more than deer poachers diving behind cover as Alicia fired blindly. Poachers wouldn't report us to the cops. Maybe I'd witnessed why so many folks went missing in the hills—shoot at enough ghosts, and someone was bound to get wasted.

We drove in silence. It was a quiet Monday morning when we reached Pine Grove. Nobody gave our begrimed visages a second gander. I dropped her at her house, then went to my motel room.

After the longest shower of my life, I guzzled a gallon of water.

Called Alicia. "Just wanted to see if you were okay."

"I was just getting ready to go to work. I'm pulling a shift at the gas-mart tonight. You going to come by for a midnight snack?"

"Yeah, sure." I felt guilty I was going to blow the day off and sleep while she went to not one, but two jobs. It felt absurd feeling guilty. After all, she had involved me in murder.

"Are you okay, Sherlock?"

"Guess so."

"Last night was my best date in ages. Say, what are you doing Wednesday night?" she asked.

"Nothing."

"Up for another date?"

"Uh, sure."

"See you at seven. I'll bring the shotguns." She hung up.

I sat down hard, putting my dizzy head between my knees. "It's going to be okay," I told myself.

I was such a liar.

The Soldier

Thomas Groh

"This one's a soldier," Bernie tells me over the phone. "A hero. You've never done a hero, have you? No? Well, there you go. Plus, he says he'll pay $50—double my normal fee, because of the late notice and all."

"I'm in the middle of things," I tell him. "The boys are at practice, and I've a lot I need to do before they get home." Though I don't tell him this, I'm sick up to here with heroes.

"We're kind of in a bind here, Donna," Bernie says. "We got Lois out with the flu, and the service is tonight. You'd really be helping me out on this one."

If that's the case, he could pay $75, couldn't he?

Bernie decides he can.

"Cash," I tell him.

"Of course."

This isn't me. I didn't used to be this way.

"I'll be there in ten minutes," I say.

This soldier's hair is fine and soft and very short, a grown-out induction cut. Cropped on the sides but longer, almost curly on top. They teach you how if you can physically grip the hair, you can style it. And I can grasp it, though I'm not sure what to do with it.

"A soldier," Bernie says again. He'll get to set out the flags, call his friends from down at The Knights. "A local hero. Was a big deal. You don't read the papers, follow the news?"

I'm not from here, I want to say. I just live here. "My boys will be home in forty-five minutes," I say instead, tying myself into the nylon apron. I step into the booties, roll on the rubber gloves.

Everyone's a hero. The store clerk who shoots the kid dead is a hero. The football player flashing gold teeth. The fireman who comforts the widow of his closest friend, eventually

28

sleeps with her, then leaves his wife of nine years and two months; he leaves her and their two sons to fend for themselves. He's a hero. They're everywhere, like cockroaches.

The hero on the steel table has a plain face, an ugly face. The nose juts like a shard of stone. But it's a young face, the cheeks pocked and downy. This hero couldn't have been older than twenty. As a rule, I don't do kids. They try to teach you about detachment, but I don't do kids.

"Terry was twenty-seven, actually," Bernie says. "And sorry, we weren't provided with a photo. Please just do what you can."

Sometimes, though not usually, it's simpler without a photo. I open the kit and affix a #2 guard, then thumb on the razor clippers.

"Wait," Bernie says. "Don't—" He moves behind me, places his hand on mine. He smells of Paulex powder and disinfectant.

This hero is soft, the jaw and chin are weak. I might airbrush some structure into the jaw—

"What are you doing?" he says. "What are you thinking?"

The pale lips are full, but slack and malleable, not rigid like you'd think. They teach you how to plant your elbow on the sternum, to balance your wrist on their chin to apply color. *My God, this soldier. . .*

"Yes," Bernie says. "From down Christian County."

. . . This soldier is a woman.

She got called up a month ago, Bernie tells me. Left her husband at home with the kids and was due to ship out Friday.

A woman. . .

"Then the parking brake failed," Bernie tells me, "on a forklift outside of Hopkinsville."

"She's beautiful," I say.

I Want To Tell You
For Nancy

Madeleine Crouse

about this day, and
a little more, too:

the sun is in charge; potent
shadows man the grass,

and, there is that ancient
unfurling of fern. The earth

quivers as acres
of corn break ground.

All the while,
my son is in Iraq

assigned to the 2nd Marine
Expeditionary Force

patrolling a trail of towns
along the banks of the Euphrates.

"With infrared goggles," he says
"our guys see in the dark—

own the night." Mouthed
between bombings, clenched

I Want To Tell You

in the jawbones of war—*How long
can he own his breath and blood?*

Each morning, in my mind,
I watch him rise.

*(Originally published in FOR A BETTER WORLD 2007, Ghosn
Publishing.)*

Orin

Woody Carsky-Wilson

Sibling mine, please accept this letter in the manner it was sent, which is to say abject desperation. Let me explain. Better yet, allow me to narrate. That way, I can pretend it happened to someone else and thus lessen the sense of utter panic I feel. And not to be too blatant about it, but kindly remember who was there for you when you needed money not so long ago.

Orin turned to descend. I sat at the purp, blocking him. Don't get me wrong, the guy had a powerful will, maybe stronger than mine. But he lacked purp access at the deeper levels. As well you know, access has been the name of the game for fifty millennia.

Orin's obsession was gonna get us both in trouble. I had to play him tight, but not overly so. He would sense that and fight me.

He used his link to push at the mental barriers operating the forward tunnel, but got murked up again. Wrong codes. Wrong attitude. Finally, he clenched his fists and opened his mouth.

"They need me."

Ah, the ultimate conceit! They needed him, not merely his message.

"Maybe later," I answered, pretending nonchalance. My mouthparts worked the purp where chemicals conveyed data. I also wore a link, which automatically kicked in when I disengaged my mouthparts, but I preferred the old-fashioned interface. It really let me get a taste of the data.

He gritted his teeth and his back tensed. Long ago, it would have been a meaningless gesture for me, but I'd worked

Orin

with his human guise long enough that it seemed standard. If one of our own people, a Wann, had emerged unannounced from back tunnel, I'd have jumped out of my skins in fright. Orin and his human shape had become the norm.

I'll describe the human body. You've dealt with gas giant derivs, and though they're not really aliens, they do *look* alien. You'd never know they were once like us, lab altered and shoved into makeform suits to brave the horrid ring storms of their intended environment.

Humans, however, are true aliens, with no relation to us. They've got two legs for walking, two arms for grasping and manipulating, brains up in a head teetering above the whole gravity-threatened affair of their sticklike bodies. There is a central nervous system coordinated through the backbone. They're really proud of the opposable thumbs located on the ends of the arms, and they're awfully obsessed with their own sexual organs, improbably located between the legs. (Frankly, I cannot see how the males walk around without crushing their own genitals, but I guess if you live with an evolutionary joke like that for two million years, you get used to it.)

By way of comparison, I'll give you the same explanation of our bodies that I gave to the Rim Wisp Collective who visited a few millennia ago. He/it/they was unable to see me, as I radiated in the wrong spectra for Wisp senses, so I purped him the following description.

We Wann have three legs for bounce-walking, but the front limb is a fusion of two smaller limbs. It's got a hook on the end for grabbing, traction and gutting. Within our two freefloating skins, we move like a small water bed filled with blubber. Our mouthparts act as hands, doing the fine work, like interfacing a perp. We're very proud of our mouthparts, but we're far more obsessed with the back fin being either notched or unnotched. You know how that goes, being a big-notched guy yourself.

As species, both Wann and humans generate disproportionate bureaucracies, which makes us more similar than different, despite our bodies.

After his mission surgery, Orin was a Wann mind in a

33

human body, but I'd argue he was less like either species than he was a unique character. Orin was simply . . . Orin. Don't try to put him in a box or label him. Ordinarily, I'd find that distasteful, but he was so well-meaning, you had to love him.

"You wasted too much of my time already," he complained. "It took me a month to fill out my travel voucher!"

I laughed inwardly. It's true, I'd fiddled with the purp every time he jacked in, lowering the frequency, deleting files, spilling fluids so he had to redo his form over and over. I kept blaming it on the maintenance plek, but guess who controlled the plek?

"Why not fill out a complaint form?" I asked, keeping mouthparts steady. "That might take *two* months."

He scowled. "Take your notchless fin and—"

"Whoa, keep it clean, barbarian!" I laughed. "That's not the sort of base insult I'd expect from a celebrated deity. And I don't see a notch on *your* thin-skinned back."

"I never said I was a deity. They did." He jerked a finger toward the forward tunnel.

That gesture could have indicated anywhere in the local star cluster. But of course he meant Earth, which was the home planet of the humans.

"Jeeeesus Christ," I said, shivering my skins in mock recrimination.

He wrinkled his brow. "What?"

"Nothing. I'm just calling you what *they* call you." I indicated the forward tunnel with my forelimb. "Hallelujah, brothers, send me your cash today and I will saaaaave you from your sins! Act now, operators are standing by. Visa and MasterCard accepted."

He stared at me for a long time. I was human-savvy enough to catch quite a few shades of emotion within his stare.

I let my mouthparts wave noncommittally to and fro.

He shook his head. "I meant something to them."

"Careful, Orin, you're not really a god," I reminded him. "You just play one on TV. When the sense of humor goes, so goes reason." It was sound advice.

He retreated to his niche with a curse. The con reformed and he was safely tucked away.

Orin

Or maybe not. I would be wary. Didn't keep my cush job this long by taking stupid chances.

Two days later, mister grumpy deity emerged.

"We've got honey and locusts in the food niche if you're hungry," I teased.

"Ha, ha," he said, grabbing an ale and twisting off the top. He guzzled the ale and tossed it aside when done.

A recycle plek caught the bottle, turned it over a few times to examine it, and scurried off on a confused path. Probably a newbie from back tunnel. Bottles were a completely human thing. Who would've thought you could make a container for liquids out of something as dangerous as glass?

By the way, they make great knickknacks. I'll send you one. Did you get that human lab skeleton I sent a few decades back? Cost me a mint, but I thought you were worth it.

"Let's talk." I let go the purp and sloshed over, settling into my chair, hindpods sinking into the floor and my bulk resting on a web of parafilament. I tapped the tabletop with my spike. "We've known each other a long time, Orin, since you were a one-skinned little baglet."

A shy smile crept around his lips. "Yeah." He fiddled with a food pack, removing the entrée and scooping out a spoonful. Beef stroganoff. Not planet fare, but a close simulation rumored to be nutritious.

"The others used to lean on you until I swear I thought you'd pop." I squatted sidewise on a pillow until it splurched out and hit the ceiling. The plek caught it, fluffed it, tamped it down beside me.

"They treated me unjustly. There's no reason for that kind of behavior." His eyes went faraway, then cleared. "That was a long time ago."

"Even longer in planet time," I said.

He nodded, taking a quick breath. "That's what I was telling you. The people of Earth have had a lot of time to absorb my teachings and—"

"They've had no time!" I said, tapping the tabletop again.

Another plek moved forward as if I'd summoned it, and I smacked it into the wall. It retreated with a whimper and I signaled the perp to keep the damned things clear of the room. "Two thousand years isn't shit, Orin. It's barely enough time for your grand lesson to sink in. These humans do better with Mohammed, anyway. He was practical, knew how to compromise and play politics. And he wasn't even our guy. He was organic."

Oh, the Arabian Conquest had been a sight! I ran a betting pool with some of the guys in the home office on that one. When the Moors took Spain, I collected quite a chunk of cash.

Which I later sent to you, if you remember.

"It's plenty of time," he objected, leaning forward. "People can learn and grow and change if they want."

I felt the intensity of his eyes like a blow to the body. If I were human, he could have compelled my obedience. But a Wann is not, as they say, human. And my fin does possess a deep and ruggedly carved notch, thank you very much, so bowing and scraping was not something I'd easily do.

"Orin, this is your first assignment, so you've gotta pace yourself." I wiggled in my chair, trying to get that deep-down comfort feel that makes debate seem like dessert. "You have a solid message, and you've got brand. The Christians are all over that planet, well organized, spreading the faith, and growing ever wealthier. But you've got to mature. Remember Meenev?"

He rolled his eyes. "Meenev was working with the pre-Indian states. That was different."

"Granted, but his philosophy was more subtle, yet radical in its way," I said. "Not so confrontational. It allowed its believers to recognize a universal truth. It didn't force them to change the world overnight. Hell, it strengthened the ones in power!"

"Leaving his believers in bondage," he said.

"So? Life is bondage," I countered. "You just have to make sure the chains aren't too tight. For example, where would I be without this job chaining me?" I wiggled my bulk. "Hell, where would you be?"

"I want to shake the foundations of authority," Orin insisted. "The priests were blocking a substantive transformation

36

of the whole society."

"Priests, hell." I scraped the tabletop in excitement, and he winced. "Sorry, forgot about those sensitive human ears. Orin, you have to look at societies from a functional perspective. Don't get so caught up in the suffering versus happiness paradigm. Every part has its function, and one function of those in power is to slow down transformation, allowing the rest of society to gradually adapt and not be blown apart."

"No!" he said, slapping the table, and this time it was I who winced. "Sorry, forgot about the Wann percussive amplifiers," he apologized. "It's just wrong to let those in charge get away with oppression."

"That's their function, Orin! It's all part of the game. Oh, you are so wonderfully naive."

"It's not a game!" he roared, and this time his eyes lit up so fiercely that I nearly rolled right back out of my chair, quivering.

It was at this point that I began to feel real fear. I was fairly cynical when it came to shaping societies. Had to be in my job. But part of me wanted to believe in Orin. Part of me sensed that. . . well, I'll say it. Part of me sensed Orin was right and I was just a fool standing in his way.

Go figure. I'm a sentimentalist deep down in my skins.

"It's not a game," he continued. "This is for real."

I wobbled hard to center myself. "Your ego is so wrapped up in success that you've lost sight of the goal here."

"And what is that?" he asked. "If we aren't leading these people as shepherds, then why drop a con halfway across the galaxy? Why seed them with Meenev, aka Buddha, and others like me?" He tapped his chest.

I resettled slowly into the chair holes, angry at myself for wanting to do exactly as he said, just tear into the corrupt Wann authorities who smothered their own people with comfortable lies. But I was also annoyed with him. Orin was asking for the truth, but I was one of the guys helping those corrupt authorities "massage" the truth to stay in power.

They pay well, after all.

"When you were younger, you wanted to be one of the

elite, a seeder of foreign shores, but you knew the mission." I waved at the purp pad, contextually synonymous with the forward tunnel, and hence the local cluster of stars. "We're like everybody else who succeeds in this universe. We're a self-interested, highly-developed civilization with a scattering of friends, and a dark glot of powerful enemies who could threaten us directly. We don't pick open fights with them. It's not to our advantage. We maintain a balance."

"So the humans—" he began.

"And all the others we mentor," I added, again indicating the forward tunnel.

"—they're all dupes who do our bidding," he said, his expressive face registering anger.

"Allies, by another name," I said.

"Proxies," he countered. "For a war—"

"—that may never happen," I finished. "It might just be one of those things you prepare millennia for and it fizzles out, so you go on to the next preoccupation. Welcome to the status quo, my friend. It's predictable, and far more preferable than chaos."

"Our work is a perversion." He set his jaw and his eyes hardened.

"Our work is a necessity," I offered. "Get used to it, young charge."

He shook his head, the black hair falling softly with ringlets around the ears, skin tanned and feet firm in the sandals. "I'm going back."

I rolled upward, hindlegs compressing and foreleg raised in a gesture he must certainly remember was threatening. The human body was an impossible marvel, but it was no match for my spike. One thin little skin would not protect its innards if I struck. "Like hell you are, Orin. I am in charge here."

The moment stretched on. I could kill him, and not be reprimanded. I did it once before on another con, orbiting a different world. The Wann I killed was wearing an alien body, and he'd strayed too far, gone native. His death was quick, but I couldn't sleep for weeks after the experience without horrible nightmares.

I did not want to kill Orin. Damn, I loved the little baglet!

He finally licked his lips and looked sidewise. "You misunderstood me."

Whew . . . Thank god he'd backed down! The boy was too strong for his experience level, that was the problem. But he wasn't stupid. He was learning the first painful lessons of compromise. I settled back into the chairholes with relief. "It's been a rough assignment on you. You went too deep too fast. We'll let you rest up and re-enter their society in, say, three hundred of their years. Is that fair?"

He nodded and took his leave, disappearing into his niche, while I sat there and considered how to handle the rest of the assignment. Orin did not understand the political reality back home. Our cons were spread in a vast three dimensional net covering half the galaxy. The enemy net lay beside us, one for one, dark for light, and the potential for a spark was great.

A spark that would temporarily disrupt the status quo.

If the spark occurred somewhere near Earth, we'd mobilize the humans, discreetly boost their warfighting capabilities, our proxy against the Enemy's proxy. In this neck of the local cluster, though, we were terribly outmatched and knew it. Earth would fall, and there would be frantic negotiations, but not before human civilization met its tragic end.

I'd be blamed. Humans and Wann both honored the technique of scapegoating minor functionaries after political disasters. Orin needed to see it from my point of view.

He'd come around.

I let the pleks back in. They tidied up.

My day began with exercise on the rollers. Oh, how my lateral cords ached! Did the rollers have to be so brutal? But a few pints of altered ale settled my skins and I fit my pods to the chairholes in front of the main purp. It awoke and I asked for logs.

The data scrolled through my mouth in discrete chemical blurbs. There were some comets being harvested as long range weapons . . . have to tag them, helluva weapon if you forget they're there. One of the Enemy clients was developing solar lensing to warp gravity and hide its moon bases. Might need intervention, but it wasn't my department. I passed it off to Mid Tech. And a small administrative note alerted me that my con was undermanned. Underpersonned. Whatever.

Wait, repeat that? My con was a two-Wann operation. Two Wann required, two authorized and two present for duty. Why did . . .

"Purp!" I asked louder than intended. "Where is Orin?"

ORIN HAS TUNNELED, came the response.

I shot upright, mouthparts spraying fluid and spike clattering the deckboard. "I told you he was not to go forward unless I authorized it!"

HE DID NOT GO FORWARD.

"But if he . . ." I remembered our last conversation where I'd come close to threatening him with physical violence. "He said he was 'going back'. Then he said I misunderstood him."

"HE WENT—"

It hit me like one of those weapon comets plowing full speed into a populated planet. This was bad! "Back tunnel," I said, my skins bumping each other in panic. "Orin went back tunnel." A plek came close, stroking my skin. I spiked it reflexively.

The plek died with a hiss of escaping air and a query laced with surprise, but I barely noticed.

"He went back to the core," I continued. "Back to the great unwashed legions of uninformed idiots who do not appreciate the stability that the status quo provides." A new thought struck me, clear and chilling. "Back where the politicians are firmly in charge and they have a function in society, yes they do, slowing it down, keeping a lid on the boiler. But they also pander to the electorate, the feckless bastards! They'd sell their own sibs out for any political advantage."

IS THERE SOMETHING YOU REQUIRE OF ME?

"Oh, god, he's smarter than the first time. This boy is warier." The panic carried me on a wave that seemed to remove me from the purp, from the con, from a sense of self. "He'll build his base of support. He ain't fighting this galactic Rome until he's damned sure of himself. They won't crucify Orin a second time, me having to pluck his body out and drop him in rejuv for a whole day, no."

DO YOU REQUIRE REJUVENATION SERVICES?

I just sat there, still stunned and trying to think. This con with its single tunnel and purp feed was all I knew, my whole life. And as long as it was business as usual, it's all I needed to know. But Orin, back there, with his intense eyes and his resolve and his experience—experience I gave him!—oh, he was a danger.

WHAT DO YOU REQUIRE?

I could hear the air whistling out of my precious status quo, just like the squashed plek now blotching the floor, about to be removed by another of its mindless fellows. I laughed within my skins until they burned with it. The fear chattered me mindless. The sense of a future I no longer controlled rose up like a dark wall.

"Yeah," I finally said, answering the purp. "I need you to send a letter to my sibling."

Which leads me to the request I now make, my beloved kindred. You work in Personnel. You're good at what you do. You have connections.

So . . . can you help me write a resume?

Redemption at Willow Crossing

Linda Arnest

People say I'as crazy. They look at me funny all the time. Some's scared; cross the road to stay out my way. I ain't never hurt nobody.

That's alright, I guess. It don't matter much what people say. Don't even matter what they think. Only thing matter's what they does. I mind what people does. I watch them. Miss Dory Maiden, the schoolmarm, says I studies them.

I was the baby of the Allen Clan. They'as all kinds of stories why I didn't come out right. Ole Mammy, who birthed me, said it was mamma's forty-five years that done it. Some said it was the curse that come with the Great Depression days.

I think it was cause I'as born on the Leaped Year. I don't get a birthday ever year. I only get one ever four years. While other babies born same year as me was learnin to talk, I'as still droolin.

Mamma loved me, though. I'd sit on her lap; she petted on me an talked to me in her soft, sweet voice. She tried to keep me from seein the people stare at church an the kids mockin me. But I seen. Before my twelfth year mamma was gone an I knowd I'as different.

After that it was just me an Marindee, all the other Allen folk gone an buried under the pine trees behind the smokehouse. Our great grand-daddy, Moses Mathis Allen, buried highest on the hill, was taken early by the asthma.

Mamma used to say, in the days before I'as born, Grandpa Allen grew the best sorghum for miles around. People come from far away to trade for it; sometimes with store-bought things. Mamma told so many stories, like the one bout the time Grandpa traded a load of sorghum to a bootlegger for a phonograph. Trouble was we didn't have no records to play on it.

Redemption at Willow Crossing

I loved the stories mamma used to tell. I could spend hours sittin in the family graveyard tellin them stories to the cows in the pasture, the crow on the fence post or Ole Tom Cat. But I couldn't live in the past all the time.

Marindee kept me round cause I has a way with animals. There wadn't no animal doctors for miles. I'd look in the eyes of a animal an knowd its pain, its fear. I'as more at home in the pigpen, the cow pasture, the hen house than any other place on God's green earth. They didn't look at me funny or hate me; they'as my only friends.

I has to be careful round Marindee. Miranda Sue Allen was her given name, but we all called her Marindee. She ain't book smart like Miss Maiden, but she can size up a sit-e-ation in seconds flat. Her eyes gets all squinty an I know her mind's aworkin. Don't take her long a'tall till she know what she gonna do.

Marindee got a mean streak. When I was just a boy, she'd whisper in my ear, tell me mamma an daddy's gonna sell me to the circus. I'd be the star of the freak show, she say. They'd put me in a cage tween Elephant Man an Chang an Eng, the Siamese twins. She say they'd take one look at my sorry face an just call me Freak Boy.

Cause I was family, Marindee let me stay in the little house out back of the big house. I wadn't allowed to step foot in the big house no more. But I had a wood stove an enough to eat. That was more an some folk in them Depressin days.

After mamma died, Marindee say I have to go to school. I didn't wanna go, had a fit, kickin an screamin. I'd never stayed away from home nor family. Marindee put me in the wagon anyways an drove me the mile to the schoolhouse an left me. That'as when I met Miss Dory Maiden. She wadn't nice as mamma, but she was real nice.

Miss Maiden come from Chicago. Peoples say she come in to money when her mamma an daddy died. All her kinfolk dead and gone now. Nobody knowd why she come to Hazel Green, Kentucky, of all places.

Ever day at school, she let me sit right in front of her

desk. She gave me colors an paper with pictures I could fill in. She told stories bout them pictures. The stories the best part of the day, that an dinner break when the other kids went out the room. She kept me behind; I ate my dinner with Miss Maiden.

She never let the other kids hurt me. But she wadn't round all the time.

One day a little colored boy come to the front porch an knocked on the door. Marindee was out in the fields workin, so nobody come. I knowd 'im from town, seen 'im offerin to help folks pack groceries or sweep the feed an grain store floor. I never seen 'im get any work, but he'd spend the whole day tryin.

I heard 'is daddy had left town lookin for minin work in the next county; been gone a month or two. Had to be hard on the boy, his mamma an little sister. The boy's mamma did laundry for rich folk in town, but times had got so bad her work fell off. They lived in a dirt floor shack out past our place in the holler. Only stove they got for heat is the cook stove.

I caught the boy's eye as he passed me by in town one day; felt the gnaw in his belly sure as if it was my own.

Hap Wasson walked the rutted dirt road as the sun broke above the tree tops on a cold spring morning. He watched his breath escape in a white cloud of moisture thinking about the work boots on his feet. His family had sacrificed over the winter, some days having only a pone of cornbread and a bit of red-eye gravy to eat so they could afford the only pair of shoes the family owned. He could walk farther and get better work with the boots. That was his hope.

Hap had walked two miles before sunrise and had two more to go before coming to the largest farm in the area. The Wyatt farm would begin the work day at 7:00 a.m. Assignments made, workers would move out into the fields and barn shortly after.

He heard Jeb Wyatt was slaughtering spring lambs this morn. He carried his butcher and fillet knives and meat hook in the burlap feed sack slung over his shoulder. His grand-daddy was taught as a slave on the Miller Plantation to slaughter and carve the annual harvest. He'd handed the craft down to this son and grandson. Hap took pride in his work. He could slit a lamb's throat so quick and clean it didn't make a sound. Maybe Mr. Wyatt would throw in a lamb shank or two if he did a real good job. A little money and some meat would do his family good about now.

The sun was up enough to know it was going to be a warm spring day, a welcome after so many long winter nights. He thought about summer as he came to the main road and headed north on Highway 25, the smooth pavement allowing him to pick up his pace.

Hap's empty stomach growled a complaint as he pondered his financial future. After the spring kills there wouldn't be much butcher work until the fall hog slaughter. Paddy told him they were hiring at the coal mine over in Hazard. Hap hated that deep, dirty work, but maybe he could save enough to get Lotty and the kids through next winter better. Lotty had her laundry work and Little Hap was earning a bit here and there. They'd make it alright.

I was sittin in the Y of the poplar tree bout half way up when that little colored boy come walkin up to the front door of the big house an knocked real soft. He knocked again, then stood tall as 'is small frame would let 'im. He only flinched a bit when Marindee snapped the door open. She stared at 'im silent with those devil eyes of hers.

"Mornin, ma'am." I thought I saw 'is pant leg shakin. "I was wonderin if they's any work I might do for y'all today, ma'am; gatherin eggs, milkin, feedin?"

"Go on. Git outa here, boy." Marindee's voice boomed. The boy jumped a foot back'ards without knowin it. "I got a boy to do all my shit work. Don't need ya. Now, git!"

Without lookin her in the eye he said, "Yes, ma'am. If you ain't got no work for me, I'as wonderin if I might do a little fishin in your pond. We ain't had nothin to eat save some poke salad greens an cornbread in a couple days, if you could be so kind, ma'am."

"I said GIT!" Marindee yelled. Even I heard "nigger bastard" as the door slammed shut.

I got to Willow Crossin before the colored boy. Willow Crossin's a restin spot in a grove of willow trees on the walkin path bout halfway between Highway 25 an East Bernstadt. Somebody long ago felled a old oak an laid part cross the creek that ran through. The other half served as a sittin bench. Somebody left a dented tin cup for passers-by to have a cold drink from the creek.

I took a haircut through Ole Man Goss's pasture where he kept that bull ever body was scared of. We had us a understandin, ole bull an me. I took 'im a few sticks of sorghum to help 'im remember.

I was sittin on the log havin myself a drink of creek water when the boy got there. He looked at me surprised.

"Howdy," he said.

I knowd he wouldn't understand my jabberin, so I just dug in the front pocket of my dungarees, pulled out three warm hen eggs an handed 'em to 'im. His eyes changed an I knowd, just like when I turn the calf so's it can be born the right way, he trusted an would remember me, like the mamma of that calf.

I hates to say it, but that trust would fail the boy, sure as they's a world.

Some days later, I was up at the graveyard spinnin old tales for a jack rabbit when I heared Marindee's heavy foot steps down below. I could see half the farm from up there. Marindee walked back towards the hen house, then farther toward the pond. Then I seen'im, that little colored boy, sittin on the end of the fishin wharf with a cane pole in 'is hands. Marindee seen 'im, too.

I got quiet an hunkered down. I slipped down off the hill quiet as a mouse an hid behind the hen house. From there I has a bird's eye view of the wharf. My stomach has a knot big as a goose egg an I'as sweatin in the cool mornin air like the Fourth of July.

Redemption at Willow Crossing

Marindee's first foot step on the wharf caused the boy to jump. He put his pole down an jumped up to face her. I think he's too scared to speak.

"What's the matter, cat got your tongue, Little Black Sambo?" she smiled a crocodile grin.

"Miss Marindee, ma'am, I know you told me—"

"Shut up, boy," Marindee snapped. "So, what did you catch in my pond?" She pulled up his line tied to the wharf post an found four small bluegill. "This will make me a fine supper."

"Ma'am, please—" the boy started, but Marindee picked up his fishin pole an poked 'im in 'is chest. I seen her eyes gettin squinty; I'as so scared for that boy.

"I told you what, boy?" she poked again, pushin 'im back toward the pond.

"You told me not to . . ." I could see the fear in 'is eyes, feel it in the air, sharp as that fishin hook.

"That's right, you bastard. So, what'm I gon do with you now?"

"I swear on the Bible, ma'am, if you—"

"Shut up, boy." She poked again. "You know what happens to niggers who steal, don't you?"

"Please ma'am, my mamma—"

"I told you to SHUT UP." Marindee poked hard an the boy fell into the pond. My heart nearly stopped. Nobody could swim in these parts, least off a colored boy. His arms thrashed as he fought the water tryin to stay afloat. Marindee pushed 'im under with the cane pole. He come up coughin an grabbin. I put my hand over my own mouth to hold back a scream. I had no doubt what Marindee'd do if she seen me there.

The boy grabbed onto the fishin pole with all 'is small strength, coughin an screamin. Marindee pushed 'im under one last time an held 'im there til the pond water was calm again. She waited a long minute then took the boy's catch an his fishin pole an left, a sick grin covered her face. I watched her go in the smokehouse; she come out without the pole an took the fish in the house.

I could only swallow a bite or two of the pan-fried bluegill

47

that night.

A few days go by an folks start talkin bout the missin colored boy. Ever'body knowd 'im cause he was always askin for work. The boy's mamma talked to Floyd Barnes, Reverend of the colored Baptist Church on Crooked-Leg Road. She say her boy went off to ask Miss Marindee if he could fish her pond. Reverend Barnes talks to Reverend Albert Houston of the white people's Holiness Church over on Laurel Ridge. Reverend Houston feels for the woman an puts together a dragin party.

They talks to Marindee. She say no boy asked to fish her pond, but go on an drag if they wont to.

This be the saddest day in my sorry life, fersure. I watch them bring flat-bottom boats an lines with big fishin hooks on 'um. They cross ever inch of that water.

I set on the hill, close enough I can see, but not too close. I shivers like its Christmas in the early August heat. I knows what they gonna find.

As they work on the far side of the wharf, Leonard Sizemore yelled, "We got somethin!" Colored boy's mamma begin to break down in Reverend Barnes' arms. They pull an pull, all the while I'm thinkin bout them hooks in that boy's skin. Finally, they pulls 'im up on the bank. I can see 'im clear as day. His hair an clothes full of mud an green pond plants, his mouth froze open in a scream; his skin grey like a March sky an wrinkled like nobody I ever seen before.

The boy's mamma walks close enough to be sure, held up ever step by Reverend Barnes. When she gets bout ten feet away she stop. An then the sorriest sound I ever heard in my life come out of that woman. It'as a wail that hit me like a strong arm punch square in the chest. I runs off in the woods an stay gone two days.

I dream bout that boy in his watery grave ever night for weeks. With his green hair an grey skin, he cries out to me; wake cryin most days. One mornin I decide, I just cain't take it no more.

* ✳ *

Redemption at Willow Crossing

Hap was broken when Lotty told him about the boy. He was so proud of that boy; a hard worker, book smart and mannered. He would make his way in this world better than his daddy had.

But now the boy was gone. Drown in a pond trying to feed his mamma and sister. He'd left a boy to do a man's job. This would weigh on Hap for the rest of his life.

Hap came home from coal mining in late August. He hadn't seen or heard from his family since he left in May. By sharing one room with another miner, he kept his expenses low and saved $10.00 in wages. They'd get through the coming winter alright.

Hap was on his way to the Wyatt farm to ask about the fall hog kill and get his name in for hire when he came upon Willow Crossing. He knelt at the creek bank, splashed his face with cool water, then scooped up a handful to drink. He was about to go on when he noticed the boy sitting on the log bench. He wasn't a boy really, but he looked and acted so strange everybody called him boy; like they did Hap, but for different reasons.

The boy was small for his age. Even as an adult, he had the frame and stature of a young boy. Born with a cleft palate and tongue attached all the way to the tip, the formation of words was impossible. His appearance was freakish, his mouth a gapping hole, teeth widely spaced, scaring most folk. But, for some reason, Hap worked hard on this day to get past the deformity and look into the boy's expressive blue eyes.

"Afternoon," Hap touched the brim of his hat and walked by. To Hap's surprise, the boy stopped him and excitedly tried to form words. His mouth worked in strange ways like a gash in his small face, but nothing Hap could understand came out.

The boy gave up trying. Hap waited, half out of amazed curiosity, half out of courtesy to this pathetic white boy-man who had no more status in the community than he had.

The boy let out a long, slow sigh as he looked into the black man's eyes. Hap wasn't sure what he saw there; pain, compassion, determination. He was compelled to try and understand the boy.

And then the boy reached out and took Hap's hand. His mouth worked, his eyes focused, he said, "C—C—Cm."

Hap's own grief was touched by the boy and so he followed him across the fields to the Allen farm and the smokehouse. Inside, the boy pointed to a partially exposed cane fishing pole. Hap pulled it out and found the initials HW carved into it by his very own hand. His eyes grew darker as he studied the cane pole.

The boy flinched when Hap turned to him. "Miss Marindee done this?"

The boy stared at his bare feet standing on the dirt floor of the smokehouse and shook his head yes.

Hap put his hand on the boy's head and tiled it back so he could look him in the eye. "You a good man, Moses Mathis Allen."

I'as didn't know what Hap might do, but I knowd I'd done all I could. The dreams had stopped; the boy must be at rest.

Then early one mornin I woke to the sound of commotion in the big house; it wadn't light yet. Pots an dishes clattered an broke. I seen the dim light of the oil lamp inside an shapes movin in the kitchen. Marindee yelled, "Git out this house, you son-of-a-bitch." An then she screamed. Not long after that, a man come runnin out the back door an off in the woods. It'as so dark I couldn't tell for sure who it was.

I wait til sun-up. When I don't hear Marindee stirrin like usual, I tiptoe in the back door of the big house. There she lay, spread eagle on the kitchen floor cold as a stone, her throat cut clean open.

I took off runnin to the nearest neighbors, Mr. an Mrs. Philpot. They bout half mile down the road. I was so excited it wadn't hard gettin Mr. Philpot to bring me back in 'is wagon.

Soon after that, the Sheriff come all the way from Springfield. He had two black automobiles full of deputies with 'im. I never seen a automobile before. I heard Reverend Houston say they's Model T Fords. Folks come from all over to watch as they took Marindee out the house. One of the police cars went on down the road an brought Hap back.

I heard Worley Barnes tellin the Sheriff that Hap was surly the man who killed Ole Marindee, with his son drowned in her pond an her throat slit; ever'body knowd Hap was a butcher by trade.

Bout that time Hap's wife an little daughter come walkin up. The three of them holds to one another like they's one person.

Miss Maiden come drivin up in her buggy. She come an stands by me just as the Sheriff come. He looks at me, then at Miss Maiden like he hopin she has some answers, then back at me again.

The Sheriff say, "Boy, you see your sister get killed?"

Miss Maiden try to help, "Mose, did a noise wake you this morning?"

I stares at the ground an shakes my head yes.

The Sheriff say, "Boy, you see the man who done this come out the house?"

I shakes my head yes.

"Was it a white man?" I heard Worley Barnes start to take exception, then somebody shushed 'im.

I shrugs my shoulders.

"Was it a negra man?"

I shrugs again.

"Was it this man here, Hap Wasson?"

I look at Hap. His eyes full of fear. We both seen colored hung on the spot with less reason. He still holdin his family tight.

I shakes my head no.

Worley an the others gets louder; they ain't likin this.

Sheriff shuffle 'is feet, takes 'is hat off an runs a hand through 'is hair. Then he look at Hap hard. "You gonna have to come with me, boy."

One of the deputies steps behind Hap an handcuffed 'im. His wife an little daughter begins cryin. Then they put Hap in the back of one of them automobiles.

Miss Maiden asks the Sheriff if he gonna charge Hap with murder. He say no ma'am, but he needs to take 'im in an let the prosecutor decide what he gonna do. Besides, the Sheriff say, it probably ain't safe for Hap round these parts right now with folks worked up an all.

Miss Maiden say it ain't right to take Hap in. They's no evidence an they cain't hold 'im without chargin 'im. She ask for the prosecutor's name.

Miss Maiden got one arm round me an the other round Hap's wife. We stood there watchin as the automobiles left with Hap inside.

Wadn't long after Marindee was killed Miss Maiden starts callin on me bout ever day. She'd cook an then sit an visit with me a while. Wadn't long after that I starts realizin all the things Marindee done I had no idea bout.

Miss Maiden understands. She takes over the paperwork an hires Jessee Lee Thomas to do the field work. She say they's no reason for me not to live in the big house again. She gits Hap's wife, Lotty, an daughter to come live in the little house out back. Lotty takes care of the house an cookin. She a good cook.

An then Miss Maiden moves to the big house. She say she went and talked to a judge an now she the closest thing to family I got in Hazel Green. She ain't as nice as mamma, but she real nice.

Life these day's pretty good. I still takes care of the animals an sit in the graveyard spinnin tales from the past ever chance I get. Miss Maiden's learnin me to talk an read an write better. An now I don't have to be watchin Marindee all the time.

We think bout Hap all the time.

For two years, Miss Maiden writes one letter ever week tryin to get Hap out of jail. She say it ain't fair, 'im never bein charged with anything. She write to the sheriff, the prosecutor, a judge, the prison warden, the state legislature an even the governor of the Great Commonwealth of Kentucky. (I still puzzle bout the meanin of that word so many of us bein poor an all.) She even write President Herbert Hoover, his self. I always said, if they's anybody can git Ole Hap out of there, it'as Miss Maiden. An damn if she don't.

Redemption at Willow Crossing

Hap come home in February when they's a dust of snow on the ground. The cold don't make 'im no never mind. First thing Ole Hap done was build a bigger house for 'is family out behind the big house. Come spring, he takes over the field work. We takes our meals together an, over time, I find out what a kind man Hap be.

We was almost like family, not blood relations, but I'as thinkin, maybe they's times when the kind that comes together by chance an happenstance in this life is the best kind of family they is.

Ancient Suite—Mound City
For Barbara Bonney

Carol Feiser Laque

Skeletons skip high noon into
    celestial syncopations.

Bones war and mirror dance
    clouds, thunder, blue skies.

I dream days around nights
    owning Earth before Pangaea.

My headstone in the mossy cemetery
    is a glossy, hidden hideout.

I wear a dead woman's shoes.
    They do not fit.

An American Blues Band in Paris

In memory of
Russell Otero Givens, Jr.
Blues man extraordinaire

Darlene Blasing

Slender branches traced dark, intricate patterns on an overcast sky as Otis and Company made their way along the Seine. The band had taken a red-eye flight to Paris, arriving minutes before dawn. After dropping their bags off at the hotel, they hit the streets for a closer look at the city. Otis, the band's leader, and Richard, his friend and bass player, were in high spirits.

As they drew near the Pont Neuf, the silhouette of a familiar landmark emerged in dawn's glow.

"Oooee, lookee there . . . the I fell tower!" Otis made a tumbling motion with his hands as a cool November breeze snatched ashes from his Cuban cigar.

Richard slapped his comrade's back, a guffaw exploding from his throat. "That's a good one, O."

The band's young pianist shook his head. "You embarrass me, man . . . two old men who don't know how to behave yourselves."

"Don't be dissing them, Jimmie," snapped Jasmine, her arm curled around Richard's. "They were playin' the Blues when you were crawlin' 'round in your diapers."

"Bare ass, mo' likely," boomed Otis, prompting another burst of laughter from Richard.

"I don't know you people," said Jimmie as he dropped farther behind the group.

"Oh, come on! They jus' funnin' ya." Sadie, their petite, sixty-eight-year-old drummer coaxed him over her shoulder as she stepped smartly alongside the 'boys', a floppy, faux leopard skin tam topping her wild mane.

"Young people have no sense o' humor," groused Otis. He pulled his wool peacoat tighter against the chill.

"You got that right. That one's got no respec' for his elders, neither," complained Richard.

"Mm, mm, mm. What ya gonna do?" Sadie posed her favorite question.

"Ain't nothin' ya can do with kids these days," was Richard's pronouncement.

"Fersure," purred Jasmine.

Jimmie was outnumbered, as usual.

Parisians love Blues and they packed the club that evening. Jasmine's voice alternated between sweet and sassy, while the sultry notes dripping from Otis' sax slithered around the room putting everyone in a mood. What kind of mood depended on each person's inclination. One thing the Blues does not do is make you blue.

After the first set, the band sidled up to the bar.

"What ya got fer us to eat, bro?" Richard asked the bartender, a dark, mustachioed Middle-Easterner.

"For you we 'ave Steak Tartar, broiled Swordfish Amande, and Shrimp Diable over pasta."

"Don't ya have any poke chops in this place?" railed Richard.

"What's steak tartar?" he asked in an aside to Otis.

"That's bloody meat, man. We don't want that."

"What we got left . . . swordfish?" Richard intentionally pronounced the 'w'. "I don't care for swordfish. I don't care for pasta, neither." He spoke the offending word with a derogatory 'a', as in 'at'.

"Does Diable mean what I think it means?" Otis directed his question at the barkeep.

"Ees spicy, veery spicy."

"That does it. We come all this way to entertain these folks and they can't give us a decent meal? That pasta dish is heartburn city. I knows it." Richard was ready to rush out in search of something closer to home cooking.

"Let's try the swordfish," begged Jimmie.

"I don't know if I'd like dat." Sadie's face puckered into a frown.

"Could we speak to Monsieur Dugas, please," inquired Otis.

"Certainly, sir." The bartender disappeared into the back room and returned a moment later with the Frenchman who had engaged the band for a one-month stint in his club.

"Monsieur Jones, Farad says you unhappy with menu. What you like?"

"Well, sir, back home we eat steak, taters, greens, cornbread. . . ."

" . . . a big pile a poke chops would be dandy," interjected Richard.

"Fried chicken is nice," drawled Sadie, "an' biscuits an' gravy. Do y'all grow okra here?"

"I'm partial to grits," said Jasmine. "Ya know, grits are the blues of food. They're simple, down home, make-ya-feel-good vittles. With a dab o' sweet butter on top they soak right into yer soul."

"That's right," said Otis. "Pipin' hot they warm yer innards. Let 'em git cold an' they're unbearable. Gotta be jus' right, like the notes I play.

The little man chuckled and shook his head from side to side. "You Americans will die by the fork."

"Look here," persisted Otis, "I'm not sure we kin digest the food yer servin'. We're not used to it."

"Right on," said Richard.

"Sho nuf," echoed Sadie, "and a band plays on its stomach."

"You got that right. I don't know if I kin play bass on a diet of swordfish and pasta."

"Please. Please. I have answer. You bring me what you like and my wife will prepare. There is an *epicerie* . . . oh, how you say . . . food mart around corner."

Not From Around Here, Are You?

"That won't hep us tonight," grumbled Richard.

"*Excusez-moi?*"

"He said, we'll make do with swordfish tonight," corrected Jimmie.

Richard made a quick motion with his hand telling Jimmie to stay out of it.

"We have no choice." Otis's voice held a note of finality. "We've got to git back on stage faster than my Aunt Abby kin pluck a chicken."

"All right," sighed Richard, "but we'd better git some poke chops tomorrow. I'll starve on a seafood diet."

Later, as they prepared to start the second set, Richard slid onto his stool and cradled his bass, Corrina, in his arms. A pained expression wrinkled his brow.

"That swordfish is gunna throw ma playin' off. I kin feel ma innards rumblin'."

"You grumble too much, Richie," whispered Sadie as she slipped behind her drums. "If I grumbled haf as much as you, I'd wear mysef out."

"You said it," seconded Jimmie, happy to have an ally for a change.

"All right yous kids, let's git this show a rollin'." Otis turned to the audience and stepped up to the microphone. "*Bon soir, mes amies!* I'm Otis Jones from Cincinnati, Ohio, in the USA. We're Otis and Company, and we're delighted to play for you tonight.

"Are you enjoying the show so far?"

The crowd responded with applause, whistles and shouts.

"That's so fine. Thank you.

"Before we start our second set, I'd like to introduce the band. On bass is my good friend and fellow veteran of the Blues for nearly fifty years. Give a hand to the incomparable Rich King."

Richard played a quick riff and bowed to all corners of the room.

"On keyboards we have jammin' Jimmie Jackson from Atlanta, Georgia."

Jimmie tickled the ivories and cast a gleaming smile at

58

the appreciative listeners.

"Our vocalist is lovely Jasmine Evans. . ."

Jasmine curtsied gracefully, her opalescent gown shimmering in the colorful stage lights.

" . . . and on percussion, the eternally young, Hot Momma, Sadie Washington!"

The applause resurged as blushing Sadie waved off Otis' compliment with her drum sticks, a grin spreading from ear to ear.

Before the audience's adulation faded, Otis slid the sax's slender mouthpiece past his lips and a low moan oozed from the bell of his instrument. It sent a summons to the bass, which in turn called to the piano. Coming in behind all three, Sadie tapped out a rhythm on cymbal and drums as they drew the listeners along to Blues heaven. The swordfish forgotten, Richard assumed his usual trance-like state, rich, sweet notes sliding from Corrina's strings, a gift from the Blues gods. Jimmie's fingers sailed deftly over the keys, at one with the music and the band.

When the first piece ended, Otis jumped into a spirited number, and Jasmine added her voice to the mix. Sadie heated up the drums, leaving no doubt as to how she earned the nickname, Hot Momma.

Otis and Company played on into the wee hours, but the French crowd did not want the evening to end. They demanded three encores before finally allowing the band to call it a night.

"You were smokin', Sadie!" Richard held the door for the ladies as they stepped out into the chilly Parisian dawn.

"You were purty darn hot yersef, Richie. I guess dat swordfish did ya no harm."

"Don't get him started," pleaded Jimmie.

"I promise," intoned Otis in his rich baritone voice, "we will have poke chops fer supper tonight, even if we haf to buy 'em ourselves."

"Hotdog!" Sadie did a jig right there on the sidewalk to the amazement of her tired friends.

"Enough of that dancin', Sadie. Git yer caboose in gear." The talk of food had aroused Richard's appetite. He headed resolutely down the street in search of an open café with the rest of the band in tow. "I'm hungry fer some bacon, eggs, an' grits."

"I doubt we'll find grits in this food-fersaken town," said Otis.

Richard paused only a second before resuming his forward momentum. "Remind me to pack a box o' grits nex' time we git a French gig."

"Sho nuf, bro," promised Otis.

Alien in Ohio

Robert Schofield

When Zaron Glov moved from Omicron-VII to Norwood, Ohio, he had a little trouble fitting in.

He tried. In fact, the first thing he did was to change his name to Elvis. It was just paperwork, his ReLocator assistant told him. Go to the naming branch and complete some paperwork and that's that. Halfway through his second hour at the naming branch, Zaron/Elvis started getting suspicious as he observed the single window, with its Official Name Change Stamper call, "Forty-three?"

He glanced at the chit in his palm labeled two-hundred and thirty-eight, and scanned the packed room of sweaty name change seekers. Zaron, not one to back down from a challenge, stood on his chair and screamed at the top of his lungs, "Is there no more efficient way?"

He was greeted by a score of faces that turned to stare at him with the dull looks of grazing cattle. The other name change seekers didn't bother to notice. The Official Name Change Stamper paused, and said, "Forty-four?"

Elvis (pending an official stamp) moved into his new domicile. . .house. The houses in his neighborhood were all exceptionally well kept: polished, clean, with neat lawns, fresh paint, and trimmed hedges. He was afraid he had moved into a slum.

"ReLocator?"

"Yes," the artificial intelligence expert system on his wrist replied.

"The houses are all so. . .complete. Is everyone in this neighborhood so poor?"

"It is different here, Zaron/Elvis (pending official stamp). There are institutions called banks where people store their

61

wealth."

"You mean they do not continually build, as a sign of their prosperity?"

"No."

"What if the economy falters? Surely it is better to have reassurances in land, and brick, and concrete."

"In that case, the government intervenes."

Zaron/Elvis, not overly impressed so far by the efficiency of his new government said, "Oh. I am not so sure I will sleep well tonight."

"Give it a try," his ReLocator said.

"I will." He paused. "ReLocator?"

"Yes?"

"What is 'installing a gas line'?"

"Nothing to worry about."

Elvis did not sleep well.

The next morning Elvis, curious, looked up gas line: A major pipeline or conduit conveying gas to smaller pipes for distribution to consumers. Which prompted a lookup of gas: Slang, Something providing great fun and excitement.

That sounded good. The move, though not his choice, might prove worthwhile after all. They would bring fun right to his door!

The gas men arrived and informed him that they would be "servicing his house later that day." Three days later, they were pounding his neighbor's door and leaving leaflets on his neighbor's porch, not having made it back to his house yet.

Elvis watched the gas men's progress daily. They started at one end of the street and serviced a few houses a day. Gas line servicing, Elvis discovered, involved digging tremendous holes in front yards, demolishing sidewalks, and leaving boards and piles of sand and dirt lying around. Finally, a respectable neighborhood, he thought.

Elvis's excitement about the fun nearly at his doorstep grew. He became so excited that he looked up gas line again on his Thumbnail Pilot. This time he stumbled upon gas line explosion: A sudden rapid violent release of energy that generates a radially propagating shock wave accompanied by a loud sharp retort, flying debris, heat, light, and fire.

He knew what an explosion was. It was not fun. And it made Elvis question the gas men's habit of lighting off fireworks from the back of their truck as they scratched their armpits and ate fried chicken for lunch every day.

"Is your gas line serviced?" ReLocator asked.

"Yes. They came into the garage and said I needed welding. They backed a large truck around the house and knocked over a tree. Now I have a safe gas line, but I feel no additional fun."

"I see. Now it's time for you to get a car."

"ReLocator?"

"Yes?"

"I miss the pod fields. The podstalks would just now be ripening."

"I know. Get a new car. Then you'll feel better. Everyone has a car. It's a way to express yourself, and fit in."

"Oh."

Elvis had noticed that his environment offered very few methods of locomotion . . . travel, and that the ability to "get around" was highly necessary, so he took this car business seriously. Elvis thought about his new situation, the name change, gas line service, his new neighborhood, and got a new, black, Plymouth Super-Fury. He soon discovered that operating a car was amazingly simple. He mastered the techniques of driving with a flip through his owner's manual, and he breezed through his driving exam, although the process of obtaining a license was dishearteningly similar to a visit to the Official Name Change Stamper.

Elvis maneuvered his vehicle with great efficiency. He noticed, however, that some of his fellow drivers did not. Therefore, he practiced defensive driving, which did little good, unfortunately, when parked. He was sitting in his car puzzling at the "sandwich" he held, a "sandwich" he had obtained by driving thru (actually, alongside) a restaurant that claimed, in past history, to have served eight times the population of this planet. He puzzled at the qualification of the restaurant and the truthfulness of their claim as he stared at the small pill in his hand, and the cellophane twist-wrapper labeled "Super Jumbo Biggie Sized Mac-Whopper".

His peripheral vision caught an object looming large as it slowly swung in next to him. He heard the scraping of polyfiber and metal and his car lurched forward. Following a thunk, and a screech from impact his car settled back into place and Elvis got out. A young female climbed out of her vehicle, which Elvis identified as a Super Caravan LXVCx. She had, what Elvis had read about, a deer in the headlights expression. "Were you parked there?" the young female asked.

Elvis shook his head in amazement.

Elvis contacted the girl's insurance company. He was surprised at their efficiency. Call routing was logical, and direct. The presented options made sense; they were even communicated in an aesthetically pleasing manner, a mechanical voice strung together with mismatched tonal inflections.

Elvis complimented the claims consultancy advisor who finally answered his call. "That was lovely. I enjoyed wading through layers and layers of automated, inflexible routing, guided by emotionless instructions for nearly one quarter of an hour."

"Thank you," the voice on the line said.

Elvis paused. Something about that accent . . . . No.

Elvis explained the situation, and presented information about both he and the young girl. "Very well," the voice on the phone said. "You will need to get four repair estimates, each from repair companies equidistant geographically from the location of the alleged incident in the four cardinal compass directions. You need these estimates in triplicate, on form number ISBS-12073-L. The repair companies will know what that is. You must fax me two copies of each of these forms, and mail me the third. The one you mail must be on blue paper. Do you understand these requirements, and approve of the fact that we have been tape recording this conversation? Be aware that a negative response will require you to call in again and start over."

Alien in Ohio

"Yes, I understand and agree," Elvis said cheerfully. What thoroughness! He paused. "I wonder if I might ask you something?"

"Threats or foul language will require you to start over," the voice said. "And we reserve the right to prosecute for indecency and harassment."

"No, it's not that. I was just wondering, I mean, are you by any chance from Omicron?"

"I . . . actually, yes."

"I was wondering—"

"Hold on." Elvis heard a short buzz followed by a click. "Monitoring is now off," the woman on the phone said.

"I am new here," Elvis began.

"We all were once."

"The podstalks are ripening back home . . . ."

"It is a difficult time."

"I have a ReLocator. But, could I call you later?"

"Yes." She gave him a string of digits.

He called her later and they talked. Elvis was morose as he explained his transition. Syrah (the closest pronunciation of her Omicron name) was sympathetic. "They do not wage battles here over inefficiencies," she said, after Elvis explained his challenge at the name changing branch. "War, in their recent history, tends to be more for economic reasons."

"It is all so strange."

"I know."

"Your company seems highly efficient!" Elvis interjected.

"It is run by Omis."

"That explains it. There are not many of us here."

"No," Syrah agreed. "May I ask why you are here?"

"Displacement."

"I am sorry. Why?"

"The Illogic Chip."

"That has changed much," she consoled.

"Yes. I thought I had a secure position augmenting machine intelligence, but then the Illogic Chip was perfected and now all subjective opinion is handled internally."

"Subjective opinion?"

"Yes, in Omicronian imbedded system processes."

"What was your job?" Syrah asked.

He sighed. "It is well known that our computer systems are the best in the galaxy. They are self correcting, with cyclic redundancy checking. Only rarely, very rarely, once in a billion-trillion times, can the computers not decide what to do. When they are stumped, they call me." He hesitated. "They used to call me."

"That does not sound subjective," Syrah said. "That sounds technical."

"The questions were things like—let me translate: if nothing rhymes with orange, is it acceptable to substitute a made-up word, such as porange?"

"Wouldn't that depend on the context?"

"Exactly. Context is ever important. And it is subjective. In fact, my title was Subjectivity Expert."

"I see."

"I was wondering," Elvis asked, "do you think I could work at your company? A job would help me fit in."

"All applications for employment must be made through the company's InterGlobalnet website," Syrah said, slipping into her work monotone.

"Oh."

"Here is the address. I will only say it once. If you miss it, you must call back in." She rattled off a four-dozen character gibberish alphanumeric string.

What efficiency! Elvis thought.

The next day Elvis posted his application on the company's InterGlobalnet website, according to instruction, and waited.

"ReLocator, I have applied for a job," Elvis said to the AI on his wrist.

"Excellent," ReLocator replied. "It may take a few days to process your application."

"What shall I do until then?"

"Learn the history of these people, what is important to

them. Learn what has been passed down from generation to generation."

"How?"

"Fairy tales."

So for three days Elvis' ReLocator told him the story of Cinderella, the Pied Piper, Sleeping Beauty, Puss in Boots, the Salt Mountain, Rapunzel, The Golden Goose, and many others. Three days later, up to his ears in dwarves and wicked witches, Elvis reposted his application. He knew that the highly efficient company computers and staff at the Omicronian run business could not have made an error, or lost his application, but maybe the InterGlobalnet had.

He waited four more days.

". . .so the wicked witch was never seen in that land again," ReLocator said.

Elvis reposted his application once more, and waited two more days.

". . .and all the little toys were happy."

Elvis phoned the company.

"What position was it again?" the voice on the line asked.

"Subjectivity Expert."

"I don't see that listed in our ad."

"It wasn't. But, you need me," Elvis said.

"Um. Oh," the voice replied.

"May I speak to Syrah?" he asked.

"Who?"

"Syrah. She works in claims."

"One moment."

He heard a click, click, click, on the line, then Syrah's voice said, "Yes?"

"Syrah, I am applying for a job at your company. I followed the process you described, but there seems to be an opportunity for improvement—"

"We are not seeking experienced hires at this time," Syrah said in her official monotone. "We are strictly a hire-the-best, and promote-from-within company."

"Oh."

"And," she continued, "we have quotas, which have recently been reduced."

"I understand," Elvis said. It was efficient of them not to waste time and resources to notify him.

"Good-bye, Syrah," Elvis said.

"Good-bye." Click.

After hanging up, Elvis realized he had been thinking about this job more than he should have. He forced himself not to think about the pod fields back home . . . back on Omicron.

He took a deep breath and reaffirmed, I am a Subjectivity Expert. A thought, perhaps that meant something else here. He activated his Thumbnail Pilot and looked up subjectivity: Proceeding from, or taking place within an individual's mind such as to be unaffected by the external world. Existing only within the experiencer's mind and incapable of external verification.

He had been external verification for Omicron computer systems. And now they no longer needed that? Incorrect! The Illogic Chip was part of the computer system. It was internal. It was not independent verification. He was still needed.

Incorrectness was inefficient. Inefficiency caused problems. The Displacement Board had made a mistake. The next step was clear. A challenge.

But how could he challenge the entire Displacement Board? Especially from this new planet?

Thoughts of intergalactic warfare popped into his head. He would contact the Earth's Xenocouncil and convince them to start a war. He would tell them he could make the Omicronian computers fail, with his access and knowledge of Omi computers. He would tell them he would give the computers subjective inconsistencies, although his access had certainly been removed, he could convince the Earthlings. What had Syrah said? Recent human warfare was waged over economics. Everyone knew Omi computers were the best, and therefore the most profitable anywhere.

It would work!

It had to.

Alien in Ohio

He spent the afternoon plotting. That evening he called Syrah at home. She listened, then said, "Let me send you something."

A file appeared on his viso-phone.

"Watch that. Think about it. Then call me," Syrah said.

Later that evening Elvis watched the video of pod fields ripening back on Omicron. Great lavender balloon stalks swelled and rose into the yellow sky. The balloons distended, became long, sinewy teardrops that turned red, then deep purple with orange streaks. Wisps of stalk-grass trailed along the ground, dragging intricate paths through the young fields of next year's crop.

That night he dreamt about wicked witches giving poison pods to innocent young girls.

The next day he continued to think about that. Pods and dwarves, Omicron, subjectivity, and his new home.

On the third day he realized, there was no wicked witch.

He called Syrah.

"I am glad you came to that conclusion," Syrah said. "You know, I am just cooking dinner. It is not pod-milk and granstalk, but you get used to it. Do you want to come over?"

He did.

On his way out the door, his ReLocator buzzed quietly.

"And they lived happily ever after," it said.

Coming Home

Jerry Judge

Your blonde wife is now brunette
and older and sleeping
with another man who looks like you,
yet older, paler and heavier.

You've not been on an odyssey —
only ten minutes have you been gone
to get some milk and bread
which has already spoiled and gone stale.

You don't have a theorem or theology for this.
Your hands go right through the sleeping couple.
Mind and memory function, but
the rest of you can't grip or permeate.

No voice says whether this is dream or death.
The man and woman awake, eat cereal
and go to work in separate cars.
All three of you are so alone.

Of Shadows and Substance

Joseph Terbeck

We are magical beings. A light shines, the inner eye. We smile perplexed and dance the night away.

The sun goes down, the mushrooms come out. Fred pulls a sack from the refrigerator and sets it on the kitchen table. I open the bag and spread them out. These are not ordinary mushrooms, I remind myself. These are magic mushrooms. *Teonanacatl*, the Aztecs used to call them, "flesh of the gods". Delivered fresh in a sealed packet the day before by overnight express from an old friend of mine at the Museum of Anthropology in Mexico City. He's heard of my research and wants to help. He'll certainly get a grateful acknowledgment in the preface when I finally complete my work.

We arrange the fungi on the table according to size. Light brown in color with purplish bruises, some have caps nearly three inches across. A few are small and deformed. That doesn't matter. There's a certain perfection even in imperfection. In all, thirty-six mushrooms. I hold a handful up to my nose and breathe in the deep, earthy smell.

"Let's eat a few now and then make some tea," says Fred. Fred is another old friend from my student days at the university. We used to room together. Hard to believe he has his own practice now. Tonight, he's abandoned his wife and two kids, nearly grown, to do a little research of his own. Another Aldous Huxley, he jokes.

We eat the mushrooms in pairs, one large and one small as the ancient priests prescribed. The taste is bitter, grows worse with each bite. I make a note of that. Not quite so awful, however, as the peyote we sampled last month. As Fred fills a pan with water and sets it on the stove, I lay a handful of mushrooms on a cutting board and dice them. When I finish, I sprinkle them into the pan as Fred adds a few tablespoons of honey to the tea to improve its flavor. Cups in hand, we retire to the living room for a game of backgammon.

It's a mystery, sometimes, just being here at all. I look up into the night sky and see stars far flung in a vast space. All is confusion there, just as it is down here, even though we strive to impose our own order onto it. Yet nothing is so beautiful or so awesome by itself as complete chaos.

It's Halloween night, quite by coincidence but appropriate to our current state of mind. Spirits freely roam the streets. Neighbors appease them with gifts of candy and gum. Meanwhile, Fred and I remain sequestered in the semi-darkness of my living room, bewitched.

Fred picks up his guitar which he has brought along for the occasion and plays for me. He plays the way he feels, improvising, and the music is strangely sweet and filled with emotion. His long fingers move down and up scales, they add a long, bending note. Each clear note sets a mood, riding on the air we breathe. As I close my eyes, I not only hear the music but absorb it. Inside the darkened theater of my brain a show begins. A curtain rises like a lifting inhibition. I see a golden palace, shimmering, outlined in a blue sky. White birds flying, soaring and diving through the clouds. Diamonds, sparkling rainbows, fringe the field of my perception. I abandon myself to a kaleidoscope of imagery.

Later, I turn my attention to the clock on the wall. I watch as time goes around in circles. Time and motion, motion and time. Something profound there but I can't quite catch it. Time depends on motion. Without motion there can be no time. And without time, what becomes of being? I wonder. If I could be still, absolutely still, I might find or become a space in time. What then? I watch the clock. The hands seem to slow but inexorably proceed.

I look up. The gray ceiling undulates. It's not a smooth surface, but irregular, stuccoed, pattered with tiny stalactites.

Of Shadows and Substance

Like molded cobwebs. The cobwebs expand, break apart and reform. New patterns emerge. Spinning wheels, intermeshing gears, whirling galaxies. The universe evolves from chaos to order back to chaos again. Eons pass, all in a moment.

The music stops, though I still hear its echoes.

"Whew!" says Fred. "Getting off yet?"

"Not me," I smile. My good mood is tempered, however, by a sudden rumble in my stomach. A secondary effect of the psychotropics. I burp, leaving a terrible aftertaste.

"Make a note of this," says Fred. "I just saw a blue ball of light shoot in through that window. It raced around the room a few times, stopped right over your head, then exploded. There were colors flying everywhere. You were drenched."

"What time is it?" I ask.

"Time we ate some more mushrooms," says Fred.

Some scientists say that the laws of physics, the very rules of the universe, are flexible, and, to a certain extent, dependent on assumptions made by the observer. There's a trick, I think, in using this knowledge to your best advantage.

I turn on the lights. I have an old oscilloscope and Fred hooks it up to a pair of secondary output channels on the stereo. The music he selects for our next adventure is something weirdly electronic. I turn the lights out again. Fred turns up the oscilloscope's brightness control, flooding the room with an eerie green luminescence. At first the light is steady, but then the band begins to play. The flat trace of electrons explodes across the screen to become a pulsating scribble, dancing at the speed of light.

Ghostly shadows, our shadows, like homemade Halloween goblins flicker on the wall. I move my arm in a flowing motion up and down. My shadow's arm waves too but in a vibrating way. Fred and I move about experimentally. Shadows loom large and furry, shadows shrink small and become more sharply defined. Shadows play, shake hands. They take on other strange shapes limited only by our imaginations. Deformed trees.

Not From Around Here, Are You?

Ogres. Fantastic birds.

The sensation of movement is incredible. I feel I am tied to my body, yet strangely detached from it. Like floating inside myself, walking in space.

When I was in the Army, in the days of my youth and before I became more serious about my research, I once experimented with LSD with a friend of mine named J.P. That evening, while sitting by the edge of a canal watching water ripple through the moon, J.P. said something to me that I have never forgotten. He said, "A trip is not a trip unless you see God." Now, I think to myself sometimes, what is life itself but one long trip?

The album ends and the green light steadies. I am looking at the wall, but I don't believe what I see. I look at Fred. He looks at me. We both look at the wall. There is something between us now. Something that wasn't there before. There's someone else's shadow on the wall.

At a certain level of experience, we come to transcend the distinction between what is real and what is normally considered illusion. They are really complementary aspects of the same consciousness. Both can be teachers. At this level we must avoid being too serious. We laugh a lot.

There's someone else's shadow on the wall.
"You see it?" I ask Fred.
"I see it," says Fred. "Where's it coming from?"
"It can't be coming from anywhere."
We look around the room just to be sure. The mysterious third shadow just stands there. It's not exactly a person. Seems to be some kind of animal, a big one.
"Could we both be hallucinating the same thing?" wonders Fred.
I have to think about that, trying to remember if I've seen any such thing in the literature.

74

Of Shadows and Substance

"Perhaps not as rare as one might think."

"Ah," says Fred and giggles. Fred doesn't usually giggle.

The new shadow seems to mock us, suddenly taking on a life of its own. It sticks thumbs in its ears and wiggles fingers.

"Incredible," says Fred.

I don't know what to say.

The Shadow turns to mine and makes a bow, like asking for the next dance. My shadow bows back. The two lock arms and begin a soundless waltz. Fred's shadow conducts an absent orchestra. Fred and I don't move. We can't move, it seems. The waltz goes on. Finally, I shrug my shoulders and sit on the floor.

"We might as well enjoy the show."

The doorbell rings, shocking us both. I know it doesn't look like there's anybody home with the shades drawn and the lights out. Fred, closer to the door, gets up to see who it is. Curiously, his shadow stays behind. A moment later he calls me.

"It's for you."

When I get to the door I can see why he called me. A six foot raccoon poses on the porch, stylishly outfitted in a plaid vest with a green derby on top its furry head. He looks harmless enough.

"It's a little late for trick-or-treat, isn't it?" I ask. In fact, it's nearly midnight by now.

"He wants to know if we've seen his shadow anywhere. Says he lost it," says Fred.

I look at the raccoon. It wrinkles its big black nose. I look at Fred. He wrinkles his nose.

"Come on in," I say.

"Sorry to bother you," the creature says politely and in a fairly normal voice. I had expected a squeak. "The name's Perkins, Hopewell Perkins."

Fred leads our guest to the living room. I trail behind. It's funny, but I don't see any zipper to this Perkins' costume. Then I remind myself that figments of the imagination don't need zippers.

Not From Around Here, Are You?

We get to the living room but all the shadows are gone. Big surprise.

"I might have expected this," says the raccoon.

"Expected what?" asks Fred.

"You were fooling with your shadows," the other replies.

"So?" I say. "Have a seat."

Perkins sits on the couch, tucking his long, fat tail gingerly beneath him. Fred and I sit in chairs to either side.

"So that's why my shadow came in here. I was in the neighborhood, passing by, when I noticed the little imp had run off. Wanted to fool around, too, I guess, and couldn't resist. They never do seem to grow up, do they? Now it looks as though they've all run off together."

Fred asks, "Is that bad?" He's having a hard time not smiling.

The raccoon makes a face. I realize then how hard it is to read a raccoon's emotions.

"Not for me," says Perkins. "But you boys might be in some trouble."

"How's that?" I ask.

"Because you might not get them back."

I guess we look puzzled.

"I can see this is going to take some explaining."

"What do you know about shadows, really?" says Perkins. "Mere silhouettes, dark copies of yourselves cast by the light? That's what most people think. But you couldn't be more wrong. You go about your daily business and as long as your shadows remain attached to you, you content yourself with your ignorance. Ah, but a shadow is so much more than what you imagine. Shadows are alive.

"Shadows aren't actually cast by the light. It just looks that way. No, they merely hide from the light as they hide their true nature from your awareness. But they aren't separate beings either. They are a part of you, a part that you cannot do without any more than you could do without your brain or your heart. They are like a side of your soul that connects you to worlds

76

your waking mind cannot grasp or comprehend. Indeed, from their point of view, it is they who have substance and you who are the shadows. They move about at night while you're asleep. They reconnoiter, commune with other shadows. They find out things for you and return to tell you these things in dreams. I don't know how else to put it. If you lose touch with your shadows, or they get away completely, bad things happen. You lack imagination. You become listless and stupid. You live, but you can't be happy. The best thing, of course, is to recognize your shadow and become friends with it. Let it open up these other worlds for you."

"If shadows only go out when we're asleep," asks Fred, "how could ours have gotten away?"

"There are other ways," says Perkins seriously. "Deep meditation for one. Sometimes a sudden shock. Chemical methods, too. Not usually recommended but effective. You know what I mean, I suspect?"

"I think so."

"That opens the gate. You relax your control. Your shadows escape."

"If they go out anyway," I ask, "why won't they just come back on their own?"

"Good question," the raccoon says, nodding. "Nobody really knows. Shadows are a mischievous lot. They return when you don't know they've been away. But they are as afraid of you as they fear the light. Now that you've seen too much the jig is up. You'll need to seek them out now, ask them back. They need to know you are not afraid of them, for your fears and their fears are much the same."

"You don't seem to be too worried about your own shadow."

"Oh, I know how to find mine," laughs Perkins. "We're on very good terms. Thing slips away all the time."

"Tell us how to find ours then," says Fred.

"Sorry, that would be like me telling you how to find yourselves. That's the problem. I can't. Each one's different. You must know them better than I. You'll have to find them on your own. I can only tell you to go look. That and maybe offer a few general rules."

"If that's the best you can do," I say, "shoot!"

A famous Zen master once said it's easy to describe the nature of the universe. He said it's just a way of talking.

"You've got to trust your magic feet," says Perkins. "At least, that's what I like to call it. You can call it anything you want. Just don't say to yourself, 'Let's try a systematic search.' Shadows like to move around, they travel in realms you know nothing about. So concentrate not on following them or on trying to get ahead of them, but on joining up with them. Intersecting with them at just the right time. That's the way to look at it. Believe in your magic feet, feet that walk where they will, but somehow always knowing the right way to go. Technically speaking, you'll have to let your shadows find you. When they do, they'll hang around for awhile to see what you do. That will be the crucial moment. As soon as you sense them nearby, you've got to let them know where you stand. Say this: 'Little shadow mine, suffer not to be untwined.' I know it sounds silly. It's a little ditty I made up myself, but that's all you need. They'll take it from there."

"That's it, then?" I ask.

"Just follow the signs."

"The signs?"

"I don't want to go into that right now," says the raccoon. "Let's just say there's a certain guiding force in the universe that watches over what's going on. It will put up signs, I can't say what kind, to help you along."

"A guiding force?" I ask. "You mean God?"

"That's just one way of talking," says Perkins.

So Fred and I go for a walk.

"Okay, magic feet," I say. "Do your stuff."

We wander around for about an hour. The night is warm and pleasant. We see a lot of nice colors, but so far no signs. Maybe we just don't know how to read them. We pause to rest at a bench near a park.

There's this crazy tree next to us. I can't recall ever seeing one quite like it before but then I've never paid much attention to trees. Little orange spiked balls hang from bare branches. One lies at my feet and I reach down to pick it up. It has a very tough shell. You'd have to work very hard to get through the cover to the nut.

"Looks like an egg," says Fred.

"A seed is like an egg," I say.

"It's a beginning," says Fred.

Just then another of the orange balls falls from the tree and rolls a little way down the walk. I pay attention to the direction.

"Let's go this way," I say.

We wander on, in no particular hurry. Our only destination is to find ourselves, even if it takes all night. I'm getting this weird sensation in my toes. A sort of disconnected connectedness. My feet do seem to lead the way. I don't have to make them go. I never noticed I could do that before. More time to enjoy the scenery that life presents.

Later, far from home, we find ourselves walking along some railroad tracks. We come to a bridge. About halfway across the span we hear a roaring noise behind us. A train. Fred and I hug the railing. The train shoves by, nearly throwing us over the edge by the force of its passing.

"That was close," says Fred.

"What a rush," I say.

It's always a rush when you're crossing over.

"Almost dawn," I say, studying the sky.

"I hope we're getting close," says Fred.

Out of nowhere, a gray cat with black stripes comes sauntering along beside us. I'm very fond of cats. The ancient Egyptians and Chinese used to think of them as gods.

"Hello, kitty," I say. I crouch down and try to get it to come to me.

Not From Around Here, Are You?

It just looks up at me with curious eyes.

"Meow," it says.

We walk on and the cat walks with us for a while, tail erect and waving behind like a banner. When we stop, it stops too and stares up at us.

"Meow," it says and walks on.

The cat leads us across the street to the gates of an old cemetery. The three of us go inside together. We roam among the tombstones and monuments. Some of the stones have shifted over the years and sit crookedly. The grass is long and unkempt. Tall weeds appear here and there. Some of the monuments are so weather-beaten as to make their inscriptions unreadable.

"It's like the end of the world here," says Fred.

"Many have gone before us," I say.

The cemetery grounds begin to slope uphill. Our guide leads us up to the top of a small ridge then disappears from sight. Beyond the ridge lies an open valley full of roads and houses and people still asleep.

"There he is," says Fred, pointing.

The cat stops by one particular stone. He rubs up against it, tail all bushy as if he's seen a ghost. We approach. But the cat is not our cat after all. It's a raccoon. He scampers away.

We examine the stone. It dates back to 1888. It reads simply "Perkins." No initial. Beneath the name is a lengthy inscription, the weather worn letters small and difficult to read in the dim morning light, a quote from the ancient Greek poet, Pindar.

"Creatures of a day, what is a man? What is he not? Mankind is a dream of a shadow. But when a god-given brightness comes, a radiant light rests on men, and a gentle life."

"Some coincidence," says Fred.

"I've had enough," I say. "Let's sit here and watch the sun come up."

"It's been a strange night," says Fred.

Of Shadows and Substance

I agree. We look out to the east, beyond a range of low hills to where the sky is beginning to lighten.

"Has any of this made sense?"

I know what he means.

"No," I say. "Not much."

"Did we just imagine it all then?"

"It's quite possible, I think."

It's a red, red sky. Sailors take warning.

The sun comes up over the rim of the world like a big, beautiful mushroom, huge and swollen. The morning now is cool and misty, but we can already feel the warmth of that great orange ball on our upturned faces. The giver of life and a marker for the passage of time.

"The dawn" I say, "is a mystical moment."

"We're back at the beginning," says Fred. "It all turns in circles."

Fred and I sit side by side, our backs against the tombstone.

"Is that significant?" I ask.

"I think it must be."

I shake my head.

"So many mysteries," I say. "We need all the wisdom we can get."

We sit silent for a while, watching the sun rise. Something about this moment feels right.

"They're close," I whisper to Fred.

"I can feel them too," he says.

We must seek to find ourselves wherever, whenever, the opportunity presents itself.

"Let's say it now," says Fred.

We say it together.

We *are* magical beings.

A Man for His Time

Dori Van Luit

His dad walked five miles to seek work—no money for
streetcars.
And mother took in ironing, sewed patches on clothes.
With grey hair, wrinkles, and bones stiff with arthritis,
he leans back in recliner, his eyes see the visions of the
40th Division on Guadalcanal - nights of fear, stories of
torture.
As Sergeant Specialist, he climbed poles, ran lines in Iloilo,
and tracks from the railroad near the town of Jaro.
Dragged a Jap for miles tied on a bumper, then gave him
cigarettes.
Got shot in the ear on the Isle of Luzon.
Had malaria in the Philippines, then again in New Britain.
Cleared Japs out of caves with police dogs.
Saw the enemy kill babies from pregnant women.
Played games with Samoans during guard duty at Schofield.

Now he fights a new war, stands each week at her grave site,
remembers fifty-two years of her lovely smile, and how with
old fashioned values, they raised prosperous children.
Alone, he limps through the house that he built
where pictures throughout tell tales of the good times.

Master Gardener

Jim Jackson

Nancy Gonzalez would be aggrieved to know we have gathered in this church sanctuary she called home to eulogize her. Today marks the anniversary of the November 16, 1989 murder of six Jesuits, their housekeeper and the housekeeper's daughter in San Salvador, El Salvador. Red, as I knew her, would have been in the front rows of the thousands who protest this year at the School of Americas at Fort Benning outside Columbus, Georgia. They call it the Western Hemisphere Institute for Security Cooperation now, but it will always remain the School of the Americas to me, and it is the reason I got to know Red.

Red would ask us, "Why are you wasting your time talking about me? I'm dead. You should be out *doing* something."

I hear you rustling in your seats, afraid I will go on one of my rants about how our government has fomented and supported abusive regimes across the globe while ignoring our own disadvantaged. Fear not. Today is for us to remember and celebrate Red's life with stories and song.

Red's nephew asked me to share how meeting her transformed my life. My guess is you are here today, because you too experienced firsthand Red's conviction that each and every one of us has important work to do on this thin crust we call planet Earth, and it changed your life.

In July, 1983, Red was on her way to meet Father Roy Bourgeois to plan the protest that landed Father Roy in the Federal pen for fifteen months when the group, dressed in military fatigues, entered Fort Benning and, using a cranked-to-the-max boom box after lights-out, played the last homily of slain Salvadoran Archbishop Oscar Romero. In the sermon given the day before he was murdered, the Archbishop pleaded for an

83

end to their civil war.

She never got to "Casa Romero," Father Roy's name for the apartment in Columbus he had rented. Since I had to head north anyway and had briefly met her once, Father Roy tasked me to find out what happened to her. How many of you know this story? A show of hands. Good, only a few.

So. . .the temperature in Georgia that July didn't get much below ninety in the evening and the humidity and temperature raced each other toward one hundred each morning. If you had to park your car during the day, you cracked the windows down so they wouldn't blow out. I had just completed a stint as a VISTA volunteer and the junker I drove didn't have air conditioning, except what we called four-forty AC: four windows down and forty miles an hour and at least your sweat would evaporate.

If you've been in a car with Red, you know she had to be the driver and she didn't cotton to Interstates. She had stopped for the night in an AAA-rated motel just south of Rome, Georgia, and let us know to expect her the next day. When she didn't show, we were concerned, but figured her for a flat tire or something that would delay her a few hours. The next morning we called everyone we could think of: her brother in New York City, friends back here, even her favorite nephew and not so favorite employer. Not a peep. She had disappeared off the face of the earth.

The next morning I started backtracking, knowing she would be taking US-27 down from Rome, just as she had the whole way from Cincinnati. I imagined an automobile accident, although we had called all the hospitals we could locate along the way. Back before ubiquitous cell phones, I dialed the operator, plunked in the requisite quarters, dimes and nickels and then she placed the call. After three minutes of holding for a hospital receptionist to check to see if they had a Nancy Gonzalez or a Mrs. Esteban Gonzalez, I'd listen to the chimes again as I deposited three more minutes of coins.

I drove north out of Columbus and passed through rural Georgia towns—Cataula and Hamilton and LaGrange — and checked ditches for a wreck. At each crossroad I stopped at the country store to see if they knew anything. Back then, Georgia accents were thick enough to choke an anaconda and there were still local restaurants with southern cooking, not fast food junk at every turn. I digress. It felt like I'd already been consigned to hell, the sun so hot the blacktop would stick to your shoes if you didn't keep moving and the whole highway smelled like freshly paved road. I don't know if you like that smell — I kinda do; course I also like a light smell of manure scenting the air in springtime. Smell of money my father used to say.

North of Reevesville I stopped at a farm stand just off the main road: a tarpaper lean-to with a toothless stick of a black woman selling plums and blueberries and late peaches. Evian and the like were just a gleam in some marketer's eye and I was parched, so I loaded up on peaches and plums, the woman steering me away from those not quite ripe enough for immediate consumption, although in that heat, everything would probably be overripe by the end of the day.

I asked the proprietor about herself while I luxuriated in the sweet pulp of fresh fruit. Miss Martha was forty and looked at least sixty. Her family had been sharecropping the same land since her ancestors were freed in 1865. Between her drawl and lack of teeth it took me two plums and a peach before I figured that much out. I returned to task and enquired whether Red had passed by.

"You couldn't miss her," I said. "She'd be driving a twenty-year-old Ford Mustang convertible only slightly redder than the color of her hair."

"Yas, suh," she said. "Nice missus. Bought her some okra and pole beans and a peach just like yourn."

Red had stopped late Friday morning and told Miss Martha she would stop back next week on her return north.

"Ya talk with the Sherriff?" I don't know if she read the concern on my face but she quickly added, "Yas suh, betta do that."

Despite my attempts to draw her out, the only thing else I got was, "I don' need no trouble. Best be goin', suh."

I doubled back south, troubled by Miss Martha's sudden

transformation from loquacious to sullen. What had she meant about talking to the sheriff? Just before a roadside sign advertising Reevesville Antiques the speed limit was posted as fifty-five, but hidden by the sign and a curve in the road, the limit dropped to twenty-five. Around the bend two county sheriff roof-racks flashed in celebration, each having captured a rabbit in their snare. If there had been a third trooper I would have been nailed as well, but luck was with me that day.

In Reevesville I stopped at the only open establishment that Sunday afternoon, the village drugstore. Outside were four codgers decked out in suspenders, two playing checkers under the striped awning; the other two in rocking chairs keeping up a running commentary.

I excused myself for interrupting their game and asked about Red.

"She that Yankee lady the deputies caught yesterday?" Rocking Chair One asked Rocking Chair Two.

"'Spect so. Heard she refused to pay and she's enjoying a stay at Ralphie's Inn."

"Ralphie's Inn?" I said. "Where's that? Pay for what?"

The game stopped and eight eyes took me in.

"I'm confused," I said, although all five of us were clear on that issue already. "I thought I had a list of all the motels in this area."

Whenever I need a soundtrack to accompany my stupidity, I replay their laughter. Finally, the player with his left sleeve pinned up to a stump of arm took pity on me. "Not from around here, are you, boy?" He laughed some more. "Ralph Bluxton is sheriff in these parts and Oren was referring to the county pen. What I heard is your lady friend refused to pay the speeding fine and the deputies are housing her at the jail until court opens up."

"Yep," Atlanta Braves Hat chipped in. "Happens once or twice a year. They ain't got enough ready money or they's dumb enough to think they can win."

Finding the county courthouse was a breeze. The Italian Renaissance palace was a block or two past the town square and shuttered tight. After some bad directions I found the Sheriff's office a mile or so farther down the road. Behind the desk sat a sleepy old-boy, puffy eyes dominating bloated cheeks and jowls. Once he finally deigned to acknowledge my presence, he asked, "Sumpin' botherin' you, boy?"

I explained I was trying to locate Red. He took off his Smokey-the-Bear hat and scratched his shiny pate. "Gonzalez, you said. 'Fraid visitin' hours was yesterday — all female inmates last name beginning A to L. Have to wait 'till next Saturday."

"So she's in jail?"

"Don't know. But if she is, you can see her next Saturday."

Telling an asshole he is one doesn't usually enhance communication, so I tried to start again from the beginning, inquiring how I might determine if Red was in custody.

"Sarge will be in Monday mornin'. He'll know." He put his feet up on the desk, leaned back in the chair and closed his porcine eyes.

A part of me wants to tell you that I grabbed his ratty shoes and flipped him onto his back and beat the information out of him, but I didn't. I walked out and after getting turned away at the jail, checked into a motel. The yellow pages listed a lawyer who promised prompt resolution of traffic violations. Bluxton was his name, not Ralph, but I figured there was probably a family connection to the Sheriff. I left a detailed message and never got a call back. I couldn't get in touch with Father Roy either. Sunday was the day he and two others slipped into Fort Benning for their civil disobedience.

So put yourself in my position. It's Sunday afternoon. You are torpid in the blast furnace called Georgia summer, enervated from the heat and intransigence of the local constabulary. You don't know for sure your acquaintance is in jail, but think she might be. You guess it's because of the speed trap. If so, maybe the best you can do is get some money to pay her fine. Your checking account has less than a hundred dollars and you are supposed to be driving home to start a new job as a management trainee the next day.

Needless to say, I didn't sleep well that night.

Not From Around Here, Are You?

Time for you folks to stretch your legs, so please stand as you are able and join me in singing one of Red's favorite songs, hymn number 108, "My Life Flows On In Endless Song." Red first learned this song from Pete Seeger way back, and always thought its title should be "How Can I Keep From Singing."

I don't know if Red had a favorite verse, but she certainly practiced the final one throughout her life: "In prison cell and dungeon vile our thoughts to them are winging, when friends by shame are undefiled how can I keep from singing?"

The Sergeant was a veritable fountain of information. Traffic court started at 10:00 am Tuesday morning. I could see her there and if she were still imprisoned Saturday. My visit could last thirty minutes. I could see her each and every Saturday if I wished.

"You want to help her? Bring a lot of money. She's got the ticket, court costs and what I hear, room rent and food costs since she's refusing to work for her keep. Add in towing and storing her vehicle and she probably already bought some clothes and soap and stuff. Should come to less than a thousand, but don't quote me on that, boy."

Red was last on the morning docket and entered the court, her dress streaked with dirt, hands cuffed behind her back. When she saw me her face lit up in a patented Red smile and she waved her shoulders at me.

The court clerk read the indictment: she was clocked doing forty-two in a twenty-five mile-an-hour zone. The ticket was $10 per mile over the speed limit for $170. How did she plead?

"Not guilty, your Honor," she said in a clear voice that filled the courtroom.

The judged looked down at the scruffy woman standing in front of him. "Where's your counsel, young lady?"

"I have no counsel, your Honor. I was not allowed to make any long distance calls to contact my lawyer. But," she shrugged, "assuming I can have the handcuffs removed I will represent myself. I'm part Italian, your Honor, so I need my hands to talk."

The judge cracked a grin and covered his face with both hands. When he spoke he was under control again. "You are ready to proceed?"

Assuring the judge she was and after her cuffs were removed, Red sat at the table; two six-foot, two hundred pound deputies stood guard. The prosecutor asked for a recess. The arresting officer needed to be called in to testify. The judge appeared annoyed, but offered a continuance until 2:00 that afternoon. Red was shackled and taken away, but shot me a smile before she left.

At 2:00 on the dot we all rose at the judge's return and the prosecutor called the arresting officer to the stand. He gave the facts, confirmed the defendant was the arrestee and stood up after the prosecutor said he was through.

Red sat him back down. "A pleasure to see you again, Officer. Can you tell me the distance between the point when a motorist proceeding southbound on US-27 first sees the 25 mph speed limit sign and the sign itself?" After a long pause while the officer looked pleadingly at the prosecutor, she added, "I'm sorry, I must have accumulated some ear wax over the last few days. I didn't hear your answer."

"Don't know," he mumbled. "Don't make no difference anyhow."

"Relevance?" the prosecutor asked.

"Would you agree, officer that it might be about 125 feet?"

After another long look at the prosecutor, the officer agreed, "Might be about that."

"The speed limit before the change to twenty-five was how much?"

This time the officer looked at both the prosecutor and the judge, who said, "She's asking you, not me. Answer her."

"Uh, fifty-five."

"And if a car pulled out in front of you, how quickly could you step on the brake?"

"Objection. Relevance?"

"Overruled. I have nothing else to do this afternoon and it's your fault we didn't finish before lunch since your officer wasn't here. Please answer the question."

"Pretty fast, I guess."

"Pretty fast," Red looked to the top of the courthouse ceiling for a count of two. "Two seconds? Or maybe your reactions are twice as good as that. A second?"

"Faster than that. Tenth of a second."

"Really? And here I thought the South was a slower part of the country. In college I did a research project that showed students averaged between a fifth and quarter of a second to respond to a flashing light. Of course they were expecting the light and didn't have to process something unexpected, like a speed limit sign hidden by a billboard and the curve of the road. And they didn't have to take their foot off the accelerator and get it to the brake either."

The prosecutor waved a hand around as though he needed permission to go potty. "Is there a question?"

"I'm sorry, your Honor." Red nodded is his direction. "I just wanted to give the officer a chance to reconsider his answer. It being sworn testimony and all."

"Maybe a second then," the officer said.

Red paced back and forth before the witness, his eyes following her movement while his head faced straight forward.

"Officer, what percentage of the people you arrest for speeding at the spot you arrested me would you say are from outside the county?"

The officer looked as though he finally understood the joke. "Prettineer all of 'em," he said, drawing a chuckle from the gallery.

"The defense wishes to put into evidence exhibit #1." She pulled toilet paper out of her pocket and waved it around. "I apologize to the court for the flimsiness of the exhibit, but it seems to be as strong as the case."

The prosecutor toppled his chair in his hurry to object. The judge gaveled the guffaws to silence.

"Oh I'm sorry, your Honor. I didn't mean it like it came

out. Are you good at math, officer?"

He shook his head and only after the judge reminded him that gestures were insufficient did he offer a mumbled, "No."

About that time I noticed a steady stream of people entering the back of the courtroom, including several deputies and looked back in surprise to see the four checkers players from Reevesville had joined the gallery.

"Can I put myself on the stand, your Honor?"

The deputy was dismissed and Red sworn in. The judge gave her free reign to ask and answer questions, unless the prosecutor objected; then she had to wait for the judge's ruling. On the toilet paper written in eyeliner because, she explained, the deputies had taken away her purse with pens and paper and she'd had to borrow the eyeliner from another inmate who had smuggled it into the jail, was a mathematical demonstration of how long it would take to slow a car from fifty-five miles per hour to twenty-five (about two seconds of braking and a second to hit the brake.) The car would travel two hundred feet.

But of course she only had 125 feet before the sign and the police radar. As her calculations showed, if she were doing exactly fifty-five when she saw the speed limit sign, you would expect the officer to have clocked her at forty-three mph.

"Therefore, your Honor, I respectfully request that you dismiss the case as it is not physically possible to go only twenty-five at the sign unless you knew in advance that the changed speed limit sign was there. The proof is no locals are arrested for speeding, just we out-of-towners."

The prosecutor had only one question for Red, "You admit you were driving forty-two in a twenty-five mph zone?"

The judge rapped his gavel to quiet the crowd, which had been buzzing ever since Red had asked for dismissal. Into the silence, he pronounced his verdict: "Guilty. Defendant will pay court costs of $200, the traffic fine of. . ." he looked at the papers in front of him, " . . . $170. Towing costs. . . ."

I was stunned by the miscarriage of justice and didn't hear the total damage. What I did hear was his summary: "Defendant will be remanded to jail until the fine is paid. . . or for

Not From Around Here, Are You?

thirty days. Time served will count toward the sentence."

The next day I presented myself to the court clerk with funds Western Unioned from her brother. After an interminable wait two deputies brought her out. She was still handcuffed and each one held an arm. "He's not going to believe us," a deputy said. "You tell him."

"I will not condone paying ransom," she said. "Send the money back to my brother and tell him I love him dearly." Her face shone with her smile.

"What about Father Roy?" I said. "What about your job?"

"I can always get a new job, Joshua. But I could never look myself in the mirror if I wasn't willing to stand up to injustice when it presents itself. To misquote someone, 'if not here, where? If not now, when?' Thanks for your help and let everyone know I'm okay." She flashed her escort with a smile. "Shall we, boys?"

As far as I know, Red never talked about her thirty days in jail. She insisted what happened to her was not relevant; what mattered was that her actions improved life for others. Now's a good time to read a letter written by one of Red's fellow inmates. I'll skip the first part that talks about several of the inmates Red knew.

I've never had the courage to tell you we were sure you were lying when you told Sarah, Marissa and me you were in for speeding. Why would they put a skinny white chick in a cell with three bad mommas like us? Figured you for a stoolie, especially when you got us all singing spirituals Sunday morning. I still remember my spine tingling that first time you got us to stomp our feet and use the bars for percussion and the whole joint joined in. Only after you left us did we get the idea that it wasn't about sassing the man. It was about celebrating us.

When they threw you into the hole for not ratting out Marissa about her eyeliner and again when you refused to work, you got me wondering.

"I will not be a slave to an unjust system," you said.

Master Gardener

At first I thought you had no right to talk about slavery. What did a honky know about that?

Turned out more than this black girl. I hawked your every move, trying to figure you out. You'd tell stories about Martin and the movement. I thought you were making stuff up—trying to fit in or maybe just funning us. That's what first got me to the library—I wanted to prove you were a fake. Now I've earned my GED.

That reminds me: Marissa and I figure we've written over a thousand letters for the ones who can't write so well. I never thought of it until you wrote a letter for Sarah that first week. "We each have to find our own ministry," you said.

Amen, sister. Amen

The letter continues, but you get the idea. Red served her full sentence and since I was fired from the management trainee job for showing up a few days late, I met her when she was released on a Monday morning and drove her to pick up her car. The interior was ruined; they had left it outside in the weather with the top down. The floor mats were moldy. Worse, the okra and beans and peaches had rotted, ruining the upholstery.

The ACLU won the suit she filed based on the Polaroid pictures we took that day and the testimony of the four checkers players who had seen a deputy drive the Mustang through town and were none too fond of Ralph Bluxton as it turned out. You should have seen the four of them the day they testified, dressed to the nines but still wearing the same garish suspenders. The trial provided them with three days' entertainment and lost the sheriff the next election.

Every time we passed Miss Martha's stand we always stopped in to buy whatever was fresh and shoot the breeze. That was Red's way.

Red testified before the Georgia legislature about her rural speed trap experience. For years afterward the billboard that had previously advertised Reevesville Antiques proclaimed "Speed Trap Ahead. Reduce Speed to 25 MPH." Nowadays, all

Not From Around Here, Are You?

over the country we have warning signs showing an upcoming decrease in a speed limit. Never underestimate the power of one motivated individual.

A couple of months ago it was clear Red was slipping from us and I told her again how inspired I had been by the way she handled herself in Reevesville. It was the trigger that caused me to go to law school and become a poverty lawyer.

Through her pain she cracked her smile. "It's nice that you think I did something," she said, "but every seed knows its time."

True, but don't you agree Red was *the* master gardener?

Before I turn the podium over to our next speaker, I'll leave you with another of Red's proverbs: "Life is not separate from death; it only looks that way." Red is never dead to us as long as we remember. Thanks, Red.

Jazzman
In Memory of Oscar Treadwell

Carol Feiser Laque

My icy lips—Keep February Blue,
Blue blood—A scat—
Skies—shocking shadows—
With a sudden shine.

Slippery verse—notes a time
when spring is shoved
back into the earth and
Frosty tulips—bend forward

To a time—yet to come—past—
But too soon—to bud and bop—
entire landscapes swoon—percussive
yellow or red—falling now.

In love with Time—upbeat—green
sliding a capricious theme
contrapuntal—you can down beat it—
up—don't hardly say it—play it cool for March.

My true face sings songs
while masks tumble trapped—
Don't be afraid to risk
a simple saxophone in the spotlight.

Going Home

Mary Fitzpatrick

"Reason for visiting the Appalachian Cultural Reserve?"

"Father's funeral." John McIntyre said as he handed his ID chit up to the border guard, along with his wife's and daughter's.

"You a native?"

"Born here."

Without leaving his booth, the guard leaned over to look into the cab of McIntyre's pickup. His belly got in the way before he bent far enough to get a good view. McIntyre doubted he could see much. Dawn was a ways off. The moon didn't shed light down between the mountains where the road ran.

Kaz slept in the passenger seat, wrapped up to her ears in a blanket against the slight chill in the air. Ella slept in her safety seat in the back.

With any luck, this stop wouldn't wake Ella. They had timed the trip so she could sleep most of the way. McIntyre wanted to be closer to his parent's home place before she woke up. He had learned the hard way that four-year-olds and long trips were not a good match.

Flying into the Reserve would have triggered alarms so there was quite a bit of driving on old mountain roads still in front of him. Already tired and uneasy about his family's reaction to his return, McIntyre felt a spike of frustration start to build at the delay. He didn't want to be held up at the checkpoint. His brain implant was working to help him concentrate on the drive; he felt it shift to keep his temper from getting out of hand. An argument with a border guard was the last thing he needed.

"My wife and daughter were born off world," he said hoping to speed the man along. "I applied for their non-tourist visas several months ago. Everything should be in order."

Going Home

Leaving the protection of the Datdsii embassy compound in London had been a risk, but McIntyre had to be there for his father's funeral. The thought of facing his mother again made his stomach churn. He would rather go up against hostile aliens than face her wrath over his prolonged absence.

The officer slipped the ID chits into his scanner, a bored look on his round, pleasant face. That changed the moment McIntyre's Alliance ID came up on the screen and he realized who was waiting at his booth. The kid in the ID picture looked brand-new, blond and blue eyed, and clean-cut as a recruiting poster. He seemed about to burst with the earnest desire to protect, serve, and right what was wrong with the universe. McIntyre could remember being that kid, but he was older now, and he hoped wiser when it came to righting wrongs.

The guard glanced toward the truck, and back at his screen while typing something on his keypad. After reading through what came up, he tapped the chits against his palm and stepped down from the booth.

"Everything seems to be in order, Lieutenant."

He leaned against the door to speak to McIntyre, but his eyes looked across him toward Kaz.

"We free to go?"

The officer paused and took off his bill-cap, pushed back his salt-and-pepper hair, then settled the hat back on his head. The harsh blue-gray fluorescent lights from the booth made him look tired and pale as a ghost.

"The Alliance dropped their charges against you. You're one of us, no matter what you've gotten into, so you have every right to enter the Reserve. But we don't need any trouble."

"I don't want any trouble."

"Sometimes it just happens. Most of us on the Reserve are live and let live types, you know that, but there are plenty who go on about cultural purity. They are not going to happy with you, or her." He nodded his head toward Kaz.

"My father's dead. The funeral's tomorrow."

"I understand."

Kaz shifted in her sleep. She pulled up her knees and

curled more deeply into the seat causing the blanket to slip down to her shoulders. She was turned away from them, but the back of her head and the line of her jaw and cheek were visible. The light from the booth made her pale, feathery mane glow, and highlighted the delicate scales on her cheek so they shown like a fine layer of frost.

"She's pregnant, right?" the guard asked.

"Yes," McIntyre answered, wondering if any aspect of his personal life had not made the news since he returned to Earth with the Datdsii treaty negotiation team.

"Is the baby human?"

"Some."

"You the father?"

"Every way but biologically."

"I see."

Surprisingly, his tone of voice made McIntyre think maybe he did.

The officer paused for a moment, then nodded toward Ella in the back seat, "She's human, but you and her mama renounced your Alliance citizenship and joined up with these new aliens. Some aren't going to be too happy about that either."

He let out a sigh that was oddly parental; obviously feeling it was his duty to point out McIntyre's poor life choices, but not wanting to insult him in front of his sleeping family. For a moment McIntyre thought he was going to get the "don't they teach you flyboys to keep your zipper up" lecture again, but the guard just went on.

"You're going to be away from any quick rescue if troublemakers come after you. Reserve Security doesn't have a lot of manpower."

"With any luck we'll be back in London before anyone outside my family knows we were here." McIntyre left unspoken that it depended on the guard's discretion.

"God willing," said the officer and started toward the booth. He realized he still had the chits in his hand and stepped back to the truck.

"Sorry, Lieutenant, I'm distracted, I've never seen one

before."

"One what?"

"An alien in the flesh. Your wife's my first." He blushed and handed McIntyre the chits then waved him into the Reserve. "Good luck. Sorry about your dad, he was a good man."

Several hours later, McIntyre turned down a gravel road that snaked its way along a narrow gap in the mountains. The closer he got to his birthplace, the worse the sour acid pressure in his gut became. He felt like he had been driving forever.

His cross-wired brain made him one of the few people who could pilot a ship as it dropped out of real-space to cheat the speed of light, but it also meant his time sense wasn't great. The implant helped with that, like it did with concentration and temper control, but jumping halfway around the globe still left him more disoriented than most people. That added to his anxiety about coming home, and was making him feel like he had swallowed a chunk of lava. Pulling over and throwing up would only postpone the inevitable. He queried the implant for the local time. 7:00 AM. Early, but his mother would be up and working.

Almost as soon as they were off pavement, the pickup hit a series of potholes. The bucking woke Kaz.

"Are we there yet?"

"Almost."

They hit another rut in the road and McIntyre swore under his breath.

"I doubt you would impress your mother with that sort of language."

McIntyre snorted. His shoulder muscles were tight enough to snap. He wished computerized vehicles weren't banned on the Reserve so he could use his implant to hack the truck's guidance system and let it take over driving.

"Are we close enough that I should wake Ella?"

"No. If she can sleep through this, she must need the rest."

Kaz stretched and looked out the window. "The road is hell, but the scenery is beautiful."

Steep tree-covered hills rose around them. Early morning

sunlight filtering through layers of leaves dappled everything with gold. The air was rich with the fecund smell of earth and the clean, spicy green smell of trees. The road was the only manmade thing in sight.

"Hard to believe it was all clear-cut and strip-mined at one time," said McIntyre, swerving around another set of potholes.

"This is all salvaged?"

"Yep. The legislation setting up the Reserve also provided funding to preserve what was left of the ecosystem and reclaim the rest of the land. But even when things were at their worst, these mountains were addictive. That's why my mother's people stayed here when they could have lived better almost anywhere else."

"You left."

"Doesn't mean I don't miss it."

McIntyre slowed the pickup and turned carefully onto a dirt road that split off and wound up the side of the hill. It was only a foot wider than the truck and had twice the dips and bumps of the 'improved' gravel road. There was a long drop back into the valley if they pitched over the side.

"Is it always this bad?" asked Kaz.

"This isn't bad. You should see it when it's coming down rain, or better yet after a snow." He grinned at her.

"Eyes on the road, please."

She gave him her raptor-angel look, gleaming scales, puffed mane, and mirror bright eyes flashing with the promise of vengeance. He suspected she practiced the look because she knew the instinctive fear reaction it caused in humans.

It was an act.

Mostly.

"The worst is behind us." Wishing that was true, he reached over and patted her on the knee.

"Careful." She swatted away his hand.

They reached the top of the ridge and the road started into a shallow hanging valley. A pasture rolled down to the right and on the left a wooden house with generations of additions sat with its back against the mountain. A deep covered porch wrapped around the front and sides. Baskets of pink and purple flowers hung between the roof supports. Flowers also lined the flagstone steps leading up to the porch and to the large vegetable plot on the hill behind the house.

McIntyre pulled into an open space at the side of the road next to a faded blue truck. Kaz took off her seatbelt and started to open the door.

He reached for her arm. "She knows we're here. Wait a bit. It's the polite thing to do."

Dropping a ship out of real space without definite target coordinates was easier than this. He wished he could kick his implant into flooding his brain with something to settle his nerves without dulling them. He needed to be in control to protect his wife from the rough edge of his mother's temper.

"Being polite can't hurt." Kaz sat back and stretched her legs as well as she could inside the cab, while rubbing a hand across the bulge made by the baby in her pouch.

"Everything OK?" McIntyre reached across and cupped her face with one hand tracing the fine arch of her cheek with his thumb.

"I'm stiff." She patted her belly again. "And huge. How are you doing?"

McIntyre was not listening; he was looking into her wide silver eyes.

"You are so beautiful."

"Not answering my question." She grinned, a human style grin, which should have been scary on her alien face, but she knew enough human body language to make it work. "You can't lie to me, John."

True enough. Thanks to their emergency use of a brain-to-brain interface that was never meant to work with her species, they kept a constant awareness of each other. The connection had saved their lives, and let her know how his smile felt from the inside. Yet, after five years they were still learning to live inside each other's head. Kaz could sense the bubble of impending doom growing behind his sternum. The last thing he needed was her considerable temper being spun-up.

"Dad was the only member of the family who gave me his blessing when I left. He was hurt bad in a fall when I was still in school, and never really got better. Now he's gone. Mother isn't the forgiving type. How should I feel?"

"She's your family, John." Kaz brushed a lock of golden-blond hair off his face and pulled him over to rest against her shoulder. "And you have Ella as a peace offering."

He swallowed the acid trying to crawl its way up his throat. This was not one of his brighter ideas; it was never going to work.

"Even getting a grandbaby as sweet as Ella won't soften Lee McIntyre's heart toward her runaway child. Nothing is harder than pleasing family. I saved your life, and risked a great deal to take you home instead of back to Alliance space, but how happy was your family about us?"

"You slept with the woman my brother loved within twenty-four hours of landing on the planet."

"I had you inside my head, and Melissa had not seen another human face in years. We were both very confused."

"I know, I know. . . ."

She rested her chin on top of his head and let her love and support settle over him. His gut calmed and he began to relax, then the sound of a door slamming cut through the morning quiet like a gunshot.

They looked toward the house. The screen door was swinging back and forth, but the porch was empty.

"So much for a warm welcome," sighed McIntyre.

He got out of the pickup and helped Kaz down from the passenger seat before reaching into the back for his sleeping daughter. Ella's mother, Melissa Stanton, was a victim of eugenic terrorists; Kaz's brother had rescued her from their research lab along with a huge brood of hybrid Human-Datdsii embryos. McIntyre had slept with her once, which led to Ella.

In Terran societies, that would have caused a horrible tangle, but Datdsii had complex and extended families. The Datdsii solution to the problem of the hybrids had been to create a family for them that included adults of both parent species. There were thousands of hybrids, but Lissa and McIntyre were the only two humans in Datdsii space. By the time Ella was born, they both were braided tightly into the hybrid's family.

Now all McIntyre had to do was get his biological family to take him back.

As they started up the stairs toward the house, the screen door opened and Lee McIntyre stepped out on the porch. She waited with her arms crossed at her waist. She was slight, thin as tree that dropped its leaves for winter. Her eyes were the same bright blue as McIntyre's. When they reached the porch, she wrapped her arms around her son and the child in his arms. There were tears in her eyes.

With his head on his mother's shoulder, and her hand rubbing his back McIntyre felt he had been worried over nothing, and all was forgiven.

"Mother," he said when she let go, "I'm sorry I couldn't be here sooner."

"Your father was a long time dying. He's at peace now." She didn't mention her own pain. She didn't have to, for it shown from every line of her face. Stepping back, she looked at Kaz. Her mouth drew up in a grim line.

"You couldn't marry a local girl, could you, Johnny?"

His stomach knotted again as if she had kicked him.

"Don't start, Mother."

She reached toward Kaz and McIntyre stepped protectively between the two women. Lee leaned past him and placed a hand on Kaz's belly. "Who is its father? Not my son, I reckon."

"SHE is one of the hybrids." Kaz placed her hand on top of Lee's and pressed so they could both feel the baby shift inside her pouch. "John risked a great deal to make sure she would have a proper family. That makes him all the father she needs."

Lee's hand shook as she pulled it back, and wiped it on the seat of her pants. Her face was white. "The one you're holding is yours, right? That's what they say on the Net. The Alliance told us you were missing, and later you were AWOL, but

103

everything else we had to learn from the gossip feeds. Not the best way to learn you made me a grandparent."

"For the past five years, I was on a planet without diplomatic or trade ties to the Alliance. I was trying to help avert interstellar war and there wasn't regular phone service."

"You were gone for eight years."

"I sent you a message as soon as I was back in Alliance space."

"You weren't here, Johnny. Not for me, not for your father. That's all that matters."

She picked up a basket of tools from the porch and headed toward the garden. Halfway up the hill she turned and called back to them.

"Go on in, you know where everything is. I'll be back in time to fix supper."

"Mother, can we talk about Dad's funeral?"

"Your brothers will be by later, talk to them." She continued toward the garden without looking back.

"That went well, didn't it?" Kaz sighed.

Still carrying Ella asleep on his shoulder, McIntyre went into the house. He stopped just inside the door as if unable to go any farther.

"I'm going to go talk to her, John," Kaz said through the screen. In their link, he felt her distress.

"Don't waste your breath. I'll get a few hours sleep and we'll leave. To hell with the funeral."

"I didn't come up that poor excuse of a road for nothing, John."

"Fine, Kaz. Whatever." He walked away from the door too emotionally drained to argue.

Kaz stepped off the porch and headed up the hill toward the garden. Part way up, she had to stop and catch her breath. Lifting her sweater she reached into her pouch to shift the baby. She didn't know how human women made it through gestation without being able to move their babies from time to time. Their daughter was large enough now for it to really be uncomfortable when she stayed in one place too long.

Going Home

Lee McIntyre knelt in the garden with her back to the house, working the soil between rows of bush beans with a trowel, the ash-blond braid hanging down her back swung viciously back and forth from the force of her movements.

"It's not the plants' fault, Mrs. McIntyre. Don't take it out on them."

"That's Doctor McIntyre," she said without a break in her work. "Just because we live by old ways does not mean we are uneducated yokels. I'm a director of the Reserve's biosphere reconstruction project, after all."

Kaz nodded. "Ecological reconstruction is considered an art form and religious calling on Datdsu. We suffered greater damage in our industrial phase than Earth. That's partly why our fringe political groups didn't want us to have anything to do with the Alliance."

"I don't see the connection."

"We have ongoing infertility problems because of trace contaminants. That may be why the radicals created the hybrids. You can outbreed us."

"Your family had no problem breeding spies to infiltrate the Alliance. That's what the news feeds say."

"We trained spies, but they were surgically altered, not bred, for their job."

"So, you weren't raised to seduce my son into treason? They got that wrong, did they?" She glared up at Kaz, then dug her trowel viciously into the soil nearly uprooting a nearby tomato seedling.

"My brother and I were raised to think like humans, but John was never part of my family's plans. A terrorist mine disabled both our ships and brought us together."

"But you did talk my son into going to Datdsu."

"Yes."

"You used his ship's control interface to get inside his head. You made him go to your people instead of coming home."

"We would be dead if I hadn't tried the interface. John couldn't fly the damaged ship by himself. I didn't know it would leave me with John inside my head for the rest of my life. Dr.

105

McIntyre, do you really think that just because our subconscious minds are linked, I can make your son do something he doesn't want to?"

Lee McIntyre stopped working and sat back on her heels. She gave Kaz a long look and there was just a hint of humor in her eyes.

"Johnny does not take kindly to being told what to do, that's for sure, but could he say no? Does he control his mind now, or do you?"

"He's in my head as much as I'm in his. I came here so he could make things right with the Alliance. If they decide to prosecute him and toss him in prison, I can't go home. If we get too far apart, we both suffer."

"Why didn't you just come here in the first place?"

"Luck and wishes were the only thing keeping John's ship going. We were closer to Datdsu. Going there was our only hope of surviving. I made John see that. When it comes to sheer force of wills, I'm no less stubborn than your son."

"I figured that out for myself ten minutes ago."

"Then you forgive him? We had no idea it would be so long before he could come home. No one knew about the hybrid children until after we got to Datdsu. They complicated everything."

"Johnny could have come home when the first Alliance negotiation team reached the planet."

"He was afraid humans would see the hybrids as disposable complications, not children needing homes. His willingness to renounce his ties to the Alliance and become part of their family did more than all your diplomats to negotiate a treaty between our people."

"Oh, Johnny values the right things. I am proud of that, but it doesn't make it any easier for me to forgive him."

"For what?"

"Leaving in the first place"

"I don't understand."

Lee McIntyre picked up a handful of soil and held it up to Kaz. "My family has lived on this land for over four hundred years. It's ours. Timber barons, coal companies, social reformers, and rich folk looking for vacation homes with a view, all tried to drive us off this land, but we stayed. The land was stripped, raped and poisoned, but we stayed and nurtured it back to health. We stayed, because this is where we belong, but Johnny left." She opened her hand and let the soil trickle out. "He just walked away."

"I thought service was compulsory for anyone with drop-space piloting ability."

"The Alliance didn't have to come looking for Johnny. He had all the paperwork ready so he could leave the day he turned eighteen."

"If the Alliance would have drafted him anyway, why blame him for leaving?"

The old woman's eyes flashed. "He never planned to come back! This is the first time he's been home since he left for training. You people only had him five years. Before that, he could have returned, but he didn't. He was ashamed of his roots."

"That's not true, Mother."

McIntyre stood at the edge of the garden holding Ella's hand. Her dark unruly hair was sleep tousled and her face had a solemn and curious expression unique to children contemplating adults. She got her wild hair and round stubborn chin from her mother, but the intense stare and bright blue eyes came straight from Lee McIntyre.

"Then why'd you stay away, Johnny?"

"I was born with brain damage, because you lived here on the Reserve instead of someplace with modern prenatal monitoring. You were proud of your heritage but ashamed to have a damaged kid. I needed a chip implanted in my head so I didn't blow up at every little thing or get lost on the way home from school. You were ashamed of me. Kids pick up on that. That's why I stayed on Datdsu. Kaz didn't seduce me. I just didn't want to see those kids treated as freaks. I knew what it felt like."

"But you're my child. I love you!"

"And that's why I stayed away. The older I got, the harder

it was to stand the pain in your eyes when you looked at me. Dad understood. We talked about it before I left. He felt I would be happier away from the Reserve where the whole implant thing wouldn't be an issue, but he knew you would never understand."

"Your father loved you without question. Is that why you came home now?"

"I've been planning to come back since Ella was born. His funeral was an excuse to push through the paperwork. Her future is with the hybrids. They are her siblings. Together, they can build a bridge between Datdsu and the Alliance, but Ella needs to know her human roots."

"John is not ashamed of growing up here, Dr. McIntyre," said Kaz. "Part of him never left."

Kaz took Ella's hand. "Your grandmother is going to tell you some stories, sweetie, so you know about where your dad grew up. OK?"

Ella nodded and Kaz walked her over to where Lee was sitting and passed her the girl's hand. Then she took her husband's elbow and led him out of the garden.

"Wait," said Lee. "What about your next daughter, Johnny, the one she's carrying?" She nodded toward Kaz. "Will I be having the same talk with her?" Her voice was guarded, but hopeful.

McIntyre glanced at Kaz, then back at his mother.

"Yes, I think you will."

He slipped his arm around his wife's waist and they continued downhill toward the house. Lee held Ella's hand awkwardly for a moment, then pulled the girl onto her lap. The doctor took a long, deep breath that tasted of surrender. She licked her lips and begin to speak in a voice as old as the hills.

"You were born on another planet, child, but this is your place, this is where your roots are."

She pressed her granddaughter's hand into the garden's rich soil.

"You will always have a home on this land."

Improving on Goodness

Marcia Eckstein

There was no good way to tell someone that life, as he knew it, was about to end.

The message arrived yesterday. Two words. *Found them.* Signed with Uncle Gerald's big "G".

My brother, Gerry, was chronologically old enough to be told the family secret, but I worried about his emotional age. Since the previous night, I'd rehearsed my speech. Sloshing through the rain on my way to work, I tried a hundred different ways to say what needed to be said, only to pitch them all and start over again.

Frustrated, soaked with the rain that had snarled the traffic, I shifted the umbrella to my other hand and raised my palm to the reader on the door.

An automated voice, too cheerful for my mood, said, "Good morning, Director Perkins."

The door opened with a gentle wheeze. "Good morning, Ethel. How's the family today?"

"Lucy is operating at ninety-nine point four seven six percent capacity this morning. Atmospheric conditions have increased moisture in the surrounding area causing a slight reduction in speed. Lucy is attending to the problem. She anticipates we will be at peak in approximately eleven minutes, four seconds."

"That's our girl. Thanks for the update, Ethel. Have a good one."

"Walk in beauty, Madam Director."

The room was dark.

That should have been my first clue, but I was busy shaking my umbrella and rehearsing my lines. I gave the command and the cavernous building flooded with light.

Not From Around Here, Are You?

"Anybody home?" I called out.

"Yissss." A voice came from the back of the building in the lockdown area we called The Safe.

"Good. I'm on my way. Let me grab some coffee and we can begin."

I walked past row upon row of old oak desks. In slumber mode, the computer screens that recessed into the desktops displayed graphics that would have won awards, if we could show them to anyone. On the off chance that an intruder managed to gain entrance without a registered palm print, they would find a dusty warehouse full of battered furniture. The wrinkled newspapers, fast food wrappers, the odd copy of *Mad Magazine*—Gerry's desk, of course—were screen-savers built to disguise the computers connected to them. Our intent was to make the trespasser lose interest and go away.

The screen on the receptionist's desk showed a game of solitaire, which told me that the unit had been shut down at some point. That meant we had a problem in The Safe where we stored the four master cells. Ethel had accounted for Lucy. That left Ricky or Fred.

A nerve twitched in my upper lip. Our four uber-computers ran a system that could take over the world, if we were interested in that sort of thing.

"Gerry!" I hollered. "Get out here now. How many times do I have to show you the proper way to lock down before you leave your station? Gerry? Gerry!"

Obscenities flowed as I stomped toward The Safe. While my doctorate had increased technical know-how, it did nothing to improve my people skills.

Our project was massive and I admired the outside-the-box thinking that had spawned it. The antithesis of most covert agencies, we let others chase bad guys. Our think tank searched for good. When we found even a glimpse of it anywhere in the world, we dumped resources into it in an effort to expand and improve the goodness.

This morning's staff meeting would decide which lucky faction of the universe would reap the benefits of our expertise next. I looked forward to these yearly meetings. We all did. Even lazy, loud, obnoxious Gerry who, if he wasn't such a genius, I would have dumped long ago, was at his best when deciding who the next lucky winner would be. An empty warehouse on the day of the big meet had Gerry written all over it. I did a slow burn at the thought of his gum popping, his goofy outfits, his utter lack of common sense.

Where were the other techs? Had that addle-brained idiot convinced them to play along with some stupid game? Any minute, I expected him to jump out of a closet and shout, "Boo!"

I didn't have time for this. There was work to do.

"Come on, Gerry, we're supposed to be making the world a better place, remember?"

"Yisss."

A tickle ran across my forehead. The voice was human-like, but not quite human enough. Last thing I needed was one of the techs' homemade robots zipping around the warehouse. How could Gerry be so careless? Why would he risk it all for a silly stunt?

I swore I would do it this time. I'd fire him.

Or maybe I'd just kill him.

I sighed. Nothing changed the fact that he was blood, and relatives weren't options. More's the pity.

The scanner on The Safe door read my palm. Inside, I heard computers buzzing with a softness that belied their power. Since the days of Tesla, humankind had toiled to create purring engines. As a species, I doubt we will ever attempt to build a silent one; that low hum is so soothing to our senses.

Lights blinked across Fred's façade. The little blue one reassured me that everything worked.

While checking the four cells, the surrounding floor and the walls, I heard the sound again coming from the air exchanger above my head. I looked up.

It was Gerry. Or not.

"Pretty," he said to me, "Mmmm, so pretty."

His little lips parted and blew me a kiss.

"What the hell?" I asked, my fingers reaching into my

pocket for the phone while my brain scrambled to recall safety procedures to use in case of attack.

He wore a smaller version of Gerry's clothes. The chartreuse corduroy pants, the orange Bengals T-shirt, no chewing gum though.

"Hi," he said.

"Gerry?" I tried to keep my voice steady. "What have you done to yourself?"

He smiled. "Yis." Pointing a slender finger at his chest, he nodded at me. "Gerry here," he told me as he jumped out of the air exchanger and, in one rubbery bound, leapt to the door. "Come."

He locked the door to The Safe as if he'd done it a thousand times before. The scanner accepted his print. It had to be Gerry, I told myself.

Strictest precaution dictated removing whatever it was from The Safe. So I followed him into the kitchen studying his features as we walked along. I couldn't lose the feeling that Gerry had somehow shrunk himself into a leprechaun and now lived inside this tiny body. The features were human-like, with extra long fingers and a head just a pinch too large. I assumed the curvy puncture marks at the side of his skull passed for ears. His enormous butt jiggled as he led me down the little hallway to the kitchen. It was cute.

Cute? Directors of international thinks tanks don't use words like cute.

I sat down at the kitchen table and watched in silence while he made a pot of coffee. When he bent to hand me my cup, I could see that the top of his head was covered by a lid that resembled a transparent yarmulke. Inside lay a snake's nest of electronic circuitry.

I did not miss the fact that he had known without me saying a word that I took cream.

The first sip added to my fears. This couldn't be Gerry. Gerry's coffee tasted like boiled weeds.

"So, who are you?" I tried to sound casual. "Why are you brewing coffee?"

"Yis. Like coffee."

"Yeah, well, I like coffee too, but I don't go breaking into stranger's offices to make a pot. How did you get inside The Safe?" I took a closer look at his eyes. "It's not you, is it Gerry?" I asked, his insolent smile so familiar somehow.

Generous lips smiled back at me. "Yis," he said, patting his forehead.

"Damn it, Gerry!" I slammed a fist down on the table. "Quit playing around and tell me what's going on."

He shrugged. "Gerry here."

"Yeah, I got that part. I don't know what you've done to yourself but I want you to grow yourself back, and I mean now!"

"Yis not Gerry," he said. "Yis Yis."

"Work with me, would you? I can't help you if you don't speak English."

"Speak fine." His face knotted with hurt. "Not Gerry. Yis. Yis." He pointed a bony finger at himself.

"Sure. Okay, short guy, I'll play. You're not Gerry." My brother's insanity had finally taken him over the hump and he'd turned himself into someone else today. "Great. Whatever. Who are you then?"

This time he smacked both palms flat against his chest. "Yis!" he insisted, "Yis!"

Then it dawned on me. Who was on first. What was on second. Yis was in my kitchen brewing coffee.

"Oh, dear." I tried to blink away the headache that had begun to lock up the blood vessels behind my eyes.

"Gerry love coffee." He smiled. "You tired? Awwww."

At that, he jumped onto my shoulders and began to massage the back of my neck. Being the director of a scientific team working in a project so secret that half the time we doubted our own existence, I knew better than to allow an alien unit to touch me or get the upper hand before I determined its agenda.

I didn't move.

Why was the question.

This thing could have killed Gerry, or absorbed him somehow. Whisked him off to another planet like Indiana, or tortured him for information. There I sat, hands warm around a mug of coffee, as sinewy fingers kneaded the stress out of my neck. I knew I was being manipulated, but I couldn't work myself into a proper indignation.

It felt good.

"Where's Gerry?" I managed to mumble, eyelids heavy. My head was on the kitchen table, spittle forming at the side of my lip. As he rubbed, he hummed. The combination of low-pitched hum and whatever magic made heat transfer from his fingers to my skin put me into a state of deep relaxation. I stopped trying to fight it and let my eyelids close. "A little to the left, a little more. That's it. Ooh, that feels so good."

"I see you two have met."

Gerry's voice slapped me out of my reverie like a cold shower. My head popped up so fast, it clobbered Yis, knocked him off my shoulders and sent him tumbling to the floor. He landed on his chubby butt, giggled and shrieked, "Gerreeee!", slamming into Gerry's knees in a bone-crushing hug.

Gerry stood in the kitchen doorway wearing chartreuse corduroys with orange and black Bengals jersey. Today he'd accessorized with a lavender ascot. An uncertain grin played at his lips.

"Well, not formally," I said.

I sat up and took a big gulp of coffee, a play for dignity that went bad when I missed my mouth altogether, spilling brew down the front of my best linen suit.

Gerry bowed. "Let me do the honors then. Yis? This is my boss, Kim. Kim?" He patted the little one on the head. "My good friend, Yis."

Yis bowed. "So pleased," he said. "Gerry, Kim pretty. Mmm."

Gerry had the decency to blush.

"What *is* it, Gerry?"

His eyes gestured toward the wall, as if I had asked an embarrassing question. He nodded to the hallway.

"Can we talk out there? Yis, will you make me a cup of mocha java, extra vanilla, with whipped cream? And sprinkles."

114

Improving on Goodness

Yis clapped his hands with glee.

"Follow me." Gerry led me to his desk. His screen-saver sported a betting form, River Downs circa 1957.

"I hate to talk about someone when they're standing right there," he said.

"Sure. Courtesy at all costs. Especially with aliens. Spill, Gerry. What *is* it?"

He ran his purple high-top up and down his shin. The way he bit the inside of his cheek spoke volumes about how hard he was working to invent the right lie.

"I guess you know I've been playing around with my communicator at home."

Gerry had inherited a communicator that, legend had it, made it possible to talk to extraterrestrials. When our former Director retired, he downsized, giving away all kinds of wonderful stuff. I treasured my volume of seventeenth century haiku. To Gerry, the communicator was the equivalent of an erector set.

"I heard you got a ping or two, yeah."

"I've been communicating with Yis for over a year. Last month he decided to pay a visit."

I let the part about 'over a year' sink in.

"From where? And why is he in my warehouse exposing the equipment to who knows what kinds of contaminants? Do you know what happens to the project now that you've compromised it?"

Gerry let out a huge sigh. "I kept him in my apartment for the first two weeks," he whined, by way of excuse. "He's sentient!"

I rolled my eyes. "How do you know that?"

"He's so intuitive, so caring."

"I cannot believe what I'm hearing."

"I don't know how to explain it. He's always so happy to see me. And he's an awesome cook. Isn't that the whole point of this project? Finding people like Yis? Cultivating good in people?"

"Gerry, honey, what makes you think he's 'people'?"

"Come on, Kim. You're supposed to stay open-minded."

He did have me there. I felt like the mom being asked,

'Can we keep him?'

"How did he get here?"

"One night, Misha and I had a few beers and started playing around with the communicator. You know the drill. You get a few pings, get all excited, then nothing. Probably a nova bursting a zillion light-years away. So I thought, why do we always aim it up and out, you know? Why do we never aim the probes directly into ourselves where the real aliens live?" He smiled sheepishly. "I guess the beer made me a little philosophical."

"I guess."

"So I adjusted the probes to point at me, then I laid down on the couch. Misha had already gone to bed. Then I heard a hiss. Of course we now know it was Yis saying his name."

"Of course."

"That kept me entertained for a while." He shrugged. "Then I brushed my teeth and hit the sack. In the morning, there was a message on the screen."

"What did it say?"

"'You like coffee?'"

"Don't start with me. I've already been through the coffee routine with your little buddy."

"No, that's what the screen said. 'You like coffee?' I was so pumped at first. Then, figuring it was Misha's joke, I asked her if she was trying to con me into making breakfast. But it wasn't her. She's not the joking type, you know?"

"And yet she calls you her boyfriend."

"So I typed back 'I love coffee. Who are you?' The usual getting to know you stuff."

"Sure."

"One thing led to another, then one day Yis asked if he could visit. We said yes of course."

"Of course." I threw my arms up in the air. What a nightmare.

"I mean, how cool is it that an alien sleeps on my couch?" He was bouncing on the balls of his feet.

"He sleeps? What is he then? Is that human tissue? He looks manufactured."

"We think he's a mutt."

"I saw wires in his head."

"Circuits. They do all sorts of things, depending on what color they are. His life cycle is different than ours."

"You don't say."

"He speaks two languages, English and this other thing that doesn't sound like anything I've ever heard. Very guttural with a lot of whispery sounds. Navaho, maybe?" His eyes found mine. "Kim, the family could learn so much from him."

The family.

Back when Queen Victoria was learning to tat collar lace, our ancestors had formed a group of scientists bent on finding ways to increase goodness in the world. Their operating tenet was endorse the good guys so you don't have to fight the bad guys. Proactive with an attitude.

Never mind that the funds used to underwrite their little scheme came, in part, from monies earned in trades best left unmentioned in polite company. Another family secret.

"You still haven't told me where he's from."

"That is the coolest part. He *is* from around here. From Earth, not outer space. The way Yis tells it, he was born in some deep cavern in the southwest desert somewhere. And get this. We share the same birthday! Not your average alien, huh?" His face glowed with pride. "Misha loves him."

"As I've already pointed out, Misha has strange taste in, well, men."

Gerry scowled. "Give him a chance, Kim."

I let my mind dance through a few scenarios, none of them career-enhancing. There was no way around it, Yis had already infiltrated our offices, the damage was done. I should have fired Gerry on the spot. I should have locked up the little urchin and thrown away the key until I had more information. But there was something about him. He made me feel good.

"Where's everybody else? We're supposed to have a meeting this morning."

"In the conference room. Waiting for you."

That didn't play. "They're awfully quiet."

"Yis taught them how to meditate."

Fireworks exploded through my brain.

"Am I the last one to meet our little visitor?" I shrieked.

"We were afraid to tell you. You worry too much."

My breathing came in pants. I locked my fists together to prevent them swinging at him.

"I'll meet you in the conference room," I said, in a voice that I hoped boded bodily harm.

My Uncle Gerald has a wild streak a mile wide. When they sent him to prison on vague charges related to sharing secrets, he escaped in less than a day. I envisioned his namesake, Gerry, in a well fortified cell where he could no longer pose a danger to himself or others.

Not my proudest moment.

After a short break to take deep breaths and gather my wits, I walked into the conference room ready to demand some answers. My devoted staff sat quietly, all faces forward, in and of itself a miracle. I usually had to bang on the table to get everyone's attention at staff meetings. It's the price we paid for genius. Creativity often came couched in child-like brains.

Gerry had warned them ahead of time, obviously. I looked out at a room full of pleading eyes.

"Give me one good reason." I kept my voice low. "And make it a very good one."

Everyone spoke at once. The cacophony was abrasive but reassuring in its normality, so I let myself relax a little. I let them shout for a few seconds before clapping my hands for silence.

"Okay, hold on!" I shouted. "One at a time." I nodded to Misha. "Why don't you go first? Gerry says you've grown very fond of Yis."

"I love him!" she squealed, bouncing in her seat. "Oh, Kim. Let us keep him. He's so, so, I can't think of a word." She ran her hands through silky jet-black hair. Misha's people hailed from Siberia and her Asian genes had blessed her. "He's *good*. He makes you feel good." She dropped her arms to her sides and scoffed at herself. "Rats. That wasn't very convincing, was it?"

"Not unless you're trying out for the pep squad, no."

"Next?" I looked around the table. "Carl?"

Carl was our most taciturn staff. The stodgiest member of our group by far, I figured if he could find a good word to say, it might mean something.

"Good cook," Carl allowed. "Like his potato soup."

Nods and murmurs of agreement around the table.

This was not working. I searched the room for a saner voice. "Della?"

Della's skin is more midnight blue than black, but her blush was evident all the same.

"It's personal, but I guess I can tell you. Devon and I were having trouble conceiving. We were too psyched up about it and got into fights. Overly sensitive, you know?" She brushed her hands in the air, flicking the bad memory out of the room. "Anyway, Yis taught us how to relax and it worked."

"What worked?"

"I'm pregnant," she beamed.

Whoops and cries of "Go, Dell!" while Devon suffered a rash of shoulder smacking.

Talk about a trump card, how was I supposed to respond to that? "Congratulations," I murmured.

"Kim?" It was Allen, project physician and former love of my life, the former part being all too recent. I had returned his ring the previous Saturday. Looking at him, I couldn't for the life of me remember why.

"Yes, Allen?"

"I've studied his body extensively. Yis appears to be some form of human-techno hybrid. He thinks he's from Earth, but we didn't create him, and I don't know who else could have. His basal body temperature, for one thing, is one hundred eleven point four."

"That explains the warmth on my neck."

Allen smiled. "Pretty good, huh?" His eyes burrowed into mine. "The first time I interviewed him, I was dressed in full moon suit in the decon room. I had detectors comb that room multiple times for any contaminant he may have left behind."

"And?"

"Nothing harmful. A trace of sand on the furniture." He gave a guilty shrug. "I know it sounds odd, but he's good for us. Like a pet, but better behaved, with cooler tricks. His only agenda seems to be making people happy."

"Kim?" Gerry's voice was somber. "We don't always get along. I know you only keep me around because Mom made you promise to look out for me."

I didn't deny it.

"Yis is good for me. He makes me look inside myself. Every year, we try to decide who's going to get our support. This year, I vote for us. The nurturer needs to be nurtured or the well runs dry, right? Yis can help with that."

I waited for the cheers in the room to diminish.

"People's lives may be at stake, Gerry."

He cleared his throat. "I want him to stay, but if you say no, I'll understand."

You could have, as the saying goes, knocked me over with a feather.

Gerry had never behaved as an adult in his entire life. At twenty-seven, his social skills remained at junior high level with his humor leaning toward boogers, farts, and immature sexual puns. He had never taken responsibility because it wasn't necessary. Every time he got into trouble, I was there to bail him out.

The door to the conference room opened and Yis walked in with fresh coffee. A lavender ascot had been added to his ensemble.

"Kim pretty," he said, and winked. It reminded me so much of something Gerry would do to try to make up for one of his stunts.

And that made me wonder. Maybe it wouldn't be so difficult to tell Gerry the family secret after all.

I turned and studied Yis' features more closely. If you knew what you were looking for, the resemblance was uncanny. Fashion notwithstanding, he did favor Gerry. That little cleft in his chin, the chubby cheeks, the alarming lack of maturity.

On the day Gerry was born, our parents left us in the care of my eccentric Uncle Gerald. The official line claimed they died in an accident but Uncle Gerald and I knew better.

We saw the other baby. The twin.

A crazy streak gallops through my mom's side of the family. She is Uncle Gerald's younger sister, game for anything. An accomplished geneticist, Mom couldn't resist using herself as a guinea pig when an interesting bit of DNA found its way into her lab. She was pregnant with Gerry anyway. I guess she figured she might as well incubate the two fetuses together.

Yis was indeed a hybrid, Allen had hit it on the head. This wiggly-butt little creature was my long-lost brother, the reason my parents had disappeared. Gerry had found him.

It is amazing what Gerry can do with an erector set.

That didn't prevent me challenging the wisdom of allowing his existence in our project.

"What if he's brainwashed every one of us?"

The room erupted in protests.

"My baby is *not* a figment of my imagination!" Della boomed, making a clear argument for the poet's warning about the female of the species.

Yis stood at my side, patting my shoulder. A low hum emanated from deep inside his belly.

"I'm worried," I admitted.

Gerry moved next to Yis and grinned. Little sparks of hope played across his face. "Could be a huge mistake," he said, his arm falling casually across Yis' shoulders. Side-by-side, the evidence was very convincing.

Maybe Gerry was right. I probably did worry too much.

"Yis," I asked, needing some sort of proof, "By any chance, would you know a woman named Marianne?"

The internal buzz escalated until his whole body hummed.

"Mmm," he purred. "Mom."

Gerry's eyes grew wide as saucers.

"Well, well, well." I straightened his ascot, whisked a crumb off his shoulder. "Welcome to the family, Yis."

Not From Around Here, Are You?

Yis slammed his head into my stomach, squeezing me in a bear hug that caused me to lose my balance. As I toppled backwards into my chair, I wondered if I was making a terrible mistake.

Then again, I told myself, he couldn't be any worse than Gerry.

Everlasting

Kim Brown

Many moons ago
The stars sang lullabies
Your soul was heavenheld.

Breath of dawn
Bright-shining as the sun
You were magically born.

Shadows of night
I no longer fear
Love comforts me warm.

Led by destiny
You chose me
To be your mother.

The Takeover

Ann Mazzaro

Grammy hugged my hand to her fat hips, shaking just a little.

"Scared?" I asked her, but she only averted her eyes even farther away from me. I guessed that now was not the right time. Grammy had her own way of answering me, and I had learned when enough was enough.

"Grammy, are you afraid right now? Are we going to die?" I asked a little louder.

"Jesus Christ, Maybell, hush up. Jesus," came her reply.

I hung my head and played with the can of tomato soup on the shelf close to me. I turned it round and round, wondering who ever could think that people would want round cans. No matter how many times you make it change by turning it around, you always ended up at the same place, and even inside the contents sat mocking you. You couldn't change them either.

The man had been only buying groceries, but the cashier had refused to accept a coupon that had been expired for more than a month. She had been polite, and he took her small smile as snobby and had put up with enough attitudes from others so he snapped.

He took a small object from his coat pocket and shot it off, screaming something about bastards and the failing economy. Grammy had almost thrown me down the aisle towards the frozen hamburgers, but when she grabbed me up I took hold of her flowered muumuu and hung on for dear life. My strength ripped it on her right side, exposing her cotton underpants, barely glowing neon green from their hiding place under her panty hose.

She screamed a high-pitched wail, flinging me from her side for real this time, and grabbing up a dish towel she tried to

124

cover her large body behind its tiny surface area.

"You insolent, no good, dirty, rotten, horrible, evil, oh of all days. If your mother could see you now. She would lock you up in her place. She never even wanted a child, and here I am in my old age, and a-a-a-and," she stammered.

I couldn't understand anything else she said, but just then the man who had caused the big bang at the front of the store came storming down our aisle, grabbing up a box of Honey Nut Cheerios and ripping it open as he got closer and closer.

"Shut up, old hag!" he screamed at Grammy, but she didn't answer him.

"I didn't mean to rip her dress. You made an-"

He slapped me.

"Get back. Movin' all you all. Goddamn it." His pale skin and scrawny body failed to match his deep and extra loud voice. His sneakers were untied, but he had on very nice black dress pants that had tiny stripes going all the way around them. Greasy hair hung limply in his face, and his sunken in eyes looked right through me. I thought he could read my mind. I grabbed a box of Fruit Loops and clung tightly to the cardboard safety net I had placed between us.

"Fruit Loops are my favorite," I said.

"Maybell, this is not the time." Grammy was whispering, but she sounded so loud. And angry.

"Mister, do you like Fruit Loops?" I asked.

He hungrily dug into his coat pocket and Grammy whimpered from across the aisle. He brought out a small box covered in a clear shiny coating and Grammy screamed. Greasy man only slid a small glance from his raging green eyes towards her as he pulled a tiny bright red container from his dress pants. Fire emerged, and he sucked in hard, sighing and breathing all at the same time.

"Aisle 4. I'm movin' all you all." He pointed with the red container. We only sat in silence, staring at him and then each other.

"Now. Jesus, people don't even listen when you got a gun. Damn society, all politics and TV." He turned, I guess to

Not From Around Here, Are You?

find others who were hiding in the aisles.

"Maybell, you stay put. I'm sure the police will be here soon. Don't you be scared now." Grammy still hid behind the dish towel.

"Are we going to ride in a fire truck?" I opened the box of Fruit Loops.

"No. Our car is still outside. Are you stealing? Maybell, those are not your Fruit Loops. Put them back." I took out the bag of cereal and closed up the empty box and set it back up on the shelf. Grammy gave me the evil eye.

"What?" I asked.

"Aisle 4," she answered.

I sat and ate my Fruit Loops rather content. Grammy had taken to trying to fit her large body into a poncho. It wasn't working out too good, but she told me we were going to play the quiet game. I think she started to get a little upset when I saw the faded design on her back. I pointed and jumped up and down as Grammy quickly shut her muumuu as much as possible to stop me from seeing. It was a bunch of little squiggles all put together right above her sagging butt. I told the woman next to me to look too, and she commented to Grammy about her tramp stamp. I didn't know what that meant, but Grammy didn't seem too pleased with the woman, and she stormed away. I brought her some Fruit Loops, but she threw the bag up the aisle. I retrieved them, and now sat, watching her curse her large body.

The skinny man with the cigarettes, that's what Grammy said they were, had taken to placing more items into a cart. He talked to himself a lot, and when he reached our aisle I asked him what he was doing. He didn't answer, but he gave me a very worried look when I asked him what he was going to do about his escaping homages. He started to ask me what a homage was, but then suddenly ran to the front of the store. I guess he figured it out.

Because he hadn't been watching, almost half the people in the store walked out the front door. I'm not sure if you can even really lock those doors anyways. Aren't grocery stores

126

The Takeover

always open? I asked Grammy, but she told me to be quiet or I was going to lose the quiet game. The place was surrounded now anyways, and Grammy had told me to stay put so I followed behind the skinny man as he ran towards the store's entrance.

"Son of bitch," he said.

I felt like I was in a movie. There were cops all over and fire trucks and ambulances and they were telling him to come out with his hands up. I put my own hands high up in the air.

"Like this, mister. This is how you do it," I told him.

He picked me up and put me under his arm like a sack of potatoes.

"Look, kid, if I go down, you go down. Understand?"

I didn't respond. I was pretending to be a potato. I hoped no one would stick me in foil and heat me up then eat me with lots of butter. I don't think I would like that very much. He paced around the front of the aisles with me for a while. Grammy stood staring from aisle 4, along with the other people who had not yet escaped. One woman was crying, something about her cats, and a man had stuffed his pants full of groceries; you could see the outline of oddly shaped boxes. Grammy eyed him doubtfully and took a couple of small steps away from him.

"All right, we need a plan. This is what I want. I want free groceries. For a year. And nobody gets hurt. One of you all is goin' to deliver my message to the cops. And tell 'em they can't shoot or arrest me and I'll let all you all go safe. You run out there, and it won't be pretty."

He had set me down and was talking animatedly with his hands.

Grammy eyed my school principal suspiciously. I had been told to wait in the hallway, but some kids from my class began to torment me and had almost succeeded with putting me in a locker when Mr. Baxley, the principal, came out of his office.

"Maybell, sit nex' to yer Gram, there," he pointed to the chair next to Grammy's.

He wiped his large hands across his face, smoothing his graying moustache and licking his palm to hold down the few unruly hairs combed from one side of his head to the other. Mr. Baxley sighed several times, and cleared his throat.

"Are you waiting for me to say something, Mr. Baxley?" I asked.

"Maybell, this is not the time." Grammy gave me a stern look. I looked out the window and pretended I was invisible. I threw my arms up and shook them, then looked to see if Grammy or Mr. Baxley had noticed. They hadn't.

"She doesn't need an institution, Mr. Baxley, she needs to stay here, under your kind and watchful eye I know she will grow out of these kinds of games that young children play. I don't understand how uprooting her would be a good idea," Grammy said. I think they were talking about me.

Sometimes when I was at school I would forget where I was and play games like I was at home. I would play Jews, and hide underneath the desk and yell at everyone else to be real quiet so the Nazis wouldn't hear us. If my teacher made me get up I would overturn my desk and say that math was for people who didn't know their colors. If she persisted that I sit and be quiet, I would cry and retell a story about how Grammy had pushed me out of our car one time when we were on the highway. A lot of times my teacher would make everyone leave the classroom, and Mr. Baxley would come and chat with me about times when he was a boy and he played soldiers in his backyard. I told Mr. Baxley he didn't know what bees were. He would look at me all funny like and nod and smile. He was a nice man, Mr. Baxley.

"Try an' undastand where I'm comin' from, the parents, the school board, even the teachers all feel Maybell would be better in a special place, for special children. Maybell?" He tried to get my attention by wiggling his fingers close to my face. I crossed my eyes and stuck out my tongue.

"Do you like Fruit Loops, Mr. Baxley? I had them when we were homages at the grocery store, but when Mama came on her Harmey she said I had to leave them there." I folded my hands neatly in my lap and ignored Grammy, who had moved her face within five inches of mine and had left her mouth hanging wide open. I looked at the little white hairs on her chin and tried to grab one but she jerked her head away.

"Jesus, Maybell, what are you talking about? Your mother doesn't own a Harley, and she didn't come to the grocery. You haven't seen your mother in so long I wonder how you even think you remember her. For Christ's sake, Maybell, she didn't want you, she didn't care about you, and she wasn't ever around you. She pawned you off on me before you had a chance to get to know her. This is not the time to be talking about someone you don't even know. She didn't hang around long enough to change your diaper, and when she did come and see you, she spent her time doped up on drugs and alcohol, pushing you on the swing and walking away when you fell off. Do you remember those things, Maybell? Jesus," Grammy said.

"See, Mz. Veldner," Mr. Baxley scratched his almost bald head and tried to ignore her sudden outburst on me, "she has a great imagination, that sorta thing jus' can't thrive in this kinda school. She needs special privileges that we can't afford to allow," Mr. Baxley told Grammy.

I thought about that day at the store, when we were homages, and I had pretended to be a potato because the man who was keeping us in there said I had to, or else he was going to shoot me and everyone else, including Grammy. Luckily, I had found a telephone, and called Mama, and she brought her Christian boyfriend, Edward, and together they rode through the grocery store's front window, sending glass spraying everywhere. She scooped me up into her arms and smoothed down my hair, cooing to me that she loved me and she wouldn't ever leave me again. Grammy only doesn't remember because she was out cold on the floor. I felt as if this was important information. It might help Mr. Baxley and Grammy reach some kind of understanding.

"Grammy doesn't know what happened because she passed out. She stole all kinds of bottles from the store, and when I asked for a sip she said I was too young for these kinds of drinks, but she finished six or seven of those bottles." I stated to no one in particular.

Not From Around Here, Are You?

"Jesus Christ, Maybell. What has gotten into you? Mr. Baxley, I can assure you that —" Grammy wasn't allowed to finish.

"Maybell, I need you to wait in the hall, now. Yer Gram and I need to speak alone. Go'n now," Mr. Baxley shut his office door behind me.

"And the next thing I know I'm here talking to you," I told Margaret. She was younger, with blonde curly hair, but she was plain and had short dirty fingernails, which she sometimes nibbled on while I blabbered on about what was on my mind. She usually wore the same outfit every time I saw her, black pants that were too loose on her skinny legs and a white sweater that seemed to eat her body from the inside out and red sneakers. Margaret said she walked to work everyday, so she couldn't wear anything else but sneakers. Grammy said she was a terrorist or a thermamist or something like that, and was going to help me get past whatever monsters I had hiding in my head, but Margaret said this wasn't the correct way to be thinking about it. She said we were just talking, like old friends did when they hadn't seen each other for awhile, but we weren't old friends. I hadn't ever met her before.

Sometimes Margaret just let me color, and I told her that I was feeling like we should color today. I drew a horse, and a cow, and Mama and Edward on their Harmey. Margaret asked who the pretty people in my pictures were, and when I told her she scribbled on her notepad. She asked me a lot of questions about Mama, but I didn't feel like answering questions just then so I started to cry. She gave me some chocolate milk and a lollipop and said maybe we should be finished for today.

"Grammy sometimes hits me," I confessed.

"What?" Margaret asked concerned.

"Yeah, when I'm a bad girl. Or sometimes she just puts me in the closet, or makes me suck on these sticks that she lights at the end. They make me cough. Or one time she just threw me down the stairs. I deserve all of it though." I looked out the window.

130

The Takeover

"Maybell, I need to know if you're telling me the truth. Are you telling me the truth?" Margaret was scribbling extra fast on her notepad, and her small green eyes widened when she looked at me.

I thought about what Grammy had said about the truth. One time she said the truth only mattered in the court of law, and I didn't think we were in the court of law, so it must not have mattered. I took off my shoes and threw them across the room. Then I took off my socks and shoved them down into the couch cushions.

"What are you doing, Maybell?" Margaret watched me.

"When I get real nervous I have to have bare feet. That's where the truth comes out." I crossed my eyes and stuck my tongue out at her.

She appeared to not understand. She must have never watched the TV shows that me and Grammy did. Everything important to learn in this world could come from TV. That's why I didn't go to school anymore, because I didn't even need to be there.

I told Margaret about the time at school when I called Mama and asked her and Edward to come get me on their Harmey.

"Harley," Margaret corrected.

"No, a Harmey. They're different kinds," I told her.

Her and Edward came and picked me up from school, I told Margaret, and we burnt all my schoolbooks then took off all our clothes and went swimming in somebody's pool. The guy who lived there came out shooting his gun because we weren't supposed to be in there. Edward caught one of the bullets in his bare hand and threw it back at the guy. Then the guy called the police and me and Mama and Edward all got on his Harmey and drove off, and hid behind a dumpster. The cops never found us, and Mama told me I was her special favorite little girl. Then her and Edward dropped me off at Grammy's house and went to their house.

Grammy was real upset with me because I never told her where I was going and all my schoolbooks were burnt and she'd have to pay for them. And I was all wet, and I caught a cold and she had to go buy medicine to make me better. After I got better Grammy smacked me in the face. She yelled at me and put me in the closet for eight days, but no one knew I was in there so no one was worried about me.

"Maybell," Margaret interrupted my story, "I think that's enough for today. I want you to write your Mama a letter in this notebook, and bring it with you on Tuesday. I won't read it, but you might decide you want to show it to me. Tell her anything you want to, ok? And if you want, we can even send it to her after we meet on Tuesday. How does that sound?"

I took the purple wire bound notebook from Margaret.

"I can write anything I want?" I asked.

She nodded.

Grammy asked me in the car what the notebook was for, but I didn't think she should know because I knew she would try and take a peek before the next time I would go and visit Margaret.

"It's for coloring in, and writing down my dreams. Margaret said if I write down my dreams, maybe the monsters will come out faster and you won't be so worried about paying her." I looked out the window.

"Jesus, Maybell," she answered me.

~~Mama,~~

~~This is your daughter, Maybell. Do you remember me? I still remember you. My friend gave me this notebook to~~

This letter thing was harder than I thought. Of course I remember her, you can't write a letter to someone that you don't even know. I had to start my letter over, but Margaret said to not rip out any of the pages and I wrote in pen so it wouldn't get all dirty looking when we sent it to Mama.

~~Dear Mama,~~

~~How is life without me? I miss you sometime when Grammy gets mad at me because you always made me feel like~~

Mama is probably having an awful time because I'm not

132

with her. Grammy looked over my shoulder and said that she doesn't ever get mad at me and I'm not allowed to tell Margaret, my terrorist, that she does.

Dear Mama,

Hello. This is Maybell. I hope you remember me, but if not I am your daughter. We used to hang out in the park with Grammy, and you would push me on the swings and laugh and giggle and push me way up high and run underneath me when I was in the air. Do you remember that? I always like to go there with you because I had so much fun. Now Grammy won't come to the park with me because she says there are too many memories there of you. It makes her sides hurt real bad when she thinks about it, like when you have to go pee real bad.

Me and Grammy were homages at the store. A man came in and got upset because of the lady taking his money so he tried to make everyone else upset too by keeping us in there. Grammy ripped her dress and I ate some Fruit Loops. Then after we got done we rode on the fire truck and I got to pet the spotted dog they always have with them, his name was Spot. I liked him a lot. Grammy said I can't have a dog because I'm not old enough to take care of him. I think if I got a dog I would make sure he was petted all the time and had food and water and I wouldn't let him eat anybody so I should get one. But Grammy says no. Would you let me have a dog if I came and stayed with you?

Grammy went and talked to Mr. Baxley at school. Now I don't have to go there no more. I stay at home and Grammy reads to me and sometimes on days when her hips don't hurt too much she gives me tests to take and she times me, just like I was in a real classroom and the bell was going to ring soon. I always get a 100 on all my tests. I know you are proud of me, even if you don't remember me. You have to be proud of someone who always gets the high score. My friends all think that I'm a genius. I think Grammy knows I am too. She said I have your eyes and sense of humor. She said I have your hair too. I hope you don't miss them. I like my eyes because I can see all kinds of things. My hair is very pretty and long. I like to wear it up in a pony tail and pretend like I'm a famous princess who can't let her hair down or someone will climb on it. Did you used to play those games when you were my age too?

Grammy says I won't ever get to see you again. She said you have to stay where you are for the rest of the time you're alive because the rest of the world doesn't want you. She said you need to say sorry to Edward's family for what you did to him. They probably won't ever want to not be mad at you anymore. You have to stay put. I asked Grammy what it was you did again, but she stared at me real hard and told me to go play outside. When I came back in Grammy asked me if I remembered going to watch Edward sleep and everyone was crying and all dressed in black. I didn't think that had anything to do with it, but she said you made him go somewhere else and that's why everyone is mad at you. Do you remember where you made him go? Because we could go and get him and then no one would be mad at you anymore and I could come and live with you. We could find his Harmey and give it back to him. I would help you, Mama.

It's time for me to eat dinner. We're having hotdogs and macaroni and cheese. You should eat dinner too. Grammy says I'm all skin and bones like you are. Bye.

Maybell

"Maybell, where's the notebook I gave you?" Margaret asked.

"Grammy burned it," I answered.

"Why would she burn it?"

"I'm a bad girl," I said. I looked out the window and took off my socks and shoes. I shoved my socks way far down into the couch cushions and glanced at Margaret.

"Is the truth about to come out, Maybell?" Margaret asked. She bit her fingernails, concentrating all her focus on me.

"I want some Fruit Loops," I whispered.

"I have your notebook, Maybell. You gave it to me when you first came in here today. Do you remember giving me your

134

notebook? Why would you lie about the notebook, Maybell? Are there other things you have been lying about that you would like to tell me?" Margaret asked.

I stared at her. Where was I to begin?

Goofy Loves Frankenstein

Donnie McGovern

There are certain expectations for first-born sons of working class families in Kentucky. Of these, having a gay son typically isn't on top of the list. Traditionally, being gay falls somewhere between getting your teenage girlfriend pregnant and becoming a convicted felon, the former at least increasing the odds that your son may indeed be virile and straight. I understood these expectations from an early age as I waited patiently for my hormones and my interest in the opposite sex to kick in. That never happened.

After years of depression and denial, and years of dating a woman who expected to be my future wife, I finally succumbed to the odd feelings I got while looking at male underwear models in Mom's Sears catalog, and the odd feelings I *didn't* get from the female swimsuit models in Dad's *Sports Illustrated*. Unfortunately for me, being gay really wasn't an option. It wasn't as if I had a strong opinion about it either way—it simply wasn't an option to even consider. I couldn't be gay. Mom wouldn't allow it.

That was the overwhelming fear in my coming-out process; that Mom and Dad would find out about my "condition" and react in some terrible way. Which way, I didn't know, but the fear was so strong I was sure I would never come out to my parents. I was convinced that I could maintain a lie that would last my entire life. I would invent girlfriends and engage in conversation that would give my parents every possible reason to believe that their son was strong, healthy, manly, and straight as an arrow. There was no other option.

This wasn't a conscious decision. I honestly believe that for years leading up to this self revelation I truly wasn't aware that I was gay. Yes, I was attracted to men, and yes I was terribly

Goofy Loves Frankenstein

depressed all the time, and yes, I was miserable but I just couldn't put my finger on the reason why. It was during this time of frustrated introspection that a plan began to form to throw myself down a tall flight of stairs (with full dramatic affect, of course.) Thankfully, I had enough wits about me to realize that my parents probably would prefer a gay son over a dead son, but who could be sure? I signed up for therapy.

I came out, as many good fairies often do, to my therapist, Marty. He was doing an internship in the student counseling office at the college I attended, and was randomly assigned to me. I was leery of spilling my guts to an intern, but one look at him was enough to calm my fears.

Marty was d-r-e-a-m-y. He was a competitive body builder and looked just like Fabio—except better looking, more manly. He had thick long hair, and a constant five o'clock shadow, very sexy in the early 1990's. He could make Pat Robertson come out of the closet. I can still picture his tight, tight pants. . . .

Anyway, the moment that the closet doors flew open for me was after one of the many sessions we had dealing with my suicidal feelings, which I could tell he was getting bored with. I desperately wanted to bring up the topic of my budding homosexual tendencies so badly, but I couldn't muster the nerve. At the end of this particular session Marty must have noticed my contemplative demeanor and asked me, "Donnie, what's on your mind?"

Marty had asked me that question before, as if he knew that there was something I wanted—no, *needed*—to say. Every time he asked, I always feigned ignorance and chickened out, leaving as if everything was a-okay, everything except for the whole falling down the stairs routine.

But this particular session I had decided it was time to take the figurative plunge, but I wasn't sure how to do it. I stared at the floor, my heart and my head racing. I suddenly tensed up and was almost immediately immobile—I couldn't move. I remember eventually looking up at him and smiling and having sudden tears in my eyes, and immediately looking back at the floor.

Not From Around Here, Are You?

Marty always ended our sessions on the mark, but this time he just let the silence continue long past our scheduled end time. After an incredibly long ten minutes I finally managed to utter the word "I'm . . .". Then I broke off. I just couldn't bring myself to say the next word. But a desperate ache in my gut told me this was the time, it was now or never. For what seemed like an eternity, I kept saying "I am . . ." over and over again. Marty just sat there in silence, allowing the moment to continue. Marty later told me that it took over an hour for me to finally say "I . . . have . . . feelings . . . for . . . other . . . men."

As clichéd as it may sound, saying those six terrifying words felt like a three ton anvil had just been lifted from my shoulders. I remember actually visualizing a wall of cinder blocks that had been right in front of my face for my entire life, exploding before my eyes leaving me in a pile of dust and rubble. Almost everything after that immediate, incredible and life-changing moment is a fog. I know that I was crying and I know that Marty gave me a hug (oh that hug!)

Finally, he let go of me, he held me up to make me look at him. He looked right into my eyes, smiled his beautiful smile and said in his deep husky voice; "Well, it's about time!" We laughed, and as scared and embarrassed as I was, I knew then that somehow everything would be okay.

That didn't stop me from panicking that Mom would eventually find out. I became very concerned about this information leaking out to the public. I made Marty swear that he wouldn't tell anyone. He told me that since he was an intern, he would be required to tell his supervisor, but assured me that he would tell no one else, including his wife (damn.)

So, by my calculations there were two people in the world who knew my secret. I was terrified that Marty or his supervisor would run into my Mother, whom they had never met, strike up a conversation and casually mention that they had just met this boy named Donnie who was a ho-mo-sex-u-al!

Marty and I worked for a few weeks on a plan for "coming out." We decided it was probably a good idea to let my girlfriend know that things wouldn't work out between us, but it was probably *not* a good idea to make her the first person that I come out to. Marty wisely surmised that my girlfriend might not be as kind and understanding about my newfound sexuality as he was. So I slowly and carefully decided to come out to a few friends first, and as difficult as it was, they were surprisingly supportive.

I was shocked at how "not" shocked they were. One of my friends actually repeated Marty's exact words: "Well, it's about time!" This was both comforting and annoying at the same time. If my friends knew about this the whole time, why didn't they bother to tell me!?

Of all the reactions I got from my friends, the first question I got consistently was "Have you told your girlfriend?!" As much as I dreaded it, I knew I had to tell her. There was no point putting off the inevitable.

Not surprisingly, she didn't take it well. We fought, we cried, and we both said things that tore our hearts to bits. It was one of the hardest things I've ever had to do. I fell into a depression again mainly because my best friend, my daily dose of love and confidence, was suddenly gone.

We didn't speak to each other for over a year. When we did finally speak it was difficult, but eventually things improved. Years later we became friends again, best friends even, but to this day she tells me that our split up was the biggest heartbreak she ever had.

Somehow I convinced her not to tell her parents or friends why I so suddenly broke things off with her. Looking back, it was such a demanding and unreasonable request, but it seemed so rational and important at the time. Now, including the smattering of other close friends I had told, the number of folks who knew my secret was roughly seven, and I couldn't help thinking that the odds that my parents would find out were increasing.

So what did I do next? I went to Disney World. I decided the best thing I could do was to move, escape to Florida, away from my folks and from Kentucky, so I could find out who I really was and what this gay thing was all about.

I took a job working for Disney as "Goofy" which was

probably the best thing I could have done. As one might imagine, there were literally hundreds of gay boys and girls crawling out of Cinderella's Castle walls making it the most 'fabulous' place on earth. Still I was afraid to publicly announce that I had more pixie-dust in my bag than most boys. I was still afraid that my Mom would find out.

During employee orientation, I had lunch with a few of my fellow cast members on "Main Street" and they kept asking me loads of personal questions. I was, and still am, incredibly naïve. I don't remember their specific questions, but eventually the conversation led to something like this:

"Donnie, you're really animated."

"Thanks" I said, assuming they were referring to my portrayal of "Goofy." While this seemed to be a rather strange and random observation, I decided to take it as a compliment.

"So," they continued. "Which team do you play for?"

I was confused. I remember hearing about an employee softball league at orientation, but I had been there for less than a week, and had not been approached to join. Again, this line of questioning seemed really weird. Besides, I hated sports.

"I don't play for any team" I said. "I don't really like softball."

They all snickered. "Seriously, which team do you play for?"

I honestly had no idea what the hell they were getting at.

Noticing my increasing anxiety, someone finally blurted: "Donnie, do you like boys or do you like girls?"

This hit me like a lead balloon in my stomach; no one had ever asked me that before, at least in such a blunt manner. It seemed so personal, so rude, yet oddly exciting. So I answered with some hesitation, still not knowing where the conversation was heading. I said, "I'm not sure."

They all squealed, "See, I told you!!!" Apparently, any answer other than 'I like girls' meant immediately that you were gay. So I was officially deemed a Disney "princess." This revelation led to some of my first gay experiences, healthy and unhealthy. Sometimes there were exciting cheap thrills but most times there were unfulfilling lows. Most of my initial relationships

Goofy Loves Frankenstein

with the gay world were relatively anonymous. It felt like a world only I belonged to. I figured I was safe here and that my Mother would likely never find out. I thought I could live like this forever which was both liberating and deeply saddening at the same time.

I joined a "men's coming out support group" at the local gay and lesbian community center. During our meetings I listened to these men share their sad stories. Most had been previously married and had children, and their coming out process had been incredibly difficult, causing serious pain and heartache to their families, more than I could ever imagine.

I was thankful that I had come to terms with my sexuality as early as I did. I felt as if I had dodged the bullet that many of the previously married men in the group hadn't. But there were other bullets still left to dodge.

Some men talked about coming out to their parents. I distinctly remember one man sobbing as he talked about how his parents essentially disowned him after he came out. He hadn't spoken to his parents for over seven years. He said he learned that week that his mother was critically ill and in hospice care. When his brother called to give him the news, he also told him to stay away and that he wasn't welcome in the hospital.

Was my sexual orientation worth this kind of pain? Why would I choose to live like this if it meant a life alone without the love and support of my family? Why would I put myself though this? I had already broken one woman's heart, how could I break my parent's hearts as well?

As I listened to the stories of these men, I wondered if this so-called 'lifestyle' would ever lead to a healthy relationship and positive self-worth. That word, lifestyle, implied that I had some kind of choice in the matter. But I was learning that my sexuality was not a choice—it is who I am and have always been—for better or for worse. And at that point, in that circle of unhappy men, many of whom had been rejected by their closest friends and family, I saw my chances of finding true unconditional love as slim to none.

I feared I was seeing my own future in those men. It was

141

more than I ever wanted to deal with. I remember thinking at the time that if there was a switch I could pull or a button I could push or even a pill I could take that would make me straight— I'd give my life for it.

Thankfully, everything changed later that same year. I fell in love. I met my partner Ron while performing in a musical at a local community theatre and experienced what I wasn't sure would or could happen in my relationships with men—true love. It was the kind that I wanted to talk about to anyone who would listen. I wanted to tell people why I constantly had a smile on my face, why I was suddenly so damn happy all the time. But of course, I couldn't. My Mom might find out.

My first professional job was working at a college in Orlando. At work I would hear co-workers discussing their everyday lives with their respective partners. They discussed their travels, restaurants they enjoyed, arguments they had, etc. I wanted so badly to discuss these same kinds of anecdotes from my life with Ron, but was too scared.

I invited Ron to a Halloween party I was organizing for the students. I had an extra Frankenstein costume that I somehow convinced him to wear, something he would never do today. The costume included a rubber mask that he sweetly wore all night, because I was scared that folks would ask questions about this 'mystery man.' One of my students took a picture of us together, with both of us in full costume, and gave it to me the next day. I framed the picture and put it on my desk. It was our first official picture together and I felt safe having it up at work. I didn't have to answer any questions about who this "other man" was and why I looked so happy with him.

In my head, I would think, "Well duh, I'm in love with Frankenstein!" And I'd smile. Ultimately, however, the picture was a sad reminder that I really wanted to see his face—the man behind the mask—the man who pumped life back into my empty, lifeless heart.

Not long after the Halloween party, I decided that keeping my life a secret was just plain silly. I was happy, happier than I ever remembered being; I planned on being with Ron for a very long time. It was time to start planning my 'coming-out' on a larger scale. Little by little I tested the proverbial waters and noticed that it really wasn't as bad as I thought it would be. And I figured out quickly that anyone who really cared about me seemed to be just fine with my sexuality. People who did have a problem with it weren't worth the energy. And most of these folks, after further exposure and education, eventually came to understand and accept me for who I was.

I was still afraid of telling my family. I was so scared that they might completely reject me that I continued to dodge any questions and made up lies to cover for my relationship with Ron.

I was living with my cousin Roger at the time. Roger was the kind of guy who had dreams of playing in a rock-n-roll band. He had long hair until it started falling out and he decided to shave it and go completely bald. Roger never held a job or dated a girl longer than a few weeks, drove cars that didn't belong to him, smoked Marlboro 100s and carried all the money he had in his wallet. We were very close.

I decided to tell Roger. This was a daring move considering we were both dirt poor and could only afford to sleep on an air mattress, which we shared in shifts since Roger worked nights. I was terrified that Roger might hate me or want me to move out or, heaven forbid, buy a second air mattress. To my amazement, when I told him, he cried. He said that he was "honored" that I would come out to him first—the first of my family members to know. It was a huge relief knowing that Roger was okay with my secret. It was the encouragement I needed as I began to tell other extended family members—swearing all to secrecy—so it wouldn't get back to my folks.

It was also refreshing to know that Roger had noticed my sudden happiness. He said, "For once in your life you seem genuinely happy."

My relationship with Ron continued to grow and as we started plans to move in together, I finally realized that it was time to tell my parents. As scary as this proposition was, Ron and I had already spent several holidays apart and were determined to not let that happen again.

I thought through the process very carefully and decided that I needed to tell my folks in person, not by letter or phone. This meant telling them when I went home to Kentucky for a Christmas visit or another special occasion. I didn't want my visits home to be "tainted" with bad news. My only other option was to tell them on our upcoming family vacation. I figured that my folks would be in relatively good spirits and the vacation would put us on neutral ground—not at home.

I insisted that Roger come with me for moral support. I don't remember much about that weekend except for being freaked out, totally scared and my stomach in knots just about the entire time. Roger kept egging me on, but I was too damned nervous, so I kept putting off the 'deed' for another hour, another day, at lunch, or even at the outlet mall— but at every opportunity, I would chicken out. I was a total mess, I could think of nothing else.

On the last night of the vacation, my heart pounding as the impending meltdown approached, I decided the time was right for me to come clean. It was 3:30 a.m. I was still working at Disney part-time, and had to work a shift the next day. So I had to be in my car by 6 a.m. in order to make the drive home in time to get suited up as Goofy. So I marched into my parent's room, where they were sleeping peacefully and dreaming of their perfectly happy and simple lives, and I woke them up. I had never done this before, not even as a child.

I had hoped that I would just say what I had to say and they would not be surprised at all. I had hoped that Mom would take Marty's words and say, "Well, it's about time!" And Dad would say, "Well, Donnie, you always were animated." And that we'd all hug and cry and that they would say they loved me. And then they'd snicker and Mom would say to Dad "See, I told you so."

That's not how it happened.

The details are fuzzy. I remember they turned on the lights and knew something was wrong. Just like in Marty's office, I struggled to say the words. I cried. Mom cried, probably thinking the worst because they had never seen me so distraught. When I finally told them, I think they may have been relieved that I didn't give them worse news. But the heartbreak in the room was palpable. I think they were in shock. Mom just stared at me and I remember at one point she faintly whispered, "I knew it." Dad could barely process what I was saying. All he could manage to say was, "Are you sure?" And the more direct, "You're sure?" over and over as if I might change my mind while I stood there.

They asked me if I liked to wear women's clothes and then proceeded to ask questions related to gay stereotypes and dangerous behavior, and of course—AIDS. I decided it was important to let them know that I was, in fact, healthy and in a stable relationship, which was the reason why I chose to come out to them in the first place.

Mostly, I think they thought they were dreaming. My timing wasn't ideal, which contributed to their fuzzyheaded confusion and muted reaction. Their only harsh words were making me swear that I not tell my grandfather. Mom also said that she never wanted to see Ron and never wanted me to speak of him, ever. That part was particularly painful, but at the time it seemed rational and reasonable.

All in all I thought the entire episode went as well as could be expected. We did hug and they told me they loved me as I drove away in my escape car. But it was awkward. The days that followed were the hardest. After several unreturned phone calls—me thinking the worst—Dad finally called me back and said that Mom had been crying for three days straight and that I "ruined her vacation." He also said they couldn't talk to me for a while and repeated their warning that they never wanted to see Ron or hear anything about him, ever.

Luckily, that was the worst of it. As painful as it was, from that point on it didn't matter what anyone else thought—my Mother already knew. Another heavy weight had been lifted.

In time, my parents calmed down a bit and even started asking questions about Ron. I started to push the envelope further and further, even freely mentioning his name and our activities in weekly phone conversations. They began to recognize that for the first time in my life I was actually happy and healthy and successful. They even said they were proud of me.

A few years later, my very uncomfortable parents met Ron at my graduation ceremony when I received my Master's Degree. We decided to drive separately to the ceremony but due to limited seating they sat in reserved seats next to Ron. I had planned on giving introductions immediately before the ceremony, but traffic was heavy and I was running late—I barely made it. So Ron, God bless him, met my parents for the first time without me in the bleachers of the gymnasium and made small talk with them during the three-hour ceremony. They weren't fast friends, but I was relieved to find that all involved parties behaved themselves. They were decent and respectful to each other. My fears of all-out bleacher melee resembling a scene from the "Jerry Springer Show" were unfounded.

Since then Ron has been to visit my family on several occasions. We've even managed to spend Christmas and other major holidays with my family as well. Mom now considers him part of the family and is actually disappointed when I visit home without him. It wasn't easy and it has been a long twelve years to get there, but clearly it was the best decision I could have made.

I consider myself lucky. Unlike many of the stories I heard in the support group, my coming-out story was not at all disastrous; poorly planned, perhaps, but not nearly as awful as I feared. Marty, Roger, Mom and even my ex-girlfriend all came to peaceful terms with my sexuality, and learned to love me for who I am. Most importantly, *I* learned to love, understand and embrace the man I am. I wouldn't dream of pulling a switch, pushing a button, or taking a pill—even if my life depended on it.

I've learned that the greatest power gay folks have in gaining acceptance and support from others is actually coming out. For the most part, the bigotry and hatred that I have experienced came from ignorance or misunderstanding from people who, like my parents, thought they had never been exposed to gay people in their life.

That's why I display my Human Rights Campaign sticker on my car, and why I participate in gay causes and share my coming out story to anyone who will listen. Most importantly, that's why I keep a picture of me and my beautiful Ron (without his Frankenstein mask) proudly on my desk at work.

My Jerusalem.

Jean Syed

And was Jerusalem builded here
Among these dark Satanic Mills
William Blake

My clogs mount the iron bridge:
The steam train comes with its tonnage,
No whit fairer than stone chimneys
Of cotton mills, houses, foundries.
It comes, it comes, the soot, the fume
An elegant but somber plume.

(There wasn't any kind of flower
In my cobbled street,
But on that bridge I did not wail
What filled my nose was sweet.)

Demoniac along the track
The fury advances clickety-clack,
It comes in clouds, the acrid smell
Like smelling salts, the sulfur swell,
The steamy jets—are all benign.
Jerusalem is Hell Divine.

Dazed Days

Angelina Caliguri

Mondays are for the birds. I detest getting up in the morning especially when I know there's still a full week ahead. Some say I see the glass half empty. I say it's overflowing, fed by a hose pelting a steady, unceasing stream of water. My alarm blares piercingly, so I pick it up and smash it into the closet door. It tumbles to the floor, leaving a slight gash in the wooden frame.

Which makes me grin.

"What the hell was that?" Darrin rushes into the room.

His voice is loud enough to rattle my eardrums. His right fist is clinched ghostly white. I say nothing, and quickly point to the alarm clock amid the heap of clothes on the floor. Darrin scares me when he gets angry. Through the black greasy strands of hair hanging in front of his face, I can see his eyes roll back. Without another word he turns to the door clomping away. He can't understand working full-time while going to school like I do. Sometimes my hands get so worn-down I'm afraid my bones will pop through my skin. He sits around and goes on binges on his days off. I don't ever have a day off.

Mondays are no big deal for him.

I met Darrin on a Saturday in October. It was brisk outside, and he was like a warm fire drawing me in. There was something magnetic and mysterious about him that made me want him in my life. I had gone to a hole-in-the wall bar right down the street from my apartment. It was the type of bar that had water marks on the ceiling and a floor that hasn't been swept in ages. I was only twenty but had been drinking there for years. Darrin sat at the bar taking shots of whiskey by himself. He had a chiseled chin covered in scruff. His ice blue eyes pierced through me as I walked in the door, but quickly veered off in the other direction.

149

Not From Around Here, Are You?

I could tell he thought himself cool, yet was unaware of his own good looks. I pulled up a chair next to him. I was wearing a low-cut top, and he didn't even take a second look at me. Most men in that bar would have been excited, but not Darrin.

I was intrigued.

For some reason I kept finding myself inside the bar whenever I saw his motorcycle parked outside. He was a man of few words, so we didn't say much to each other. We never really went through a "getting to know you" phase. Darrin preferred it that way then and he still does.

I once was filled to the brim with independence.

That was four years ago. We work together in the tattoo parlor now. His artistic abilities have always attracted me. He could have been a painter and actually made a living. I get so frustrated when I think of his innate talent. It's so honest and real, yet he wastes it in a grimy tattoo parlor. When I met him, I only had one tattoo, a miniscule clover on my right hip. The only time we seem to get along anymore is when he's tattooing me.

I'm on tattoo fifty-three and counting.

As I throw on my cracked leather jacket, I feel a slight twinge in my neck. Ever since my first fall, it has never been the same. I step outside into the chilly February air and hop onto the bus. I am finishing my degree in Fine Arts but what's the point? Working in the tattoo shop, I make more than enough money to support my lifestyle. I have been in school for eight years, just switching around from here to there. I've attended three colleges and still haven't earned a degree. Originally, I wanted to be an elementary teacher, but realized I was too selfish to put the needs of thirty whiny school children ahead of my own. Next, I majored in Criminal Justice. Until I realized I hated authority. How could I possibly be an authority figure myself? Finally, I figured out a major where I could be selfish with and never have to answer to anyone but myself.

I found my niche in the arts department.

The first time Darrin saw my artwork he said, "It's nowhere near as gloomy as you are."

Dazed Days

That was a compliment coming from him, the nicest thing I have ever heard his lips utter.

When I look into the future I picture myself walking down the aisle with cap and gown. It may be the proudest moment of my life, but what will I do in May when I graduate? The other graduates will pose for pictures with their proud families; I'll be lucky if anyone shows up for me. I will still live in my crappy old apartment. I will still be with Darrin. I will still be working at the shop.

My phone vibrates in my pocket and I look down to see "Laura" on the screen. Laura is my mom. I insist on calling her by her first name. Why call someone "Mom" if they have never been one to you? I throw the phone back into my satchel. My dad was never around much and Laura wasn't either. It's a good thing I didn't have a bunch of bratty brothers and sisters to take care of. She calls me when it's convenient.

I erased her message without listening to it.

Tuesdays are miserable. The alarm beeps until I muffle the sound with my pillow. I had to set my phone alarm last night because the other is broken. I worked last night until one in the morning and here it is six o'clock already. Darrin was decent last night. He didn't get excessively drunk and he waited to smoke until I went to bed. I suppose that's a step. Laura called me again last night while I was at work. She must really need something. Sometimes I want to call her and scream at her until my voice goes bad. Other times I just want to go to her house, scoop her up and hold her in my arms.

When I was in third grade, my face turned green in class and I got sick all over my desk. I went to the office but was petrified for them to call Laura. When they took my temperature they discovered it well over a hundred degrees. The school nurse told me they had to send me home. I screamed and cried for them to let me stay and they thought I was being ridiculous. It took them three hours to get hold of Laura. When she finally

151

showed up she was in hysterics. I'll never forget the sparkly green mini-skirt and scuffed white boots she had on that day. She scooped me up and gave me a million kisses all over my face. I was relieved and comforted by the smell of the cheap perfume in her hair. I forgot why I was so terrified of her coming to get me in the first place. She thanked the office ladies over and over for taking care of her "baby girl." She carried me to the car and laid me in the passenger's seat. When she got into the car on her side, she turned towards me and slapped me across the face.

"Don't you ever make the school call me out of work because of a stomach ache. Unless you are ten seconds away from falling over dead, I don't want to hear it. You can sleep on the floor when we get home; that'll make you wish you'd never complained like a whiny baby."

I am going to school today. I enjoy using school as an escape from life. While most people go to school drudgingly, I am secretly relieved. I still grunt with the other students as we shove our cigarettes butts into the ashtray sand before heading into class. Those grunts are a vicious lie.

When times were simple, I enjoyed escaping to school as well. I pretended even then that my favorite class was recess. The truth was I loved the safe, warm walls that the elementary school provided me. Crusty macaroni and cheese with cold pizza cut into a square was better food than anything I would get at home. The crack where the wall met the ceiling in the classroom was homier than the crack in the window overlooking the fire escape of my bedroom.

It was Mrs. Springer who showed me a glimpse of what a real mother could be. She would sneak apples to me and excuse me to the bathroom to go eat them when my stomach grumbled in the morning. Mrs. Springer smelled like peach cobbler and she wore outfits that matched the color of her shoes. She had a four-leaf clover tattoo on her ankle that I would only catch a glimpse of when her pants rode up just a bit. It made me think she was more real than the other teachers; imperfectly perfect.

Dazed Days

She probably wouldn't remember me now, but I don't think I will ever lose my memory of her.

As I doze off in my art class remembering Mrs. Springer and her brown ringlets, I smile. When I realize I am sporting a big grin for no reason, I feel instantly dumb. Everyone else is incessantly taking notes while I'm daydreaming. The professor dismisses us, and I walk outside to catch the bus.

The air is swift and cold once again.

"Your mom has been calling up the shop looking for you. Call her back so I don't have to hear her whiny voice bitching about your lack of respect."

Darrin tells me this during my lunch break phone conversation with him. He doesn't care if I make amends with Laura or not. I never had a falling out with her per se. We have always been at odds. Darrin is lecturing me about all the things I have forgotten to do around the house, so I start daydreaming again. I can picture him eating Doritos, plopped down on the couch, not lifting a single finger, except to point it at me. I daydream into Wednesday.

As I eat Fruit Loops saturated in milk, I see the bruises taking over my knee. My eyes avert but wander back to the purple and yellow splotches. As soon as my eyes rest on the spot, they dart back up to the putrid yellow tile of this decrepit apartment I call home. It looks almost the same as the yellow in the bruises. I find it poetic the way that the bruises seem to go with the color in the flower tattoos growing up my shin. I flash back for a second to the last time I went to the hospital. Three cracked ribs and a hope that it would never happen again make my eyes well-up. I clinch my teeth and pull my pale blue jeans overtop of the bruise, concealing it.

I never thought I could let anyone just toss me around. If I was physically stronger, Darrin would be the one going to the hospital with strangle marks on his neck. I am a strong woman. Regardless of how I may appear, I am proud of myself. On this gloomy Wednesday, I have so much to look forward to in life.

Not From Around Here, Are You?

In three months, I will be the proud owner of a BA in Fine Arts.

I pick up my cell phone as I wait at the bus stop. There are no missed calls. I scroll through the names in the phonebook with my thumb. My half-painted black nail stops at a name, James. James is my oldest and dearest friend. I am lucky he still lets me talk his ear off when I need to. He is always there to listen. I hit send. It rings once and then again. He picks up. It has been weeks since we last spoke, but it feels like minutes. We converse. I convince him that Darrin and I are fine. I even take time to listen to stories of his life. It sure isn't perfect but it always appears ideal compared to my own.

"Jess, I know what this is all about. I wasn't born yesterday," James says.

"I know you do," I reply.

"You need to get out; you need to go pack and get lost. Leave this town. That's what it will take," he says.

"Nonsense," I say.

The bus brakes squeal as I leap in, finding my usual seat in the back. James has a lot of good ideas. He gives honest, often times gut-wrenching advice. We have been friends since elementary school. His dimples press into his chubby cheeks today the same way that they did fifteen years ago. When he told me that he was in love with someone named Rico, I was the only person in his life who didn't shut him out. He is forever grateful. It's like I have my own free personal psychiatrist and even then I can't follow his counsel.

Maybe someday I will.

After school lets out, I hop on an alternate bus line. I have to go to the grocery to buy some basics. Stretching $14.38 out for the next two weeks is a talent. I grab the first cart I see and of course it's the one with the wobbly wheel. I'm too lazy to take it back, so I suffer through its madness. While strolling down the bread aisle, I hear familiar chords from behind me say, "Jessica? Is that you?"

Dazed Days

I whip my head around. Through the bright red strands of hair in my eyes, I can see a familiar face. The smile lines on her cheeks didn't used to be there, and she wears them proudly. Her brown ringlets are painted with grey streaks. Her nails streaked with the same bright red polish on slightly wrinkled hands.

I flip my head back around as my heartbeat pounds into my ears. Why would running into a former teacher cause this much anxiety? I grip my cart until my knuckles turn white. It reminds me of Darrin's fists before they touch my skin. The thought of him and this moment makes my eyes swell. I hurl my cart into aisle six as I pummel my feet into the ground harder and harder with each tread toward the front door.

A tear streams down my face as I fumble for my phone. When James answers, I can tell by his raspy voice that he fell asleep. He can tell in my quivering voice that something is wrong. He doesn't care that I have awoken him.

"I. . .I. . .I saw Mrs. Springer."

It's all I have to really say for him to understand. James knows me well enough to know who Mrs. Springer is to me. I sob uncontrollably around the corner of the supermarket. James says everything a good friend is supposed to say and I tell him that I am going to take his advice.

"I love you so much Jess. Call me whenever you get wherever it is you're going."

"No news is good news," I say.

I wipe my stinging eyes, and click end on my phone. I feel relief. I am on the verge of doing something for myself. I don't even bother to tell Laura or Darrin that I am leaving. She'll put on a show for Darrin and all her neighbors just like she did for the school nurse back in third grade. Except this time they won't be fooled.

They already know she's a shitty mother.

I sit at the bus stop as the sun begins to break. I chew on the side of my mouth so hard it becomes numb. One of Mrs. Springer's apples would taste good right about now. I remember the last time I saw her before this. I had stayed late that day, as I often did, to help her do things around the classroom. I never wanted to leave her side, but the time had come for an eight year-old and her third grade teacher to move on into the summer.

She gave me a hug and I inhaled her peach-cobbler scent for the last time. As I turned back around to wave at her silhouette in the doorway, I caught a glimpse of wetness just below her eyes. We promised to stay in touch. I told her I would come see her next school year. I planned on helping her after school and still having our little talks. I wanted to help her hang posters, grade papers, read "Highlights" magazines, and beat her at Connect Four.

Mrs. Springer understood it was never going to happen.

Laura yanked me from the school district come August. When I realized I would never see Mrs. Springer again, my heart split open.

I finally see a bus number and name I like, "Clover Meadow: number nine." The name conjures up images of the tattoo on Mrs. Springer's ankle. I stand up and step up into the bus. When this route ends, I will be somewhere I can stay for the night.

I rest my head against the bus window and stare at the bare trees as they fly past. They are framed by a dark grey sky boasting a big, bright, banana-shaped moon. My eyelids shut and I drift off to sleep, pressed against the cold metal wall of the bus. I'm not sure where this Wednesday will take me but I am content. The bus jerks as it comes to a complete stop but I keep my eyes closed. The bus driver notifies me that we have arrived at our final stop. I step out of the bus and inhale the crisp evening air. I am aware of my new surroundings.

I am here.

The Mockingbirds, Delta

Jonathan Burns

Mamaw lives just over the river but doesn't want us picking her up on the way. She's coming to stay in our new house on Delta Avenue for three days before we leave for the Oscar family reunion, but she wants us ready to go when she gets here. Nobody knows why. Maybe Frank does but he can't say because he's a dog. She said she'd be here by four. It's 2:30. It's Saturday. I've been in the shade of the porch since noon watching reruns of The Munsters while everyone else is mad-housing to get ready for Mamaw.

Dad's home from work at the mill just up north where he cold-rolls steel all day, turning long flat sheets of shiny metal into big, rolled up wheels of it. He traipses out past me into the dead air of the yard with the historic tags for his Cadillac and yells back into the house at Mom.

"Brenda! Move that Buick out back."

And Dad talks to himself a lot. "Just put it back there when you get home. Christ." He swears Mom leaves it out there to get him griping.

The washer top claps shut upstairs as Dad rolls the sleeves of his blue work shirt and plays with his salty collar to crouch in the driveway behind the bumper. Patting the car he whispers through his crooked teeth.

"Oh . . . Daddy's Caddy." The summer sun beats his neck and crew cut.

He yells "Shit" into the air and stamps back inside for a screwdriver, stepping over Frank's electric-wire dog fence which skirts the yard and yells at me on the porch.

"Get that damned TV off your lap and get inside. Or at least take it out back. Christ."

He shakes his head and shadows past Mom as she

157

comes out to move the car, clip-clopping in electric pink thong shoes with her strawberry hair in curlers. She yells back into the house at my older sister.

"Jeanie! Get down the suitcases. And Frank's caddy."

Mom calls it that, but it's just a wire-mesh box Dad hooked up with zip ties then covered with leather from the seats he replaced in the Cadillac. Mom yells again.

"And clean up Mamaw's room before she gets here."

She starts the *Blue-ick,* and it farts a choking cloud of smog into the air that lingers around the constant gray flow of the street's joggers and fancy cars. Then she rattle-traps the piece of shit out back because Dad doesn't like her car out front, even though we have room for two in the driveway.

But Jeanie doesn't hear Mom. She prances out, cradling Frank's stubby body to bathe him in sunlight and coo at him over the driveway heat.

She's nine years older than me and loves the dog and hates that she has to leave him once she's at college at the end of summer. She thought about staying here for beauty school so she could keep after Frank but says she misses Kentucky too much. I don't think beauty school will make her beautiful.

We'll be headed back from the Oscar Family Reunion so close to Jeanie's leaving that she's going to stay there with a cousin and catch a ride everyday to The Lenny Lewis Academy of Cosmetology in Harlan. She'll be our first college graduate.

Dad comes back out with the screwdriver as Jeanie asks him, "What did she say?"

"Wash out the cooler and get that brother of yours off the damn porch." He points at me.

Jeanie looks at me, then at the dog and puckers a kiss at his shriveled face. We got Frank after Mom got wind of the dogs the people had up here when we were still back home. Dad picked him up as a puppy when he came to look at the house. Frank is the first dog we've paid for and I'm as curious as my father; who the hell would mix a Bulldog and a Chihuahua? And what do we call him?

I should not have joked, "Hey, name it after me."

The Mockingbirds, Delta

Perfect. We'll call it Frank.

Christ.

The dog's sun bath is short-lived as Jeanie bumbles past me with him tucked in her elbow like an empty football and says nothing as she passes me in time to look back at the taxi pulling up to the house. I hear her clumble upstairs.

From my porch I can see Mamaw's head through the Community Taxi window as she slides down onto the street, the sun lighting up her wire-mop of gray-purple hair while she waddles around to the trunk. The driver pops the lid but does not get out to help Mamaw, or to shut her door. He doesn't even put the car in park and waits while Mamaw curses and hauls her bags out onto the curb. She slams the trunk and he tears off, fogging her with road dust and old-car smog.

"Rotten son-of-a-bitch. Can't drive. Christ! Frankie!" she yells. "Come get these bags."

She beckons me with a wide sweep of her arm. The skin on the back of it flaps in the hot air like a running-rooster's cockle. When I don't move, she pokes her monkeyish mug at me and yells again, "Frankie. Get these bags!"

Mamaw is a clumpy old woman, with sloping shoulders and forearms that lurch out from her elbows well below her waist. She's barely upright and looks like a landslide that started at her forehead and stopped at her orthopedic shoes. Her denim skirt is held up under a set of old boobs a foot from each other.

Mom comes out and asks me, "Frankie, why didn't you tell us she's here?" She likes to ask questions with stupid answers.

Because Mamaw is a scary ape.

Mamaw yells, "Brenda. Tell that Frankie to get this stuff."

Mom sighs and looks at Mamaw. "Ginny," she says, but changes her mind and says she'll help with the bags that Mamaw will not. She whispers "sorry" to me and razzes my hair as she passes into the house with the first of the luggage, headed for the downstairs bedroom Mamaw says we're to always have ready for her. Says she hates climbing up and down.

I look at my TV as a Rolex commercial fuzzes back to

Not From Around Here, Are You?

Eddie Munster, and the poor reception sends a toothy spear through his head while the sun bakes what Dad calls "The Acre, Oscar." It ain't even close to an acre, from what Dad says. But it gets Mom laughing. Mamaw waits at the curb, knee-deep in luggage, her ape arms drooped under two bulbous brown leather bags as she stares through her glasses at the houses and yards and joggers and cars. The way she's breathing, seems she's exhaling the whole block little by little, trying to keep it out of her system. And I watch that fuzzy spear dance through Eddie's face while Mom plays fetch with Mamaw and her stuff.

So Dad is hell-bent on fixing dinner tonight. Ever since next-door Roger bugged his ear that "the complete man cooks," he's been warpathing. But he still asks, "What about the *real* man?"

We've a gas stove in the kitchen and tonight's the first time he's used it. Mom's been asking why he's so set on cooking when he jawed off more than anything when he had to do it down home. Seems Dad's been overflowing with new ideas since we moved up here. He shaved his beard and hung fancy paintings on our walls. He's fixing up the Cadillac and trying to learn to cook real gourmet-man-style. And he wants to get Frank "town-trained." That's what he calls dogs what mind on a leash. Frank didn't know what a leash was until he came to Delta Avenue with its Bichons and Labradoodles. He's getting used to it but still vibrates like a crooked wheelchair when Jeanie digs it out of the porch cooler.

The water should be boiling soon in the kitchen and Dad comes out clean-shaven with his shirt tucked in.

"Don't you look complete," Jeanie says.

Dad's demand comes in a question. "Where is your grandmother?"

Jeanie smirks. "She's inside telling Mom to not unpack her clothes. I heard her yell, 'Not yet, Brenda,' a second ago."

"Well tell them that we're eating supper soon and to get ready. You, too. Go clean up. And don't worry about your brother just yet." He glances at me and disappears into the house.

The Mockingbirds, Delta

I can hear Mom and Mamaw bickering at each other from the porch as the sun burrows into the tree tops. It's not cooling off, but I don't care because they've restarted The Munsters marathon and I'm back to the first show.

Out on Delta, the mockingbirds drift here and there, imitating the calls of the other birds from the pruned branches and white fence posts of the street. The joggers are on the sidewalks again, bouncin' this way and that against the heat, all coming or going, sweatin' both ways. Seems every one of them wears a little radio and stretchy running clothes, even the ones who are walking. Down home if you were running it was because something was on fire or the animals were loose. And if you're walking it's because you got somewhere to be. We never needed no radio.

Jeanie comes out and eases Frank off the porch steps, reminding him to "Watch your fence, Francis."

I hope he doesn't watch it.

"I know you hate Frank, but you don't have to snort like that when I talk to him," Jeanie says.

"I was breathing. Christ. Go play with one of your boyfriends."

"Frankie, that was back home."

"Then shouldn't they be lining up by now?"

She stands up quick and says, "At least I can move."

Frank's out in the grass pissing on a faded-pink, heart-shaped chew toy he's eaten half the stuffing from and staring right back at me. Jeanie's shadow kills the glare on the TV, and Marilyn Munster stares straight out of the screen, laughing through her ruby-red hole of a mouth.

Dad pokes out wearing an apron and glares at Jeanie who gets the message, scoops Frank out of the yard and heads inside.

An apron?

At supper, Dad puts food I've never seen before on the table, little sliced rolls of white stuff wrapped in green, laid out on shiny, square plates I didn't know we had. Everyone gathers

161

in no real order. Then Mamaw moves Jeanie to sit across from Dad. Her old boobs catch the table top as she plunks into her seat and says, "I'm saying grace."

We're all silent after *amen.* I can hear our eyes darting around the table, and the house creaks as it settles. Jeanie has Frank cradled in her lap and Mamaw stares through the bottom lenses of her bifocal glasses at the food, at the walls, then at Dad, who's traded the apron for a fancy-gray, collared shirt.

"So Harold," Mama says, "what're we eating here?" She grips a fork in each hand like she's holding two steel hammers.

"It's sushi, Mom," Dad says.

"You mean raw fish."

"No, not raw fish. It's a way of preparing rice."

"Preparing? You mean fixing." Mamaw lifts a piece for a smell and draws back at it. "Stinks like raw fish. . . I suppose." She puts it back on her plate and leans on an elbow toward Mom.

"You aren't trying it, are you?" Dad asks.

"The fish? I'll get to it. You just hold on," she says, her headlight eyes glaring at Mom. "Now, Brenda. . . what you think about this then? You like raw fish?"

Mom squeezes my thigh under the table. I can't feel it, but I see the muscles in her arm tense up.

Dad starts in quick. "Now Mom, you know this ain't down home." He sounds like he's asking, not telling.

"You're goddamn right it ain't down home," Mamaw fires without looking at him. "Now . . . Brenda . . . what do you think of this raw *fish*?"

Mom hasn't lifted her eyes from her plate, hasn't even touched her fork or spoon or knife. I was her I'd use the knife first.

"It's not bad," Mom says. "I'm getting used to it."

"Used to it, huh?" Mamaw leans back, banging her two hammerforks down beside her plate. "How many times you have to try it before you know you used to it? Shouldn't have to get used to it. Ought to like it right out the gate. That's how you know it's good."

The Mockingbirds, Delta

Mom's eyes dart around like one of those mockingbirds trapped flying out front of a big city bus, beating its wings and flying in the air with no escape but up if that bus doesn't take a side-road or pull off to park.

Mamaw turns to me, forks in hands.

"Well Frankie, how about you . . . *you* like this raw fish?"

I don't even know how to even eat it. I stare at my empty lap, wishing I was back out front with Eddie Munster, but I know I can't go unless I eat supper. Mom eyes me out of the corner of her face. She's still looking down. Dad holds his breath a bit.

"Why don't you ask Jeanie?" I say.

"'Cause I don't have to." Mamaw leans back again and pats Jeanie's arm. "'Cause she don't need pushing around all day. 'Cause she can take care of herself." She slides her plate to the middle of the table. She's had enough of this raw fish.

Jeanie looks up from Frank. "We done with supper already?"

"Yea. We're done with supper," Mamaw says, but doesn't get up.

We're all stiff, waiting for Mamaw to pick a road to turn down to mangle parked cars and mockingbirds. I'm guessing it'll be Dad. Then Mom gives my leg a quick, stiff squeeze and looks up. She stares at the walls, then long at Dad, then right at Mamaw's headlight eyes.

"Bullshit, Ginny," Mom says. "Supper ain't over."

"The hell it ain't," Mamaw snaps. "I ain't gonna sit here staring at food that ain't food, seein' you all trying so damn hard to fit in with these folks around here. Christ. Like you've forgotten where you come from. Not one of these fancy neighbors of your's knows what a mountain or a coal mine is. Probably never even smelled mountain air. Jesus, Harold, your father saw you trying to live up here with these people he'd chew your ass off."

Dad takes a breath to talk but Mom cuts him off, her strawberry curls catching a breeze from somewhere far off and lighting up electric red.

"We ain't forgot, Ginny. We know where we're from. But you ever thought we don't want to *be* where we're from? Ain't

163

nothing down there for us but the same shit-old coal stories. Everybody blaming the coal mines. Everybody blaming the coal. Blaming the mines. Can't get their heads outta their asses long enough to see there's more to life than laying down blame for problems, and I ain't gonna have Frankie sittin' around listening to sorry folks and learning how to make excuses for himself cause of that wheelchair. Ain't gonna have him listenin' to folks juggle the reasons why they ain't left the holler. Ain't gonna do it."

Dad's hands are folded on the table and he's looking at Mom, his mouth dropped, half-open. He hasn't blinked. Jeanie has forgotten about Frank, who has jumped down to the floor, and even Mamaw is stuck for words, if only for bit.

"Brenda, them coal mines put the food on your plate when you was a child. Don't you forget that. Harold's too. Them mines fed us, and fed us good," Mama says.

"Christ. Fed us *good*? Union potatoes and bread for days. That's good? Shit, I'll show you good."

She stands up, buries a fork it in a piece of sushi and eats the whole thing at once, chewin' like she ain't never held such sweet food in her mouth. She leans back and grins at Mamaw from ear to ear, chewin' through that big smiling mouth full of food and grabs another piece before she's done with the first one.

"This is *California Roll. . . Ginny,"* she says, and buries the second piece in her mouth while she's got a third one ready to go.

"See, Mom," Dad instructs, "that's the way it's *supposed* to be eaten."

"Damn, Howard," Mom hollers through her mouth of food, "this the best damned raw fish I ever had. Christ, a gal could get used to this!"

She grabs pieces of sushi and lays them on everyone's plates, walks around the table and slides Mamaw's dinner onto her own and stuffs that piece into her mouth, and we start sucking down raw fish left and right.

Mamaw sits like the world is spinning around her, and

164

she can't do nothing about it. Like a wheel unhooked from a hub that has no rule on what that wheel is doing, while it just keeps picking up speed and swallowing up the ground beneath it.

Mamaw leans in, but quiet, and asks one more question.

"Frankie. Tell Mamaw what you think of this raw fish and this livin' up here."

I look to Mom, see that spread-out chomping sushi smile, and somewhere Herman Munster is walking straight through walls, destroying the floor with his booming steps, somewhere deep in that marathon. I can hear them big boots breaking the land and see my own chest spread out like the front end of a city bus walloping through every other damned bus what won't get out the way.

"I think you wanted us ready two days early so you could get us up and outta here if you didn't like what you saw," I say. I look to Mom, and she smiles wide through a mouth still full of food. Her eyes, blown up like big sundials, bounce from me to Mamaw. "And I know how to eat sushi."

Mamaw tosses her forks on the table and starts saying something, but I don't hear because Mom's laughing the food straight out of her mouth. She pops another piece in and grabs my TV, chewin' away, and wheels me back out to my porch with Frank following and the kitchen table as quiet as the evening Delta air.

Mamaw's taxi pulls up right as Dad finishes hauling the rest of her bags to the curb. The sun is just coming up over "The Acre." It's going to be a hot day, but I'm in the shade, and I'm comfortable. Things have quieted down and Mamaw hasn't said much since dinner last night. She was the first to go to bed, making sure to ask Dad if he'd call her up a taxi early this morning. Mom tried to convince her to stick around for a few more days, joking that, "Maybe you'll get used to it, Ginny." Mamaw didn't laugh with the rest of us. Just gathered her purse and some small items and went to bed behind a locked door. There wasn't any sound from her room through the night, but the house settled in the dark hours anyway. As did all the houses on Delta Avenue.

Not From Around Here, Are You?

Dad called the taxi place early and cooked up biscuits and eggs for everyone. Mamaw wouldn't eat any. She didn't say why. The only one of us who cared was Frank, 'cause he got her portion. Mom ate with me out on the porch and was just finishing when the taxi pulled up.

Her and Mamaw and Dad are out by the curb now, and though I'm back to my Munster's marathon, I can hear what they're saying.

"Mom," Dad says, "you know you can stay for a few days if you like."

"No. I've got things to do down home before the reunion."

Mom looks up and down the street, watching the mockingbirds drift here and there, shadowing her eyes with her hand. The three of them are quiet. Searching for something to say.

Mamaw turns to Mom.

"You all still coming down for it though, right?" The growl has left her voice and she sounds like she wants to know.

"Of course we are, Ginny," Mom says. "We wouldn't miss it. Why you think we wouldn't come?"

Mamaw looks past the two of them, up and down the street, up to the rooftops of the houses, then across the yard at me and back to Mom.

"Tell ya what, Brenda. Why don't you take that bottom room there and give it to Frankie. I won't be needin' it anytime soon. Have him sleep there. I'm sure you all play hell getting him up and down those stairs every night." And for the first time, she smiles.

Mom doesn't tell her that the room is already mine, that they hauled me upstairs for just last night. They don't tell her yesterday's busyness was them making sure it didn't look like a kid's room and that there's another room upstairs anyway. Dad doesn't tell her either.

"Thanks, Mom," Dad says. "I'm sure Frankie'll love it."

"I know he will," Mom says.

Mamaw, staring at the curb, takes a few breaths, her hair deep-purple in the morning low-sun.

166

The Mockingbirds, Delta

"I'm sorry," she says. "Really it ain't that I don't want you livin' up here among these folks. I'm sure they're alright people."

Dad squeezes her shoulder and says, "I know."

"And I just don't want you livin' anywhere but down home with me." The sun bounces a twinkle I can see from here off of Mamaw's cheek. She's crying.

Mom puts her arms around her and hands her a little hanky and says, "Ginny, you know, we're trying real hard to make sure Frankie's got," but Mamaw cuts her off.

"I know. Everything he needs. And he don't need those half-ass lazies down in them hills feeding him ideas on how to make excuses for not doin'. He needs the both of you. Needs you so he don't end up back down in that holler, stuck in the mud."

Dad snorts. "We'd have to get him different tires."

The laugh that bursts from the three of them bounces off the tidy trees and spooks all the mockingbirds out into the sunlight. For a second the gust from their beating wings blows away the smog from the taxi, blows away the hot air of Delta Avenue, and shadows the three of them still laughing away on the curb. Dad's always had a good sense of humor about him.

They all hug and Dad loads the trunk with his mother's bags. Mamaw looks back across the yard at Jeanie and me, not looking so monkeyish, and hollers at us.

"I'll see you all in a few days. Don't let that father of yours drive like a madman in that Caddy. And why don't you bring that damned little dog with you." She looks to Dad and asks, "Seriously, Harold, who the hell would mix a Bulldog and Chihuahua?"

She climbs in and the taxi putters down the road. I can hear her cussing the driver all the way down Delta, cussing him up and down in the heat as that gray flow of joggers and runners just keeps rolling by.

You know, Mamaw's laugh just now was the loudest of all of 'em.

I'm looking forward to seeing her again in a few days.

167

Without Wings

Jerry Judge

My Uncle Henry swore aliens captured him,
kept him for three years in their zoo and then
rewarded him upon release with an inhuman power.
Only three minutes of Earth time had passed.

He showed off at a family gathering, flying
around the sycamores and oaks like a blue jay.
Nobody believed it for a minute, but all said
he could be the next David Copperfield
       (if he was better looking).

Henry took to flying around the world
claiming the human population was blind,
but crows followed and pecked at him incessantly.
There was a little boy in Peru who waved.

The CWP Mandate

Mary Fitzpatrick

The mandate of Cincinnati Writers' Project is to promote and develop a writing community, and by extension enhance the general Arts community in Greater Cincinnati. The most visible way CWP does this is through critique groups that are equal part classroom, peer review and social network for their members. Through the CWP website, Yahoo Group, and newsletter Rough Draft CWP gets the word out about, readings and publications by members, because, while it is an ego boost to get something in print, it's even nicer to have your work sell.

Putting together an anthology of work by local writers every few years is another way CWP enriches the local writing community. This year CWP did two new things to spread the enrichment around.

First, the cover art for the 2008 anthology was selected through a contest open to all area artists. The art winning art came from Tina Clyburn of Cincinnati. Second, the anthology accepted, one short story and one poem, from high school students taking part in the Kentucky Governor's Scholars Program. Established in 1983, the Governor's Scholars Program is a five week residential summer program for outstanding Kentucky students completing their junior year in high school. It promotes academic and personal growth through a strong liberal arts curriculum, with classes ranging from physical science to cultural anthropology. CWP member Ryck Neube has been working to shape young minds in the creative writing portion of the Governor's Scholars Program for a number of years and was instrumental in including work from some of the students in this anthology.

Twilight Runners

Evan Holbrook

Gliding above the earth and through the trees, their white forms lit up the forest as they swept across it like ghosts in the night. They were not ghosts, however. Death had not taken its hold on these lifeless beings. They were approaching their destination quickly, but were in no rush. They needed to arrive just as the sun was about to peek over the horizon, which gave them an hour. That was the time for retrieval. The twilight hour.

Their dazzling cloaks shone brilliantly in the dark forest, chasing away the shadows and even the night itself. But the group of four could not reveal even an inch of their bodies to the night air for fear of being consumed by it. Trapped within their cloaks, their only escape was the twilight. Only then could they remove their cloaks. Only then could they retrieve a new runner.

They longed to feel the night's chill, the warmth of sunlight. These would never again be theirs. They were stuck in between day and night, just as they were caught in between life and death. They were runners of the twilight, creatures of the blue hours. Their only purpose was to increase their ranks so that they might remain forever.

Their destination was a certain town, with a certain hospital, where a certain boy laid dying.

Randall's body was powerless, but his mind was ablaze. He had never felt such anger. He wanted to fling his bed through the windows, and break the hospital equipment. But he could do nothing. He had reached the end of his life, and his body had accepted it before his mind could. Tears streamed down his face. He wanted to yell, but he felt too weak to manage even that. Cancer had beaten him. After months of treatment, they realized that they were too late to stop it. He had known for awhile that he would die, but it had never seemed as real as it did that sleepless night when he lost all hope.

"I won't accept it," he whispered to himself. "I won't die."

Randall looked out the window. Light poured over the horizon, but the sun had not yet risen. There was a strange blue hue to everything around him. Randall's tears stopped. The twilight was beautiful, but it was also sorrowful. Randall would never see it again, like so many other things.

He would die here, alone.

Randall's eyes caught a shimmer of movement in the distance. At first he thought it was a car catching the first rays of the sun, but the sun had yet to show itself. The light grew brighter, four tiny suns heading towards him. They zigzagged across the land at incredible speed. A ping of fear ran through Randall when he realized they were coming towards the hospital, but it left him just as quick as it had come. He was dying, after all; what was left for him to fear?

The four white figures passed through the glass of his window, like the ghosts he'd seen in movies. Each was painful to look at, like staring into the sun. Randall had to shield his eyes as the four ghosts moved towards his bed. He could have reached out and touched them, but he wasn't able to. He was too weak.

Their dazzling bodies seemed to billow up around them, like a cape in the breeze. The room was silent for a full minute.

"Are you angels?" he croaked. His dry throat pained him.

The glowing figure closest to him answered, "Far from it."

If they were not here to carry his soul away to heaven, then there was only one other alternative. Fear rammed through him.

"You are demons then."

"Just as far from that," the figure answered again.

The response confused Randall and sent his tormented mind spinning.

The figure closest to Randall bent his head and pulled off its hood. The other figures followed suit, removing their dazzling cloaks. Underneath they wore thin, dark outfits. The clothes seemed terribly cold to be wearing that time of year, but Randall figured that the glowing cloaks must have been terribly hot. Each held their cloaks in their left hand, letting the shining material drape to the floor. Each looked fully human. The one that had been speaking looked at Randall with pale green eyes.

"We are not to be feared. We have come to see you."

"Wh-who are you?" Randall managed to get out.

The people who stood before him all seemed to be perfectly normal now.

"We are the twilight runners," the man said. "We are the essence of the night and day. Both have more right to our souls than we do. If the sunlight touched our skin, it would dissolve into light. If the darkness crept onto our bodies, we would fade away into shadow. So in the day, we shroud our faces in dusk, and in the evening, we wear the dawn on our shoulders. Light keeps away the shadows, and darkness chases away the daylight. In this way we are immortal. In this way, we have ceased to live."

The man's voice was haunting, yet melodic. It enchanted Randall and made him sleepy. He struggled against the feeling.

"Why are you here?" he asked with as much force as he could.

The pale-eyed man gave him a strange look and answered, "We have come for you."

"What do you want with me?"

"Do you fear death?"

Randall was taken aback by the question. Having fought death for so long, he wanted nothing more than to rid himself of it for good.

"Yes," Randall whispered.

The man eyed him strangely. "What do you want more; to live or to not die?"

At this question the three others of his group turned and glared angrily at the pale-eyed man. There was a woman with dark hair and dark eyes, a man with white hair who looked very old, and a boy no older than Randall. They looked angry.

"I do not want to die."

The three others seemed to ease at his response.

The pale-eyed man looked at Randall sadly. "That, I can grant you."

He offered his hand. Randall felt a sudden burst of energy and rose from his bed, staring at the outstretched hand. Randall began to reach for the man, but he stopped short. The man glared at him, as if trying to tell him something. The three behind him were holding their breath, as if frightened by Randall's sudden pause.

Randall closed his eyes and looked into himself. Did he really want what he was being offered? What was the cost of living?

He grasped the hand.

The day had cooled. The sun settled below the horizon. Five figures flew across the open, rocky land. Their dark cloaks fluttered behind them as they ran at an impossible speed towards their destination. The cloaks were as black as night, darker than any shadow. They reached the base of a cliff, but darted up the slope against the pull of gravity, running in a zigzag pattern. They reached the summit and continued on their graceful flight.

They felt empty, without meaning. They kept on running only because they had to. They were beyond emotions, having left them behind with their lives. They feared death so much that they were now trapped on the brink of it, unable to plunge into its sweet release. They were not alive, but they were not dead.

The group halted at a landslide. Rocks and debris still trickled down the slope. A man, half buried in the rocks, laid bleeding in front of the group. He looked wan and near death. When he looked up at the ghostly black figures, he showed no fear. He had realized his own end.

"Y-you—" the man gasped out the word, but was unable to articulate anything more.

A moment later, the sun sank below the horizon. A semi-darkness covered everything, but night was not yet upon the group. It was the twilight hour.

Randall and the others pulled their cloaks away from their bodies and looked down at the pitiable man.

"We are the twilight runners," he said emotionlessly. "You will soon be dead. If you fear death, you may come with us."

The man looked up at them, but said nothing. Randall and his group waited tensely for a response. Then, the dying man focused his eyes on Randall.

"I do not fear death," the man coughed out with surprising control. He looked at each of the runners, one by one, with a serene look on his face before he died.

Randall looked at his companions. The pale-eyed man was smiling, but the others were disappointed. Randall didn't feel happy for the man. He couldn't feel anything. He did, however, wish that he would have made the same choice. But it didn't matter now. He was unable to go back and change his mind. So he began to run, followed closely by the others.

All he felt was the emptiness of twilight.

Cubist Self-Portrait

Abby Kirk

I feel like my mouth is where my
Left eye should be
Like a pirate patch blinding my judgment
Only worse.
I can only see the situation now
From one pupil—
One perspective
(mine)
So my mouth short-circuits
And spits out whatever word vomit
Is within the tongue's reach

My only eye is flipped upside-
Down. Even the brow is underneath
Soaking up any tears
That might have—
Theoretically—
Fallen there
From my hard, blueluminous eye
They say that we see
Upside-down, and our brains flip the image
Right side-up
I guess for me, I see
Things as they are
But then my brain twists them backwards
To what it thinks it should be seeing.
(denial at its best)

Not From Around Here, Are You?

My nose is bent sideways
Sticking out past my profile
No profound psychological reason here
Just roller skates and a
very fast approaching
very stationary
Wall.
The only part of my mangled face that's
Exactly where it should be
Is a shiny pink zit
Smack in the middle of my forehead.
Teenage karma.

Werewolves

Jerry Judge

Take note of this safety tip that I learned at a writers' conference. You're aware, of course, about the recent documentation and research by Briggs and Stratten proving the existence of werewolves and their growing numbers. Many people are uneasy about this even though werewolves don't kill any more people than Grizzles and poisonous snakes. They're mainly just a nuisance—both to people they meet and themselves and their families. Just the new clothing bill alone is staggering for werewolves. (As an aside—scientists haven't yet figured how werewolves can burst out of their clothes while transitioning and yet always be clothed, albeit tattered and ripped, when they return as humans.)

The tip you have been waiting for is this—werewolves are usually not dangerous, just grouchy. They get gigantic hemorrhoids during the changing process. The most painful hemorrhoids are what cause the killings. We can all understand that. Forget the silver bullets. They don't work and really piss off the werewolves. Instead, always carry a tube or two of Preparation H when you venture out at night. It will save your life and gain you a valuable friendship.

American Tea Party

Jean Syed

One fall I planted daffodil bulbs
in our not quite English wood
and with milky tea I sat on a bench,
an English interlude.
I thought about Wordsworth's daffodils
alongside the blue bay,
wishing that I could have Windermere waves
in the soily clay.
So I planted English bluebells
beside an oak tree's grass,
the waves were there most jocundly
in spring when the wind would pass.

Yet I and mine are happy here.
Now I plant a native tree,
the redbud's not found in English woods
and I am contented that we
may sit to see them all with cups
of American iced tea.

Angel of the Wal-Mart Big-N-Tall

Doug Clifton

Roscoe Long went to his mother's house every Thursday for their special day, and as he sat in her living room on that particular Thursday morning, he recalled something. In a forward to THE OCTOBER COUNTRY, Ray Bradbury explained how he'd come up with that title. All the stories in that book were so bleak and mournful that Mr. Bradbury had wondered what the most downright dreary, miserable time was that he could imagine hearing them. He settled on 3 A.M. on a Thursday in mid October.

Roscoe allowed as how he might be a bit off remembering the exact hour and the part of October that day was in, but he was certain of the day. He looked around his mother's living room as he waited, and nodded. Yep, old Ray had damn sure picked Thursday.

"Roscoe!" His mother's voice poured down the stairs like the gift of a busted drain pipe from a toilet. "Are you ready? I don't want to be late because of you!"

"I'm ready! I been ready for half an hour now. And you won't be late on account of me. You'll get there because of me!"

Christ Almighty! Just once she could say thank you.

"Now don't you act like that!" Her drain pipe voice was closer to the top of the stairs. "You know how I look forward to our special day together. Me and my baby boy at WAL-MART! What could be more fun?"

Roscoe thought about that question. The first thing that came to mind was a do-it-yourself vasectomy but he brushed that idea aside. Instead he settled on how nice it would be if Ima B., his older sister, would put down her AMWAY case long enough to get her ass over to Momma's just one Thursday for her own special day. He could see it all. It would be Thursday and he'd be home sitting in his recliner in boxers and T-shirt. He'd have a

179

cold beer in one hand and a JIMMY DEAN breakfast burrito in the other, and JERRY SPRINGER would be on the tube. Funny how it was the simple things that brought so much joy.

"Roscoe! What are you doin' still sittin' there?"

Lord, that voice could raise the little hairs on his neck. He'd been so enraptured contemplating the finer things in life he hadn't noticed her come down. She was at the foot of the stairs in all her lavender sweat pants glory. Her almost matching sweatshirt, size XXLG, had hearts and moons and stars all over it with WORLD'S BEST MOM in bright red glitter across her bosom. Ima B. had bought it for her. . .on sale at WAL-MART.

"We need to get goin'. WAL-MART waits for no man. I want to see if they got any new angels. I just feel the need for some more angels."

Roscoe looked around the living room. It didn't matter which direction he turned or what height or angle he chose to hold his head, all he saw were angels. There were angry Old Testament angels with fiery swords, prissy Victorian angels, even tight waisted, big boobed angels he thought would sure look fine on the back of a Harley in some magazine.

They were everywhere, both flattened in picture frames and three dimensional on little pedestals and bases. He especially liked the big boobed angels in three dimensions. But he couldn't begin to understand where his mother might put even one more, be it two dimensional or not.

"Why?" he said, being a man of deep thoughts but few words.

"Lord, Roscoe, don't you know what's goin on in the world today. All that pornography and drugs and wars and gay marriage and gas prices and all. And don't forget about those Muslimists. I just feel like I need some more angels around me."

"Momma, do you even know what a Muslimist is? There ain't no Muslimists around here."

"Have you seen my new mailman?"

"What?"

"We got us a new mailman on the street and he's awfully dark."

Angel of the Wal-Mart Big-N-Tall

"What do you mean, dark?" Roscoe thought of THE OCTOBER COUNTRY again and how the stories in that book all seemed so dark. But that was more a darkness that came from inside the people involved and couldn't be readily seen.

"Well, I don't mean to say he's a . . . black man." She whispered those last two words so that Roscoe had to lean toward her to be sure he could hear. "I think he might be an Egyptian."

"Momma, the Post Office is a government job. I don't think they're allowed to hire Egyptians."

"Well, just the same I'm gonna keep my eyes on him. And I need me some more angels. I hope they got some new angel books there. I just love those angel books. It makes me feel good to read those stories about how some angel pulled somebody back onto the curb when they was about to step out in front of a city bus or garbage truck or some such and get flattened and have to go to hell before they got a chance to get saved. Would my Egyptian mailman do that? I don't think so. He'd probably give that poor Christian a push so's he'd get hit by that garbage truck mid grill and do the job up right. Yes sir, I need to get some more protection around me. Lord, Roscoe, come on. We need to get to WAL-MART before those angel books get all picked over."

Roscoe followed his mother out the door trying to picture a swarm of women, all in sweat pants of various colors, putting hammer locks, full Nelsons and even sleeper holds on each other as they fought over the meager remains of a once great stack of angel books. He figured his mind must be too attuned to the simple things of life; the image just wouldn't come.

So he got into the car with her like a man climbing into a gas chamber to sit beside a big, lavender cyanide pellet. All the way to WAL-MART she prattled away about Regis and Kelly and how stuck-up Oprah was so that by the time he pulled into a parking space he'd just about decided that if Ima B. didn't take over the next special Thursday with Momma, he might have to shoot her; Ima B., that is, not Momma.

As they walked into the store Roscoe made a point of

Not From Around Here, Are You?

ignoring the greeter. The old man kinda scared him the way he seemed so happy with his lot in life. That same grin was probably on the faces of half the folks in Jonestown while the other half mixed the KOOL-AID. Maybe, too, one reason the greeter was so scary was that things were not going well at the paper bag factory where Roscoe worked. Seems like people had finally taken to heart that man's advice in THE GRADUATE; plastics.

If the bag plant went under he might just have to stand at a store entrance and ask. . . .

"Would you like a cart, Ma-am?"

"Lord yes," his mother said. "We always find so much in here we never expected. Don't we, Roscoe?"

"Got any angels?" Roscoe asked the poor old guy.

"Why, I truly don't know. You can ask at the Customer Service Desk if we got any in lately, though."

Roscoe decided not to ask if they had any devils. He was afraid that if enough interest was shown WAL-MART just might try to stock them.

"Come on, Roscoe, we don't need to ask. I know where they keep the angels. Lord God, I ought to. I own enough of 'em."

"If you own enough, why are you after more?"

"Oh, don't tease me. Come on. I can hear my next angel callin'."

His mother led them on a labyrinthine path up and down aisles, past lug wrenches and flip-flops, until he was near to being motion sick when she finally turned into the row for magazines and books. That's when he left her. His mother turned and Roscoe kept to the straight and narrow and just walked. He'd have kept right on walking too, even if he went so far as to find himself in a desert where he was sure to keel over and die of either hunger or thirst without the sudden helping hand of a real Egyptian mailman, if it hadn't been for the skinny woman with the wide shopping cart.

She barred his way like a heavy chicken wire fence with a very light chicken behind it, so he turned right, into the men's BIG-N-TALL section. Roscoe was not ignorant of the irony of

182

the situation as he was neither big nor tall. But he was alone, mercifully alone, and out of both sight and, hopefully, earshot of his mother. That last, if true, would certainly be saying something for that woman could cast a shot at one's ears for a goodly distance.

Just to be sure, Roscoe delved a bit deeper into the BIG-N-TALL and wound up next to a display of big Hawaiian shirts. He looked at those shirts. They had pineapples and parrots and palms and birds of paradise in shades of orange, yellow, red and green so bright that they almost screamed at him. Each of the price tags had an addition to it that said HALF OFF. Roscoe reached down to the nearest tag, tore that addition away and slipped it into his pants pocket. If anyone was going to buy a shirt loud and jarring enough to be a polyester version of his mother they needed to pay the full price just like he did.

That's when the flash of light hit his eyes. It wasn't like a flashbulb or one of those strobes that could put an epileptic into conniptions, but a little glint just bright enough to get his attention. He decided to cast about to find the source of that light so he could avoid it. He had a good view of a couple of aisles, but could see nothing shiny enough to flash in his eyes like that until he looked down right beside him, and there it was.

It was a little girl, maybe four years old at most, with light brown hair and big brown eyes, standing there with her head thrown so far back you'd think it had to hurt. She was looking up at him and smiling and, Oh Lord, that smile. To call it a smile would be like calling the Mona Lisa just another painting of a woman, and a pretty plain woman at that. Like calling the face of God just another old man with lightning in his eyes.

Roscoe knew she had to have seen him tear that HALF OFF part of the price tag away. That little girl had him red-handed. For all he knew, she wasn't a little girl at all but maybe a dwarf store detective hired to skulk about and peer at the shoppers from an unexpected angle. The light in his eyes may well have come from her tiny store detective badge.

"Shoo!" Roscoe said to the dwarf spy or whatever she was. "Go on, get out'ta here!"

Not From Around Here, Are You?

But she didn't shoo. That little girl, for Roscoe was finally convinced she wasn't a dwarf at all, simply stood there at his feet and continued to give him that radiant smile.

That smile was so open, so beautiful it was . . . well, it was pure. And in that purity he knew that she saw him for what he was; a man who could abandon his mother and just run off, then try to find a pitiful bit of joy in ripping price tags asunder. Yet she not only accepted what he was but also, dare he even think it, loved him simply because he was. She had found him in the BIG-N-TALL where neither of them belonged, both strangers in a strange land. Had found him a bitter man filled with bitter thoughts worthy of THE OCTOBER COUNTRY, and she found him worthy of love.

It was too much. Roscoe needed distance, not because he feared her but rather he feared that by standing too near he might somehow defile the ground whereon she stood. He actually staggered back from that little girl's smile and stumbled right into the waiting arms of a rack full of loud Hawaiian shirts.

The pineapples and parrots and palms and HALF OFF price tags were all around him clutching at him like his mother used to do when he was little, and she would threaten to jerk a knot in his tail. Roscoe wanted to scream but that little girl had stolen his voice and wouldn't give it back. He thrashed about and wrestled that shirt rack near to the floor before he was able to extricate himself from all the short, clutching sleeves and take a step away.

It was when he stepped back and had a new perspective that he saw them. That little girl's legs were each imprisoned in a set of braces that came almost to her hips. The flat steel bars that ran up the sides of her legs were padded and wrapped and left only the knee hinges exposed. The metal there was polished and bright, and it was from those that the light from the overhead fixtures was reflected into Roscoe's eyes. That little girl and her light held him like a bug in amber.

A thought came to Roscoe. He figured it must be his own but it spoke to him as if someone else and it said, If she can stand there with those things on her legs, see you as you are and still give you a smile like that, what right do you have to complain about or judge anyone? Then the thought was shooed away.

"Roscoe! What are you doin' with that child?"

His mother was standing in the aisle staring at them. Roscoe wanted to answer but just plain couldn't. Something in that little girl's smile had entered him and was burrowing down deep inside and it left him mute.

"Come over here, honey." His mother held out her ample arms and beckoned. "Where's your mommy?"

As that little girl hobbled toward Roscoe's mother one of her feet in its big, clunky brace shoe caught on the floor tiles so that she pitched forward. And Roscoe saw a miracle or so it seemed. His mother, slow and ponderous by nature, moved so swiftly that she all but sizzled through the air in her effort to catch that child. He had visions of senseless biblical retribution as when that nice young fellow reached to steady the Ark of the Covenant, and God laid him out dead like a peevish old neighbor who would send plagues to bedevil anyone who dared to step on his grass.

But neither plagues nor lightning nor even one decent-sized boil came to afflict his mother. She simply caught that little girl in mid fall and then set her down steady on her braced legs like a little Colossus of Rhodes bestriding a one-foot floor tile. That child stood with upturned face, and Roscoe saw his mother's expression melt. Then his mother gave him one last disgusted look, like he should have known what to do and not leave it to her to do it, took that little girl's hand and led her off toward the Customer Service Desk.

"Don't you worry, honey," she said. "We're gonna find your mommy even if it kills us."

As they walked away, that little girl gave Roscoe's mother another of those smiles that he knew was the bestowing of some profound gift. He just wasn't sure how to accept his. He stood like that, transfixed and astonished, until he was jolted back by the PA system.

"Attention WAL-MART shoppers. We have a lost little girl

185

at the Customer Service Desk in the front of the store. She has brown hair and eyes and won't tell anybody her name. And she has. . .issues with her legs," the voice said with tact. "Will her parents please come forward and claim her. Thank you."

And that little girl's mommy responded. Roscoe never saw her but marked her passage from the back of the store to the front by the wail of her voice.

"Oh, baby! Mommy's comin'! Mommy's right here! It's gonna be okay, baby! Here I come!"

It's the way you might expect that Mary would have sounded if she'd been shopping at WAL-MART and got separated from little Jesus. Maybe the way she truly wailed as she wound through the streets of Jerusalem hot on the trail of his cross.

Roscoe figured that little girl's mommy made it, for there were no further announcements over the PA about little lost girls with leg issues. But still he stood there in the BIG-N-TALL unsure where to go or what to do next. Whatever it was he suspected he might have to go beyond the BIG-N-TALL section, maybe even outside of the WAL-MART altogether to accomplish it, but he couldn't will himself to move. It was like he was waiting for something monumental to come along and give him a shove.

"Lord, Roscoe! You still here? Have you gone simple?"

Roscoe shook his head and focused on his mother.

"Yes, Momma," he managed to say, for he figured anything as big as what was happening to him at the moment had to be simple.

"Well, that's okay. Come on. They got some new angel books, and I need you to help me pick one out. Let's go before they're all gone."

Roscoe reacted without a single thought. He looked at his mother and smiled the same smile that he'd seen on the face of the little girl. It was like he was watching from deep inside, and he could hardly believe what he was doing. He was smiling at his mother and he loved her, and he knew that with a surety that was astounding. It was an all pervading fact that held him, a willing captive. His mother took his hand and gave him an

Angel of the Wal-Mart Big-N-Tall

uncertain smile as if she wasn't quite sure that the person she was about to walk off with was indeed her son.

As Roscoe went along with his mother he reached into his pants pocket, pulled out the HALF OFF half of the loud Hawaiian shirt price tag and let it flutter to the floor. At the same time, in that place deep inside, he sat back in an embrace that was so warm and sustaining he knew that not even his recliner, even with JERRY SPRINGER on the tube, could come within a mile of it; maybe even a hundred miles. And the light! Oh Lord, the light was so bright you'd have thought it had to hurt his eyes, but it didn't.

It just sparkled a bit like it was reflecting off the knee hinge of a little metal leg brace.

Pipe Dreams

Jane Biddinger

It's quiet now. Time to relax and get tidied up. Ethel comes each night, and I look forward to her visit. I welcome her as I would a personal masseuse coming to rub down my tiles, scrub my bowls, and scour my sinks. It makes me feel more permanent because you always clean what you plan on keeping. These days, things are changing so much in the mall; it gives a gal reason to take pause. What with this company buying that one, and this one closing down, and something else taking its place, I sometimes get a little flushed. Once in a while, they'll slap some new countertops or hang new pictures, trying to make me look all new, and big-city like. Like somebody's going to burst through my doors, all in a hurry to take care of business and say, "Wow! I feel like I'm in Tuscany, and it's so much better than peeing in Cincinnati."

I feel right at home now. But let me tell you, it wasn't always this way. When they first started building, I was a rookie and had never rubbed elbow joints with a bunch of architects and designers with their plans and hoity-toity notions. Arguing all the time. Tile versus marble. White versus almond. Brass versus silver. They even fought over the sign on my door, until they finally settled on a tan plaque with WOMEN in white letters. Almost drove me crazy in the process. Those people made the job so much more complicated than it truly was. Dependability and comfort are what people are looking for, and that's my responsibility. When you're a public servant, you have to prove yourself. You've got to earn a position of trust, and that takes time. A backup or an overflow and you're right back to square one. Not to mention those nightmares about giant plungers and two-mile long snakes.

Pipe Dreams

Mama wasn't thrilled with my career path and that caused me to have second thoughts. She always wanted bigger and better things for me. When I was little she told me I could be anything I wanted to be. "Jonnie," she would say, "in this great country the possibilities are limitless. If you just set your mind to it, why you can even grow up to be a White House lavatory." But I just don't have the stomach for politics even if I'd be sought after more often than those Congressional seats. I did entertain thoughts of joining the CIA or FBI with all their intrigue and adventure, but I've always considered myself to be a little on the private side, and the thought of being bugged just didn't set well with me. Deep down I always knew I'd be in retail. Maybe it's something in the water, I really don't know, but I could just feel it in my pipes. You got to be true to yourself, I always say. Besides, Mama herself knows the allure of department stores; she worked her way up to the coveted position of lounge in an exclusive dress shop downtown. She had an attendant who turned on the water for the ladies and offered each one a towel as she finished her business. Mama even had a red velvet couch that those women called a settee. Now I may only have two mismatched chairs and six stalls, but I like it here in Tri-County. I prefer the suburbs.

Mama questioned my choice, but I said, "Now, Mama, I really like living on the edge." When I said that, she was really upset. Then I assured her, "I mean living on the edge of the big city—not on the edge of sanity, morality, or whatever else you may be thinking. I just don't feel comfortable smack dab in the middle of all that hubbub and traffic." I personally think this suburb-city argument is a sign of the times and part of the battle of the generations. Besides, I've got a bit of my granddaddy in me. He was a two-seater behind the older general store in a small town. Got pushed aside by indoor plumbing in the name of progress and personal hygiene. But to hear him tell, Granddaddy had pretty much gotten his fill by the time he was forced into retirement.

Now as far as spaces go, you may wonder why I am content to be a ladies' room rather than, say, a shoe department.

Not From Around Here, Are You?

Well, I look at it this way. I've got job security. Now they can stack shoes just about anywhere or decide not to sell them at all. But to be a restroom, you need to be plumbed, and I have indeed been that. I don't like to brag, but I've been told that I have some of the best-looking PVC fittings in these parts. And the likelihood of my services not being in demand is highly unlikely from what I've observed. Even with all of the high-flying technology, some things just never change. I guess I could work myself into a dither thinking about those astronauts and the suits they wear, but I don't see that coming to the general public any time soon. So for now I feel pretty good being what I am where I am.

There's a lot more to being a restroom that what you may think. I see a different side of people, if you get my drift. I consider myself the great equalizer. Except for some variations in skin tones, everybody looks pretty much the same to me. I see people with their guards down along with just about everything else.

I notice that women like to come here in pairs, leaving their men in the hall scratching their heads. I can't tell you how often I hear, "No, I really don't have to go, but I'll come with you." I guess that women have spent so many years dragging some little one along with them, either one of their own or a little sibling, they don't realize that they can come in here alone. Besides, most ladies are pretty sociable and take advantage of any opportunity chat. I'm amazed at how they manage to carry on a conversation while choosing a stall, passing paper under the partitions and adjusting panty hose, all without missing a single word. They grumble about it being a man's world and complain about glass ceilings, but I get the idea that they like having this place where men are off limits.

I provide refuge for mothers of young children. I have an alcove they call a baby-changer. Now when they first installed this apparatus, I pictured mothers coming in with bratty kids they didn't like, trying to pass them off on someone else. Sort of a human flea market. But then I realized it was for changing babies' diapers, not really for swapping the tykes themselves, I warmed up to the contraption right away. Up until then, these poor women balanced those little ones on laps in my stalls, or sometimes plopped them right down on my cold hard tile floor desperate for a place to remove those soiled and wet bottom coverings. And while my two chairs may not match, they have been the sites where many a hungry infant has been satisfied by bottle or breast. I am my own mini food court.

I offer a challenge for mothers of little boys. The sign on my door displays an image of a skirt-wearing person. The little guys don't balk at coming in here for the first few years of their lives but then comes the day of reckoning dreaded by every mother. The lad doesn't feel comfortable here anymore and mom agonizes and tries to delay the inevitable. "Maybe next time." But sonny pleads, "Mom, I'm not a baby and I'm not a girl." I witness this rite of passage day in and day out. It still tears me up. The mother is frightened and doesn't want to see him charge off into the unknown—through that door marked MEN. Mom can't go in and keep an eye on him. Can't keep him under her wing. But deep down, she knows that she has to send him off alone. She watches him go, knowing that this is just one step of many that will take him away from her and through that door of manhood. She holds her breath as she waits for him, her eyes moist as one of my bowls on a hot summer morning before the air kicks in. And mark my word, she will continue to tuck his shirt in for another year or so.

Teenagers love me. My stall walls give them a free place to advertise the loves of any particular day. Scrawled in lipstick that Ethel will later massage away, Heather professes her love for Scott. The next day, Heather can proclaim her affection for Justin. The younger girls come in to experiment with makeup they've bought at Wal-Mart. They paint their lips black and polish their nails with dark colors. They want to prove to their parents and to the world that they are independent and unique. After they've applied layers of stuff, they gaze into my mirrors. And I chuckle and think to myself, what a waste of time. I guess it just doesn't occur to any one of them to look at one another. The face staring back would be so similar to her own. These young ones take a stab at acting like grown women, and they think that their mothers don't know, but my guess is that they do. I offer them paper towels to remove the evidence just in case.

Every now and again here in the store, we offer special savings to senior citizens. Let me tell you about my last Golden Buckeye Day. I was sitting here admiring my freshly scrubbed gray carpet that lies in my entryway, its nap standing up as straight as bristles on a new toothbrush. The picture of a vase of red roses was hanging straight as any plumb line. My tan wall tiles were all but sparkling and I must admit that I was feeling pretty smug as I admired them in my full-length mirror. My matching floor tiles have a splattering of darker brown ones here and there. I could smell the pine aroma of the cleaning solution Ethel had used the night before. You know, there are times when taking a deep breath here is ill advised, but I was feeling the effect of an intense fall cleaning and breathing a little easier than usual. My stall walls glimmered as the soft lights from my recessed bulbs overhead bounced on their gray imitation marble sides. It was early. My paper holders were full and my garbage cans empty.

My door opened and I set to guessing who was coming. I can generally tell by the feel of the footsteps. Light, tiny ones signal a child. When they get a few more years, they can fool the inexperienced with their jumping and hopping, but the size of the feet gives them away. Rubber wheels can be either a stroller or a wheelchair. Time and practice have allowed me to sense the difference. Well, on that particular day, I recognized the touch of low-heeled Hush Puppies shuffling over my tiles. The shoes made their way to the green tweed chair and a body plopped down and I heard a deep sigh come from that direction. Before long my door opened again followed by the same shuffling, but this time Keds dragged over me. Another chair, another plop, another sigh. The silence was as thick as that new Lysol Cling bowl cleaner Ethel tried not too long ago. Finally the two gray-haired persons, each with a firm grip on the purse in her lap, caught sight of one another. Blue eyes met brown. The blue ones said, "I'm just lost without Sara. We did everything together." The brown eyes understood. "My sister Kay passed on just a while ago. It's really hard."

Pipe Dreams

Well, these two ladies commenced to talking and reminiscing about the lives they didn't share but understood so well. To make a long story not quite so long, they each cried a bit, comforted each other a lot, and took off for the food court at 10:30 AM for lunch together. Now maybe it was just my imagination, but those feet seemed a little lighter then when they came in. Every now and again, they come in here together. When it's close to the day for Social Security checks, they sneak tuna sandwiches in here and stink the place up, but I really don't mind at all.

Now I don't mean to sound boastful, but sometimes I just get this warm feeling all over—and it's not just Ethel hosing me down, or someone with poor aim. I draw a certain satisfaction from my work here. Not too long ago a young woman was studying for a citizenship test right here in my confines. She dropped a pamphlet as she left. It had a picture of the Statue of Liberty on the front. I read the words, "Give me your tired, your poor, your huddled masses." I chuckled to myself and said, "My, my, that's just what I've been doing here all along. Wait till I tell Mama. She'll be proud of me yet."

When a Black V of Geese Fly Over the Neighborhood

Madeleine Crouse

I shift my mind to where I lived for thirty years:
fields of green corn, cattle grazing a hillside,
the scent of fresh plowed earth. I want

the quiet of no car door slamming but mine—
no dog barking but mine—no Metro bus,
taxi, no motorized scooter whirring

by the door. I wish mist to roll in
from the creek and a thousand fireflies
to rise from the grass. In late July,

let the Big Dipper stretch large across the sky.
On clear nights the full moon will silver
the backs of my horses white. I like

widening circles from stones tossed into water
as they press into the next and next
circle measuring lack of boundary.

(Originally published in Maze from the Median, CWP Press, 2004)

194

The Haven of the Green Lady

P. Andrew Miller

As I pulled into Aunt Ruth's gravel driveway, I could feel the knot in my stomach tighten. It had been getting steadily worse on the hour drive to her house from my apartment in the city. Now, I just wanted to turn around and head back without even seeing her. Instead, I pulled up between the main house and the old barn that she now used for storage, came to a stop, and turned off the engine. *This is it,* I said to myself. *You can do it.*

I got out of the car and walked up to the gate in the picket fence that surrounded her house. Even though it was still a half hour to sunset, she had lit the old metal lantern that hung from the gate post. It was half rusted, with a pattern of stars and crescents cut into it. A fresh green candle had been placed in it and now flickered with the slight evening breeze. I wondered if she lit it every night, since I hadn't called and told her I was coming.

In fact, I hadn't been to see Aunt Ruth for over a year. The last time I was here was when I came to borrow some money from her. The new riverboat casino had been too much of a temptation. I had been desperate then and had even been stupid enough to ask for it as a loan on my inheritance. Aunt Ruth had given me the money, but the look she gave me, the suppressed anger and supreme disappointment, was the real reason I had stayed away. I didn't want to face that again, especially since I had never paid her back.

Aunt Ruth was in fact my great aunt, my father's aunt and had never married. Now in her eighties, she still lived on the old family farm by herself. She had refused to move into any type of assisted living or closer to the city, and I had to admit, I knew no reason for her to do so. At least when last I had seen her. But apparently, my sister Carol and our cousin Len thought otherwise. Both had called me over the last week, trying to get me to go out to the farm. Of course, neither one of them knew about the loan.

For the last two months, Carol had been calling to nag me about coming out here to "talk sense" to Aunt Ruth. I had kept putting her off, not telling her why I didn't want to do it. But Carol thought something was wrong.

"Look, Allan, Mrs. Pettit called me again this week. She said she saw more strange people skulking around Aunt Ruth's barn."

"Mrs. Pettit lives a half mile away. The only way she can see Aunt Ruth's house is with binoculars."

"That's not the point, Allan. The point is, she's all alone out there and it's not the 1970's anymore. It's not safe for her out there. Len agrees with me."

I sometimes wondered if my sister and my cousin were concerned for Aunt Ruth's health and safety or for the inheritance they both thought was coming. Of course, I was the only one that I knew of who had already tried to get that out of Aunt Ruth.

"Then why don't one of you go out and talk to her?"

"I tried last month. She gave me some tea and told me to leave and to mind my own business. And you know Len lives four hours away. Besides, you were always her favorite."

I doubted that was the truth anymore. But that was why I decided to drive out. Aunt Ruth was in her eighties. Even if she was still in good shape, I wanted to make amends. I wanted her to know I was sorry for what I had done. So I made the drive, violating Aunt Ruth's rule of always calling first since I hadn't wanted her to tell me not to come.

I steeled myself for our meeting as I made the short walk up to the front porch and knocked on the door. I knew it would be unlocked, but still, I didn't think it would be a good idea to surprise someone in their eighties.

I heard some muttering in the house and a footstep hit the creaking floorboard in the living room. Then the door swung open and Aunt Ruth posed in the doorway, hands slightly to the sides, the palms of her hands facing me. But the pose was nothing compared to her outfit.

She was wearing a long green velvet dress with flowing sleeves of some sort of sheer material. Gold sparkles glinted in the material. I stared, taking it all in, and then I noticed the tiara resting on her gray hair.

"Allan!" she said.

"Aunt Ruth," I said. "Um, how are you?"

"What are you doing here, Allan? And why didn't you call first?"

She looked behind me as if she were expecting someone else to come up the path.

I didn't want to tell her why I hadn't called. "Sorry, about that. I, uh, thought, I would, you know, surprise you."

"I'm not lending you any more money, Allan."

I winced. I deserved that. "I know, Aunt Ruth. And I didn't come for that."

"I'm sorry. But I don't have time for a visit right now," she said, looking around me.

"I need to talk with you, Aunt Ruth. It's important," I said, as I pushed past her into the living room. I realized I was being rude, but I didn't think I could work up the nerve to drive out here again on the same errand. Besides, dressed as she was, I thought maybe she might be suffering from sort of dementia.

"Allan, really, I don't have time for this," she said, looking towards the old clock in the corner.

I didn't know why she even kept it. It didn't work right. It kept getting stuck at different times. I glanced at it as well and noticed it had stopped at ten after seven, just a minute or two from now.

I walked toward it, then turned and walked back. I had rehearsed what I had wanted to say all the way out here, but now I couldn't remember what I wanted to say first.

"Aunt Ruth, I wanted to come out and well. . . ."

"Allan, whatever it is, it will have to wait. I need you to leave now."

I stood my ground. "I can't leave yet. I need to talk to you."

Not From Around Here, Are You?

"Not. Now." She actually grabbed my hand and pulled me towards the door. For a short, slight octogenarian, she had a good grip.

"Aunt Ruth. . . ."

"Dammit, Allan, I need you to leave!"

I didn't want to hurt her by resisting and I felt too stunned to try. Did she really hate me now? She kept pulling me towards the door, and then swung it open just as the broken clock bonged once. At 7:10?

"Oh, no," Aunt Ruth muttered.

I looked back at the clock and then at Aunt Ruth. A motion in the doorway caught my attention.

Standing outside on the porch, one hand poised to knock at the now open door, stood a tall man with long dark hair and a beard. He wore what I think was a tunic with a leather belt. A sword hung from it. He wore dark pants and leather boots.

I could make out others behind him. One was short and nearly as wide as he was tall. He wore armor, a spiked hat, and had a sledgehammer swung over his shoulder. An old man, even taller than the dark-haired fellow, towered in the back. While he had no hair on his head, his beard clearly fell far down onto his chest. To his left was a young woman who stepped into the open to look at me and Aunt Ruth. She had a quiver of arrows on her back and held a bow. She had long silver hair, braided and hanging down her back. This style revealed her ears which look pointed. She wore a tunic and boots and *nothing else.* Just lots of smooth skin between, smooth . . . light green skin?

The man in front suddenly dropped to one knee and bowed his head. The short guy and the young woman followed his lead.

"Milady, I am Hykar, whom some call the Brave, and these are my companions, Zeron, Master of the Arcane Arts; Rocksplitter, prince of dwarves; and Kalyxta, warrior of the Eternal Forest. We have come far to seek your aid in our quest for the Sword of Dalatha and my rightful place on the throne of Ardwanna."

Aunt Ruth looked at them then looked back at me. She

looked a little ill.

"They're not from around here, are they?" I asked.

Aunt Ruth sighed.

She made me wait in the kitchen as she saw to the comfort of her "guests" in the barn. I thought the old beds and furniture in there were for storage. I never realized Aunt Ruth put it to use.

I had no idea what to make of the strangers who were now taking shelter in the old barn. I had a few friends who were in the Society for Creative Anachronism back when I was in college. I figured this was something similar, though I must say they went to a lot of trouble for the look of it. What surprised me was that Aunt Ruth had gotten involved with them. I mean, how did she even hear about it? But it did explain the people Mrs. Pettit had seen. However, knowing who they were didn't make me feel any better about it. Aunt Ruth seemed a little too trusting of these guys. What if they did decide to take advantage of her? Damn, I was starting to think like Carol.

Finally, Aunt Ruth came in the back door, plunked down at the table, and took the tiara off of her head. She twirled it around her fingers.

"I guess you want an explanation."

I nodded. "Well, I am mostly curious about how you got involved in this group. I would never have thought you would be into roleplaying."

She stopped twirling the tiara. "Roleplaying?"

"Well yeah. Those people out there are in some sort of roleplaying society, right? How did they get you to join?"

Aunt Ruth blinked once. "I have no idea what you are talking about, Allan."

Now I was starting to get really worried.

"You really shouldn't have come here tonight," she continued.

"I had to, Aunt Ruth. I wanted to make sure things were all right between us and that you were okay." I paused. "Are you okay?"

Not From Around Here, Are You?

"I'm fine, dammit," she said. "I wish you and your sister and your cousin would stop treating me like I'm some crazy old lady." She folded her arms across her chest.

"Aunt Ruth, you just had some stranger come to your door, say he was on a quest with a wizard, a dwarf, and a warrior girl. *And you let them sleep in the barn.* Plus, you're dressed in a gown and wearing a tiara."

"Your point?"

"Well, it sounds crazy."

"I'm perfectly sane, Allan. Believe that and leave the rest alone."

I reached out to hold her hand. I wanted to be understanding and comforting, if she would let me. That's when the old cow bell started clanging in the yard.

"Shit!" Aunt Ruth exclaimed and jumped up from the table. She ran out into the living room. I followed.

She held the curtains back and peered out the window. I joined her, looking out into the yard. The sun had set some time ago, and fog had started to collect in the yard. Which was really odd since we weren't really near any rivers or water.

"Aunt Ruth, what's going on?"

"We're about to be attacked by Dark Forces," she said.

I could hear the capital D and capital F in her voice. And then the first one popped into view in the yard.

It looked like a man. Or an ape. Or something in between that had been squeezed into an old kettle stove. I realized it was supposed to be armor of some sort. The hairy ape-man held a huge club and bellowed as he trudged forward. Behind him, a second apparition solidified. It looked even less like a man. It hunched forward, and had large spikes protruding from its spine. It held a mace of some sort in its scaly hand. That was when I finally started to think that Aunt Ruth might not be crazy.

"They're going to head for the barn after the heroes. We have to help them. Come on," Aunt Ruth ordered.

"Help them?" I couldn't imagine what I could do that could help.

Aunt Ruth darted back into the kitchen and flung open

the pantry. She felt along the side of rack of canned goods and the whole shelf swung out revealing a secret closet. *Aunt Ruth had a secret closet.* I felt like the whole world had gone insane.

"Here," she said, and handed me a slightly rusted crossbow.

I held its weight in my hands and then she thrust a leather pouch containing the arrow-like bolts at me.

"What should I do with this?" I asked.

"Fire it at the monsters, Allan."

"What? Are you crazy? I could kill someone!"

"That would be the point, yes," she said as she continued to root around in the closet. She finally came out holding a battered disc of metal and a sword. "It's been awhile since I used these," she said, and swung the sword in an arc. It sliced right through a can of creamed corn.

"Where did this stuff come from?" I was close to screaming.

"Oh, different questers have left them behind over the years, either as gifts or toss offs. Okay, follow me," she said. Then, brandishing her sword, she strode across the kitchen towards the screen door that led out into the yard. Did she just say over the years?

"Aunt Ruth, wait," I said.

She paused long enough for me to catch up.

"Are you serious? You really want me to fire this thing at, at those things?!"

She nodded. "Don't worry, dear, it's enchanted. It doesn't miss no matter how bad your shot."

"But, that's not what I meant, I mean those things. . ."

My words fell on deaf ears as she threw open the screen door, waved her sword, and ran off towards the barn. I did the only thing I could. I followed.

A full moon and Aunt Ruth's back house light illuminated the yard and glinted off a variety of metal weapons and armor. Already the earlier group had come out of the barn, wielding their own weapons as they met the hoard rushing them. Hykar gave out a war cry and charged into the mass of monsters.

Not From Around Here, Are You?

Kalyxta had strung her bow and I could hear the twang of the string. I thought I saw the hammer rise and fall. One of the monsters dropped with an arrow protruding from his chest. What the hell were these people doing?

Aunt Ruth was almost to the edge of the Dark Forces. She swung her sword and the ape guy's long spear-like weapon was cut in half. He held it before him, staring at it, then let out a bellow and lifted the half he still held up above his head. I knew what he was going to do. He was going to bring it down on Aunt Ruth's head.

I swung the crossbow towards him and squeezed the trigger. I felt a slight recoil and then looked to the ape guy. The bolt was in his heart. He blinked once and toppled over.

Oh dear God, what had I done?

Aunt Ruth seemed unfazed, however, and continued to hack her way through the monsters. I reloaded the crossbow and watched her back. I fired four more times before I saw Zeron suddenly appear in the doorway of the barn.

"Demons! Dark creations! You will no longer sully the Haven of the Green Lady," he yelled. Then he held up his staff in his right hand. "Salanzalla!" he shouted into the night. Immediately, orange lightning erupted from his staff, streaking out among the Dark Forces. They screamed in a variety of ways, from shrieks to bellows. I nearly dropped the crossbow. It wouldn't have mattered if I had or not. None of the creatures were left standing.

The questers stood, surveying the carnage. Kalyxta started going through the remains, retrieving her arrows. Aunt Ruth panted a little from her exertions and her long sleeves had gore on them that I didn't want to really think about. Otherwise, she seemed to be fine, possibly even exhilarated.

I think I was still in shock.

Hykar approached Aunt Ruth. "Milady, we thank you for your assistance and beg your pardon for bringing such filth into your domain."

"My dear Hykar, I regret that my domain was not the haven I promised you. But fear not, Master Zeron and I will assure you that no one else disturbs your rest. I will see you in the morning and provide some aid in your quest."

"My thanks again, milady," he said, bowing his head.

I felt a small tug on my shirt sleeve. I swung about, trying to use the crossbow as a club. Kalyxta jumped out of the way.

"My pardons, milord. I just wanted to return these to you."

She held out her hand and I stared at it for several seconds before putting my own hand out. She dropped the five crossbow bolts into my palm. Some of them felt wet and sticky. *You will not vomit, you will not vomit,* I told myself.

Kalyxta hadn't moved and I realized that she was waiting for something.

"Um, thank you. Um, you're a really good shot."

She lowered her head and blushed slightly. It was very attractive.

"Thank you, milord."

"You're welcome."

I continued to stare at her when I heard Hyrak call out, "Come, Kalyxta, we will all need our rest come morrow."

She glanced at me, smiled, and then walked back to the barn. I watched all her all the way, at least until Aunt Ruth grabbed me on her way back into the house.

"C'mon, Romeo, we need to talk."

Aunt Ruth and I sat the table, sipping hot chocolate. I would have preferred something stronger, but the only thing alcoholic she had in the house was mead. I didn't have the appetite for that.

"So, you've been the Green Lady for thirty-four years?" I was finally willing to believe that the people in the barn were not members of a roleplaying group. For one, if I were to believe that, I had killed several people tonight with an enchanted crossbow. And it had to be enchanted or I never would have hit them. But that Aunt Ruth had been doing this longer than I had been alive? That was hard to imagine.

"Yes, I took over from my Aunt Judy. Her cousin Peter had been in charge before that."

Not From Around Here, Are You?

"How long has our family been doing this?"

Aunt Ruth took a sip of her hot chocolate. "I think Peter was the first. Before that, I believe the Haven was in New Zealand."

"It moves?" How much did she expect me to absorb in just one night?

"Perhaps, I can help explain?" came a deep voice.

I turned around and Zeron stood at the screen door, his staff still in one hand.

Aunt Ruth beamed to see him and got up to let him in. He strode in (I don't think he could have just simply walked anywhere) and took a seat at the table. Aunt Ruth got up and went to the refrigerator and came back with a Diet Coke. Zeron's eyes gleamed as he took the can, pulled the tab, and then took a long swig. "Ambrosia," he said softly.

Then, his hand still curled around the can, he looked over at me.

"The Haven of the Green Lady, or sometimes the Green Lord, and even once, the Green Dolphin, is a mystical place that has its own rules. Ages ago, it existed solely in my world, but during a particular nasty magical war, the Great Powers moved it to your dimension. In addition, they put further enchantment on it so that it moves from place, sometimes in just a few years time, in other cases, decades or more. It has been here in its current location for over seven decades. The longest it has been in one place, as far as I know."

I was curious. "Why so long here?"

Zeron shrugged. "I can't be positive since the original spell was cast millennia ago, but I suspect it stays the longest where it has the best guardians. Your family has provided three strong caretakers. Whether it provides a fourth, remains to be seen."

He stared at me when he said that. It took a minute for the implications to set in.

"A fourth?"

I turned to Aunt Ruth. She was staring at the table.

"What do you mean a fourth?"

Aunt Ruth sighed and looked up, meeting my eyes. "It's

204

time for me to pass the mantle on, Allan. I'm old and tired and . . ." she looked at Zeron and smiled, ". . .and I want to have a few years left to enjoy my retirement."

The wizard met her gaze and the connection between them could not be missed. But then Aunt Ruth turned back to me. "Zeron and I have been thinking hard about this, Allan. The omens in his world have all indicated that a passing of the guardian was about to occur. I was looking forward to it, and was trying to figure out which one of the family was going to show up and claim it. I didn't think it would be you."

I could hear the disappointment in her voice. It felt like one of the bolts from the crossbow in my chest. Except for no blood or dying of course. But still it hurt. I never wanted her to be disappointed in me.

"Aunt Ruth, I . . . well, I'm sorry. I, hell, I made a mistake and I'm sorry. But I understand. Someone else would be better."

I met her eyes and couldn't tell what she was thinking. Finally, she gave a small smile. "We'll see. I still have a few days to decide. Zeron has to take this group a little further along on their quest, after I give them their quest object."

"Quest object? What's that?"

"You'll see in the morning. Now, we all need to go to bed. Allan, you can take the guest bedroom."

The two of them stayed seated at the table and I took the hint. I stood and said good night and went up to the guest room. I plopped down on the bed, sure I would never sleep with all the stuff going through my head, but I soon felt myself yawning and my eyes growing heavy. Then a terrible thought hit me. Had Aunt Ruth put something in the cocoa? I would never have thought so but then, I would never have believed anything that had happened tonight. Would I even remember the night? That was my last thought as I fell asleep.

"Allan? Wake up, the questers will be leaving soon."

My eyes snapped open and I looked at Aunt Ruth and remembered everything from the night before. I felt so relieved. She hadn't drugged me and she trusted me to remember what had happened.

"Come on, get up and come with me."

I blinked a few times and got out of the bed. Aunt Ruth was already dressed and headed out the door. She was wearing another green dress, though no tiara this time. I followed her down the stairs and into the garage. She went to a cabinet and opened it. Inside were boxes of green glow sticks. She took one out.

"That's the quest object?"

She grinned. "Yeah. I buy them wholesale. The green light of the Haven to carry with you. Used to just give them a flashlight. From what Zeron says, these work wonders in their world."

"Have you been in their world yet?" I asked.

She shook her head. "No, I haven't been able to cross over, though Zeron says I will when the time is right."

I reached for her free hand. "And you want to go?"

"Yes," she said, without hesitation.

"Then I'll be happy for you. And if you want, I will take on this job for you and I swear I will not disappoint you."

Her smile was bright and was reflected in her eyes. "I believe you, dear. Now, let's send this quest on its way."

Waiting

Scott Heile

The angel fish cut a path behind fake seaweed, turned at the glass and made its way to the front of the tank. Fins unfurled like a victory flag gave Martin a feeling the majestic creature had some sense of entitlement, being the only fish in the tank. On the bottom, a small crab scurried its way among the tiny orange pebbles, foraging for algae and bits of fish poop. Martin patiently waited for one of those little claws to reach up to clip off a bit of tail.

Damn popinjay fish. He realized the comment might have been loud enough for someone else to hear and looked around to see if anyone else had noticed. The receptionist was busy finger popping on her computer while chatting on the phone simultaneously.

Martin knew she was called Carla but never uttered the name. In fact, he had never addressed her as anything. A second choice to the prom sort of pretty was off-putting to someone who had never been to a school dance. Even with the big nose and not so perfect skin. Martin could see himself married to Carla, but not talking to her the way real couples did.

Every relationship has its obstacles.

"Uuuuaaag!"

A guttural sound across the room belched forth from a stranger who definitely was not Mrs. Hemorrhoid. Rising to ask Carla about this stranger, Martin was iced with a glance. Something Mother would have done. He liked being on the same page with the receptionist even if it meant getting chided. The best couples could communicate without so much as a word. People in this business were trained to overlook certain behaviors seen as disruptive in another setting. Not so much trained as initiated.

Not From Around Here, Are You?

A cursory glance at the new guy revealed messy hair and mismatched socks. Both were blue, but one a slightly lighter shade. Martin scratched his leg, just a little bit.

"Haamph!" The man banged his temple twice and attempted to smooth his hair. Failure to check if anyone had noticed his actions was an insult. Where in the hell was Mrs. Hemorrhoid? She was a reliable woman, even with all the digging into that big butt of hers.

Martin lost his patience and shot over to the reception desk, too quick to receive another stern glance.

"Who is he?" A quiet whisper would not only keep the conversation private but make him suspicious.

"Sharing another client's information is discouraged, Mr. Willis.

"But where is Mrs. Hemorrhoid?"

"Who?" Carla asked in surprise.

"I mean, you know, the lady who's always here today, on Wednesday."

"I'm can't discuss any of this with you, Mr. Willis, and you know it. You wouldn't want me leaking all your personal information, would you?"

If they were married, she'd tell him everything while they spooned in bed and laughed at the guy's deficiencies just before falling asleep. Martin wondered how her hair smelled, wanted to kiss, despite the big nose. Not something Dr. Gilford would look favorably upon.

"Please have a seat. I'm sure it won't be long now."

The angel fish continued to circle, the way a tiger beats a thin, muddy path along its fence at the zoo. Being locked up does that to people. Makes them clink a pilfered spoon on cell bars all day until the paint is worn, stopping at the sound of footsteps.

Dr. Gilford had surely placed the tank in the waiting room to instill a sense of peace in their clients. It had the reverse effect.

"I'd get out of here if I were you my friend," he whispered to the fish.

Waiting

The crab seemed better off among the algae and orange rocks. Despite the fish waste.

"Gu . . . gu . . . gooog!" The guy began banging on his temple again, followed by a funny little foot kick.

The door opened and jarred Martin's wandering mind. It was Delivery Man.

"Hey Carla, what's up?" Without waiting for a response, he followed with, "Got anything today?"

"I wasn't expecting you for another hour. I need to get this sent, but I don't have enough packing material." She pouted.

"Well I'm sure we can figure out something." He leaned in slightly on her desk making sure to expose his biceps. "For one of my favorite clients."

"Are those new tattoos?"

"They're matching tribal designs. Picked them out myself."

Carla smiled and ran her fingers over the flexed muscle. "I bet it hurt."

"Naw. How 'bout I finish the rest of the building and come back when you're ready for me." Flashing his unnaturally white teeth to Martin, he said, "What's up, chief?"

"That's so sweet. I have to go buy some bubble wrap and tape so it might be a little while." She laughed nervously and teased her long brown hair.

"No problema." Delivery Man turned his two-wheeler towards the door. "You're gonna' owe me though."

Engrossed in the soap opera, Martin had forgotten the new guy whose hand fumbled in a coat pocket. A faint but familiar sound jumped the gap of patterned carpet and glass tables to tickle his eardrums. It was a pill bottle.

Without warning, this interloper, who had no clue how things ran in Doctor Gilford's office, looked at him. What was he thinking? Was he going to get up and walk over next? It was a clear invasion of personal privacy and enough to enrage a person.

Carla hadn't noticed, being so busy with the package. The fish on the other hand, had sensed tension and darted to the back of the tank. If only he were privy to all the juicy drama that fish had seen. Suddenly, and while still staring at Martin, the man shook his head so violently it moved the whole couch back and forth, a mini neurotic earthquake.

Carla looked at her watch, picked up the phone and spoke a few words into the mouthpiece. Standing and carefully smoothing a diaphanous skirt, she walked over to the man. He hoped she would tell the guy to shut up.

Martin enjoyed the glow of her tanned legs as she bent slightly to speak. Her tone was calm and quiet, and the guy was smiling. Why the hell did she have to get that close? Was she saying something nasty about him? A quick little quip to demean, help the jerk feel superior. Damn! Why couldn't he hear?

She stood and walked across the room. He felt like ignoring her for going to the other guy first. When she drew near, he smelled roses, or lilacs, something flowery. Pleasant as it was, the scent made him slide back a little.

"Mr. Willis, I need to step out for a few minutes. Should be back before Dr. Gilford is ready for you. You have the water cooler if you need it, and of course, the magazines."

Oh God, Martin thought, *the damn magazines*.

"What about 'hurky jerky' over there?" he asked.

"We discourage labels, you know that."

"No, I mean is he here for my doctor also?" Martin tried not to be too obvious in the question. Carla bit her lip.

"He's waiting for Doctor Palmer, Mr. Willis. I'm sure he'll keep to himself."

"Buuuooaag!"

The guy's breath was clearly cutting a swath of nasal destruction through the room.

"How can I be comfortable in a room full of spasms and shrieks?" He spoke loud enough for the guy to hear and hoped it would hammer the point home. There was no sense asking him directly when it could be done through Carla.

"You can get over that for me, can't you? Just try to read an article." She motioned to the spread of ladies magazines and one Field and Stream on the coffee table.

"It won't be long until you see the doctor, so please don't

go into his office on your own." She raised her eyebrows.

"I explained that a hundred times already. It sounded like he called me in there." Martin wondered if he would ever live down such a tiny mistake.

He began scratching again, but stopped when she looked at the leg.

"Thank you so much," she added on her way out.

He rethought his marriage to Carla, nice legs and all.

Now it was just the two of them, and the fish and crab. New Guy was wringing his hands under his coat. He hoped it was just hand wringing. *Who knows what someone like that has in his pocket?*

The man suddenly stood up, opened his mouth wide and let out a loud "Gheeeee!"

Head flung up and mouth open wide like a baby bird, he punched his temple three times. Familiar feelings welled in Martin's gut, and he rapped on his own forehead with his open hand in a mocking way. *This jerk isn't going to intimidate me.*

The guy's T-shirt was visible through his open coat. It read: THERE'S ONE TOO MANY OF US HERE RIGHT NOW AND I THINK IT'S YOU

Who would have the audacity to wear that to a doctor's office? There was no limit to the depth of a needy ego. Dr. Gilford would see right through him.

Pushing magazines aside on the glass tabletop, Martin kept an eye on his counterpart. Carla's perfume still hung in the air. He wondered if any magazines might have been hers. The address boxes had been blacked out.

'Angel' suddenly changed direction, its fins curling back on themselves like the ribbons of a gymnast in that Olympic sport. The fish was very likely trying to mess with the little crab. As if crapping on it several times a day wasn't enough.

New Guy was fumbling around in his pocket again, and

like the fish, making a spectacle of himself.

"Uuuuuaaag!"

Itching returned, stronger this time. Rubbing against the aluminum table frame helped scratching at the scabs, but was far too smooth to provide any real relief. He needed a nice hard edge to get in there good.

While walking to the water cooler, Martin tried not to scratch his calf in the spot, but dear God it was bad. And right before he was to see Gilford. He knew the doctor would ask to see first thing. Maybe just rubbing it a little would manage the problem. The fish tank stand caught his eye. It had a sharp wooden corner like the one on the china cabinet in mother's house. He hadn't seen that cabinet or his mother in over four months.

The angled wood provided instant relief. His eyes strained to check on New Guy, who appeared to be minding his own business. But looks could be deceiving. Most people were way too sneaky to be caught.

A ripping sound startled Martin. The stand's flimsy laminate had torn and a large piece was hanging toward the floor.

A sick feeling ran through him as he tried to fix the laminate. He realized his hand was scratching hard and the scabs were bleeding. With socks pulled high, he stomped his leg down in hopes the itching would stop. Dark colors helped mask the scratches and blood even in tennis shoes. Martin continued to the water cooler, not because he wanted a drink, but because the man might otherwise wonder what he was doing.

New Guy stood and Martin prepared himself for any accusations which might be leveled. The corner was already ripped and he had only brushed against it as far as anybody knew. What was the word of a stranger against his, a six year patient?

Back at the couch but not seated, he carefully listened with back turned to the stranger. If the guy approached, he would hear, and deal with it any way necessary. There was shuffling and a rattle, but nothing to cause concern. It might have been another bothersome tactic.

"Oooooaahhhhhh"

This sound was more muffled than usual. Shortly after, gurgling and coughing, unlike previous instances. A tense moment of silence was followed by a thump. Martin turned, half expecting to see the man coming at him in a rage, but not expecting at all to see the guy crumpled in a pile in front of the couch. Hesitating in case it was a ploy, he could see the body convulsing in a way a person just couldn't fake. With caution he drew near the man.

"Hey, bud?"

Wanting to touch, but with the memory of too many zombie movies in his head, it was better to keep hands off.

"C'mon, man, get up."

Martin looked for something with which to poke the quieted body. He grabbed a net hanging from the fish tank and gently pressed it into the man's leg and saw no reaction. There would be no check for breathing. No way, no how. He pushed with the tip of his shoe. Still no movement, so he kicked the guy a little.

Martin started to pace in a circle as he tried to think of what to do. He couldn't let anyone see what had happened. They might suspect him. Maybe he should call 911. 'That's all I need, the cops asking me questions.'

On his knees he rolled the guy under the couch, carefully using his own coat sleeves to keep from actually touching skin. As the body flopped over, Martin glimpsed the pale, strained face. 'Oh God, what if this freak wakes up while I'm rolling him?'

He managed to get most of the limp body hidden except for one very stubborn arm, which he managed to wedge under the guy's back. The stench of French fries was ruining the memory of Carla's delicate scent. A deep breath of fresh air was necessary. Something was needed to mask the body. The table with magazines was close. He pulled it over and put it against the couch, but pulled it away a little to avoid it looking suspicious.

One ladies magazine had fallen off the table and Martin put it under some others in an attempt to make the scene look as natural as possible.

The itch was back, and strong, but there was no time to lose concentration now. Martin's sock was stuck to his leg from the dried blood. It was useless to over-think the situation. Once he was in session with the doctor, New Guy (or perhaps Dead Guy) would become someone else's problem. Carla would know what to do. She had experience. He shifted his attention to the fish tank, but just as quickly decided to take one last survey of the room.

On the floor, in front of the table was a cell phone. He hurriedly walked the four steps and bent to pick up the evidence. Carla's voice could be heard just outside the door.

"I just need to finish packing and tape it up. Give me five more minutes."

He didn't have time to move the table again and couldn't just throw it in the trash. As the door opened, Martin quickly lifted the flaps of the box on Carla's desk and shoved the phone under some fancy wooden frames.

"I told you I'd be back before you went in. Just need a minute more in the back to get a label." She disappeared through a door which had the words 'Staff Only' clearly displayed.

The only loose end which remained was the fish net. At the tank, he could see the angel was quite disturbed. It was swimming erratically, practically accusing him. Exactly the kind of thing Gilford would spot. The toilet was the only proper place for a water breathing snitch. A few seconds of chasing with the net and he had it. Grabbing the slimy animal and returning the net to its hook, his ordeal was almost over.

With a sudden jerk of the handle, Delivery Guy walked in backwards carefully making sure the door didn't slam into his two-wheeler. In a panic, Martin slipped the fish in the pocket of his shirt.

"She's not back yet?" the white teeth chattered.

"No, not back yet."

Waiting

"I can see why she needs so much filler. This box is too big."

"Yeah, some boxes are like that." Martin wanted to tell him to get the hell away from the package, but stood motionless, putrid water soaking through to his chest.

Carla walked in and saw her package being eyed. "Hey nosey."

"You have too much extra space in here Carla. Use a twelve by twelve by six"

"I know it's big but it's all I have," she said in a teasing voice.

Why the hell was he using her name?

Bubble wrap was carefully folded around the frames as Martin held his breath. The phone rang as Carla was finishing the shipping label.

"No, I thought he was in your office, Dr. Palmer. No, sir, I had to step out for a minute. Yes, I'll try now. I have the number right here."

She keyed in something on the computer and asked, "Martin, did you see the other patient leave?"

"No, I didn't see a thing. I think I might have been in the bathroom or getting a drink or something."

The fish wriggled.

Dr. Gilford popped his head out of the office. "Ready, Martin?"

"Uhhhhhh."

"A problem?"

Carla explained the situation as she dialed the phone, prompting the doctor to exit his sanctuary. The fish flopped against confining fabric as it tried to breathe.

Seconds passed as days, and then...a reggae song faintly twittered from the sealed box.

The look on Delivery Guy's face was almost worth it. "What the hell?"

Pulling a letter opener from her desk, Carla began to open the package. She uncovered the cell phone.

"I saw him with this," she said, walking to the couch, "but

I don't remember that table being there."

The scream was inevitable. Delivery Guy pushed the glass and aluminum table aside with ease and rolled the body over.

"I think he's still alive."

Doctor Gilford looked squarely at Martin, reminiscent of his mother's 'O dear God, what have you done now' stares.

"Carla, get an ambulance." Without turning his head and in a half whisper he said, "And the police."

"What's all over your shirt, Martin?"

"Oh, this? I forgot all about it." He pulled the fish from his pocket, dropped it into the tank where it swam wildly to the bottom. Martin cleared his throat and tried to act casual.

Doctor Gilford just stared, until finally, the silence was too painful to bear.

"Considering all the progress we've made, doctor," said Martin. "I hope you don't consider this a relapse."

Subway Blackout 2003

Dori Van Luit

Everything stopped and it all went black Caught in a
casket far under ground Fear gripped at hearts
fiercely pounding Hands with white knuckles held the
straps tighter Breathing dense from the heat and the
stillness Stench of garlic and perspiration. Children
cried and some said prayers And they all thought
"Nine Eleven again?"
Then somehow they got the doors open and
one by one placed their feet on the tracks, down
the long and treacherous tunnel, making their
way, holding on in the dark, some with cigarette
lighters to lead them up the steep steps to light,
air and safety.
No riots—no looting—a few mild tempers flaring
When the power went on, life resumed as before.
The New Yorkers proved they were cool, and strong
and maybe cared just a bit for each other.

Originally published in Let the Robin Sing *SongBird
Publishing, 2003.*

The Visa

Jenny Engleka

I descended the jetway stairs, leaving the rusty TU-154 behind in the November chill of an Uzbek night. After I forced the quadruple stench of jet fuel, airplane bathroom, cigarette smoke and Old World body odor from my lungs, I paused to refill them, while a heavyset man in a faded, wide-lapelled suit scurried his family of four past me to get seats on the shuttle bus.

I was in no hurry to get anywhere. I would be here for the next two years.

Once I boarded the half-empty shuttle, I stood near the elderly, head-scarved woman—your classic babushka—from our flight. She had paced back and forth between three rows on the plane, serving and catering to her extended family, and was now on the bus doing the same. She nudged her grandchildren into the remaining seats, fretted over her daughter to feed the infant in tow while pushing the husband, who was busy lighting another cigarette, to stand closer to his family. We only needed a goat or a chicken or two and you had Borat's Caucasus Vacation.

The babushka was so busy prodding people into their seats, that when the bus suddenly jerked into motion, she didn't have one. Even though she was as close to a Weeble as human form could get, she needed to grab on to a strap or pole or she would fall over. I was hanging onto a leather overhead strap, swaying back and forth with the bus, when she dug in with an iron grip right below my armpit. At four feet something, that was as high as she got. She winced at me, half-apologetically, half-babushka, but I smiled at her anyway.

I hadn't even started and already they were suspicious.

* * *

218

The Visa

It was my first day at the interview window as a Junior Officer for the State Department, running the Consular Section of the U.S. Embassy in Tashkent, Uzbekistan. The Visa Lady for short. I stepped into the small booth and spotted the customized immigration by-laws and poverty income charts posted on my left, familiar from my training back in the U.S. A dull headache took hold.

Junior officers often got assigned running small, obscure posts in countries I couldn't have found on a map before language training. Or else they'd be sent off to the "Visa Factory" in Mexico City. One step above working at the DMV.

From day one in Consular training, I was terrified of being the unlucky officer to allow some future terrorist or serial killer into the U.S. The odds were minute, but in this post-9/11, 24/7 cable news world, I had nightmares of Inside Edition tracking me down.

My first gig in diplomacy. My feet were about to get wet.

That's why the Ambassador, with an arcane knowledge of all things Soviet, couldn't pass up doling out some advice.

"Don't let your guard down. Eighty percent of the people are lying to you when they come to your window. They all say they want to visit Disneyland or see a dying uncle, but really that uncle is planning to put them to work in his restaurant.

"Watch where they say they are visiting. The Armenians go to Glendale, California. The Lebanese go to Dearborn, Michigan. Lithuanians, Chicago. You know, I don't know where the Uzbeks go."

Neither did I.

The first applicant that approached my window in the visa waiting room had written down New York City.

"Hello . . . Mr. . . . . Karetov. How are you?" I asked in Russian.

He smiled. "Good morning," he answered back in the same.

He was a middle-aged man with Asian features, wearing an outdated blue suit with stains at the collar. I noticed he sweated a bit too much for the pleasant sixty-five degrees outside. It was probably good that I couldn't smell the other side of bullet-proof Plexiglas.

Along with his non-immigrant visa application, he presented me with his business card, a brochure of the "Rug Outlet" in Brooklyn, and a bank statement showing his personal savings at the equivalent of $1,300. That put him well above the average worker in Tashkent. But the card and the bank statement could have been printed for a small fee at a tiny kiosk next to the embassy's metro stop.

Or so I was told.

"Where are you going to in the U.S., Mr. Karetov?"

"Only to New York City. In the borough of Brooklyn." He sounded like he had been studying a map.

The picture of the store in the brochure looked legit. I rummaged through his passport looking for the telltale 214(b) symbol at the back of the passport that marked an applicant's refusal.

"214(b)" was the legalese in the Immigration and Nationality Act, in which Congress deemed anyone not overcoming satisfactory burden of sufficient ties to their home country, blah, blah, blah.

No 214(b) in the passport.

"So, how long will you be in New York City, Mr. Karetov?"

"One week. It is a long flight, yes."

"Have you done business with this store before?"

"No, I hope to make a strong contact."

According to his passport, he had entered New York four times since it was issued. That was a good sign. He kept coming back home.

"Have you done business with other rug shops, sir?"

"No, they said my rugs were too expensive. So now I try him on the picture." His pudgy, wrinkled index finger, with a slightly dyed-red hue, pointed at the smiling mustached man in the brochure.

"Thank you, Mr. Karetov. You may pick up your visa at the first window after 2 p.m." I placed his passport and application

The Visa

on top of the plastic "Yes" box on the cart to my right.

One down, thirteen more to go.

A busy day for Tashkent.

If this had been Mexico City, my fifteen colleagues and I would each have been through five applicants already with another ninety-five to go.

The next applicant was a young, Russian-looking man, who spoke to me in English. He had a form from INS approving his student visa to study violin at Oberlin College in Ohio. If he had brought his instrument with him, I could have asked him to perform for the waiting room, but that wouldn't have been necessary. Not necessary because his papers were legitimate, but it would have been enjoyable to listen to.

The next eight or nine applicants were textbook for me. Forged documents, unrealistic stories, or refusals in the passports from two years ago. Unlike other, better off countries, the $75 non-refundable visa fee was out of reach for average Uzbeks, but these guys tried anyway.

The most memorable of these was the young guy who said he was going to visit his sick grandfather.

"What hospital is your grandfather at?" I asked in Uzbek. He was young enough that he hadn't been forced to learn Russian.

He had handed me a suspicious letter from "Dr. Johnson" in spotty English, explaining the grandfather was "dead sick".

"He's, uh, at home. At his restaurant," he said.

"At his home or at a restaurant?"

"Restaurant."

"Well, how sick is he? What disease does he have? Dr. Johnson's letter doesn't say what disease he has."

There was a long pause and then held out his hands, shrugged his shoulders and let out a big laugh.

"I'm sorry," I said. "I have to refuse you under 214(b), Mr. Khudaybergenov."

I opened his passport to the back page and stamped the dreaded refusal as he nodded in agreement and smiled. "If you get proper documentation from the hospital and from your employer stating you will come home, you may come back."

At 11:45 a.m., the last applicant hurried to my window but put her head down as she handed me her passport, her application, and an invitation to attend a conference at the University of Central Florida.

Where had I seen her before? On the subway ride? I'd only been taking it for four days. Was she another regular commuter?

She recognized me too. She was a beautiful woman, with a classic Slavic look that stood out among the Asian majority.

"Hello, Ms . . . Golubov," I said in Uzbek. "Ms. Golubov, why are you going to the United States?"

She looked down again. "To Orlando. School of Applied Math and Science," she said from memorization.

Had she been another passenger on the plane? Maybe she traveled a lot. "What will you do at this conference, Ms. Golubov?"

"There is a math lecture, there." She pointed to the logo on the crisp piece of paper that had not been folded and probably had never seen an envelope.

"Do you study here at the University?"

"Yes, I study math." She looked down again and ruffled through the papers she had not given me.

Had I seen her at my apartment building?

That was it. I had seen her coming out of my neighbor's apartment, mop and bucket in hand. She was a maid. I remember being shocked to see such a striking face and lovely blond hair with that job. But this wasn't DC. She looked much more at home in the pale green business suit and slacks she was wearing.

Now I was sure she was lying. I should have refused her immediately.

Nicely, but immediately.

But I was a math major too until I took a break from college to get out and see the world. I came back to change majors to International Relations, which only whetted my appetite for more travel. I then headed to Germany and worked "under the table"

The Visa

as a nanny. In the ten months I was there, I walked every inch of the small town, learned the language, and fell in love with a German.

Technically it was illegal, but it felt like a rite of passage.

After checking those experiences off my list, I went back to the States.

What was her plan?

Thinking about Germany gave me a wonderful rush of nostalgia. I smiled at her before the next question as I recalled the taste of Bavarian pretzel rolls, fresh from the oven. Even though she most likely planned on being a maid to send back money, I didn't want to deny another's worldly adventure.

And we looked like each other, Svetlana and I. Her high cheek bones and fashion model's jaw line notwithstanding. I was sure there would be love affairs in her future in the U.S. I hoped at least one would be real love.

Would she really go for only a few years then come back?

I needed to refuse her, but I sensed her need to get out of her current situation.

Maybe it was my need twelve years ago.

"Ms. Golubov, our computers are down right now. Will you come back tomorrow?" I lied.

The Ambassador encouraged this—the stalling part, not the giving in to youthful adventures part. "You know when Lisa was in Yekaterinburg, it was full of Russian Mafia, and she knew this one guy was trouble. He was in the mob, but she didn't have anything solid to refuse him by. So she told him the computers were down and to please come back tomorrow. That night he got whacked. End of problem."

I should have refused her.

Later that evening, I knocked on the door where I had seen Svetlana. I knew the neighbors were a French couple, in which the man managed the newly-built Hotel Sofitel. I knew my questioning about Svetlana would not seem suspicious because I needed to hire my own maid.

"*Bonjour.* Oh, hello, welcome to Tashkent. I'm Sophie

Tripard." She had a sophisticated chestnut bob and coal-colored eyes. "You are replacing Mr. Urdahl, yes?" The stylish woman in her forties motioned me into her equally stylish apartment that was a skillful mix of antique and modern furniture and gorgeous, red Turkmen rugs.

"*Bonjour.* I'm Sue Olsen. *Enchante.* Nice to meet you." And it would also be nice to be invited to a cocktail party at their place. Their living/dining room, with several oversized couches, chaises and chairs-as-art, was ideal for entertaining.

After the initial round of where you're from, how long have you been a diplomat, and how do you like the city so far, we got to the essentials.

"The landlord said that you really like your housecleaner." I was hoping she would say Svetlana was the best and loved working for them.

"Oh yes, she's a sweet girl," she said. "But she just told me she's going back to her home town. I think she's trying to get away from her boyfriend. She was so agitated last time she was here."

"Why?"

"I'm not sure. I think the boyfriend is trouble." She paused and then took a deep breath. "I wish I could take her to Paris with me when we leave this spring. I think every young girl should get a chance to see the world, don't you?"

I nodded.

"I did that when I was twenty," she continued. "I was an au pair in New York and it was wonderful. I loved exploring Manhattan and all the boutiques and little cafes there. And my English is fluent, *oui*? I bet she would love Paris."

No doubt, if Sophie dressed Svetlana in Paris's finest, the two would make the Society pages in Paris Match.

"And she needs to get away from that boyfriend. But he has money, I think." She shook her head and rolled her eyes.

This is not what I wanted to hear.

But then she perked up, "Don't worry, Sue, it's easy to get another housecleaner. Svetlana is already our second. You know, it's a prized job to have here."

The Visa

"Yes," I nodded. I wished Svetlana didn't want to leave hers.

The next day, I adjusted the appointment schedule so Svetlana would be last. I could stew over her case while I interviewed the other applicants.

Beaten up by her boyfriend? She had to get away. If I reported him to the police, it would only be worse for her. Her personal welfare was at stake now.

"Hello, Ms. Golubov. Thank you for returning today."

Despite the outdated turquoise slacks and stained white tunic she was wearing, she still was stunning.

"May I see your application and paperwork? Do you have any other documents of supporting ties?"

Along with her passport, application and phony invitation from the university, she handed me a reference letter from Ms. Sophie Tripard. The date at the top was two months old, so it was likely that Sophie did not know of Svetlana's real plan. If I were to issue a visa, I didn't want anyone, especially Sophie, to think I could be influenced.

Only my conscience knew I could be influenced.

And my conscience reminded me that she needed to get away from the boyfriend.

"Thank you, Ms. Golubov. You may pick up your visa after 2 p.m. Enjoy the conference."

Not a great day for my diplomatic track record.

I vowed not to let any more personal connections interfere next time. No more saving stray puppies, because more were sure to come sniffing about.

I was glad I had not told Sophie I'd ever seen or asked for Svetlana's full name, so I could claim I didn't know it was Sophie's employee.

If it came up.

Perhaps Sophie knew all along, but she never talked about it.

Until four months later when Sophie and I had become

225

good friends. It was our typical late Saturday morning of chatting in her glamorous apartment, drinking the best café au lait that side of the Silk Road, that she blurted out the news.

"Sue, I have to tell you what I found out about my last maid? You should know about this for the visas." She hurried me in and forced me to sit down.

"My husband heard from his employees at Sofitel, that a bunch of girls from Samarkand were forced into a sex-ring in Manhattan. Samarkand's the town where Svetlana's from. I thought she was back there, but she really went to New York. Oh, it's terrible, yes."

My empty stomach seized up.

"They thought they were going to be maids at some hotel, but the police found out when one girl escaped and ran to the hospital. When she told the police where they were held, they found a dead body."

I should have refused her.

Sophie started to choke up, but I was already numb.

"It wasn't Svetlana, but all of the girls are gone now."

If only I'd refused her.

"Oh, Sue, now we don't know what's happened to Svetlana. You have to watch for any pretty girls that come from Samarkand. No matter what they say they're going to do, you've got to refuse them."

"Stray puppies," I mouthed, forgetting where I was.

"What?" she asked.

"I'll refuse them. Next time I will."

Finding Religion

Thomas Groh

It was cold outside, more than cold. The sun rose slowly, frosty and dim. Perhaps I saw the warm light inside, heard the reassuring roll of organ music and thought, *Why not? I can't go home, not with these impractical hands, these empty pockets.*

It was the holidays, almost Christmas. The church was always packed on Christmas and Easter. Catholic guilt explains a lot.

Last time I sat in church was ten years ago. It was one of those longish Easter masses set up like a play, where the congregation played the role of ill-tempered mob, hollering "Crucify Him!"

Uncle Martin was up on the carpet at the side lectern, solemn expression on his face as he delivered the parts of various Sanhedrin high priests, subtly altering his voice for each character. Up there smiling with his new teeth, wearing his blue suit, a silvery tie and those boots he always wore.

The year he ran for town council and lost.

I remember when the lady with the hat narrated one of the longer stretches and this big old crow *thunked* against the stained glass window and got stuck. I really remember the dull *thunk* and the dark silhouette of a big bird splayed and fluttering against the glass.

Then Uncle Martin's subdued chuckle amplified through the sound system.

A lot of folks proclaimed the discovery of profound meaning that morning. They realized some essential truth which they applied to their lives in fruitful way, helping them raise honor students, Junior Olympians and future astronauts. I wasn't one of them. Didn't raise one, didn't become one.

Might explain why I'd been away so long. Divine

providence has limits.

That's what I thought when the old ladies shambled in out of the snow, one after the other, swaying hump-backed in their faded woolens. They placed each foot carefully on the slick tiles, then plodded forward cautiously, one foot after the other like a parade of elephants.

Some lingered in the back, lighting prayer candles, sharing holiday greetings with old friends. Then hunched beneath quilted overcoats, assorted wraps, elaborate knotted scarves and dark ropey frocks, they stomped slush from their boots and filed into the pews.

Heads down, they maintained a respectful separation. They filled the church back to front, settling onto the heavy oak benches in the same arrangement I'd observed last week, and the week before, perhaps going back twenty years.

The old women took care getting settled. They disentangled scarves and removed coarse, woven hats. They set aside shiny, beaded handbags and shucked wet outer garments, shaking and folding the bundles over the benches in front of them.

I'd come early and chose a folding chair along the wall against a heat register, a few feet up the aisle from the left side entrance, tucked neatly behind a large polished sculpture of Saint Dismas. The statue obstructed my view, but the metal register was still warm when I arrived, and I could imagine the glory of moist, super-heated air to come.

A few minutes before seven, a tall woman in white, conspicuously elegant and erect, glided through the side door behind me. Her pale face was smooth and flawless, rose-colored dots highlighting the balls of powdered cheeks. Her white, fur-lined coat draped nearly to the ground. Her jeweled handbag glistened and her eyes sparkled in the dim light. The corners of her mouth drew into a frown as she surveyed the crowd to discover the church nearly full.

Two slouch-backed boys, wearing canvas robes too short to hide ridiculous gym shoes, entered and began lighting the thick candles about the altar.

Finding Religion

The Woman in White glanced at me, sniffed disdainfully, then swooshed past and slid into the bench across the aisle. She was right; I shouldn't be there. She was no less beautiful for her observation.

At two minutes past seven, an anxious jangling of bells signaled the start of Mass and a brightly robed priest emerged from an anteroom at the rear of the church. He was a bear of a man with a shocking head of rusty hair and a shaggy beard to match.

The congregation rose as the organ rolled into a familiar holiday song. The priest's baritone thundered over the crowd as he proceeded up the center aisle. Mounting the steps to the altar, he swept his gaze over the stooped congregation, compelling old ladies to stand taller, sing louder.

I knew the melody though not the words, and so I remained seated, humming quietly, resisting the impulse to withdraw further into the shadows.

The song faded and the priest began. *May the Lord be with you.*

And also with you, we intoned. Just like I'd never been away.

I know I don't need to explain the significance of this day. . . .

As he explained the significance of the day, someone entered through the side door. Icy tendrils of air rushed over the marble floor and up my pants leg as a short, stocky woman clomped in. My irrepressible sneeze was sudden, powerful and loud. Unsettled, the Woman in White turned vaguely in my direction, then drew her narrow shoulders together in a controlled shiver.

"Bless you," the solid old gal whispered. She laid her hand on my shoulder as she hustled past. A cluster of elongated skin tags dangled from her eyelid. She favored me with a wink.

"Forgive me," she said, burling into a pew, stepping on toes, squeezing past the Woman in White. "I'm so sorry," she whispered. Her overstuffed handbag, a woven wicker affair complete with a dangling sunflower, had snagged on the shawl of the Woman in White.

I confess to Almighty God . . . the priest said.

The stocky woman brought a warm garlicky grandmothery smell with her, a smell of old sweat on yesterday's clothes and steam rising from a pot of boiling potatoes.

. . .the Lord is good and righteous, revealing the way to those who wander . . . he said.

The Woman in White smelled her, too, and wrinkled her elegant nose before turning away.

. . .We have become like unclean people, our good deeds like polluted rags. . .

The stocky woman shook out of her coat and noisily unburdened her bundles, making a pile on the bench between herself and the Woman in White. She removed a black-beaded rosary from her wicker bag and closed her eyes to silently pray.

. . .Whoever has two cloaks should share with the person who has none. And whoever has food should do likewise . . .

My stomach grumbled noisily, causing the old Woman in White to turn again in my direction. I dropped my head and hunched forward; nothing solid in my belly since rice and beans yesterday. Soon, with the heat pouring from the register, hungry and tired, I dozed.

I was a child, just four or five, and it was Christmastime. Large multi-colored lights were strung loosely from the gutter outside my window and snow was falling. Something had woken me. Tat-tat-tat. Tat-tat-tat. Several black birds gathered on my window sill, pecking at their bright reflections in the glass. Their eyes were blacker than the night, and sparkled with a deep intensity as they attacked the glass. Tat-tat-tat. One bird, larger than the rest, was not pecking the glass, but was looking straight at me. Abruptly, he squawked and swooped away. The other birds went silent, kicking and scratching in the snow. They scattered as the larger one shot out of the night and crashed through my window.

I woke in a panic, worried I've missed my opportunity. My last good chance for redemption! But no, thank God! The old women were just beginning to rise and file into the center aisle, shambling up to the altar and its grizzled bear-priest. Their singing was out of step, croaky and woefully off key. But together, as a group their song was somehow beautiful and melodious.

They flowed up the center aisle, received the Body of Christ on their tongues, crossed themselves, then with heads bowed, spilled out along the marble rail and reclaimed their seats from the outside aisle. The first row emptied, then the second, on back. Heavy oaken kneelers, which had clashed and clunked on the floor tiles for half an hour, were now lowered reverently into place as the stooped women knelt to pray.

The Woman in White straightened her hat, preparing to rise. She glanced in my direction, wrinkled her nose then leaned to whisper something to the woman in front of her. Then she set her feet and rose straight up. She arranged her gold-beaded handbag out of harm's way, retrieved a hymnal and with her perfectly pitched voice took up the song and proceeded toward the center. She worked her way slowly to the center aisle, bright red nails trailing over the back of the pew, gold lamé shoes stepping lightly, narrow hips rocking subtly beneath the fleecy shawl.

Forgive me, Lord!

My left arm had gone numb, tingly. I flexed and unflexed my fingers, preparing to rise as their row emptied. I was trembling. My heart thumped in my chest and I was gooseflesh from head to toe. As the song reached crescendo, I found myself singing, singing loudly: *"Joy to the world! The Lord is come: Let earth receive her King! Da Da Da Da Da Da-ahhh. . ."*

Forgive me!

Quietly, I rose and slid behind the last bench as it emptied. I scooped up the gold-beaded bag and shoved it deep into my coat pocket.

". . .and heaven and nature sing, and heaven and nature sing . . . Da Da Da Da. . ."

Passing behind the pew, my arm dipped instinctively and grabbed another handbag, then another, and another, moving down the line. The purses were light, flimsy, practically empty, and I easily looped several over my wrist. Six bags, seven, as I traversed the center aisle toward the far door, the crimson Exit light glowing overhead.

Forgive me!

". . .*Repeat the sounding joy, repeat the sounding joy, repee-eet, repee-eet the sounding joy. . .*"

At the front of church, the massive priest was radiant, bathed in candlelight, as the double line of old women shuffled forward with eyes pinched, tongues unfurled and extended in anticipation.

As I passed behind the pew on the opposite side, my left arm dipped rhythmically, securing more bags. Hastily concealed beneath a shabby pea coat, the black leather purse made eight, the light blue clutch the color of the morning sky found its way into my pocket. Nine!

"*. . .No more let the sin and sorrows grow, nor thorns infest the ground . . . Da Da Da Da Da Da. . . .*"

My skin was flushed and tingly, my hair stood on end as the organ pulsed and thrummed. Ten bags, eleven, twelve!

I spared a final glance over my shoulder at the bulging wicker purse, its bright sunflower turned heavenward, before I burst through the door and into the light.

Colonization

(A science fiction poem mostly found in a flower catalog.)

P. Andrew Miller

Starblazers,
the disease resistant Darwin Hybrids make a spectacular
showing:
Violet Queen with burgundy eyes
Muriel's dark mysterious color,
violet blue with a crystalline purple fringe.
Starblazers,
shipped in special climate controlled containers,
strong, long lasting and disease resistant,
perfect for naturalizing.
These hardy wonders
will arrive
at the first hint of spring
in fantastic red blooms outlined in white blaze.

Earth—An Immorality Play
(a dialog on life, birth and other disasters)

Carl Morris

The couple settled into comfortable chairs at the fashionably clandestine cabaret.

The man, tall and slender, carried the imprint of dominance. His skin was smooth, fine grained, old ivory white. A sprinkling of gray peppered his hair and a few betraying crow's feet accented eyes that were ten thousand years old.

The lady, Senator Alyson Brandt Copers, mid forties, purveyor of currently popular causes, blinked and scanned the dimly lighted loft. Smoke-haloed, paper lanterns, like miniature Saturns, orbited above small tables circling a postage stamp dance floor. Most occupants held cigarettes, inhaling the smoke, seeking the exhilaration of lungs absorbing another nicotine hit.

Scantily-clad beauties, canvassing the room, quietly hawked illegal cigarettes from their trays.

The underground Smoke-Easy, stashed on the third floor of an apparently deserted warehouse, was a throwback to the nineteen-twenties, an era too remote to be remembered, but the nostalgic decor was based on fact. As Santayana wrote, "Those who forget history are doomed to repeat it."

Executive types puffed rare Cuban cigars. Several men stacked burned matches after lighting their pipes. Most tables held drinks, though the primary purpose for attending this illicit bistro was the inhalation of the great god nicotine.

Alyson turned to her companion. She was not aware of how or when she had met him, unsure of why she had accompanied him here. "You're a lobbyist." She turned away. "I do not talk to lobbyists. Who are you? Why did you bring me here?"

"My name is Messenger. I lobby for no one you know."

"I don't believe you."

"Surely you were aware of these nicotine dens."

"I should not be seen here. This place is illegal."

"Senator Copers, you lead the People First zealots. You rammed the smoking ban through Congress. You precipitated the birth of these places. I hope to reveal that the enjoyment of life sometimes precludes the prerequisites of political correctness."

"P.C. has nothing to do with it."

"Professional meddlers such as yourself forced seat belts on the masses."

"Seat belts save lives."

"You helped ban assault weapons."

"To save more lives."

"You passed legislation to abolish smoking, and drove smokers underground."

"I make no apologies. I am proud of that."

"Now you have proposed a bill to outlaw fast food enterprises distributing high-cholesterol food."

"A law for the people's own good," the senator protested.

"You true believers are bent on protecting and saving people who have no desire to be saved or protected. You call it humanitarian. We call it meddling. The function of government is protecting citizens from each other. It has no right of intrusion, no prerogative to save anyone from himself."

"The tobacco industry was exposed," said Alyson. "The F.D.A. proved nicotine an addictive drug. I make no apologies."

"Who did not know?"

"We have saved people's lives."

"There was money to be made. People were pressured into thinking they had been duped into smoking those terrible cancer sticks and coffin nails they inhaled of their own volition. Lawyers oozed from the slime, suing in their name. Ignorance was bartered for innocence. No one accepted responsibility for his actions."

"You make light of it," complained the senator. "Cigarettes

kill people."

The man smiled. "Some quote Andy Rooney from your so-called enlightenment period, "Cigarettes don't kill people, smoking cigarettes kills people."

"That's like saying seat belts do not save lives."

"They don't. Fastening seat belts saves lives, sometimes. Sometimes a fastened seat belt may kill you," said Messenger.

"That's air bags. Some air bags kill children," admitted the senator.

"And smaller adults."

"We should abandon lifesavers because, sometimes, they do not work?"

"You should abandon them because they sometimes do."

"I suppose you would allow everyone a gun. You're mad."

"Guns do not kill people, pointed guns kill people."

"If there were no guns to point, you'd need knives for the killing," said Alyson, triumphantly. "It's been proven that. . ."

Messenger smiled. "It's a pity you latter day geniuses have not recognized that unsafe sex makes mothers."

"I talk about people dying. You poke fun."

"There is too much emphasis on the saving of lives on an overcrowded planet."

"That's crazy!"

"I'm talking sense. Zealots out there crusade to save lives while the human race screws this planet into oblivion. You do nothing to solve the problem."

"You're talking blasphemy."

The man laughed bitterly. "You allow religious lunatics to picket birth control institutions and abortion clinics. Does no one recognize that the most virulent disease on this planet is pregnancy? The blind prophets lead those who refuse to see. They rally against any vaccine, any method that can ease the population plague. They preach sacredness of life and make living a sentence served in misery rather than a gift. A higher birthrate translates, always, to increased poverty."

"That's anti-Christian."

The man shook his head sadly. "Pro-sanity."

"Some hold every life is precious."

"Not one condemned to hopelessness. For votes, you have aligned with fanatics, true believers who would kill those not bending to their beliefs."

"How dare you call motherhood a plague?"

"A virulent scourge infesting the world."

"Liar!"

"Every male a carrier and every female of child-bearing age a potential victim."

"You are preposterous."

"I offer a final opportunity to stop this insignificant outpost from sinking into the slime of man's seed he spewed indiscriminately."

"That's sickening."

"The wail of a hundred million hungry is sung every night."

"Then the more fortunate must find a way to feed them."

"Each succeeding generation breeds more hungry mouths to share fewer resources."

"Science always finds a solution."

"Your planet drowns in pollution. It is buried in its own garbage."

"We can colonize space. God will provide."

"So more humans may pollute the Universe?"

Alyson buried her face in her hands. "You confuse me. You question everything we have been taught."

"You were taught wrongly."

"You are saying that my life has been a lie?"

Messenger appeared weary. "The time has passed for erasing foolish mistakes. It is time to replenish the earth."

"You make very cruel jokes."

"Has it occurred to you," Messenger asked, "that the human species has reached a dead end? Man cheats the worms with embalming, caskets, burial vaults. He befouls perfection, spoils the air, ruins the soil, pollutes the water. He has ripped raw metals from the ground and burned the fossils hidden beneath it."

"We will find solutions," breathed Alyson. "We always

have."

"I recall an ancient legend. Ideally conceived beings were settled in a flawless garden."

"Eden?"

"They grew restless in perfection and. . ."

"They found themselves naked. . ."

". . .they discovered that, in joining, they became more than themselves."

". . . and the serpent came between them?"

"The serpent was the appendage of man."

Alyson frowned. "God was angry."

"The plague visited upon this world was pregnancy. The begats began. Also delivered on this earth were pestilence, disease, conflicts, wars, upheavals, disasters and death to keep this species in check. Over the millennia, man subdued all other beasts. He failed to master himself or his superstitions. He has bred himself to the brink of disaster. Man has fouled his nest."

"It was written, Man shall have dominion."

Messenger sighed. "A man wrote that."

"I do not believe you."

"You enact laws to protect your citizens from every possible danger."

"Isn't it humane to want more people to live longer, to have fuller lives? Cigarettes were killing them!"

"Tobacco brought solace and contentment to troubled souls. Besides, you have eliminated one more effective method of population control."

"People live longer, healthier lives without tobacco. More can enjoy old age."

"Length of life is little measure of its richness. A hungry girl in Bangladesh; what chance, what fulfillment do you see in her life or millions like it?"

"If she accepts Jesus as her savior. . . ."

"She will starve as a Christian."

"But she will be saved."

"For what? From what?"

"God's grace. His love."

238

"Will not buy a cup of good coffee."

"We must save the children. We must send more food."

"So that child matures to procreate before it starves. You perpetuate the problem and compound it."

"Life is precious. We must save the weak. It is the Christian thing to do."

"The concept is sadistic. Man has abandoned the natural law."

"He was given that power."

"He appropriated it."

"No!"

"The inevitable logic is: man does not make pollution, man is the pollution."

"We can make a beautiful earth."

"It was already an Eden."

"It can be again."

Messenger shook his head, sadly. "There is no problem on this perfect earth that cannot be solved by the elimination of the human animal."

"That's inhuman," cried the woman. "This illegal place will be closed tomorrow."

"It will not be here."

"You mean they can move this operation that quickly?"

"We're canceling." The strange man shrugged. "I wish it had turned out better."

"I've heard enough of your crap," said Alyson. "I'm leaving.

"There is no place for you to go. I am sorry." Messenger moved from the bar and was gone.

Messenger, Master of the Galaxy, stepped back. He watched a distant speck flicker once and fade. He foresaw a greener planet, inhabited by more intelligent life forms, ones not likely to overly reproduce. Dolphins perhaps.

Earth should be ready for a reseeding soon. Give or take ten million years.

Torn

Sujata Vishwas-Rekha Naik

I perch myself
between two spaces.
Memories I dare not
lose(for sanity):
Dusty streets choke,
pushing off noisy cars.
Noisier folks (quite
verbose,) on the streets
sing and dance
drums deafening. . .
Become caricatures
as the rain pours, drenching
the drunk un-drunk.
Festivities mask
want and rift. All gods
live together, in piece.
Then
Saffron rage.
Riot speaks subduing streets.
All this is home
once a nameless place
of forgotten embrace.
I'd tried to give it a face-lift
searching roots,
grasping denied cords. . .
Friendship
drowned anguish in chatter.
Friendship a deep river
ran for ever.

Torn

Perched,
I stand dazed
Don't belong to either space

'Til Death Do We Part

Charles Sroufe

With her car packed up, Linda looked around the house one last time and told me, "Robert, you are ungrateful, rude, and narcissistic," then bolted out the door.

She left me the house, the bills, two dollars and forty seven cents in the checking account, credit card debt from places I'd never heard of, a large pile of my dirty laundry on the floor, a days worth of dishes in the sink, and her two damn cats, Steamboat and Pudgy. I hated those cats!

Pudgy is very obese and can't jump up on the furniture anymore. She drinks water by dipping her paw into it and scooping it up to her mouth. She makes a puddle of water every time she takes a drink. Steamboat is a young stud who scratches everything that's stationary and attacks anybody who walks by him. He tries to jump Pudgy's bones every chance he can but gets nowhere with her. Then ten minutes later, they're grooming each other with their tongues. These cats drive me crazy but my wife couldn't be separated from them when she was home. So why did she leave them? Torture, I thought, or maybe she was planning to come back.

After a week went by with no phone calls, I guessed she wasn't coming back anytime soon.

Taking care of the cats was a pain. They were never let out because they would've run for sure. I kept them only because, if Linda did come back, and they were gone, she'd walk right back out the door for good along with an important part of my anatomy. So, when their water and food bowls were empty, I would refill them. I discovered a cheap brand of cat food at the discount store, none of that fancy crap my wife bought for them over the internet. But I damn sure wasn't going to interact with them. There'd be none of that touchy feely crap with me.

'Til Death Do We Part

One night after work I went upstairs to get my reading glasses from the dresser. I noticed a hole in the wall as soon as I entered the bedroom. It was a foot and a half above the floor and near the master bathroom. I stood there staring at the hole for a long time, my mind racing through reasons for its existence. Nothing came. I know I didn't do it accidentally. While I was standing there, Steamboat and Pudgy came upstairs and started sniffing and meowing at the hole.

How did that large hole get there? I started thinking the worst; somebody was in here casing the place, dropped one of their tools, maybe got scared, and then just split without stealing anything.

There had to be a rational explanation, but I couldn't think of one. Several bizarre and scary scenarios, from zombies in the basement to some neighborhood whacko running amok, went through my mind.

A week later, another hole appeared near the first one. I lost it and called the police. Their search of the house was thorough and found something I'd missed; the holes were made by the small repair hammer I keep on the bottom shelf of the linen closet. It still had paint and drywall dust on it.

The officer who asked me questions was not friendly. "Mr. Winslow, is this a game you're playing?"

"No."

"Did you do this to throw suspicion on your wife?"

"No."

"Mr. Winslow, are you on any medications? Are you seeing a doctor for any unresolved anger issues? Are you having a hard time at work?"

"No to all, officer. Someone is breaking into my house and doing this for god knows what reason. Will you please have an officer watch my house?"

"Yes, Mr. Winslow, we will."

Yeah, sure you will, I thought. After they left, I realized I should have given them the hammer. But, I was still a bit confused.

Walking in my sleep started sounding like a possibility,

but then, the holes appeared while I was at work. I took a few afternoons off hoping I would catch the culprit in the act. All I ever found was Steamboat, once, sniffing at the hole. When he stopped sniffing, I'd swear that he deliberately turned his head and looked up at my eyes.

The mystery was resolved when a freakish storm from the southwest blew into town. Hours of lightning and rain came that night. I usually sleep soundly through thunderstorms, but since that storm and the incident, I haven't been the same. I probably never will be, either. Who would believe me? I don't!

At two-thirty in the morning, a flash of lightning along with a tremendous clap of thunder woke me up. The lightning revealed Steamboat standing on his hind legs, next to my face, holding my little hammer over his head, claw side towards me. He was smiling and all those sharp little teeth looked deadly in the lightning. The sight scared me witless and I screamed at the top of my lungs. Screaming saved my life. It startled him and threw him off balance. The hammer went too far behind his head causing him to fall backwards off the bed.

When Steamboat landed on the floor, he and Pudgy made the strangest cat sounds I've ever heard and then they both ran downstairs to the front door and began meowing loudly. I was in shock, so I just went down and opened the door for them.

It's been over a week now and, at least twice, I know I've seen Steamboat grinning in the bushes near the house. I don't leave or enter the house when it's dark anymore, and I never turn off the lights when I'm inside. I thought about telling all this to the police and my best friend at work, but decided against it when I realized how ridiculous it would sound.

My life has become a mess. The theme from The Twilight Zone plays in my head and is now my new alarm clock. I've lost weight. My work is suffering and my boss asked me yesterday why I was staring so long at a blank computer screen. I've even thought of taking in a boarder for company, or for a witness. I keep hoping that whatever happened that night was just a nightmare and I will wake up from it sometime.

But, there is a problem with that idea. I found a new hole

today after work, considerably bigger than any Steamboat could have made, right next to my pillow. The bedside phone was off the hook and making an annoying sound. It reeked of stale cheap cat food. I can't help but think the worst—and the scariest.

Does Steamboat know how to use the phone?

Does he know Linda's phone number?

Intensive Care Waiting

Karen L. George

He paces in a black double-breasted suit,
white silk shirt, charcoal tie,
supple leather wing-tips
that shine money.
Dark circles, etched deep like tattoos,
underline his eyes.
His skin hints Sicilian, Egyptian.

A woman enters.
He enfolds her in his arms,
pats her back, loud,
as if to drown out her sobs.
Together they rock
in a solemn dance,
riding out the grief.

The same dark circles rim her eyes like kohl.
Is she his daughter, sister?
Her nails are French-manicured,
his moustache sumptuous with silver.
They hold their age close
like a hand of canasta.

The man lays out the sequence of events
like a pre-game strategy,
(the blackout, the fall, finding her,)
his voice creamy as caramel,
warm as wool.
His hands spread palm up
in his lap
to receive absolution and grace.

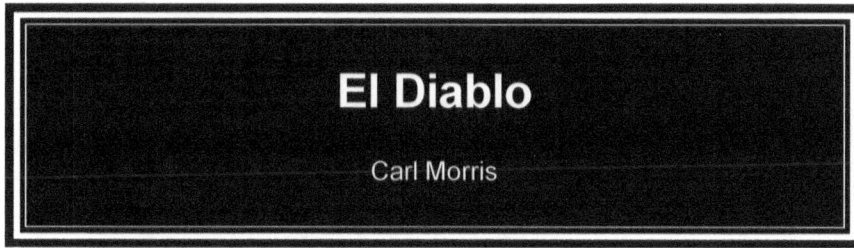

El Diablo

Carl Morris

"Señor?" The gaunt man had a battered glove tucked under his arm and a small valise in his right hand. He edged his way toward the man squatting outside the third base line. He looked too tired, too old to play ball.

Zack Savvy, manager of the Bradley Hornets, looked up into the cold, empty eyes of the ugliest man he had ever met.

"I play baseball." The strange man spoke softly.

"That's a rarity." Zack had seen them all in this baseball end of the world, this Mecca where has-beens, never-weres and never will-bes accumulated. The Bradley Hornets had lost their stingers.

"I pitch."

"Good for you."

His leathery skin, brown from years of exposure to a relentless sun ended in long fingers on large hands, claw-like, brushed too far along the seams of his patched jeans. His black hair showed little gray. His thin lips approached a smirk but he spoke humbly. "I wish to throw the baseball."

"I wish someone could throw the baseball," said Zack.

"I have a fast ball."

Zack's sore arm had worsened while pitching in triple A. His choices were: leave baseball and amount to something, or play-manage these misfits, rehabilitate his arm and work his way back from The West Texas League, Bradley Hornets. He had taken over as manager in mid-season, the previous year. This was Zack Savvy's end of the line. He pitched every fifth day on guts alone.

Zack nodded.

"A change-up also."

Clinton Eastwick, the Hornet's owner, died the year before

Not From Around Here, Are You?

Zack arrived. Minnie Eastwick, Clint's widow, had been a secretary in a Pontiac dealership before their marriage. He died at seventy-three, Minnie admitted to forty-seven. Minnie made the decisions. She fired the Hornet's general manager a week after the funeral.

After twenty faithful years, Minnie approached middle age a free woman. The Hornets became Minnie's personal playthings. She found even aging men more fun than a rowing machine or a Stairmaster. When Zack arrived, he pitched seven of their last ten victories. Attendance improved minimally. Minnie looked on Zack as a minor miracle.

Zack was handsome. He had almost made it to the majors. Minnie took Zack Savvy to her bed for the rest of the season and left managing the team to him.

Zack started at the interruption to his musings. "What did you say?"

"I have an excellent change up," said the stranger.

"Kids down here don't know the meaning of change-up."

In the second week of the season, the Hornets had a win and four losses under their belt. Though his arm was rested after the winter, Zack was not sure he could pitch all summer in the West Texas heat. He had roughnecked in the Beaumont oil fields during the off season and had been assured steady work if he stayed on. Were it not for Minnie, he would not have returned to Bradley.

The Hornets needed pitching. They needed a starting rotation. He needed an outfielder. The second base combination, comprised of the Tex Twins, was improving. What he needed most was somebody to get the ball across the plate. He eyed the gaunt man with the drooping mustache. Giving in to desperation Zack said, "What the hell. Go inside, tell them to give you a uniform."

Zack pondered talent. Jimmy Dean (no relation to Dizzy or Daffy) was a bright spot. He blocked the plate and handled off-speed pitches. He was smart and called a good game. He hit a curve on occasion. A problem was: his left leg was an inch shorter than his right. The kid said it was easier making the turn

El Diablo

at first. Some figured he needed a double to get that far. Zack wondered if his job hinged on managing, his pitching or a talent that kept his middle-aged boss moaning pleasurably in her four poster. Zack's back ached. The season had only begun.

"They call me El Diablo." The man looked thinner in a faded Hornet uniform. He came, he said, from somewhere south of Sonora and had spent time in a small Mexican League, but Zack found no record of him. "That's your name?"

"I am Lucifer Adlero," said the man, "but they call me. . ."

"El Diablo. You told me." Zack waved to the kid catcher. "Jimmy, warm up this guy. Let's see what he's got."

Jimmy Dean nodded, smiled, eager to please. "Right on."

Zack waved Mike Jackson in from the mound where he was serving up batting practice.

Jimmy dropped into his crouch. "Okay, Señor Pops," he yelled at the man old enough to be his father. "Let's see what you got. Put her there, Baby."

El Diablo nodded. He kicked the dirt and scratched his left foot on the dusty mound. He peered from beneath the brim of his cap. He nodded and lifted his right foot. He appeared to move in slow motion. He came to a full stop, his pitching hand hidden behind the battered glove at his chest. The ball exploded in Jimmy's mitt.

Everyone heard the pop. No one saw it arrive. Jimmy dropped his glove and raised his mask. He shook his left hand. "Jeezus! What do you call that?"

"A fast ball, Señor."

Jimmy blew on his hand, put on the glove and flipped down his mask. "Let's see a curve."

The thin man went into the same lazy wind-up. The ball cut in and dropped six inches as it crossed the plate.

"You said you had a change-up," yelled Zack. "Let's see it."

The ball floated, no rotation, and plunked into the mitt, taking an intolerable, hypnotizing time getting there.

The old southpaw had a whiplash arm. He threw a screwball, a vicious fast ball and change-ups in three speeds.

Not From Around Here, Are You?

Those facing him in the batter's box that day vowed El Diablo came from hell.

Jimmy Dean followed Zack into his tiny office. "He's good."

"Too good. Why haven't we heard of him?"

Jimmy shrugged. "He could have been big time before I was born. Maybe he changed his name."

"To Lucifer Adlero? A man throwing that hard could pitch a no-hitter every time he hit the mound."

"I can't catch that man nine innings," said Jimmy. "He'd make mush of me." He blew on his red, swollen left hand. "I only caught three really fast ones. I swear I never saw any of them. I don't like catching that man."

"Maybe we can talk him into easing off the fastball."

"The man is a magician," said Jimmy. "What he is, is Señor Smoke."

"Someone else was Señor Smoke. Was it Valenzuela or was it Marishal?"

"I got no idea, but I bet neither one threw like that man. He ain't human."

"He's as human as you or me."

"He gives me the creeps," said Jimmy.

"Tell you what." Zack wrapped an arm around his catcher's shoulder. "You shower and soak that hand in Epsom salts. I'll talk to Minnie about a bigger mitt for you and a contract for Mr. Adlero."

In twenty years of marriage, Minnie watched Clinton Eastwick rise from used car salesman to owner of the city's leading Pontiac-Oldsmobile-Cadillac dealership. Along the way he acquired a bank, a newspaper and the franchise of the West Texas League Hornets. He installed them in the city's municipal park after wrangling a dollar-a-year, twenty-year lease. The Hornets were still a losing proposition.

Lower level franchises could not exist without working agreements with major league clubs whose tentacles extended downward from AAA through C. Each level cannibalized the layer below. Cream rose to the top. The Hornets were dregs tarnishing the bottom of an empty talent bucket.

Here, almosts and not-quites gathered, players who loved the game and refused to grow up, hanging on to one more year before seeking gainful employment. They endured organized ball's lowest level for the privilege of calling themselves professionals.

Zack entered Minnie Eastwick's mahogany paneled office. Minnie, bent over, sorted a file. Her auburn hair, flecked with silver threads, fell forward, masking her features. Viewed from the rear, enough good stuff was packed into that leather mini-skirt to elicit whistles.

Minnie looked up. "What was all the excitement out there?"

"We've got a walk-on pitcher. He's pretty good."

"I thought you had the line-up set."

"This man has a fast ball you can't see. He could win us some games."

"Why didn't you call me?"

"I thought evaluating talent was my area."

Minnie placed her finger under his chin and raised it until their eyes met. "It is, but I sign the checks."

"Sign the man."

"Where is this kid?" Minnie drew a blank contract from her desk drawer.

"He's forty if he's a day."

"Then he's not going upstairs. No way."

"Satch Paige did."

"Everybody knew who he was. The color line kept him out in his prime."

"He claims he pitched in some little Mexican league. I checked, nobody's heard of him. He calls himself El Diablo. Claims he's a citizen, born in El Paso."

"Obviously an alias," said Minnie. "We'll offer a standard contract with options. If he doesn't produce we can let him go."

"Are we offering incentives?"

"Sure." Minnie smirked. "A thousand for a no hitter, five

grand for twenty wins."

Zack wrapped his arms around her waist from behind. "I'd halve those bonus figures to be safe."

Minnie looked up. "When do I see this marvel perform?"

"He starts tomorrow night, if you get his ink on a contract."

Minnie freed herself from entangling arms to go behind her desk. "Let's do it."

Diablo sat on the corridor floor outside the locker room, hugging his knees. A battered sombrero, tilted forward, hid his eyes. He raised his head at the approaching footsteps. "Let's go," said Zack.

Diablo followed Zack into the owner's office. Seeing a woman behind the desk, the man removed his hat and pressed it to his chest.

Minnie scrutinized the man with an evaluating eye having little to do with baseball. "Mister Adlero, I hear that you want to play ball for us."

"Yes. I pitch."

Minnie gestured for the men to draw chairs nearer the desk. "We offer a standard contract, with options." She passed several pages, stapled together, across the desk. "Look it over. If everything is satisfactory, we can do business."

Diablo's smile was sincere. He revealed uneven, yellowed teeth. "Señora, I do not wish this contract. I pitch the ball. You pay when I win."

Minnie shook her head in disbelief. Zack was the only Hornet pitcher within memory that had won more games than he lost. "What did you have in mind?"

"I win first game, you pay me $100. Second game $200. Game three, $300."

"Game four, $400.?" said Minnie.

"I will win game ten for $1,000," said the man, confidently.

Minnie did a calculation on her scratch pad. "If you win ten games over the season you would make $4,500. My way, if you last the season, you'd make more."

"What if you lose a game?" asked Zack. "It's bound to

happen."

"I win the next one for $100 dollars again."

Minnie continued her figuring. She brushed the thick auburn hair from her eyes. "My God! If he won twenty in a row we'd pay him $56,000."

"Not likely," said Zack, "that's more than the whole pitching staff won last year."

"We'd fill the stands," said Minnie with awe in her voice. "We might break even."

"I win," said Lucifer Adlero.

"I'll type it up," said Minnie. "Damn! Zack, if your arm lasts we could wind up in third place." Minnie restrained herself from hugging him in the presence of strangers.

Lucifer Adlero took the mound.

The morning paper had predicted a new sensation was pitching that night. It helped that Minnie Eastwick owned the paper. It was basically a come-on the Bradley Standard used each time a new pitcher arrived. This time Minnie almost believed it.

Zack played left field when not on the mound. The kid in center was one of three kids on the team wanting to be called Tex. "Call me Tex," he begged. Didn't every rookie from the state say that? Eventually everyone on the team called him, Call me Tex. The kid had an arm, not much accuracy, but a cannon that rifled the ball from deep center to the vicinity of home plate on one bounce. He swung a respectable bat as long as no one threw him anything resembling a curve. In the fourth, the opposing pitcher blazed one across the outside corner. Call me Tex rounded the bases to the applause of three hundred and fifty-nine paying fans.

Diablo threw mostly junk. Side-arm curves started, it seemed, somewhere near the first base line, then lazily danced toward the head of the batter who looked foolish when the ball suddenly dipped and crossed the plate. His knucklers were bounced weakly to the mound. Diablo fielded them easily and tossed out the runner. He struck out eleven, allowed one hit.

Not From Around Here, Are You?

The Hornets won, one-zip.

In Bradley, Texas, women did not enter men's locker rooms, not even lady reporters. Minnie Eastwick occasionally dropped by. However, she called out a warning before entering. This time, in the excitement of winning, she forgot.

The Hornets were celebrating. The first case of beer vanished quickly, the second almost as fast. Jocks, fresh from the showers, sat before their lockers replaying each amazing pitch. Others roved the locker room in their jock-straps, hoisting a second or third cold one. Zack had been delayed by reporters wanting to interview Diablo and his catcher. Now the three, having leisurely soaped themselves, enjoyed the muscle relaxing needles of nearly scalding water.

Minnie crossed the room unfazed by nudity. She had encountered most of the veterans at least once. It was a rite of passage. Damp towels quickly draped most male crotches. Call me Tex blushed. Tex Horne and Tex Too, the shortstop-second base combo, being green rookies, hid behind their locker doors.

Big John Thomas, the forty-year-old first baseman, had retired from double A ball three years earlier to return home after inheriting the family undertaking business. He played when there were no funerals to conduct. He usually managed to arrange with the bereaved to avoid conflict with an important series. Totally nude, he strode to the cooler and uncapped a fresh bottle of Lone Star. He minced up to Minnie and doing a perfect bunny-dip, his eyes on her hemline, offered her the bottle. "I see you come to help us celebrate, Miz Eastwick."

"I did that." Minnie tipped the bottle to her lips, then beamed down on the big first baseman. "I thank you kindly for sharing."

There were wagers as to where her gaze fell and to what she referred. Most gave her benefit of the doubt and assumed it was the beer.

Minnie took a healthy swig. "Where's Zack and Lucifer? I want to congratulate them."

Big John nodded toward the showers situated next to the whirlpool. Most pitchers used the battered Jacuzzi to ease the tension on their pitching arms. Minnie strode forward expecting to find them there. She paused at the sound of the showers. Three men lazed under separate shower heads. The kid catcher had his back turned. Her eyes roamed the smooth, hairless buttocks and the stocky, hairy legs with a connoisseur's approval. Zack and the older man stood at an angle, not looking up. Eying the two lathered bodies, her eyes glazed over like cheap pottery. The gaunt man with the scarred body looked up. His taunting eyes mocked her.

The Hornets won four of their next six before taking to the road. Alpine was an overnight trip in their lumbering, converted school bus. Minnie and Zack traded off at the wheel, with occasional relief from a utility infielder who had a spiked leg and did not expect to play next day. Minnie was encouraged with the gate receipts for the home stand. Diablo's second start saw the stands almost half full.

El Diablo volunteered to play right field on the days he was not pitching. With Zack in left, when he was not on the mound, the Hornets had a passable outer defense. It amazed Zack, the number of fly balls lofted his way when Diablo pitched. In the ninth inning of their first road game, Zack went to the fence to seal Diablo's third victory and put the stamp on his first no-hitter.

Minnie cheered and winced at the same time. She owed Diablo $600, plus a bonus for the no-hitter for the two week pay period. She called home that night and found advanced sales for the next home series was going well.

Mike Jackson pitched a six hitter the next night. Diablo and Zack each hit a home run with a man on board, The Hornets won 4-3. The following night Zack pitched his third win of the season. They swept the Alpine Angels for the first time in memory.

Zack lay face down. Minnie methodically rubbed alcohol into his back and tender pitching arm. The heels of both hands, under her full weight, worked the ridge of his spine and, with a twisting motion, moved lower with each grunt until Zack moaned with contentment.

Not From Around Here, Are You?

"What's the fine print say about the days you win?" asked Minnie.

"It says," said Zack, "the boss lady stays on top and does all the work."

"I like that clause," purred Minnie.

In San Angelo, while playing the Abbots, a pinch-hitter stepped up in the bottom of the ninth. Crouched over the plate, a gold chain with an attached crucifix dangled from the man's neckline. Diablo's inside fast ball clipped the chain and embedded the cross into Jimmy Dean's new catcher's mitt. The batter was awarded first base. Diablo then struck out the side. Zack had never seen his star pitcher so infuriated.

The Hornets came home to face the Del Rio Devils, after their most successful road trip in memory. The won lost record stood at 11-8. Five of those wins belonged to Diablo and three to Zack.

Minnie sat in her box, looking over the first-ever sellout crowd.

The Hornet's pitching sensation threw his final warm-up pitch. Zack handed the umpire the line-up card. He was headed toward left field when he saw a stranger leave the owner's box. Minnie waved. Zack waited until the man had found his seat.

"What's up, Minnie? What's that blood sucker looking for, as if I didn't know?"

"He's scouting for the Houston Rockets. He's here for a look at Lucifer. They'll steal him sure as hell."

"Damn and double damn."

"It's that 'effing working agreement. We can't play without them, and they won't let us win with what they leave us."

Zack shook his head. "I'm not sure Diablo would be happy in the big leagues, but we got no right to hold him back. He deserves a shot at something better."

"This is what I've got," said Minnie. "This is what I hold on to. I'm paying him more than he could make two steps up. He'll be in the money come September."

256

El Diablo

"I was wondering," mused Zack, "can you pay him if he keeps winning?"

Minnie eyes swept the crowd. "With advance sales rolling in, I can handle it. Damn it, Zack, I'd like to win this rag-tag league, just once."

"It better be this year. My arm won't last forever. I want to make it through the season. If you want me next year, I'll stick to managing."

Minnie nodded, soberly. "If we pull this off, you'll be General Manager. You know Clinton left me other irons in the fire."

Zack stopped at the mound on his way to left field. "We got to talk, amigo."

The gaunt man nodded. "There is a scout in the stands."

"I know moving up might mean more money, but we'd be mighty pleased if you don't look too good out here tonight."

"He is looking at our young catcher also," said Diablo.

"God! I forgot Jimmy Dean. The kid needs seasoning. A year down here would do him good."

"That is so."

"I know you got a streak going. It's money in your pocket." Zack paused. "If you can find it in your heart, I wish you wouldn't look too sharp."

The man's eyes glowed, a cat toying with a hypnotized mouse. "I think they will not want me and not, perhaps, young Jimmy."

Zack nodded, gave Diablo's shoulder a slap, and trotted to left field.

Diablo gave up three walks in the first inning, but no one scored.

The Houston scout shook his head. "Lucky s.o.b."

In the top of the second, Jimmy Dean was charged with a passed ball. He had no idea how it got by him. Luckily, no one was on base. The Devil's second baseman, a lefty batting eight in the order, came to bat. A glint from his left ear lobe called attention to a dangling gold cross.

El Diablo wound up. Rage reflected in eyes that had

become amber slits in onyx. A fastball buzzed the man's ear, a swarm of angry bees. He believed one stung him. He touched a tender lobe that felt strangely bare. His fingers encountered slick traces of blood mixed with sweat. "The bastard hit me!" He started to charge the mound. The pitcher's cold eyes stopped him short. He turned to the man behind the plate. "Hey man, the bastard hit me, he nicked my ear."

Doc Newby attended the games because he got in free. He examined the torn lobe. "Clipped it, neat as can be," said the doc. He daubed the ear with antiseptic and pressed the torn flesh together with tape.

The ump gave the batter first base. Zack, who trotted in from left field, did not contest the decision. The Devils scored three runs that inning.

The Hornets got one back in the last of the sixth on a beat-out bunt by Call me Tex, a bloop single by Tex Horne, and a long fly to right by Tex Too . Zack homered with one aboard in the eighth to tie. Diablo was still on the mound in the top of the tenth. Zack got all three outs with his back against the wall, the last one, a flying leap with hard contact.

They were in her office, on the couch, his head cradled in Minnie's lap. It was an effort to open his eyes. "What's going on?"

"We won," said Minnie. "There's a slight concussion and you bruised your left shoulder. The fine print says you sleep alone tonight, owner's orders."

Zack woke late. Diablo had not occupied his room next door. Since Zack seldom stayed at his rooming house, he was not aware of the Mexican's nocturnal pursuits. He believed no woman would be so desperate as to sleep with El Diablo. The man was uglier than Dennis Rodman.

He found Diablo in the greasy spoon across from Municipal Park. Zack's head ached. The bump on his head was beyond sore, it was tenderized. His shoulder ached. "I hear we won. I guess we were lucky."

"I don't think so."

El Diablo

Zack checked the morning paper. "Box score says you gave up nine hits, hit two batters, and walked thirteen." Zack peered over the top of his folder paper, "The man tags it your poorest outing."

The older man shrugged. "It was the most difficult."

"He says Call me Tex walked, stole second and third, then came home on a passed ball while you were at bat."

The gaunt man nodded.

"Who gave the kid the steal sign? He hasn't stolen a base all year."

"Miss Eastwick did. I suggested it, Señor."

"Who made you manager?

"Someone must take charge. Mrs. Eastwick suggested I not be the one who wins the game."

Zack nodded. "Is Mrs. Eastwick in her office?"

"I believe so."

Zack finished his ham and cheddar omelet and downed his third cup of coffee before crossing the street to talk to his boss.

She wore dark circles under tired eyes. Minnie viewed him through the same false eyelashes she had worn the night before. "You look better. Can you pitch?"

Zack shrugged. "I don't know. The arm's no worse than usual. I'll have to loosen up to see if my equilibrium will let me stand up on my follow-through."

Minnie nodded. "Dan Hooks stopped by."

"The scout from Houston?"

"He says the kid needs seasoning. We've got him for the rest of the year."

"And Diablo?"

"Too old, too wild. Says he threw at the kid's head when he clipped his ear."

Zack shook his head. "If he aimed to hit him, the kid's head would have popped like a spoiled melon falling off a tailgate."

"The man was wild. He walked eight or ten batters last

night."

"Thirteen. He worked a 3-2 count on most."

"God!"

"He nicked the cross off that kid's ear like a surgeon. He controlled the game from the first pitch."

"He told me, this morning," confided Minnie, "he's only thrown one no-hitter because he didn't feel I could afford the bonus."

"Sometimes I think Diablo uglies the ball across the plate. His looks scare some of those green kids half to death."

Minnie swept the hair from her face. "He is rather rugged looking."

"I heard you visited the locker room the other week. I guess what you saw in the showers appeals to you."

"Don't intimate what you can't prove." Minnie focused on the document in her hand.

"Those dark circles didn't come from sacking out solo."

"Remember who owns this club." Minnie's tone definitely cooled. "We've got a game tonight. You best get to your job."

That night, Zack lost 3-2. Afterward, his arm throbbed more than usual. Minnie was not around to give him his post-game rubdown.

The Hornets lost the following night, then had a day off before the Saturday game El Diablo was scheduled to pitch. Friday night Zack watched the gaunt man enter Minnie's front door around supper time. Diablo had not left when the last light went out in Minnie's bedroom. Zack went to his Hornet's nest under the stands, made out the next day's line-up, put his feet on his desk, and slept in his chair.

The Pecos Padres were back Sunday. Zack and Minnie had not spoken in two days. She looked as miserable as he felt.

By the second inning Zack knew the Hornets were in trouble.

Having won his game Saturday, Diablo patrolled right field. He fumed each time Sanchez, the Padre's first baseman, approached the plate and made the sign of the cross. Sanchez

El Diablo

tagged Mike Jackson's second pitch over the right field fence.

Diablo retaliated in the third. Sanchez tagged another in the fifth with a man aboard.

In the dugout, when the Hornets came to bat in the bottom of the seventh they trailed 5-2. Diablo sat next to Zack.

"Sanchez is killing us," said Zack.

"Put me in. I will kill the man." Diablo spewed pure venom.

"You are in," said Zack. "You're in right field."

"Make me the pitcher. I will handle him."

"You pitched nine innings yesterday."

Diablo shrugged. "Another inning, two? Who counts? Next time he comes up, I will put him out."

Zack nodded but did not promise.

There were two on and two out in the eighth when Sanchez approached the plate. The Padre first baseman flashed the sign of the cross and stepped in.

Zack trotted in, took the ball from Mike Jackson and waved his ace in from right field. He gave Diablo the ball. "Don't show him anything good."

"It is not good baseball to ask a deity for help," said Diablo. "It is not right that a man should invoke spirits for what he should be man enough to do alone. He should not mock us."

Zack smiled. "What about the devil? Can he help?"

Diablo smiled, bitterly. "The devil helps himself. Sometimes he throws strikes."

"Sometimes, so do we."

"This man should not make signs and mumble to provoke others," persisted the man twisting and screwing the ball into his worn glove.

Zack watched Diablo's warm-up pitches before trotting out to left field.

Sanchez made the sign of blessing and stepped in.

The first pitch was a fast ball so far inside Sanchez felt the breeze. The man stumbled, fell backward and hit the dirt.

Ball One.

The Padre brushed the dust from his uniform. Again he made the sign.

Not From Around Here, Are You?

A sidearm curve breaking in front of the plate caused the batter to bail out a second time.

Strike!

Sanchez picked himself up and entered the batter's box. He crossed himself.

An unearthly wail rose from the pitcher's mound. Diablo went into a full wind-up. He did not bother holding the runners on. No one saw the pitch. Everyone heard the ball rip the bat into splinters and the ball strike the backstop.

Foul! Strike two!

The batter wrung his hands in obvious pain. The umpire called time. Zack trotted into the mound. "Take it easy. You'll ruin your arm."

Diablo shook his head. "The man, he should not ask for help." The voice was more gravelly than normal and deeper. "He would take unfair advantage."

"You're ahead in 2-1."

Sanchez took his position in the box.

"Do not provoke!" shouted Diablo.

Sanchez waved his heavy replacement bat in anticipation. Then, as though he had lost something, he bent forward and knelt. He crossed himself.

The pitch turned his head obscenely. Everyone heard the "THUNK!" a dull, hollow sound, a wet bean-bag, thrown by a giant, smacking a mound of wet sand or perhaps an over ripe honeydew falling a great distance to smash upon cobble stones. The crumpled figure did not move.

Diablo stood, unmoving, on the mound, head bowed, arms at his side.

No one had called time. Five thousand versions from five thousand witnesses, did not explain why Sanchez had lowered his head into the strike zone. Only Jimmy Dean saw a small crucifix fall from the batter's gold necklace. In the confusion he collected it to join the earring pried from his glove after the Alpine Angels game. Jimmy swore the ball would have been a strike had not the man's head interfered.

El Diablo

Some called it murder.

The game was called on account of rain. Not one dark cloud tainted the sky. Those part-time umps knew no rule covering a dead man blocking the plate.

Sanchez was taken to the hospital, but no one doubted he was dead.

The sheriff took Diablo to the lockup until someone could decide whether it was manslaughter, murder, or a terrible accident.

Next morning, Lucifer Adlero was gone, with him the dreams of a Hornet's winning season.

Zack sat in the Hornet's Nest staring at the ceiling. He squeezed a rubber ball to strengthen his arm. He had not spoken to Minnie for days.

Minnie entered without knocking. "Advanced sales have fallen to zilch." Her eyes looked tired.

"Just like old times, and they weren't so good."

"He brought in the fans. They shouldn't have taunted him."

Zack shrugged. "Jimmy says that last pitch was a strike."

"He was a gentle man," said Minnie, "though he was a devil on the mound."

"He cultivated the image. But he didn't have horns."

"Or a tail." Minnie bit her tongue.

Zack shrugged.

"My husband once said that folks would do business with Satan if he gave them a big enough order for pitchforks."

"It makes sense if making pitchforks is what you do."

"He won," said Minnie. "He wasn't hurling thunderbolts or making lightning."

"Until the last, he never hit a batter. He clipped a few pieces of offending jewelry. Sanchez blocked the plate. He put his head in the strike zone."

"He pitched like the devil." Minnie moved behind Zack's chair. She massaged his right shoulder. She worked down, strong fingers digging into the biceps.

Until Zack, her romps had been no more than the

sampling of available goodies. Her last peri-menopausal romp had taken her into a meaningless roll with a man who disappeared in the night. She did not know what she felt but she wanted to explain it to Zack. "I'm sorry."

"Why? The man was ugly beyond belief," said Zack.

"I was getting older."

"His skin was like leather chaps worn through the brush. He was a mass of scars."

"He was tireless," breathed Minnie.

"Maybe I should move on."

Minnie's voice wavered. "I have a contract I want you to look over."

"With fine print clauses?"

"Dozens." Minnie giggled. "But only a few I'll hold you to."

"Maybe you should warn me."

"Well, the big print makes you general manager of the ball club."

"I could handle that. Are you buying me?"

"Only if you want to be bought."

"I'm thinking."

"There are things you can look into. Like breaking away from the Mama hen and hitching up with an organization that can put us in a league with better players. Dallas has offered to stock us, maybe move us to single A. You negotiate."

"I'd like that," said Zack.

"There's an option clause that says you should move in with me."

Zack scanned the page. "Where does it say that?"

"Very fine print. I doubt if your eyes are that good, but it's there."

"Do I have total control?"

"I think I can promise satisfaction."

"Got any more fine print?"

"Pages and pages," said Minnie.

Garbage

Katey Brichto

I rip a Hefty garbage bag off its perforated roll and start making my rounds. The rite of refuse has begun.

Judy, my Husky Beagle mix, regards me suspiciously as I belt out a line from a song we sang as kids Friday nights to welcome the angels of Sabbath peace. *Bo'achem leshalom, malachei hashalom, malachei el elyon, mi melech malachei hasharei hakadosh baruch hu.*

Arusha and Abdul follow my every step, tails wagging. The joy of Friday's ceremonial garbage ritual is no less exciting to them than it is to me. You'd think we were kids on an Easter egg hunt.

Zeide, my grandfather, knew I was lost to rank and file traditional Jews. Still, he must've hoped I'd settle down to a life of domestic tranquility, a husband who was circumcised and nominally Jewish and most important, children to carry on the line.

"Lizeleh, Lizeleh," he'd once advised me. "Enough with the foreign travel and universities. No man wants a woman with so much knowledge."

I didn't heed my *zeide's* warning. You can't expect a person long drunk on experience to stay in her seat and color within the lines of convention. Already well-acquainted with Europe, I set my sights further east to India, Malaysia, Thailand, Indonesia and a Masters in Comparative Literature. I sublet my West Village apartment and moved to the highlands of Guatemala. I started a multilingual school with scholarships for Mayan children. I went through lovers like a kid through Halloween candy.

It took me ten years, but the prodigal daughter, now in her forties, returned to the United States. But not to New York or

Not From Around Here, Are You?

Chicago. Instead I made a home in the same rural backwater where my brother had long ago set his stakes. Apart from Ari, a half-hour's drive away, there were no other Jews. I had fallen in love with a *goy* and chosen to live among simple country folk who'd never even met a Jew. My neighbors knew I was *other,* but like Red Tail hawks circling high above the woods and valleys, they rode their own wind currents and studied interlopers like me from a safe distance.

I asked Robbie for a separation and now I live alone. I skinny dip in my creek, sleep with my dogs, talk to myself. The daughter and granddaughter of rabbis happily heaves her heavy-duty trash bags into a rusty old pick-up instead of baking *challahs* and roasting the *shabbos* brisket.

A sudden chorus of howls can only mean one thing: an unfamiliar vehicle has turned into the driveway. I look out the window and, sure enough, see a shiny blue Jeep inching up to the house.

Joan is one of the few friends from high school with whom I never lost touch. This means we've been friends for thirty-five years. Like me, her life has been a journey down unconventional paths. She is one of the precious few unafraid to venture this far to catch up with an old pal. It's been a seven-hour drive from her home in Milwaukee, through, she tells me, "shit-assed icy roadways."

She's tall, willowy and black. The erstwhile Angela Davis afro she sported in college is now closely cropped. Middle age may've tempered her Pantherian passions, but her eyes still sparkle.

We embrace while a gust of wind howls past us. Even through her down jacket I can feel her bones. She has always been thin.

"Fucking February," I say.

Coatless, I am a Russian refugee, Lara in Doctor Zhivago. I reach for the leather overnight bag on the front seat of her Jeep. Joan opens a rear door, grabs two shopping bags and follows me into the house, past the Hefty bag in the mud room to the kitchen, warm and still redolent of the Lemon Pledge I'd

266

smeared into the downstairs wooden surfaces.

"This place is massive," Joan says, looking around.

Joan visited once seven years ago, when we were still in the old cabin, before it was struck by lightning, before I'd decided there were no more good reasons to remain with Robbie.

"3,800 square feet, still unfinished. Don't ask me what I was thinking."

"Since when have either of us been rational?"

I watch while she empties the contents of her Cosco shopping bags onto my kitchen harvest table: three bottles of Chardonnay, a basket of ruby raspberries, a chunk of Jarlsberg, two monster artichokes and a package of chicken pesto sausage.

"Just what the doctor ordered," I tell her. "The most gourmet we get around these parts is deer jerky and chewing tobacco." I look beyond Joan at the wall clock. It's already five-thirty. "You're just in time for Garbage Friday. I'll explain on the way."

I pick up the Hefty bag, quickly noticing it has already leaked a trail of coffee grounds and egg shells onto the kitchen floor.

"A good time always makes a mess," Joan laughs.

"I better rebag this. Otherwise, I'll be in trouble with the garbage police. I'm guessing the hole is the work of Sherman."

"Garbage police? Sherman?" Joan looks around.

Abdul, who has been eyeing Joan's pesto sausage on the counter, cocks his head as though he, too, is wondering who Sherman is.

"Is Sherman the dog outside?"

"No, that's Judy. Give me a hand. I'll double-bag this."

We fit a second, prophylactic garbage bag around the leaky one. Then Joan insists on carrying the stinky garbage bag outside. We heave our Hefties into the truck bed. She hoists herself into the passenger side with a swift and economical grace any teamster would be proud of.

It always takes three or four minutes of aborted tries to start up the ignition in Robbie's '75. Old Fords, like old maids, are famous for slow starts. It gives me time to explain.

Not From Around Here, Are You?

"The fearless Sherman is a vole, a field mouse in search of the perfect cracker, an annual uninvited guest. He visits when the first leaves turn. Unlike my cat, Giza, who prefers to live in the barn because he's afraid of the dogs, Sherman skips right past their snoozing snouts. But you know what bugs me most?"

"Those little calling cards he leaves all over the place?"

"How did you know? Are you in cahoots?"

We laugh.

"I hate his miniscule droppings on the counters almost as much as the scent of vole pee in my cutlery drawer. But it's his eating habits that drive me to distraction. He'll sample fourteen separate Triscuits at a time, chewing a tiny corner off each cracker. Why can't he just concentrate on one cracker at a time? You know, finish what's on your plate and *then* help yourself to more?"

Joan nods. "Kids nowadays. Such bad manners."

I throw Joan a look of love. The years that elapsed since we last saw each other disappear into the same sort of oblivion in which unpaired socks must surely hide.

"Speaking of mice droppings," I continue. "Why can't they dump it all into one neat little pile like any other decent member of the animal kingdom? Instead, they leave Hansel and Gretel shit trails all over the place."

The truck finally fires up, and I accelerate slowly down the gravel driveway. The horses, hearing the approaching motor, collect at the pasture gate, unashamed of their Pavlovian response.

"So we're going to the dump?" Joan asks.

"Not quite. It's a truck that comes once a week for us billies who live in the boonies without curbside pick up. It's the most sublime moment of my entire week."

Joan looks at me over Judy's pointy Husky ears. "It's possible you've been here too long. Perhaps it's time for an intervention."

Strange comment, I think, for an African-American lesbian from a broken home.

"You've got this tranquil paradise which must be a great

Garbage

place to write. But the garbage thing? This I gotta see."

We climb out of the valley, almost a mile to the stone house on top of the hill where TJ Meekers, my nearest neighbor, lives. I don't see much of him in passing on the road between our homes. But one day, about a year ago, Meekers stopped his Halflinger-driven pony cart in front of my house to chat.

"How's the house comin'?"

I saw my chance to prove I wasn't a rich city slicker. "Slowly. I've run out of money."

"That's a big house for one small person. I know what that's like. Now that our boys are all up and grown, me and the missus rattle around like marbles in that old house."

A few months later, during Bethel's annual bean and frank dinner at the firehouse, Alva Kretch saw me nod and wave at old man Meekers as he left. She took me aside to ask had I heard that Vanda Meekers had left her husband of forty-four years.

"The quiet was drivin' Vanda crazy. She moved in with her married daughter, accrost the river over in Kentucky. Now she has one of them finished basements all decorated with shelves for her doll collection. And," Alva's voice lowered with emphasis, "Meekers never even tried to stop her."

Recently, Meekers has taken on a new project. He picks up the empty Bud Lite and Michelob cans the rednecks throw out their truck windows and sticks them on the ends of branches. The brush on each side of the road stretching between our properties now sparkles in the morning sun with aluminum flowers and, in the moonlight, glitters like possum eyes. Every month or two, I walk the road with a trash bag and pluck the cans from their branches.

I roll down my window so that Arusha, his chin on my head, can sniff to his heart's content.

"So what makes you think you just have one mouse? Or mole?"

"It's a *vole*. But it's not just one, there must be hundreds. I nail a new guy every couple of days with a peanut butter trap."

"How'd you know the one who chewed into the garbage

269

Not From Around Here, Are You?

bag was Sherwin?"

I round a bend, careful to hug the right shoulder, knowing this truck could squash a rhino. Sure enough, I'm rewarded on the other end by the grateful salute of the driver of an oncoming Toyota. He was way too close to center, his Pygmy pick-up dwarfed by my Ford.

"You mean Sherman. All mouses are named Sherman," I say, turning to meet Joan's bemused gaze.

"Don't you mean 'mice'?"

I laugh. "Maybe I *have* been here too long."

As I pass neighbors coming the opposite way, I lift my index finger off the steering wheel in traditional greeting. The response today, in every single case, is not just a raised finger, but a broad smile. Everyone on this side of the county, from Splinters Ridge to Shirks Hollow, is wending their merry way down to the gravel lot in Bethel.

Bethel is more a cluster of houses than a town. Its two white churches face one another across Back Street, like gentlemen cowboys at a duel. Behind them is the fire station, a one-truck garage complete with a mint green, high-tech firefighting engine. The building is also the site for Bethel's frank and bean suppers, its summer fish fry, town hall meetings and voting booths for this corner of the county.

Bethel has no post office or bank and there aren't any shops or restaurants. Commercial industry functions out of private homes. Alva Kretch cuts hair and gives perms in her boutique called 'I'm Hair For You', built onto the back of her garage. Benny Fissel hung a barnwood shingle on his shed that says, "Taxadermie and Bate." Martha Mudd painted a sign on her corn crib which advertises "Collectibles 'N Such."

As we round the bend from the cemetery into the small quadrangle of the town, I wonder if Bethel doesn't have a memory like that of my Alzheimered mother. Perhaps, in its collective consciousness it still retains some rosy recollection of its former glory even while, in the benevolence of its dementia, it is mercifully unaware of its present shabbiness.

We pull into the gravel lot behind two pickups and a beat-

Garbage

up SUV, queued in happy anticipation. Despite the chill of February winds, vehicle doors are open because, after all, a party's a party. The driver in front of me steps out of his truck, stretches his arms heavenward, retrieves a box of Camels filters from his shirt pocket and goes over to the rusted Isuzu in front for a smoke with his neighbor.

"I thought hippies were dead," Joan says, gesturing with her head.

The Isuzu driver she refers to holds his cigarette between his lips while retying a bandana around his long head of hair.

"That's a redneck." I roll down my window. "Lookee over there and wave to the Garbage Police." I point to the far edge of the lot where six people sit in a makeshift row of white plastic chairs. "They come to watch the weekly show, from four to six every Friday."

"They sit in the cold to watch people throw their garbage in that smelly old truck?" Joan's articulate laugh indicates that this is just *too* much. "I'm witnessing a garbage dump audience?"

My response is drowned out by the groans of the dinosaur garbage truck, grinding its latest feed deep into its entrails. Joan and I watch Chester, the latest trash truck boss, as he skillfully pulls the truck's alimentary levers.

Its meal digested, Chester reopens the rear jaws of the beast.

I shift to first gear. "Do we know how to have fun or what?"

"Damn. Wish I had my camera."

I tell Joan, who is a man-appreciator in spite of being gay, that Chester is one of my favorite classic hillbilly types.

"Look at him. See how great he looks from behind? Tall, slim, broad- shouldered. He's got those hot, lean legs packed tightly into worn Levi's and he's just bowlegged enough to be sexy."

"There's a *but* coming."

Chester turns around. He's missing a mess of teeth and his beer gut precedes the rest of him by a foot. College may not make the man, but I'll be damned if Chester ever finished second grade. He's got that clueless look, as though contemplating the complexity of Dick, Jane and Spot.

Joan manages to cease laughing long enough to ask. "So what's with these Garbage Police?"

We inch up to the garbage truck, obediently ingesting its diet of pregnant Hefty bags. I fill Joan in. "It all started with Butch Scudder, the obese one in the overalls and T-shirt."

"He isn't cold?"

"It could be snowing, and he'll be out here without a coat."

Butch's arms, elongated chunks of silly putty, are folded across his corpulent belly. His doughy face sits atop an impressive pile of spreading chins. He stares straight ahead, no expression on his features.

"That is one weird look," Joan says.

I look back from Joan to Butch and notice that the woman on his left is saying something to him with her hand shielding her lips. Then they both turn to look at us. It occurs to me they've just realized that the short girl in the big truck who's been comin' here for years now, even-though-she-clearly-ain't-*from*-here, has a passenger beside her who looks to be one of them Niggra types. Butch, I imagine, is whispering back to his sister, "See that Niggra? That is one weird look."

I go on with my story.

It started six or seven years ago. Come garbage time, you'd see Butch emerging from the ramshackle garden shed beside his house with a white plastic lawn chair. Butch would situate the chair just so on his postage-stamp lawn, take his seat and fold his arms across his chest, no doubt feeling as privileged as a Roman emperor front row at a gladiator fight.

Soon after, Butch's sister Wilma began joining him for the two-hour show.

"Which one's Wilma?" Joan asks.

"Look for the woman whose corpulence matches Butch's." Wilma's dressed in a puffy pink ski jacket, wool cap and black stretch pants.

"They look like twins."

"The Hoosier version of Tweedle Dee and Tweedle Dum."

The way Alva told it, neither Butch nor Wilma ever married.

272

Garbage

For that matter, neither one ever ventured further than the Madison Wal-Mart, a twenty-five minute drive and Bethel's closest approximation to a big town. Their parents are long since gone and a brother named Maxwell left years ago for a place called Dee Troyt. Butch and Wilma sleep in the same beds in which they lay as children. They fry their eggs and grits in the same iron skillets and brew their ice tea on the same kitchen stove, despite the fact, Alva added, that their stove is old enough to vote three times over.

"Some folks is just different," Alva says.

Alva can afford to be compassionate. Her husband Herb has been at the steel plant across the river for twenty years. They've got medical insurance, one of them 401 K things and, for an entire week every year, they get to stay at a Hampton Inn in Orlando, complete with cable television and free continental breakfast.

"Is Alva sitting there, too?" Joan asks.

"Alva isn't on the garbage team. That kind of behavior doesn't go with perms and manicured nails."

Abdul jumps into the front seat. In the process, he steps on Judy's delicate paws. She responds with an irritable snarl, a pointed canine version of "Fuck off, creep."

"Hush up," I push Abdul back like a giant stuffed toy. "Mama's talking."

I move the truck up another foot. We're next. In the meantime, I return to my history of the Bethel Garbage Police.

A month after Butch and Wilma became Friday fixtures by the gravel lot, Benny Fissel began joining them. He'd bring his own chair from his Taxidermie and Bate shop, across the road. Within a few weeks, Hazel and Barney Mounce were regulars as well. Soon there was no telling who else might drag in a lawn chair to watch the show. Some afternoons they'd bring coolers and Styrofoam cup holders to make sure their Cokes didn't get too warm.

"One Friday, I think it was in June, we'd had this huge downpour all day. It let up about 3:30 and to take advantage of the lull, I arrived a few minutes early. There's nothing nastier than wet garbage bags. Believe it or not, Butch and Benny were rigging up a tarp."

"Kind of like postal employees, rain, snow or sleet?"

"The show must go on. I love the Garbage Police, even though they make me self-conscious about my garbage. Imagine those eyes with their secret x-ray vision."

"They know when you've been bad. . ."

". . .or good. . ."

". . .so be good for goodness sake."

Our turn has finally come. I take a deep breath, pretending not to notice the riveted gazes of the Garbage Police and open my door cautiously. Abdul, like a Jack-In-The-Box, seizes the moment. He jumps over the seat into my lap and bolts out of the truck. With malice aforethought, he races around to the side of the garbage truck, pees on one of its tires and heads straight toward the Garbage Police. I hear the impotence of my own tinny voice as I call out his name.

"Who wants a treat?" I call out, hoping the Garbage Police won't condemn my permissiveness.

Abdul ignores me but Arusha, milking the chaos, now jumps into the front seat. I hurriedly step from the cab, slam the door and race around after Abdul, desperate to grab him before he gets any closer to the Garbage Police. I know he sees the coolers, recognizing that usually means food.

As I approach, Abdul circles behind the end of the row where Benny Fissel is sitting. Wilma cranes her neck and says something to Butch. Butch, arms still crossed around his vast chest, stares straight ahead, at me. I wonder if I should advance on bended knee before His Majesty, King of Garbage.

"Sorry," I say. "He's not very obedient. Abdul! Come here, boy."

I get no response from either dog or king. I watch as Abdul sniffs around the back of the chairs, praying he won't mistake one of Butch's stocky limbs for a tree trunk in need of watering.

"He's a big 'un," Hazel Mounce says.

I shoot her a grateful look. "He's really just a puppy." If

they so much as suspected that these oversized beasts actually sleep with me!

Abdul suddenly spies a squirrel. We all turn to watch him, his magnificent full tail quivering in high alert, the poise of one uplifted paw and the pride of his noble wolfish head. Slowly, he sinks down to a leonine crouch, then takes a running leap. The squirrel does an about-face and runs up the nearest tree for dear life.

"Don't look like no puppy to me," Bill Mounce says, spitting in front of his feet. "I never seed a pup that big. What's his race, anyways?"

Just then I hear Joan's voice.

"Yo, Abdul! Look what I have." She's gotten out of the truck and found the silver bullet, straight out of my garbage: an empty forty-pound bag of Old Roy Lamb and Rice dog chow. Abdul looks up from beneath the tree, cocks his head like the Victrola dog and runs over to Joan. She grabs his collar and hoists him into the truck. The Garbage Police, one and all, clap.

"Thanks for saving the day," I say to Joan.

I reach over the side rim of my truck to grab the neck of a Hefty bag but a mighty arm reaches over me, lifting up the bag with one smooth swoop. The arm belongs to Chester, Garbage Man par excellence.

"Thanks, Chester. This is my friend Joan. We went to high school together."

"Weez already met," Chester says, lighting up a Basic filter. "When you was chasing your dog. And I told your friend here how I always make it a point to help out the ladies. Garbage ain't for the dainty."

It's true, he does. Just the same, I go through the motions every time, getting out of the truck, circling around back and reaching for the bags. Chester, of course, allows men to display their machismo. He'll stand by smoking, flexing his garbage-lifting biceps as they sweat over their own refuse bags. But he's tougher than a Hefty bag in his resolve to free the fairer sex from that defiling task.

"I appreciate it, Chester. I just always think that if I make it, I can take it."

"Takin' and tossin's two different things." He flicks his butt and stomps it beneath his grubby work boot.

"What would we ever do without you?" I say in a faux coyness he may or may not understand.

In any case, he changes the subject. "That dog of yourn needs some 'struction."

"I know it. He's spoiled rotten. They all are." I motion toward the three snouts in the pick-up cab. "*Mea culpa.*"

"Say what?"

"Um, I'm not much on dog discipline."

I notice a slight and subtle change in Chester's expression, a non-garbagesque narrowing of the eyes. "They said you're deevorced."

They who? Oh you dope, I think. *Butch. The Garbage Police.* They know everything. I allow myself a stupid moment of shock. *They must know as much about me as I know about them!*

"I didn't know you was deevorced. I hate to hear that." Chester shoots me a toothless, blue-eyed look which is as much a fishing expedition as it is an expression of sympathy.

I'm suddenly conscious of the buttons on my work shirt, the fit of my jeans. In the following half-second, I ask myself why. Must I establish my desirability in the eyes of the Garbage Man?

"We're not really divorced. We're separated."

But Chester cuts right through my bullshit. "What'd he want a deevorce for, anyhowz? Did he get him another woman?"

I look at Joan whose climbed back into the truck with the dogs. She looks back at me, a mischievous smile on her lips. I know she can't believe she's listening to me discuss the intimate details of my failed marriage with Chester the Garbage God of Bethel, Indiana.

"We just grew apart, you know?" I kick my rubber boot on a tire, displacing a bit of gravel from its rut. I feel his eyes on me and still can't look up so instead, I bend down and pick up a Campbell's Cream of Mushroom Soup label.

Garbage

"Your truck will be wanting this," I say, handing it to him in hopes of making my getaway.

"Tell you what," Chester says. "If youz ever wantin' help disciplinin' them dogs. . . ."

I look up to see if the Garbage Police are monitoring this conversation, taking notes. There's a momentary distraction as Butch accepts the can of Coca Cola his sister hands him, but he swiftly looks back in our direction. So do Wilma, Benny, Hazel and Bill.

"And another thing. I just have to say it like it is."

"What's that?" I ask, country-casual.

"Your husband? He's a damn fool."

I give him a sort of *oh-shucks* smile and mumble, "Have a great weekend."

I quickly step up onto the running board, climb into the cab and push off in first gear.

I'm not sure what just happened. Did the Garbage Man come onto me? If so, were the Bethel Garbage Police applauding the move? Are they claiming me as one of their own?

"You're right," Joan says, interrupting my reverie.

"About what?"

"This garbage thing. I wouldn't have missed it for the world. It's a truly post-modern event."

I hug the side of the road to make way for Curtis Spurgeon. He drives a '69 Chevy despite the fact that, according to Alva, he is legally blind. His rope-tied trunk lid flaps over a collection of shiny black plastic bulges.

"So," she continues, "Did the Garbage Man make a play for you? Now that you're deevorced?"

We laugh at the absurdity of me, daughter and grand-daughter of rabbis, world traveler, multilingual sophisticate and one-time Ph.D. candidate, going out with a billy boy with missing teeth and a Bud Lite beer gut. But beneath my glee, I hear the echo of a loneliness I'm loathe to acknowledge.

We drive on in silence for a moment, and then the traitorous thought sneaks in with the stealth of a chigger. Is there a law that says every man I date needs to have finished second grade?

"He's a nice guy," I say, diverting her attention to the faltering fawn at the edge of the road.

The Famous Last Ride
Of Elfreido de Dark

Jim St. Clair

On a dusty old sofa
In a rundown cabana
Off of Highway Trace Quatro
Outside of Havana

There sleeps the dreamer of dreamers
The schemer of schemers
A Kahlua and creamer
A midnight canteener

A pretender affluent
A proletariat truant
A half-assed mechanic
When he gets around to it

A seniorita's heartthrob
Quick with the flattering remark
A son of the revolution
Elfreido de Dark

The son of his mother
A poor peasant pineapple packer
And the son of his father
A poor peasant sugar cane whacker

Yes a son of the revolution
A Marxist society backer
He makes a fair living
As a poor peasant taxicab hacker

Not From Around Here, Are You?

Though it pays for his nightlife
His Kahlua and creams
This restless revolutionary
Has capitalist dreams

His life as he knows it
He finds quite appalling
In the bight lights of Miami
He hears his destiny calling

So he plans and he plots
And he plots and he schemes
To find him a way
To follow his dreams

And on the night of March seventh
He says good buy to his slavings
Bids farewell to his parents
And borrows their life savings

Then it's down to the shore
To a boat he has stashed
A seaworthy vessel
Made of washed ashore trash

A bathtub, some beer kegs
Bound together with fence wire
Old lumber, some milk jugs
And some used radial tires

As the sun starts to rise
He prepares to embark
On the famous adventure
Of Elfreido de Dark

Last Ride of Elfriedo de Dark

At sea for an hour
Then three, maybe four
He's awakened form his nap
By a boat motor's roar

A rescue patrol boat
Searching for folks just like him
Helping float them to freedom
So they won't have to swim

Soon the boat's captain 'Lenny'
And his first mate named 'Chuck'
Dropped him off in Miami
And wished him 'good luck'

"You're some brave kind of hero!"
The people on shore all shouted as one
And they showered him with gifts
A welfare and green card, and told him to 'have fun'

Then when the cameras were turned off
And the lights had been turned down
And the hoopla had vanished
He was all on his own

A son of the revolution
Now on American land
Things were going his way
Just as he'd planned

It had been a full day
But now nighttime was falling
When suddenly he heard sounds
The local nightlife was calling

Not From Around Here, Are You?

What could it hurt
To have a few beers
He as much as owed himself that
Now that he finally was here

Yes the land of the free
Where the air smelled so sweet
The music was seductive
And the night had a beat

Champagne was the order
He had three ladies in tow
He was the life of the party
He was hot on a roll

Yes, the land of the free
Of that there was no doubt
But freedom isn't free
He was about to find out

Because in a turn of his head
All his money was spent
When he couldn't pay up
Out the door he was sent

He was a hero non-gratis
Another dumb schmuck
A loser, a washout
Who'd run out of luck

He wandered for hours
In this self pitying condition
When he found a custom black caddy
With the keys in the ignition

Last Ride of Elfriedo de Dark

He'd only borrow the car
For a short little tear
Nobody would notice
No one would care

The Caddy's new owner
Didn't share in this fun
And he pulled out his cell phone
And dialed 9 1 1

The call it went out
The place to surround
The police now alerted
The alarm they did sound

Hot on his tail
Nearly right from the start
On this the famous last ride
Of Elfreido de Dark

Up Collins, down Lincoln
Across North Ocean Drive
Down Flagler, up Biscayne
To I-Ninety-five

Through Hollywood, Miramar
And Hollandale Beach
He was hotly pursued
But still out of reach

Through Bal Harbor and Deerfield
And North Oakland Park
Continued this the famous last ride
Of Elfreido de Dark

Not From Around Here, Are You?

His driving was shakey
But his speed lacked restrictions
As units pursued him
From ten jurisdictions

His mind it was racing
But he had only one thought
He surely would be sent back
If he happened to get caught

With his speed off the dial
He was leading the pack
He was pulling away
He might not have to go back

Yes, he might have escaped
But his chances diminished
When he turned on Jefferson Causeway
Which wasn't quite finished

The witnesses were amazed
They said it was a great leap
He might just have made it
Given another three feet

He hit the water at one-twenty
The cops estimated
It caused a small tsunami
The newspapers related

The car was recovered
But no body was found
The police nodded and winked
They were sure that he'd drowned

Last Ride of Elfriedo de Dark

The case they marked closed
He had been food for the sharks
So ended the famous last ride
Of Elfreido de Dark

On a dusty old table
In a rundown cabana
Off of highway Trace Quatro
Just outside of Havana

There sits a small shrine
His mother prepares
With wonderful stories
With the neighbors she shares

She knows he got away
That he lives his life free now
Still dancing the night
In some far off canteena

Some day to return
She holds dear in her heart
Her son of the Revolution
Elfriedo de Dark

Bayo Bob

Woody Carsky-Wilson

I'm only telling you this because you're my best friend ever, and it's a dare, so I have to. But don't tell anyone else, especially that creep Anthony you're going out with. Does he even own a bar of soap? Anyway, my weirdest experience . . . that's easy. It was Bayo Bob.

The thing is, he wasn't human, kinda like Anthony, but I imagine he smelled cleaner.

No, I did not sleep with him! Not really. Well . . . kind of. It wasn't the classic boy meets girl like my parents said would happen, but then my parents live in another world and rarely visit this one.

I met Bayo Bob on the Web in a chat room, thought he was a stalker at first!

Welcome to TreeHuggerz-n-love.com for individuals seeking the ecologically likeminded. Name?

julie from San Diego.

Thank you, julie from San Diego. Meet your hopeful companion, Bayo Bob. Good luck! (Doubleclick on a system administrator for any problems.)

julie says hi, Bob. you spelld Bayou wrong.

Bayo Bob says Hi, Julie, you spelled 'spelld' wrong.

julie says ooops! i'm a goof.

Bayo Bob says It's okay. What shall we talk about tonight?

julie says i dunno. i'm easy.

Bayo Bob says My favorite type of female.

julie says bad boy!

Bayo Bob says Honest boy. Do you know how I would make love to you?

julie says um, you're pretty fast, Bob. even San Diego

286

Bayo Bob

guys attempt a few milliseconds of foreplay.

Bayo Bob says Sorry, I'm trying to spread my seed before season. Shall I describe myself?

julie says spread your. . .??? nevermind. go ahead with the description.

Bayo Bob says I have great, widespread arms, a huge barrel chest and I am well-rooted.

julie says well rooted? you mean you live in one place, don't move? doesn't that get boring?

Bayo Bob says I will never move from this spot.

julie says a homebody, hmmm. . .then how would you make love to me, huh?

Bayo Bob says First I would—

That's when my cat Phinny batted the cable modem. It's an iffy connection at best. I was so pissed, he only got dry food that night! Then Rachel came over, and she had just broken up with Ramone, and had to tell me all about it. I didn't get back to the chat room until much later.

julie says how long did you wait?

Bayo Bob says Five hours.

julie says you waited that long? i'm so sorry! i got caught up in other stuff.

Bayo Bob says I have all the time in the world. I'm not going anywhere.

julie says you're a patient man. that's different from most.

Bayo Bob says It is the nature of my people.

julie says who are your people? don't worry, i've dated Hispanics, African-Americans, Chinese, Japanese. race doesn't matter. it's what is inside the person that makes a difference.

Bayo Bob says I am West African, though I hold no passport or citizenship papers.

julie says oh, you're like a smuggler, then. just kidding. what's your skin tone? my African-American friends have so many words for skin color, it's almost like they see more colors than i do. are you latte brown, moche suave, dark chocolate, ebony blaze, golden-yellow?

Bayo Bob says Maybe. I don't know. I've never seen a picture of myself. I only have descriptions from books. Probably dark chocolate.

julie says kewl! but you've never seen yourself? let me guess. you're a tribal prince in a small village whose parents wanted to keep the modern world at bay. that included mirrors. but now you're reaching out with electronic arms to embrace the world that you can never experience in person.

Bayo Bob says Very inventive! Very wrong. Are you a writer?

julie says nah, my ego's too small. that's why I'll never be a doctor or politician either. who would care what I have to say?

Bayo Bob says I care. You're an interesting person.

julie says thanks, Bob! that's sweet. by the way, i have to be honest. julie is not my real name. i don't give that out on the Web for obvious reasons.

Bayo Bob says That's okay. I don't need your name. I have access to your mind.

julie says don't scare me! you might be a pervert.

Bayo Bob says You might also be a pervert. I am equally at risk.

julie says touche.

Bayo Bob says I described myself, dear. Now describe yourself.

julie says okay, i picked the name julie, because i look like Jewel the singer, but it would be trite to spell my logon the same way. what would I be? jewelie? i'm a dishwater blonde, five foot four, blue eyes and i won't tell you my weight, but i'm not fat, although there's still some chub in places where the chub is good . . . at least, my boyfriends tell me that. i do aerobics and sometimes i skateboard.

Bayo Bob says I do *not* do aerobics, or any activity that requires a well-developed respiratory system.

julie says why not? it's good for you.

Bayo Bob says i'd fall over. i have no legs.

julie says oh, i'm so sorry! did you have an accident or

Bayo Bob

was it —

Bayo Bob says No accident. None of my people have no legs.

julie says huh?

Bayo Bob says Let's change the topic.

julie says okay, okay. . .fine. no prob. um, tell me about the ecology where you're from. do you have forests? we're destroying ours at a terrible rate. it's criminal.

Bayo Bob says There was once a forest where I lived, but thankfully it was leveled.

julie says omigod, that's terrible!

Bayo Bob says Why? A forest is a ghetto. Too damned many inhabitants, too damned little sunlight and water. The competition is painfully fierce.

julie says are your people headhunters? not that I'm judging your culture! I cherish other cultures.

Bayo Bob says My people fight to the death for access to the sun and for water rights when there are too many crowded together. It's internecine warfare on a scale you cannot imagine. But after the leveling, there's just me, and I am happy.

julie says was there a massacre? why didn't the U.N. do something? you said you live in West Africa, so I guess you're not in Rwanda or the Sudan. i'm looking at my inflatable globe.

Bayo Bob says I live in Sierra Leone.

julie says wait a minute. you're legless, your people have all died, but you're still alive. Bob, just who are your people?

Bayo Bob says They are trees, Julie. I am a baobab.

Weird, huh? I mean, the guy really thought he was a tree. He was so convincing, it had me tied up in knots. I spent fifteen minutes arguing with him, but no good. He still swore he was a tree. That kinda' scared me, so I told him I had stuff to do and didn't revisit the chatroom for a couple weeks.

But you know me. I got lonely, so I went back.

julie says don't you ever sleep, Mister Thinks-He's-a-Tree?

Not From Around Here, Are You?

Bayo Bob says I go dormant during cold snaps, but we don't get those often. Other than that, I'm always aware, but not as active as you mammals. No one is!

julie says uh-huh. if you're a tree, then why talk to me about making love?

Bayo Bob says Why not? You're fun. Let's pollinate.

julie says okay, i'll play along in the interest of good conversation. how?

Bayo Bob says Can you move your computer?

julie says i've got a long extension cord and a surge protector with a bunch of sockets. the cable is easy to move.

Bayo Bob says Set your computer up outside where you can lay under the open stars.

julie says i have a small patio attached to my apartment. i could go there. it's not heated or anything, but I am in California, so i won't freeze.

Bayo Bob says Do it. I'll wait and prepare a batch of pollen.

I sound like such a desperate slut, don't I? There I was pretending I wanted to be pollinated by a guy I never met, but it seemed so innocent and safe. A few minutes later I was lying outside under the stars wearing nothing but a bathrobe and holding a keyboard. I went back to the chatroom. My heart was pounding!

Bayo Bob says Are you ready, dear?

julie says i think so. i'm not really sure what to do.

Bayo Bob says Lie back and think of me. Think of how my voice would sound, wind across the grasslands. My strong branches shelter you from storms at night. During the day, my leaves protect you from the intense sun. I am larger than any man, broader, stiffer, ready to spread my seed much further than any mammal. I let myself loose upon the wind so that my seed, like dew, may fall upon you. Are you with me?

julie says oh my, yes! just make sure you wear condoms on your branches.

Bayo Bob says Don't spoil the mood, sweetheart. I am

thinking of you now, and letting go into the air, releasing my essence. I surrender part of myself to you. I know you are waiting for me. Are you nude?

julie says under my robe, yeah, very nude.

Bayo Bob says Take it off. Give me a broad expanse of receptive skin to touch.

julie says hope the neighbors can't see! i'd have a hard time explaining this.

Bayo Bob says Are you nude yet?

julie says patience! there, i am now.

Bayo Bob says How do you feel? Aroused?

julie says yes. maybe confused, too, but I am definitely excited.

Bayo Bob says There is a bond between us. I fill the air. Like a sandstorm, my pollen gathers and moves, crossing the ocean, the mountains, the plains of your wide country, coming at last to your home. Can you see it in your mind, this storm?

julie says i'm trying. yes, i almost think i can!

Bayo Bob says Feel it kiss your skin with the lightest touch. It builds, coming harder, wave after wave of me upon your body... You may stimulate yourself if you like.

julie says i, uh, already am. i'm thinking about you and me together.

Bayo Bob says Perfect. I'm moving against you, my seed entering your skin through your breasts and legs and mouth. I'm on you and in you, and there is only the eternal now, the joining of two soul-similar beings, merging souls. . . .and now it happen! It is a starshine in your mind's eye, a twinkle that becomes a fire, roaring into a conflagration, on and on and on while we mate and love and learn each others' ways. . .

julie says don't stop, Bayo Bob, do not stop!! yes, Yes, YESSS!!!

Bayo Bob says Lovely. . . . I will leave you to your thoughts for awhile.

julie says mmmmmm. . .

My god, I'd been pollinated! I really was a tree hugger in

Not From Around Here, Are You?

every sense of the word. Even if Bob was a seventy-year-old man with no legs living alone in Sierra Leone torturing baby seals for a hobby, I'd let him have his way IF ONLY HE'D KEEP SENDING ME THOSE DELICIOUS WORDS!

I felt yummy, like a warm pile of organic pancakes smothered in free-range syrup. The next night after work, a heroin addict waiting for the next needle, I rushed home to my computer.

julie says last night was wonderful, Bob!

Bayo Bob says Thanks. It's the first time I was able to communicate with a sexual partner. It's difficult to speak with another tree kilometers away.

julie says I bet. Just out of curiosity, how does a tree get access to the World Wide Web?

Bayo Bob says It involves a National Geographic camera crew on assignment, a T3 cable entangled in my roots, a lightning strike near my trunk and a long, difficult experience making sense of electrical impulses. A boring story, and not one I feel like telling.

julie says sounds rather unlikely.

Bayo Bob says Life is unlikely.

julie says well said, my wooden romeo. interesting, but can we talk about something else?

Bayo Bob says Does it involve you lying nude on your patio with me sending pollen on a warm breeze?

julie says mmmm huh.

Bayo Bob says Set up your computer, my dearest, mammalian slut.

julie says as you command, sir. my robe is lying beside me and I await your seed with open mind.

Bayo Bob says Egads! I have created a monster...

We had so little time remaining, Bayo Bob and me. It was like when Jeffrey got busted at that rave and was awaiting the judge's sentencing, then got busted again for smoking dope in the courthouse bathroom. Or like Franklin before he joined the cult and moved to Honduras and had to purify himself with jimson weed and none of our conversations made any sense

292

after that. Even like Freddie when he found out his mom wasn't sending any more money for him to live in California, and he had to go back to work at Seven-Eleven, except he had that drunken driving thing hanging over him. . . .

Story of my life. I think I meet the perfect match, then something happens to ruin it. Anyway, here's our last conversation.

julie says Bayo Bob, may i consider you my boyfriend?
Bayo Bob says I would like that very much.
julie says yeah! i have the tallest boyfriend ever.
Bayo Bob says I'm happy to please your sense of aesthetics. I would be the envy of all the other stud trees, were there any remaining here.
julie says i bet. on a serious note, did you mean what you said about the forest, that it was like a ghetto? and you're glad they cut it down?
Bayo Bob says Yes, I did.
julie says but, Bob, it's like the holocaust! first the bad guys come for the Jews, and you might be a bigot, and think that's fine, but then they come for the Communists and Gypsies, which you still might think is good, but pretty soon they're through killing the obvious scapegoats and they're down to rounding up left-handed lithuanians with a lisp.
Bayo Bob says I don't have a lisp. But seriously, I get the point. Let's change the subject, Julie. I suddenly feel my own mortality. . .

Like I said, that was the last time I spoke to Bob. The next day I logged onto the chatroom, and he didn't answer, but when I checked my email, there was a message from BayoBob@TreeHuggerz-n-love.com. At first I was a little scared. I mean, the guy knew my email address! I never told him that.

I opened the file.

Julie,
The National Geographic team is pulling out, taking its

Not From Around Here, Are You?

T3 cable with it. I don't know how much longer I have. It's kind of like you said. Now they've come for me, but they're not killing me, they're disconnecting me from someone I dearly desire. We've only known each other a short time, but I just want to say that I—"

The message ended.

Pretty weird, huh? As you can see, I still cry when I think about him. Real? I don't know. It sure felt real to me. Was I angry the message cut off prematurely?

No. I knew what he was going to say. My heart knew the words, even if I couldn't see them written down.

Goodbye, Bayo Bob. And yes, I love you, too.

The Rule of Babloo

Sujata Naik

Every morning, Babloo, the music industry magnate, took the road from the deserted seaside to visit the Shiva temple where he spent forty-five minutes doing *puja,* prayer ritual. He dressed in traditional attire, a loose *kurta*-shirt and *pyjama*, strictly white.

Such was Babloo's morning.

That temple was his favorite, a place of pride and peace. He had it renovated in a new style, red brick, the year before last. One day, though, the temple would be all black marble. Babloo saw the vision clearly: his Shiva would sit atop a massive, white marble rock, like the very Himalaya, his Lord's true abode. The snake slung around his Shiv-Shankar's neck would be lifelike, maybe one of those new digital things—an illusion created by the computer—even emitting sounds recorded in Babloo's own studios. The tiger skin around his waist would be real, and the proverbial third eye would be a computer-generated image projected on to the statue, one that would open and shut at intervals.

After prayer, he would usually visit Padma, his love, to give her *puja* sweets and listen to her melodious voice and words of solace. She was the lady with a *koyal*—nightingale—sweet voice. Babloo loved that perfect cliché.

He was devoted to his lady-love, would see her every day after the *puja*, but today decided to break that routine. They had argued again last evening over his continued vendetta with the musician Tehseen. The altercation left him restless the whole night. Padma was his soul, his noble side after all.

Babloo had no illusions about himself. He was rough, with power and Lord Shiva on his side, while Padma was refined and talented. The whole world could hear her voice only because

Not From Around Here, Are You?

Didi, Big Sister, of the Indian music industry and therefore of Bollywood, had retired some years back. This helped Babloo give Padma a break. For it was always true that without a hit music-and-dance score, there was no hit Hindi film. While Didi ruled, there could have been no hit music score without her.

No Didi, no film. It was the Didi Rule, an immutable equation of earlier decades.

Doubtless, today *he* was the only word in the music industry, controlling all music from recording to distribution. That was the Babloo Rule, and it wasn't changing any time soon, for he was in his prime.

At five foot four, he became taller with the thought.

His pace slowed, so the route of twenty minutes would take thirty. A stray bird perched momentarily on his balding head.

He had killed Tehseen's music as naturally as he had lifted Padma. Thinking of her always humbled him. She was his lotus Padma, or Padma*ji*, now that she was famous by his hand.

He sighed.

After meeting Babloo, Padma found life with her aging husband, a fellow singer, meaningless and so there were. . .impossible possibilities. Babloo had not meant for this to happen. After all, did he really love her, or did he only admire her music? Did she care about him, or was he merely a stepladder to success?

Babloo stopped mid-stride. A handcart rested on its narrow edge off the footpath. The man who had made it his home was still asleep. Not an unusual sight this time of the day, but Babloo was moved. It could have been him so many years ago, making his living off a hand-cart. A rustic from the north, Babloo had worked hard to get ahead. His own gift was small, a heart with strings that stirred to the rhythm of music. A heart that could spot talent in others.

But did he truly celebrate those melancholy *koyal* strains, or did he merely get a kick out of it all, a kick making an artist, a kick breaking an artist?

An artist like Tehseen. Now there was an artiste to be admired as well as condemned. Babloo spat, despite the *puja*

The Rule of Babloo

basket in his hands as he walked to the temple. A red flower dropped through the emptiness of the silver carving.

He walked faster.

Tehseen. Damn his ego, nonchalantly looking at others over the rim of perpetual goggles. Babloo could see him clearly in his mind's eye, Tehseen new to the industry, Tehseen who could conjure tunes the public loved. Babloo remembered the notes of that first hit.

As he took another step, the music in his mind gave way to the remembered sound of Tehseen's arrogant laughter as he looked at Babloo over the rim of his goggles. But Tehseen got careless. On more than one occasion, he had introduced Babloo as a *bhaiyya*. To disgrace him with the title of "brother", the Bombay phrase for a working-class person from Uttar Pradesh, hit on Babloo's raw spot, his northern roots.

It violated the Babloo Rule.

Babloo's speed slackened. He paused to catch his breath, and looked up. Another leafless tree. Where he came from, a small town, trees grew lush. Unable to conjure a single clear picture of his hometown, his mind formed the pleasing image of Lord Shiva.

He had always confided in Shiva during his daily prayers, had admitted to his Lord that he wanted, in his heart of hearts, to marry Padma. But he would not and he could not, for she was wedded and her husband lived. He could not marry her even after the husband died, for she had changed, while her husband had not. They were Padma, the lotus one, and Padmakar. Educated middle-class Maharashtrians, both had once held jobs. Padma had sung only as a hobby before Babloo found her.

She struggled to give her husband all due respect, but he was an unsuccessful man, one she no longer loved. The world would not understand if she divorced him, nor would her two sons.

Last night at the party she said flatly, "You have taken away Tehseen's music, his soul. So don't pretend you are a musician."

True enough. For eight months, he had canned the man.

297

Not From Around Here, Are You?

But Tehseen had crossed the line. To appease her, last week Babloo had suggested a reconciliation measure to Tehseen's partner Ranga. A simple apology from Tehseen was all that was needed.

The world acknowledged Babloo's greatness. Tehseen had not. Babloo clutched hard the metal basket handle. Not only had Tehseen refused to apologize, but he had used threatening words. Babloo had a full report. Not from Ranga, but one of the Tehseen posse:

"I will teach that *bhaiyya* Babloo a lesson," Tehseen had sworn in public, as he sat drinking with his posse. He had even made a scene. Babloo tore his thoughts away from this image and focused on the *puja*.

His Shiva was the most powerful, the destroyer of the universe, and hence the beginning of all creation.

"*Om namo Shivay, Om namo Shivay,*" Babloo invoked Shiva as he legged the last stretch of the thirty minute walk. He entered the temple and there he sat at the feet of his Lord. Immersed in invocation, his back was to the entrance of the temple. The celebrant went about his duties, lighting candles and taking gifts to the halls beyond.

The door to the temple moved aside, making a grating sound.

A slight disturbance in his dedicated ritual, thought Babloo. His back remained to the world outside Shiva's temple.

The entrance bells were struck a harsh, discordant note.

A slight disturbance in his devoted praying, thought Babloo, facing the Lord Shiva.

"*Saala!*" came a harsh curse, followed by, "Get up! Your god has come to meet you in person."

Babloo was kicked from behind, and fell flat at the feet of Shiva. He stretched out his hand to the celebrant, a six foot, hefty priest clad in a cream dhoti and cream scarf on bare, hairy chest. The priest scurried into the inner sanctuary, closing and locking the newly renovated, ornamental door behind him.

The attacker came around to the front, with demon-fierce bulging eyes. Hands on waist, he stood confronting Shiva's holy

298

bull, Nandi, as though challenging the presence of both Lord and vehicle.

"Let us see how your god saves you!" he laughed.

His laughter rang louder and more discordant than the insulting bell-peals.

"Give him a chance, *yaar*, give a chance to the god," said a mocking young voice from some unseen lad to the rear.

"*Bhago!*" Run!" said the Demon Eyes, striking Babloo across the back with a stick.

"How much time do we give his god to save his life?" the young voice asked.

"Time enough to say his last prayers, what else? Eight minutes."

"He told you to run!" The lad, now visible from the corner of his eye, pointed to the door of the temple. He was a small man, precise. He could have been a Brahmin.

Babloo, five feet four, balding and clad in snow white but soiled *pyjama-kurta*, was heaving. All his pain and fear became a flaming arrow. He shot for the door, then ran outside.

He crashed into the first door to the left across the street, a small hut. But all doors and windows around had been bolted tight at the first sign of violence.

He wasted a whole minute trying to pry open the door or look into the windows, before giving up. Babloo, on a seven minute lease of life, now ran to the next hut. Banging desperately, his voice was shrill, devoid of music, a despondent plea: "*Bachao! Bachao!*" Save me! Save me!

Six minutes.

At the next door, he regained his wits, offering any sum asked for. "Take all you want! Shiva's sake, open the door!"

But the closed doors and windows merged into one picture before his blurring eyes. He fell down at the next door, defeated, and turned to face the temple where his attackers stood by the door.

"Think you are a big man?" asked Demon Eyes, descending the steps, pulling Babloo up with one hand like a huge, soft toy. "But you're yesterday, and yesterday is dead."

Not From Around Here, Are You?

Babloo was dragged into the temple. "Two minutes more," announced Demon Eyes, with his back to Lord Shiva.

Babloo looked up, but saw no Shiva, only the goddess Parvati, Shiva's better half. Her face was kind, her eyes like those of his lady love. A heavenly light, forgiving.

She would forgive him. That's all he had left now anyway.

Babloo did not see the sword passed to Demon Eyes as he was pushed forth like a sacrificial goat, his neck entreating the shining sword.

"Die." The sword flashed once.

It was done that fast. Babloo, the music industry magnate, was dead. So ended the Rule of Babloo.

Having struck the fatal blow, Demon Eyes pulled back the blade. Then he offered the blood on the sword to Shiva, as if in apology. He withdrew a smart, black cellphone, and dialed a number.

"Sahib? It is done."

And so began the Rule of Tehseen.

Contributors

Linda Arnest has been a member of the CWP fiction critique group since 1998 when meetings were held in the vault at Ward Six. Her short story, "Jaley Walker," was published in the *Licking River Review*. Her play and short story "Astral Sex with John Wayne" appeared in two previous CWP publications, *Feral Parakeets* and *Someone Has To Die*. Her writing has also appeared in the *Hamilton Sun News* and *GLBT News*. She is currently working on her first novel.

Jane Biddinger, a graduate of the College of Mount Saint Joseph, lives and writes in Fairfield, Ohio. Formerly employed in the accounting field, she now devotes her hours to words. She co-chairs the Mad Anthony Writers Conference held each April in Hamilton, Ohio to raise funds for the Butler County Literacy Council of the YWCA. She writes a column for the Cincinnati PFLAG. Her essay "A Family Death" was included in the *Someone Has to Die* Anthology published by the Cincinnati Writers Project in 2005. She is currently working on her first novel and when not glued to the keyboard, she enjoys spending time with her grandchildren.

Darlene Blasing was a frequent attendant of the Wednesday night CWP critique fests until she hightailed it back to Michigan, her home state. Her articles and short stories have appeared in *GreenPrints*, *Grand Haven Tribune*, *Midwest Business Alliance Journal*, organicgardening.com, and *Cappers*, as well as the previous CWP anthology. Her story about the power of the blues to bridge generation gaps and cultural divides was inspired by her friend Russell Givens' misadventures in Paris. A master musician, Russell played bass guitar for B. B. King, Ray Charles,

Not From Around Here, Are You?

Lou Rawls, Howlin Wolf, and James Brown, among others. He had a heart as big as his talent, and regularly organized benefit concerts to aid ailing musicians. Though he appreciated good food, he was easily lured away from a meal by anyone in need of assistance (to the annoyance of those cooking for him). Russell passed away November 10, 2007. He is missed.

Katey Brichto is a rabbi's daughter from the NYC area. She spent her life traveling and setting down stakes in the most unlikely places. After a ten year stint in Guatemala, she now lives in a rural pocket of southeastern Indiana where she teaches yoga and aerobic dance, interprets for Hispanic migrant workers in the local courts and writes in her spare time. She enjoys getting bucked off her horses and sleeping with her dogs. She's working on her latest novel *Jewbilly*.

Kimberly Brown is a native of Cincinnati, Ohio. She graduated from the College of Mount St. Joseph with a B.A. in Paralegal Studies. She has been a member of the Cincinnati Writer's Project since 2003. Kimberly has been published in the *Maze From The Median* (CWP Press, 2004) and *Tread Well with Sweet Love* (CWP Press, 2006). Poetry is her passion and her life; a life she is ready to pursue.

Jonathan Matthew Burns is currently coming out of a career teaching high school English and journalism in the Cincinnati area. He loves teaching, but is taking time off to focus on his writing, and perfect the art of the ramen noodle. He was born in Findlay, Ohio and studied English and Psychology at a number of colleges, including Leicester University in the United Kingdom, before receiving his M.Ed. from Wright State University in Dayton, Ohio.

Jon's love of writing came to him during his grade school years. His second grade teacher, upon reading one of his stories, told him, "This is too long. I wanted only one page." That evening his father said to him, "She doesn't know what's what. Don't let your writing be normal." This has in many ways translated in Jon's life, as well as his absorption of literature, writing and the use of language.

Though the experience was short-lived, Jon learned more about writing during the two years he taught high school Journalism than during his time writing for Wright State University's student newspaper, *The Guardian*. Hence, proof: To teach is to learn twice.

Angelina Caliguri is a senior at the College of Mount Saint Joseph majoring in Liberal Studies. She enjoys fictional creative writing, which she will choose *not* to do professionally so her love of it never runs dry. She is an avid reader (books still get her going), reality television addict (she should be ashamed but is not), art show frequenter (free cheese & wine!), and dog lover (they are better then most people she knows.) She is currently planning her wedding in April of 2009 where she looks forward to enjoying a bohemian life with her graphic designer fiancé Jeremy.

Woody Carsky-Wilson has published thirty-eight short stories and is working on some novels. He attributes any and all his publishing success to critique he received from the CWP fiction critique group. Without them, his writing was well-intentioned, but unmarketable crap.

Woody commands a detachment in the Army Reserves, and he's a stay-at-home dad. He's forty years young, and continually amazed that everything in life just keeps getting better. The Reserves is improving itself on a daily basis, the kids are great to be with, and he couldn't imagine a more beautiful or interesting wife than his best friend Meg. Also, the Cincinnati Writers Project keeps encouraging and producing great writers and poets.

Not From Around Here, Are You?

Kudos to Woody's awesome parents Shirley and Woody Wilson in Southport, NC who encouraged him over many years to write. And Opie . . . thanks for the cruises! The kids will talking about them for years. Lucas, Andrew, Marcus and Erik, you can read this anthology when you're old enough!

Tina Clyburn After 25 years as a hair stylist, Tina decided to follow her dream and go back to school to pursue a degree in an art-related field. She will graduate with a degree in visual communications in 2009, after five years of working full-time and attending classes. After graduation, she plans to work as a graphic designer while continuing hair design part time. Tina is passionate about painting and illustration. She loves the city of Cincinnati, the Art Museum and Rookwood Pottery

Madeleine Crouse has been published in *The Comstock Review, The Journal of Kentucky Studies,* and in several anthologies sponsored by the Cincinnati Writers' Project. She has studied at the Fine Arts Center in Provincetown, the Kenyon Writers' Workshop, and the Indiana Writers' Conference.

Doug Clifton. He is a fifty-nine-year-old Postal Service retiree and veteran of the Vietnam War during which he was a crew member on over 150 combat missions over Laos. He was married twenty-seven years until his wife's death, and has two daughters, five granddaughters and one grandson. He has tinkered with writing for decades and had two short stories published in Northern Kentucky University's now defunct literary collection *Collage*. One of those stories was noted as one of the three best submissions that year. He finally started writing seriously in the last two years, and in that time has written one novel, yet unpublished, and is working on a second.

He has lived in this area all his life but enjoys domestic and foreign travel as a way to expand his horizons and maybe get new perspectives on the world.

Contributors

Marcia Eckstein is a seasoned short story writer, but this is her first rendering in the sci-fi genre. She lives in Loveland, Ohio with her husband and five basset hounds and is currently at work on a mystery novel. With five brothers, she drew from a wealth of background to develop the character of Gerry. This is the third time her work was chosen for the CWP anthology.

Jenny Engleka blames the wait staff at the Bistro du Coin for getting her into writing. While dining there five years ago, spouting off yet another tale of her life in a traveling two-bit ice show, she declared, "Somebody needs to write a book about this." Since there were no takers at the restaurant, she gave it a try. Now she has a completed manuscript, "Ice Charades" to call her own. She currently works out of CWP's satellite office in Mexico City.

Mary Fitzpatrick lives in Norwood, which is a way cooler neighborhood than most people think. In 1981, she graduated from Xavier University with a Political Science degree, and has been wandering through a series of eclectic jobs while trying to decide what to be when she grows up. She met her husband over a dead body. It belonged to a dinosaur, and she was a volunteer fossil-prep tech. Since she was fifteen, she has been a volunteer education program animal handler at the Cincinnati Zoo, so she knows many weird animal-related facts and may be in your vacation pictures. Dinosaurs, science fiction, and working as a volunteer science educator have been her life long passions. Writing is a new addition to that group. Ms. Fitzpatrick has been writing seriously since 2001. In 2005 she put that PoliSci degree to some use by becoming president of CWP. She's a redhead, allergic to rhino urine, dyslexic, and a breast cancer survivor, not that those things are in any way related. She's has several novels in the works, and she blogs at Flying Whale Productions - http://maryfitz.typepad.com/

Not From Around Here, Are You?

Karen George's work is forthcoming in *Arts Across Kentucky*, and has appeared in *The Cortland Review, The Barcelona Review, Drexel Online Journal, Timber Creek Review, Wind Magazine*, and others. The Kentucky Arts Council awarded her a grant, she's won Creative Writing Awards from Thomas More College, and has most recently received The Janice Giles Holt Award. She's halfway through Spalding University's MFA in Writing Program, where she served as Student Assistant Editor of *The Louisville Review*. By day, she writes and debugs computer programs. Not all the rumors circulating about her are true.

Thomas Groh spends most of his days at home taking care of his beautiful daughters, Elizabeth and Anna. His lovely bride, Amy, brings home the bacon. Tom loves bacon. Crispy.

From 11pm to 3am, Tom writes. He likes to say his stories are of the "realism school," but only because it sounds so cool to tell people that. Many of the characters in his tales are drawn from real life friends and family, and, should they ever visit a library or, better yet, open their wallets to buy a copy of this anthology, they might be flattered, or, conversely, offended. As neither event is likely to happen, we won't dwell on it further.

"Finding Religion" and "The Soldier" are his first published fictions.

Scott Heile is a writer of both prose and poetry. He resides in Cincinnati, Ohio with his wife and children, and enjoys spending most of his time in their company. Mr. Heile has also been known to be outdoors and, on occasion, on large bodies of water. If you ask him a question, you will most certainly get an answer. Right or wrong, it will never be "I don't know."

Jeff Hilliard is one of the few CWP founders standing. Writer, poet, rebel, he is currently at the head of the most interesting webzine you've ever seen. Check out www.redwebzine.org. We

Contributors

promise, you will learn things.

Evan Holbrook was born in Ashland, Kentucky, in 1991. He is a senior at Paul G. Blazer High School in Ashland and a member of the school's football and wrestling teams. He has enjoyed writing fantasy and science fiction stories since fourth grade. In 2008, he attended the Governor's Scholars Program where he was chosen among the other writers in Frank Ward's creative writing class to be published in this anthology. "Twilight Runners," written while in the program, is his first short story to be published. He plans to continue writing and hopes to submit his stories to various publications in the future.

James Montgomery Jackson claims that after fifty plus years he finally found a legal outlet for his warped mind: writing fictional accounts of crimes. His father reports much earlier evidence of Jim's fictional self-help program occurred with the 1961 publication and public reading of "The Case of the Red and Green Striped Zebra," wherein our hero learned the difference between oil-based and water-based paints when his scam washed down the drain. Jim's other writing credits include "Christmas Story," part of CWP's anthology *Someone Has to Die*, "Hands Up" a short memoir piece published in *UU World* magazine and a couple of dozen homilies delivered in Unitarian Universalist churches in Michigan and Ohio. Jim is seeking representation for his novel *Bad Policy*,

Jim lives most of the year in his cabin on a remote Upper Peninsula of Michigan lake with his life partner, Jan Rubens, their dog, Morgan le Fay, and sibling cats, Electra and Orestes (and no, they did not kill their mother.) The clan resides in their Kentucky condo for the portion of the year when the cabin is inaccessible.

Jerry Judge lives in Cincinnati with his gorgeous wife, two active cats and a dog who walks him regularly. He is a social worker for Big Brothers Big Sisters of Greater Cincinnati. His youngest son studies at Ohio State University, and his oldest son fights fires and attends to injuries as a fireman/paramedic in Dayton, Ohio. Jerry has published four poetry chapbooks, the most recent, *Writing at the Waffle House* (Pudding House Publications). He has a fifth collection entitled *Luna Moth* due out in late fall/early winter by Finishing Line Press. He has published many dozens of poems in journals and anthologies. Several of his poems have been read on the radio, and he has been a featured poet in *Artspike Magazine* and Little Pocket Poetry's website at http://littlepocketpoetry.org/pocket_poems. He has read his poetry on WVXU Public Radio and at the Performance Time Arts (a project of the Contemporary Dance Theatre). He has also read at the Hamilton County Public Library, Mt. Washington Poetry Festival and at the SOS Peace and Justice Show.

Abby Kirk is a distinguished creative writing student in the School for the Creative and Performing Arts program in Lexington, KY. This summer, she was chosen to study under the guidance of Frank Ward's Creative Writing class, in the Kentucky Governor's Scholar Program. She carries a 4.0 GPA into her senior year in the Pre-Engineering Program, and participates as a member of the award-winning Lafayette High School Marching Band. When she is not doing anything else, she prefers to write short stories and work part-time on her ice cream dipping skills at a local retail outlet.

Carol Feiser Laque failed the third grade because she could not spell. Not much has changed. Her favorite class was recess. She has a new collection of poems titled *Queen Anne's Lace*.

Ann Mazzaro is a senior at the College of Mount St. Joseph in Cincinnati, Ohio, majoring in English. When she isn't pouring

Contributors

over novels and writing, she enjoys spending time outside with her family and friends. She likes the beach, sunsets, fish, and summer. She continues her search for deciding what to do when she grows up, but hopes to fully utilize her degree in English in any future endeavor.

Donnie McGovern is *not* from around here, but after stints in Louisville, Orlando, and Seattle – he's happy to call Cincinnati home. He is an actor, performing in numerous local theatre and film projects – including a 7.5 second appearance in *Cornhole: The Movie.* He'd like to thank Linda Arnest for her unending friendship, support, guidance, and prodding. Thanks to Linda, Donnie's story was performed by the Know Theatre Tribe of Cincinnati as part of their 2007 National Coming Out Day Project. He'd also like to thank Ron for giving him a reason to write this story in the first place, and reasons every day to keep writing more.

P. Andrew Miller is currently associate professor of English at Northern Kentucky University where he teaches creative writing and literature. His fiction and poetry have appeared in a number of places, such as *Dragon Magazine, Sword and Sorceress #13 and #19, Twice Upon A Time, Someone Has to Die, Inscape, The MacGuffin*, and others.

Carl Morris is an internationally unknown writer, poet, artist, sculptor, floral designer, postal clerk, lover, drinker, and tired, retired dirty old man. He has completed five unpublished novels and a number of short stories, a few of which have been published. A native of Hillsboro, Ohio, he has lived in Cincinnati for over fifty years.

Sujata Naik has published articles and papers in diverse domains. Her poetry has been published by the British High Commission, All India Poetry Circle competition, and *City Beat-*

309

Not From Around Here, Are You?

Inktank writing competition. She is bilingual; English has been her medium of instruction. She undertook a journey of poetry in her mother tongue, along with her teacher and renowned critic. Sujata's short story in Marathi, "Just like That" won third prize.

She has also published theatre reviews and interviewed a playwright for Sunday Review of *The Times* of India. She is working at present on a novel and a play, "A Small Town in Cincinnati."

Sujata is an educator, and teaches children here. Back home, she taught graduates Organization Behavior and worked in change management. In her early forties, Sujata is an enthusiastic student of films, and has been learning about films and writing from friends in UC—notably Prof. Arner and Mark Philip, Media Bridges, the Inktank Writers' Salon, and now the CWP. She appreciates Prof. Michael Griffith for his faith in her writing, and is grateful to all teachers and gurus, her mother for her artistic sensibilities, uncle for his love of the language, and father for his love of Wordsworth.

She thanks her family, notably Aditi for her editing and critique.

Ryck Neube has been the anarchic non-leader of the CWP fiction critique group since 1993. He's a great mentor for new writers, because, hey, he's been there! (It took him fifteen years of reject slips before he learned proper submission techniques that scored him a major paying market for his fiction.) Now he's a regular in *Asimov's* and has sold a bunch of stories over the years.

Ryck had the distinction of earning a nine month case of Legionnaire's Disease and a bout of amoebic dysentery for his sins. If you ever get him drunk enough, ask him about searching for the legendary, hallucinogenic white tobacco plant bred over the centuries by Mayan shamans in the shade of a jungle tree. (One cigarette's nicotine content equals ten cartons of regular smokes!)

Ryck lives with his wife and a bunch of constantly

Contributors

bickering cats in Covington, KY, where the stories walk past your door on a daily basis. His wife Lorraine makes awesome lasagna, but pretends it's a simple recipe.

Robert Schofield has been writing fiction since 1990. He has had stories, articles, and interviews appear in various publications since then. Robert's story "Interrupt Vector" appeared in Volume 17 of the Writer's of the Future contest anthology. He has had stories in the two previous Cincinnati Writers Project anthologies, *Feral Parakeets* and *Someone has to Die*. Robert's novella "God Box" was recently published by Padwolf Publishing. Robert makes his home in Cincinnati, where he is an IT business consultant. Following a recent move from downtown, he felt a bit like an Alien in Ohio.

Charley Sroufe is married with three grown children. He is a drug and alcohol counselor and social worker, and works at a state hospital in the Cincinnati area. He enjoys writing and drawing.

Jim St.Clair

Age	54
Married	Wife, Geneva
Native of	Saginaw, Michigan
Currently Residing	Burlington, Ky
Hobbies	Short story writing, song writing, paranormal events
Famous people met	Bob Seger, Richard Nixon, Clayton Moore(The Lone Ranger)
Working on	First mystery novel
Biggest thrill	Riding out Hurricane Andrew
Favorite saying	"Why, thank you for the million dollars, Mr. Trump"

Not From Around Here, Are You?

Jean Syed came to the United States from England in 1980, and she has been in Loveland ever since. She accompanied her husband who had a job at G. E. President of Queen City Writer's in the 1980's, she is now a member of Greater Cincinnati Writers' Guild and Ohio Writer's Project. In those days she had three short stories published, but now she prefers poetry. Her poems have been published in *The Lyric*, *St Anthony Messenger*, *Bird Watcher's Digest*, *Common Threads*, *For a Better World* and Writer's Haven Press. She has won several competitions. She has also been broadcasted by Oscar Treadwell on WVXU.

Joe Terbeck is a sloppy, unkempt, over-weight, insensitive, unprofessional, slightly deranged, aging baby boomer with long, thinning red hair, usually tangled, a scraggly beard, bad teeth and a keen sense of humor that borders on the not-funny. Aside from these positive traits, there is little else to recommend him. In his off moments, which seem to be occurring more frequently these days, Joe likes to write stories that take place in time and often involve characters. His writing style emphasizes a limited vocabulary that does not require spell checking and sentences that need little punctuation. He has been a member of the Cincinnati Writers Project for about fifteen years, including the twelve somewhere in the middle when he wasn't. Currently, he spends at least five minutes a week continuing to work on a novel he began in a previous life.

Dori J. Van Luit was born and raised in southwest Ohio, has two children and eight grandchildren. She has an Associate Degree in Business from University of Cincinnati, attended Cincinnati College Conservatory of Music, and has a Career Diploma in Journalism and Short Story Writing. A member of the Cincinnati Writer's Project since 2001, her poems have been included in five different poetry collections and anthologies. She has written articles for alumni and reunion projects and for senior newsletters, and recently won second prize in the A.O.P.H.A.

Contributors

southwest Ohio regional writing contest, and is leader of the Creative Writing Group at the Sycamore Senior Center. Dori also served for fifteen years as a church choir director, and directed and appeared in many tri-state musical theater presentations.

www.ingramcontent.com/pod-product-compliance
Lightning Source LLC
Chambersburg PA
CBHW031202020726
47499CB00002B/451